TEESSIDE MISSED

May 2014

Cheers

TEESSIDE MISSED

JOHN NICHOLSON
Nick Guymer Series
No.3

HEAD
PUBLISHING

Published by Head Publishing
Edited by Sarah Winterburn
Copyright © John Nicholson 2013

Printed by Berforts Information Press Ltd

ISBN 978-0-9926640-2-2

http://www.johnnicholsonwriter.com

Dedicated to the Teesside diaspora

*"Out the way, out of fashion and ignored,
we grew, built on fire and steel and ore,
the sweat of generations, hard and funny and fair,
wherever we went, wherever we are,
our soul is still there."*

CHAPTER 1

'I always thought the expression 'blow job' was inaccurate. I mean, very little blowing actually takes place, does it? Plenty of licking and sucking, but no actual blowing. Not if you're doing it right, anyway.'

'Giz it 'ere, then. I might pick up some tips.'

Nick Guymer passed the binoculars to his girlfriend Julie Wells. A warm breeze blew across Roseberry Topping on a hot July afternoon. They'd been walking in the Cleveland Hills all day and had sat down on a north-facing slope for a rest and a flask of tea, taking in the view over Teesside as they took the weight off their hiking boots.

Roseberry Topping was sometimes called the Yorkshire Matterhorn because of its distinctive wonky peak, the result of a quirk of geology and a mining collapse in the early 20th century. Visible from anywhere on Teesside, it had long been a local landmark and a popular area for walking. A hundred years previously it was a huge, noisy quarry, but now it was quiet, rural and beautiful.

He'd been looking at a passing rosefinch when he'd spotted a couple lying in the corner of a wheat field half a mile or so away. Tucked into a hedge and totally out of view of any passing walkers or motorists, the woman was vigorously pleasuring the man, blissfully unaware that two dots on the horizon a mile and a half away could watch their every move with the aid of powerful binoculars.

'She's giving him a good seeing-to here...oops and there he goes,' she laughed. 'Oh dear, he's wiped himself off on his t-shirt and he's already zipping up, job done. You blokes don't hang around, do you? You're so ready to move on. I'm usually a quivering wreck after you've had a go on me.'

'Possibly the most defining thing about being male is the total lack of interest we have in sex exactly five seconds after just having had sex.'

'My God, he's got a face like a tortoise which has smelt something bad.'

'Not one your ex-lovers, then?'

'Given we're on Teesside and given my sexually prolific past, that might not be so unlikely, but no, thankfully. He's also hung like a snail. I'd have remembered that even if he'd had a bag on his head. And he'd have had to have a bag on his head. Oh, he's having a go on her now, dining at the Y.'

'He's what?'

'Dining at the Y!' she said, gurgling a laugh.

'Where do you get these expressions from?'

'Oh dear, he's started filming her on his phone now - you'll regret that lady. There are no movies of you in circulation, are they? You didn't get work as a public fornicator at any time?'

'Aye, that's me in the *Joy of Sex* books. I didn't know you were such a voyeur, Jules.'

'I love to peep, who doesn't love to peep?' she laughed.

'Call me old-fashioned if you like but I'm a bit squeamish about watching people having sex of any sort, be it in a field, on TV or on the internet. Am I weird?'

'For a bloke aye you are.'

Nick stretched out in the sun. It was a cloudless, blue day. The heat haze shimmered in the middle distance making the industrial weave of factories and chemical plants that stretched across the horizon blend into the land like a man-made mirage.

'I used to hike up here all the time as a kid and not once did I ever see anyone ever having even as much as a kiss, let alone oral sex. That was the sexy 1970s for you.'

'It's the heat. It makes everyone horny.'

'I'm hot but I'm not horny, are you?'

'I could quite easily be persuaded to be horny. And so could you if I put my hands down your pants.'

'True, but that'd be the case if it was snowing up here and, in fairness, we've been shagging like dogs in heat since we moved in together.'

'Aye, I don't think I've ever had it off as much, not even when I was younger.'

'We should have kept count.'

'I have.' She grinned and pushed her fair hair off her forehead.

'Gettaway. Have you?'

'Yeah, most of my diary is about sex. Always has been. Times, places, sizes. All the good stuff. Have you not had a peek? There's a huge boxful from the last 40 years in the spare room.'

'Certainly not. It's your private stuff and I'm not sure that much porny depravity is good for my moral soul. So what's the total?'

'52 in 26 days. I can break it down by position too if you want. And that doesn't even include hand jobs, blow jobs or dry-humping. Not bad for a couple in their 40s, eh.'

She grinned at him again, proud of their achievement.

'Bloody hell. Given that startling statistic it's surprising it's not us down in that field.'

'We did once have it off in a field, remember?'

'Oh yeah, where was that now?'

'St. Abbs, up the Northumberland coast. We'd only been going out for a few weeks.'

'I wonder if anyone was watching us with binoculars.'

'They'd not have got much of show; you were so worked up you only lasted about 30 seconds.'

'My seed was built for speed in those days, baby. Here, take your eyes off the sex show for a minute and have your tea.'

He handed her a cup.

'Thanks. Eeee, I'm clamming. It's proper maftin today. Nice spot this, tucked away out of the wind and with all of Teesside spread out in front of us, like.'

They sat in silence. A skylark rose from the fields below twittering a mellifluous song. The sun felt glorious and nourishing.

'From up here you can see just how small Teesside really is.

When you came up here in the 70s, the whole area would be sitting under a strip of impenetrable brown smog, no matter what time of the year it was, but now it's so much cleaner, you can see for about 50 miles in any direction on a day like this,' he said

'Yeah, but you know, sometimes I miss the smog,' she said.

'You miss that vague burning sensation in your nose?'

'Yeah. The smell of ammonia and sulphur is literally the smell of home, isn't it? And it was our thing, wasn't it?'

'What do you mean?'

'The smog, it was our thing. It was what made Teesside a distinctive place to grow up. It had a bleak sort of romance and that always made me feel that I wouldn't want to be anything other than a Teessider. The smog forged us. When I sit up here and look out at it all, it makes me feel proud to have been raised here. I bloody love being a Teessider, me.'

'Yeah, I know what you mean. The smog was our unique *eau de cologne*. Can't say I'm sad not to be choking on it now, but there is something brilliantly mythic about Teesside. It's not a county; it's got no precise definition and no boundaries that can be found on a map. Is Teesside even real? Does it really even exist other than as the TS part of the local postcode? Yet the funny thing is that we all think we know where it is, where it starts and stops and we know we are, above anything else, Teessiders. Wherever we go in the world, wherever we live, for our whole lives, we'll only know ourselves as Teessiders. It's tattooed into our cultural DNA. All because of this small strip of land either side of the river. It's weird...but a good weird.'

Julie finished her tea and picked up the binoculars again.

'Let's have another look at our two lovebirds then. Ah, they're all done and walking back to the car. Eeee fizzin' hell, she's no age, y'know. '

'She's young?'

'Yeah. She can't be more than 16 at most now that I've got a full look of her.'

'What about the bloke?'

'He's in his early 30s I'd say. Odd-looking bloke.'

'Maybe he's only 18 but just looks old. He might be Scottish.'

'I hope she's not under-age.'

'Is any sort of sex illegal if you're under 16 or just the old wang dang doodle?'

'I think it's just the actual humping. If it isn't then I broke the law for about a year.'

'I'd better take you and your over-active loins down the police station then.'

She followed them with the binoculars until they got into their car, which was parked up in a lay-by next to another car. Both cars drove off in opposite directions.

Nick got to his feet. 'Come on then lady, let's get down this hill and get back home.'

She tied her hair back into a ponytail and pulled on a baseball cap to shade her eyes from the afternoon sun.

'It's funny isn't it?'

'What is?'

They walked north and then west down a slope and back to a well-worn track.

'Going back home together.'

He grinned at her. 'Yeah it is...well, it's only been a few weeks, hasn't it?'

'Aye, no regrets though?'

'Nah 'course not. It's great, man. And we were lucky to get this place, really. Nice old farmhouses don't come up to rent that often so near to Yarm. Certainly not the sort of places we can afford anyway.'

'I reckon half of our neighbours must be footballers.'

'Well they've always all lived around Yarm, haven't they? I must have interviewed dozens of players over the years that lived within a couple of miles' radius of the town. Funny that they don't choose Billingham.'

She laughed. 'I can't see the WAGS being happy with an address near Ammonia Avenue.'

'Ah, the very accurately named Ammonia Avenue - also a very good album by The Alan Parsons Project.'

She groaned. 'Rock trivia about Billingham? Bloody hell.'

'Of course. And Alan Parsons is most famous for producing which album?'

'Too easy - *Dark Side of the Moon*. Even I know that.'

'Good work, just keeping you on your toes.'

'...ah ha...I've got you! He didn't produce Dark Side; he was the engineer...ha! The band produced it.'

She slapped him lightly on the top of the head in triumph.

'I suppose it's too late to pretend I meant Al Stewart's *Year Of The Cat* album, isn't it?'

'You're busted, son...and it's Julie 1 Nick 0.' She punched the air.

He laughed as they climbed over a wooden gate and then pointed to a figure coming up the track that led from the road.

'See who this is?' said Nick.

She perched on top of the fence and squinted

'Ah yeah, its Jimmy Repp isn't it?'

'It is indeed, The Dutch Diver himself, Boro's finest reserve goalkeeper.'

'He never gets a game.'

'Nah, Schwarzer's too good and Repp was injured most of last season anyway. He's a nice bloke though, I know him a bit...I've done some interviews with him. Not your typical footballer; he's into art.'

'Ah that's funny because I actually know his girlfriend really well. She lived three doors down from my mam's house on the Hardwick Estate. I used to babysit her, actually. '

'Really?'

'Yeah, apparently it was the talk of the estate last year when they got together. They hooked up as soon as he arrived on Teesside a year ago.'

'Hey Jimmy,' said Nick waving at him as he approached.

The tall goalkeeper broke into a smile as he recognised him

'Hey there Nick, what are you doing here?' he said with a distinct Dutch accent.

'We've just been having a hike around the hills. Great view from the top - you can see for miles up there,' he said, grinning to himself about what they had seen. 'This is my girlfriend, Julie. She's a big Boro fan as well.'

'Just since 1971,' she said with a smile.

'Hi Julie, nice to meet you,' he said and held out his hand.

'How's Pinky?' she said

'Pinky is great. You know her?'

'Yeah, she grew up three doors down from my mam's house. I sometimes used to look after her. God that makes me feel old.'

'Ah great. I'll tell her that I met you.'

'How's pre-season training going?' asked Nick, swatting flies away from his eyes.

'It's going okay. No injuries for a change.'

'Do you do much hiking up here?' asked Julie. 'We don't see many footballers on the hills.'

'...we don't see *any* footballers on the hills, you mean. Hiking isn't most footballers' idea of a good time really, is it?' said Nick.

He laughed. 'No, shopping for watches is of course their favourite...err...what to say...err pastime, yes?'

'We've just moved to an old farmhouse about a mile out of Yarm, so we'll probably be seeing a few of your mob around town,' said Nick.

'Ah really? That is good. Hey, you can't be far from my new place then. We just moved out of the hotel last month.'

'Where's that?' asked Julie.

'You know Egglescliffe? Well, it is just down the Aislaby Road. It's set back from the road. Nice place. Very private, you know. You guys should come round. I'm having a housewarming at the weekend.'

'Free drinks? I'm all for that, like,' said Julie with a broad smile.

'Great. Give me your e-mail and I'll send you the details.'

Nick wrote it on a scrap of paper and handed it over.

'Thanks Nick. I'll see you guys.'

He gripped Nick's hand in a brief iron hold and then walked off into the distance, heading up towards Roseberry Topping.

'He does seem nice...,' said Julie watching him go, '...and rather good-looking.'

'Yeah, he is. A bit of a gentle giant. It'll be interesting to see his house. I bet it's a big new-build.'

The next day, Nick had to drive down to Hull City to interview the chairman for the Yorkshire Post. When he got back home he found an e-mail from Repp in his inbox with the details of the party on Saturday night. It was only a couple of miles from their house as the crow flies. He went into the bedroom to tell Julie. She'd just had a bath and was wrapped in an enormous blue towel.

'It's a really formal invite e-mail. An HTML image of a gold-embossed card: 'Jimmy and Pinky invite you to an evening of food and drink'.'

'What, like the digital equivalent of an RSVP invite?'

'Aye, it says we've got to confirm. Pinky is an odd name, eh?'

'It's a nickname that's sort of become her name.'

'Oh right, like Sting?'

'Yeah. She would only wear pink when she was little. Even now, she always has something pink on. That's how it came about.'

'Doesn't sound like my kinda chick. Pink-obsessed girls are too...you know...too girly for me. I never know what to say to that sort of woman. It's like they're the female equivalent of macho men...uber women, maybe...you know what I mean?"

'Yeah, she's definitely a bit too girly-girly for your tastes. Good-looking kid though. Glamorous.'

'Well she's fallen on her feet getting hooked up with a footballer. Jimmy will be on decent money by most people's standards.'

'According to my mam - who reckons she knows everyone's

business - Maggie, that's her mam, encouraged the relationship.'

'I bet she did - even the crumbs from the footballer's table are always tasty.'

She shed the towel and put on some lightweight cotton pyjamas. He stripped off his t-shirt and jeans and went into the bathroom for a wash. It was steamy, damp and fragrant from Julie's bath. He looked at himself in the mirror. He'd grown a full beard since they'd moved in together and it had emerged in black, shades of grey and a fleck or two of white. His dark hair was nearly to his shoulders.

'Do you think I should get my hair cut, Jules?'

'No. I like it longer, especially with the beard.'

'I do look like a tramp though.'

'Being an unkempt sort of animal is your thing,' she shouted back. 'I like you looking a bit rough. You don't suit being tidy.'

He went back into the bedroom while brushing his teeth.

'Unkempt? Me? I'll have you know it costs a lot of money to look this cheap, baby.'

'Did those underpants come with a hole in the arse, like? Is it a design feature?'

'Yer jokin' aren't ya? I paid extra for the hole.'

He spat out the toothpaste and laughed to himself while he got washed, then got into bed naked and put his arm around her shoulder as she cuddled into him.

She yawned.

'Oh God, I'm dog-tired after all that walking. Do you want to have the old Percy Filth?'

'Well...if madam needs to be slipped a length...I am prepared to have a bloody good go at it.'

He rubbed her torso with the flat of his hand, circling the rim of her belly button with his finger. She looked up at him and smiled.

'God, there's a blast from the past; I haven't been slipped a length since the 80s.'

'Yeah it's a phrase that seems to have lost its popularity but it's got a nice graphic quality.'

She idly stroked his cock.

'Well, I do fancy a length...at least in theory... but I don't think I've got the energy to do it justice and it's so hot tonight.'

'Aye it is a hot one, like, and it's warm in here as well.'

She kissed him on the lips. 'Mmm, very funny, let's bank it for later. Now turn over, I don't want your pork bone poking up my bum all night. It's very distracting.'

'You do say the most romantic things.'

He put out his light and turned over so his back was facing her.

She fell to sleep almost immediately but he lay there in the soft blackness of night listening to her breathing, feeling relaxed. Living in the countryside, well away from a road, was so quiet and dark compared to living in his flat on a main road in Harrogate. Exactly how different had really taken him by surprise. You get so used to noise that it's merely a constant, ever-present soundtrack. He'd handed in the keys to his flat with mixed feelings. He'd loved the apartment and he had established a life in Harrogate. His best mate, indeed his only real friend, Jeff, still lived there. Moving to rural Teesside meant a change of lifestyle, but not for one moment since they'd made the decision to move in together again had he thought it was the wrong choice. Quite the opposite: he was pretty sure he'd never been happier.

They had spent 18 months under the same roof in Harrogate - 18 bad months which had eventually seen them go their separate ways. But that split was over two years ago now. It had been a long, slow repair job to fix their relationship but it had been worth the wait and the work because now they'd never been more in love. A mixture of therapy, quitting alcohol and a low-carb diet seemed to have kept the depression which had cursed him for decades at bay for the last few months. It was like having a weight lifted from his body and soul. Life felt good, unusually good and unusually happy, which, as a man brought up to expect the exact opposite, was in itself a bit worrying.

CHAPTER 2

'Will blue jeans and this do, do you reckon?' asked Nick, holding up a fitted white shirt.

She came out of the bedroom. 'Aye, fine. I'm just going in these linen jeans and a black t-shirt. It's just drinks round someone's house, it's not a wedding, like, is it? I daresay I'll look under-dressed next to any footballers' wives though.'

'They'll probably think you're a lesbian because you don't wear any make-up.'

'Almost certainly, yeah. In that case, you can be my gay boyfriend.'

'No problem. As long as I don't have to pretend to like show tunes.'

He drove them over to Jimmy Repp's house. It was a large newly built redbrick, Georgian-inspired affair well set back from the road.

'Blimey, this makes our old farmhouse look like a small ruin,' said Julie as they drove up on a warm, breezy, blue sky Saturday night.

'Aye, it's massive. Look at the size of the grounds. What's that? A six-car garage?'

'You could park Belgium in there and still have room for Darlington,' she said with a snort.

'I bet there's a pool at the back as well,' said Nick as they approached the house.

The front door was wide and tall with double doors and finished in high-gloss white paint. He pressed a button beside the door and somewhere in the distance a bell rang.

A clip-clop of heels on floor tiles approached and opened one of the doors. It was a short-ish young woman in her early 20s with shoulder-length, loosely curled blonde hair and a low-cut black blouse, worn with tight bright pink jeans, heavy black eye-liner and pink, glossy lips.

'Hi there, it's Nick and Julie,' he said pointing to himself and then to her.

11

She gave him a big smile.

'Oweee in youse two,' she said in a very broad Teesside accent, similar to Julie's.

Julie stopped and waved at her,

'Pinky. It's me, Julie from the estate, like.'

The girl looked her up and down forensically and then pointed at her.

'Eeee God, Jules, I'm sorry, I never realised it was you...eeee you look dead smart you like. I've not seen you for a while have I?'

'No, not to speak to anyway. It doesn't feel that many years ago since I was babysitting you for Maggie. How is your mam?'

'Mam? She's alright...though her nerves have been playing up recently. She's been on pins, like, but I'm sure it's nowt really. How are you, then?'

'Great. Thanks.

'And where do youse two live?'

'Just a couple of miles away. We've got an old farmhouse out in the country. Nick's a football writer; I'm at Durham University - mature student, like.'

'Oh okay, that's good. God, I couldn't wait to get off the estate. I swear down there was no way I was staying there any longer than I had to. I'll take you through to the pool.'

'How long have you two lived here then?' said Julie as they walked.

She turned and pushed a blonde curl off her face.

'Not long. It's only just been finished in the last couple of months.'

'It looks huge,' said Nick as they passed between two curving stairways which led to the first floor.

Pinky stopped and laughed. It's stupidly big. You could fit my mam's house into this about 20 times. We rattle around in here like two peas in a drum.'

She gave them another big attractive smile and led them down a passage tiled in a black and white checked pattern, surrounded on the edges by a Romanesque block pattern. Large modern art paintings hung on the walls as they walked through to a kitchen area where a team of three caterers busied themselves preparing food. They looked up as Nick and Julie came in and smiled.

'Hi there...,' said a woman with black hair clipped up on the back of her head.

'Can I help with anything?' said Julie. 'I'm a good chopper.'

'I'm not but I'm good at beating meat if that helps,' said Nick.

The caterers laughed. 'That's fine, we don't need any meat-beaters. We've got everything under control,' said a thin man who was busy making salsa while wearing a white apron.

Adjoining the kitchen was a conservatory well-stocked with palms, other hothouse plants and cane furniture. An alabaster white sculpture of an abstract nude woman with what looked like a snake or perhaps a rope wrapped around her stood centrally.

'That's a Phyllis Plant sculpture,' Nick said to Julie as they passed by.

'Who?'

'Famous painter and sculptor. Originally from North Yorkshire. She was briefly part of that whole Barbara Hepworth, Ben Nicholson crowd. Her work is super-valuable now. She died about 15 or 20 years ago.'

'Blimey, it looks like something you might find in a garden centre to me.'

'Philistine.'

'Phyllis Stein? I thought she was called Phyllis Plant.'

He laughed as they walked out to a pool area.

'Guests, Jimmy!' shouted Pinky.

The big footballer looked up. He was fixing a large gas barbecue.

'Ah, hello guys. Make yourself at home. Pinky, can you get the guys a drink? I'll be right over.'

'What would you like?' said Pinky, dutifully but still with her fixed smile.

'I'll have a white wine if you've got it,' said Julie.

'What sort? He's got like hundreds of bottles in the cellar.'

'Chablis would be good.'

'Okay and what would you like, Nick?'

'Just fizzy water is fine for me.'

'No problem, I'll get those for you.'

In the distance a bell rang, announcing more arrivals. Engines revved and tyres crunched on gravel as a glut of people arrived.

The evening was sunny and warm in a way which seemed entirely alien to anyone who spent any time on Teesside. As this was the sixth day of temperatures in the mid-70s and summery blue skies, some were already saying it must be a sign of an onrushing apocalypse.

Pinky brought their drinks just as Jimmy approached brandishing a pair of long tongs.

'Right, that's fixed now, yes...ah, you have your drinks,' he said, speaking with a classic Dutch 'sch' at the end of some words but otherwise in flawless English. 'It's good to see you guys, it's a beautiful evening, yes?'

'It sure is. Thanks for having us over. I suppose some of the Boro lads will be here soon,' said Nick.

He shook his head.

'Nah, I see them all the time, so...no...this isn't for them, it's for everyone else. Anyway, we've got a little announcement to make and it really wouldn't be of interest to any of the lads.'

'An announcement?' quizzed Nick. 'You're not getting married, are you?'

Jimmy laughed. 'Oh my God, no. Ha. No no...it's a little venture I've undertaken...all will be revealed. Now, I must go and get the meat ready for the barbecue.'

'He's unusual, that's for sure,' said Julie as he walked off, 'not a regular knuckle-headed footballer.'

'God no, he's probably thought of as some sort of weird intellectual in the dressing-room. By the look of the paintings in the hall and kitchen, he's something of a collector. Though his taste in music could do with a reboot...is this Coldplay?'

'Sadly, it is. Footballers never have good taste in music though, do they? It's traditional. Funny seeing Pinky here playing the host. Not sure it suits her really.'

'No, I know what you mean; it's a bit as though she's doing it through gritted teeth.'

'Well she's lived with him in that hotel for months so this will be her first time doing this sort of thing. I mean, we're not brought up on the estate to host glamorous drinks parties in big posh houses. Not unless watching the telly while drinking white cider counts as glamorous.'

A group of people all talking at once moved out of the kitchen and into the conservatory. Nick turned to look at them.

'See that bloke in the blue polo shirt and white jeans?' he asked.

'Shaven head? Yeah, he looks familiar.'

'That's Trevor McMahon, inevitably known as Macca, bit of a journeyman player, retired last year.'

'Ah yeah, he played for Sunderland for a bit, didn't he?'

'Yeah, famously got into a fight with the chairman. He spent most of the last few years playing in the lower leagues, ended up at Brentford. He wasn't a bad striker in his day, mind. I'm pretty sure he played for England under-18s about 20 years ago. Strange to see him here.'

'Is he not local?'

'He's a Cockney or some variant thereof...born in Upminster. Don't know why that sticks in my mind.'

'Probably because it's an Ian Dury album, isn't it? *Lord Upminster.*'

He turned to her and nodded. 'You never cease to amaze me, little miss rock 'n' roll.'

She grinned. 'It's years of hanging round with you, man, it rubs off. He's lovely-looking though isn't he with those blue eyes?'

'...and built like a brick shithouse. He's from the old Mick Harford school of strikers. You wouldn't want to run into him, would you?'

'Not unless you actually enjoy lying unconscious on the ground, no. He's a big boy and he seems very friendly with Jimmy, look, he can't keep his hands off him.'

As the two big men talked, Macca kept pawing at Jimmy Repp's arm, shoulder, slapping him on the back and generally being very tactile.

'A lot of footballers are like that though, aren't they? They're the only men in society who feel a compulsion to rub and slap each other's thighs. Just look at them on TV, they're always doing it. I dunno where they get it from these days. I'm sure Billy Bremner never got his thighs slapped by Jack Charlton.'

'Big Jack'd have laid him out for even thinking it,' said Julie.

Soon the house was full and very noisy with the chatter of about 70 people. They had just been served some delicious hot dogs from the barbecue when Julie gave him a nudge in the ribs.

'Look who's coming over here, three o'clock...remember him?'

'Err...not really.'

'The blonde bloke.'

'Yeah I see him...is he a footballer?'

'I don't know but I do know he was the bloke we saw in the field. Mr TP.'

'Mr TP?

'Tiny penis.'

'Ah, our nature boy?'

'The very same.'

'How weird. I wonder how he knows Jimmy.'

'Strange that we saw him in the field and then met Jimmy and now he's here,' she said, frowning at Nick. He shrugged. It did seem an odd coincidence.

He was tanned, about 5'6", quite skinny, probably in his mid-30s and dressed fashionably with a silver necklace and a silver bracelet on his left wrist.

'Mind, he's not exactly a looker, is he?' said Julie. 'Dear me. He's lucky to be getting any action with a face like that and a nadger that small.'

'Don't be nasty to him. He can't help it. You're born with what you're born with. You'd be really annoyed if I said that about a woman and her tits,' said Nick, taking a quick look. Christ, he was stop-a-cheap-clock ugly though. His face looked like it was offended by itself and was trying to crawl off his head.

She laughed. 'Sorry, you're right, that was mean of me. It's just that he is...well...unusual-looking.'

'Maybe he was brought up next to a nuclear power station. There's a touch of the radioactive mutant about him.'

Julie snorted and nearly choked on her wine, slapping him on the arm as she did so. 'Don't make me laugh like that...I nearly bloody drowned.'

They listened in on Mr TP chatting to another guest. He talked quickly in an odd, rather high-pitched voice and kept letting out little staccato bursts of fake laughter. After a couple of minutes, perhaps sensing them looking at him, he turned around and smiled, revealing white, uneven teeth.

'Hi there...how are you? I'm Yashie,' he said, doing his little laugh and holding out a small, flabby, pale hand.

'I'm Nick, this is Julie.'

'What do you do, Nick?'

'I write about football.'

'Ah...a journalist?'

'Not really. I mostly do books and opinion pieces. I do a bit of freelance work covering matches as well, like.'

'Ah right, right. You know a lot about football then?'

'He's a *Rothman's Football Annual* on legs,' said Julie.

'It's a *Sky Annual* now, actually,' said Nick.

'So tell me, who you think will win the league this year?'

He spoke like someone from the Far East but wasn't oriental in the slightest.

'It'll be Man United just ahead of Chelsea. Ronaldo will make the difference for them, though I fancy Torres to do well at Liverpool,' said Nick who, at this time of the year, always had to have predictions ready for the coming season.

'Ha yeah yeah...tell me this, you put any money on it?'

'No. I'm not a betting man really.'

Oh okay. You wanna good bet, you come see me. I give you great tip. You make money. I'll see you later,' he said, turning and walking off, just like that.

'What a strange man,' said Julie. 'He's a non-Chinese Chinaman.'

'Yeah. An NCC. Weird. Right, I'm just going for a whazz,' said Nick. 'I bet the bogs are great here.'

He walked into the house and ran into Pinky.

'Can you point me to the toilet?' he asked.

'The nearest one is just through the passage and on your left,' she said, again with a big smile. 'Are you enjoying yourself, Nick?"

'Yes thanks, lovely. Well done on remembering my name too, I'm terrible at remembering names unless they're especially memorable like yours.'

'Well, I looked you up on the internet earlier today, didn't I? So it stuck in my mind, like.'

She gave him a small, wry smile.

'There was all sorts of stories about you getting into one scrape or another in the last couple of years. You're a right trouble-maker you aren't you?' She said it like it was a good thing.

'Yeah, well sometimes trouble just seems to find me.' He shrugged and grinned mischievously.

'Hmm...well, it may have just found you again, son,' as she raised an arched eyebrow.

'I've never actually met a Pinky before.'

'I've always been called Pinky, me, since I was a little kid. I always loved the colour pink and wore pink clothes...so it sort of stuck. My real name is Kelly...Kelly Gull...but no-one ever calls us that.'

'Gull? Is that Scandinavian?'

She nodded. 'My dad's family were originally from Sweden. So

I'm probably the only WAG with *real* blonde hair. She shook her curls at him.

'And very nice hair it is. Well, a lot of us have Viking blood around here don't we?'

She had delicate features, sharp cheekbones and a small nose, but a hard look in her pale blue almond eyes; a hard look that told of being brought up in poverty. It stuck with you and even affluent living couldn't wipe it away.

'I remember there were two puppets called Pinky and Perky when I was a kid. I'd rather be Pinky than Perky, I reckon. If I had to choose, like. I've never been a perky fella. In fact nothing about me is perky.'

'No, but I bet some bits of you are pink,' she said, giving him a cheeky smile from the corner of her mouth and putting her well-manicured hand on his bare, tanned arm. It can't have been the first time she'd used that line.

'Only the really big important bits,' he said, raising an eyebrow.

'Eeee don't brag,' she said with a rising inflective, laughing. When she smiled directly at you, it really stuck and you wanted more. It was both flattering and exciting all at once.

'So you were staying at the Teesside International before you moved here? That's a lovely country house hotel.'

'Hmm, it is. I loved it, like. Waited on hand and foot. It makes you dead lazy though.'

'So where did you meet Jimmy?'

'In Spain when he was playing for Seville. I was on holiday but I didn't know who he was 'cos I know nowt about football. I just met him in a hotel bar. We had a bit of a fling over there, like, but when he signed for Boro he called me up and that's really how it started, like. Dead quick really.'

'Well they do say when love comes to town you gotta ride that train,' said Nick making a forward gesture with his hand.

She nodded but seemed a bit puzzled by his comment. 'Eh? Oh, err, yeah...yeah...something like that, anyway. It's a very different life with Jimmy, like...God, aye.'

'The money is crazy, some might even say obscene,' he said, looking around at the ostentatious wealth.

'Aye, but life without money is such bloody hard work, isn't it? I've had my bloody fill of that,' she said with more bitterness than he expected.

'Tell me about it. I've made being skint an art form.'

'...maybe I should have gone to college. Maybe I still will, like.'

'What would you have studied?'

'I fancied doing maths, me...don't look so surprised. I'm bloody good with numbers.'

She arranged the glasses on the tray. 'See...there's seven glasses on here.' She grinned up at him.

He applauded. 'Excellent. You'd make a glamorous mathematician. They don't usually look as good in tight pink jeans as you do, mind. Tweed jackets are more their sort of thing, traditionally.'

It was easy, natural almost, to flirt with her.

She threw her head back, laughed loudly and looked at him with her head on one side, a curtain of curly blonde strands hanging down.

'I like you. I dunno...I reckon you're my sort of bloke. Maybe I should've met you instead of Jimmy, what do you reckon?'

'I reckon I couldn't keep you in this kind of luxury and anyway, you don't wanna know me baby, I'm trouble,' he said in a film noirish American accent.

'I might just say the same thing to you, though, eh,' she said, raising an eyebrow. 'Do you have a card with your phone number? Just in case I need you, like.'

He always carried a card and he fished one from his back pocket.

'Well look, there's still time to go to college. Julie went back last year to university to do an MA when she was 41.'

'Really? She's always been dead clever though and she looks much younger than 41 an' all. Maybe brains keep you looking young.'

'That would explain why I look so bloody old then,' he said.

'Rubbish. Jimmy's got your books in the library. You can't be stupid if you write books, can you?'

'I wouldn't be so sure.'

'And you don't look that old to me. How old are you, like?'

'How old do you think I am?'

'35 or 36?'

'As much as I like to be flattered by a good-looking young woman, you know that isn't true, Pinky. I'm well over 46 and I bloody look it,' he said.

She laughed. 'Eeee well I think you look quality for an old bloke, like,' she said, resting the flat of her hand on his chest and fiddling with a shirt button. 'Are you and Jules close, then?'

'Close? Yeah we just live a couple of miles away.'

'I didn't mean that sort of close. I meant, close close. I mean, you're not married are you?'

'No, we're not into marriage. But we really bloody love each other, y'know. We drifted apart a couple of years ago and just moved back in with each other. I've never been happier.'

A look of disappointment played across her face briefly and he almost felt like he should apologise.

'Aw, that's dead nice. Well I suppose I'll have to get on with playing at being the tarty servant lass to Jimmy's friends.

'It's a big turn-out. There's a lot of tarty servanting to be done.'

She smiled at a middle-aged man in a linen suit who walked passed and then she sneered as soon as he was gone.

'I wouldn't trust any of them as far as I can spit,' she said. She turned to a kitchen bench, put down some empty glasses, picked up full ones and put them on her tray. 'They're all blood suckers, liars and arseholes. Don't believe anything any of them say to you Nick...really...,' she glanced from side to side, her face set in sneer and added, 'you and Julie are probably the only real people here. Don't believe anything anyone says to you about almost anything...most of them are totally fake, including Jimmy. Now, I must get on...I'll see you later.'

She pursed her lips together, blew him an invisible kiss and moved off with her tray of drinks. Man, she was really something.

The boobs, tight pants and blonde curls suggested she was just another footballer's bimbo but that was obviously far from the truth. This was a smart kid with a unusually bright spark.

The bathroom, predictably enough, was huge. The floor was pink marble and the shower unit alone was almost bigger than the flat he'd lived in as a student. When he returned to the party, Julie was talking to Trev McMahon.

'Ah here his is...you know Macca don't you?' she said. 'Excuse me while I go to the toilet.' She gave Nick her glass and winked at him.

Nick held out his hand. 'Yeah I interviewed you about 15 years ago, didn't I?'

'To be honest mate, I don't remember,' he said in a broad Cockney accent. 'What I do know is that you've got a quality looker on your 'ands there, my son...very tasty indeed, if you don't mind me saying so. I was about to move into your manor, I'm thinkin', now there's a Doris for Macca, but I got the old red flag. Tragic. Ha ha. Some lovely birds here though eh, especially young Pinky there. What a cracker she is ...oof dear me...you would wouldn't you?'

Nick laughed. It was like being trapped in a conversation with a stereotypical Cockney character from The Sweeney; he even had the jerky head movements to go with the sexist banter.

'Aye, she's both Pinky and Perky isn't she?'

Macca laughed loudly like a malfunctioning foghorn.

'Now that is quality,' he said, nodding up and down, 'I'll catch you later, yeah?'

As Nick waited for Julie to return, he watched Pinky move amongst the knots of people with trays of drinks and bowls of wasabi peas, smiling and nodding. As she picked up some empty glasses, she noticed him looking in her direction and wiggled her fingers at him with a grin.

'Put your tongue back in, lad, she's a bit young for you,' said Julie, coming up behind him and taking her glass out of his hand. 'Mind you can't miss her in those pink jeans, like. Must be Versace's most fluorescent creation.'

'I was chatting to her when I went to the bog; she was thinking of going to go to college to do maths but I think she put it off when she met Jimmy.'

She shook her head. 'Yeah, I seem to recall mam saying she was a bright lass who was good at exams. Silly girl. Gave it up to be a kept woman. I mean you can see why, I suppose, but even so. Her mother is a real scunner and would never have paid a penny to help her go to college. That kid has been bloody dragged up on that estate.'

'Well, so were you and you did alright. Your lot were the hard knocks of the estate. Half of Teesside is still shit scared of your brothers. Even I'd heard of them a few miles away in comparatively genteel Fairfield.'

'It was all a bloody ton of hard work just to get a small step above what I was born into but life got much better as soon as I got out of that bubble. There's nothing romantic about growing up on a tough estate, so I know why she jumped at the chance.'

'Hmmm...well she seemed quite disillusioned about being a WAG and was very cynical about everyone here - she reckons they're all fakes.'

'Well there is a bloke over there with a wig on. Terrible.'

'A well dodgy syrup, as Macca would say. Oh and you'll be pleased to learn he thought you were a Doris.'

'A Doris? What's a Doris?'

'A Doris Day.'

'But I don't look anything like Doris Day, though I can slap my thigh and belt out a verse of The Windy City.'

'It's rhyming slang. Doris Day – easy lay.'

Julie laughed and then frowned. 'So he thought I was an easy lay, like?'

'...and a quality looker.'

'Do I give off the easy lay vibes, like? It's not as though I've got my tits out like Pinky.'

'...well, you've got that in your locker, to use a football cliché.'

'I've got easy lay in my locker? Yer jokin', aren't ya? I'm just being me, me,' she said, deliberately slipping into the local vernacular.

'Maybe you give off a 'shag me' pheromone.'

'Dogs have been known to follow me in the street...maybe that's why.'

'There you go then. Anyway, Pinky said we were probably the only two people here who weren't fake.'

'Oh she was just chatting you up, man. Flirting, like. It's second nature to stunners like her. It's how they get what they want. It's an art they learn young. When you're born with less than sod all, your looks and your body is all you've got so you learn how to use them. Or you try to, anyway.'

'Yeah maybe...I had the feeling she thought it was true though.'

There was a shriek from the other side of the pool where there was a wrought iron table and some other outdoor furniture. It was Pinky, standing toe to toe with Jimmy. Hardly a fair fight, he was almost a foot and a half taller than her.

She leapt into the air, slapped him in the face with all the power she had and then pounded her small fist on his chest, her face contorted in anger, screaming in his face: 'How can you let him talk about me like that?! You don't bloody give a shit, do you? Oh...just piss off. I'm fucking sick of this whole stupid fucking game! Who the hell do you think you are? You're nowt, you are. Nowt, son! You think you're something special but you're fucking nothing! And all these fucking tossers – you're all the same!'

She threw down a tray of at least half a dozen glasses, smashing them into shards, and ran towards the house. Stopping for a moment, she spun around to face everyone was who staring at her.

24

'What are you all looking at? Just ignore me, I'm nobody, just a bit of fluff, me...apparently.'

She kicked a glass and stormed off.

'Trouble in paradise,' said Nick, raising an eyebrow. Julie bit her bottom lip and watched her go into the house.

'Poor kid,' she said. 'That was from the heart wasn't it?'

'Yeah, it's probably been boiling up for ages. These sorts of things don't come out of nowhere, do they?'

There was an awkward pause of near-silence, interrupted by Jimmy.

'Sorry folks...a bit of a disagreement I'm afraid, err...yeah...she'll be okay,' he said, holding up his hands and then walking into the house looking embarrassed.

'The party row is a bad row to have,' said Julie. 'Dirty washing in public and all that.'

'Social functions put so much pressure on you to have a good time; that's why I've never been a party animal or celebrated Christmas or had planned holidays. The moment you know you're supposed to be enjoying yourself but aren't, it makes you feel twice as bad.'

'I hope she's okay,' she said, casting a glance towards the house again.

'She did seem really upset but then we don't know if this is typical for them or not. Some people fight all the time, don't they?'

'She's a tough little madam. She wouldn't typically show that amount of emotion in public. I think I should go and see if she's okay.'

'Give her a couple of minutes to calm down first,' said Nick.

As he spoke, a middle-aged, well-dressed man in a sharp suit, close-cut grey hair and rick oak-coloured tan came out onto the terrace.

'Can I have your attention please? Yeah? Thanks. So, we've got a bit of an announcement to make.'

Jimmy came up alongside him, now smiling again.

'I hate people who inappropriately start sentences with 'so',' said Nick into Julie's ear.

'So, I really hate it too. That and the rising inflective. Should be illegal unless you're Australian or from California,' she said.

'As some of you know, I'm Frankie Gray and as Jimmy's business manager it's my job to invest his money in interesting projects and, as I'm sure you know, the big man here has always been very interested in art and has amassed quite a collection. So one of the reasons to get you all here is to celebrate the fact that we're very excited to announce we'll be opening the Jimmy Repp Gallery in Yarm later this year. We've just signed the lease on a place in the High Street. It'll be a fully commercial gallery, not just some rich guy's plaything. We aim to make it one of the most prestigious galleries for modern art in the north. As part of the project, Jimmy will personally be curating exhibitions of some of his own collections.'

Jimmy was grinning widely.

'It's very, very exciting for us. The first exhibition will be of my Phyllis Plant collection but I have arranged a little preview for you guys, yeah? If you follow me into my private gallery...'

As he said 'private gallery', he gave a rather camp roll of the eyes as if to indicate he knew it was very pretentious.

'Should we be pleased for him, do you reckon? I mean, okay, you want to open your own gallery but I'd wager most people here couldn't care if he was opening a gallery or a cake shop,' said Nick.

'Footballers think the world rotates around them though, don't they? They're always the centre of attention. Even the nice ones,' said Julie.

People followed Jimmy from the patio and into the east wing of the house. Nick and Julie stayed towards the back of the queue as they all filed into a large room which had been modelled on every modern art gallery, with its white walls, blond wood floors and two large oblong central black leather seats.

Around the walls were around 50 ink drawings on white paper

from miniatures up to larger poster-sized works, all mounted and framed identically in thin black wood. They were arranged around six large oil paintings and towards each corner of the room stood a sculpture on a marble plinth.

Nick looked at one of the artworks as they entered. It appeared to be a preparatory sketch for a sculpture of an abstract nude woman. Another was a complex shaded bio-form drawn in charcoal, a third a pen and ink of a head with two hollow eyes. There was something really impressive about them. Drawn with a quick, firm, positive hand, they had an effortless energy that suggested Phyllis Plant had a strong vision and could manifest it quickly. Each picture was signed with her distinctive stacked PP with the stem of the second capital P stuck into the round of the other. He'd seen her work quite frequently over the years, particularly her sculpture, and it had grown on him as he'd got older. At first it seemed difficult and pretentious but now, to his older eyes, it felt complex and deep.

'Are these expensive?' asked Julie, sipping from a fresh glass of Chablis.

'Oh yeah, I'd have thought so, she's a big name is old PP.'

'Is she? I've not heard of her.'

They had rarely seen eye to eye on art. During their worst arguments he'd all but accused her of being wilfully ignorant but the real truth was that she just struggled to 'get' abstract impressionism and the like, which was very much his favourite kind of art. Since their reconciliation they both now accepted that you could no more persuade someone to enjoy your taste in art than you could make them like the music you enjoy. This was an emotional and intellectual leap for him, but it had stopped them having any more arguments.

'So how much money is in this room then?' she asked as people filed past looking at each work in turn.

'God, I've no idea. Millions. Do you like this sculpture, Jules? I think it's ace.'

It was a bio-form of two interlocked shapes. Perfectly smooth and carved from quartz, it had an inner luminescence. Discoloured lines innate to the stone ran through the piece like veins, suggesting the whole thing was an internal organ from a calcified creature.

'Yeah. I like the stone. It's a huge piece of quartz, I think,' she said, resting her chin on her hand. 'I know I shouldn't ask what it is, but that's the first thing that actually comes into my mind. I want to know what it's supposed to be. I'm just a common lass from Hardwick, remember.'

'We weren't brought up to like art, were we? We were brought up to mock it, if anything. Not for the grubby working-class oiks like us. I just love this though. It's like you can almost see it breathing.'

'Do you like it?' said Jimmy, walking up behind him. Nick spun around and smiled. 'I love it. Does it have a title?'

'Yeah, *Woman Heart*. Not Woman's Heart but *Woman Heart*. So it doesn't belong to a specific woman, it is really a...a kind of representation of the female heart. Great huh? It's my favourite too.'

'I didn't realise you were quite such a big collector,' said Nick.

He shrugged and looked bashful. 'I don't like to talk about it much when I'm on football duty. Yeah, it's my passion – more than football really. Much more.'

Julie excused herself to go and use the bathroom and check on Pinky while Nick looked at the rest of the sketches and drawings. Imagine being rich enough to amass your own art gallery collection by the time you were 30. Boro didn't pay the biggest money in football by a long way and even if he was on good wages in Spain, it wouldn't have paid for all this. This was worth many, many millions and this was only his PPs; he had a lot of other artworks too.

As much as Jimmy and Nick liked the art, it was clearly only of passing interest to almost everyone else. Polite interest was paid but soon it became just another background to the conversations and arguments.

'Pinky is in tears y'know,' said Julie as she returned. 'I just saw her as I came out of the toilet. The downstairs one was busy so I went on the first floor. She was in a bedroom, sitting on the edge of a bed and had her head in her hands, poor lass. I went over and put an arm around her but she wouldn't say anything about the row. She seemed very vulnerable, somehow. She's only a kid really. Felt really sorry for her but didn't know what to say or do.'

'Aw, poor Pinky.'

'I hate the idea of someone being so upset and on their own. No-one else here seems to give a shit. I mean, where's Jimmy? Why doesn't he go to her? He doesn't seem to be paying her any thought. And she doesn't seem to have any other friends here. She's on her own.'

'Jimmy's over there with Macca and the rest of them. They're all too busy talking at each other if you ask me.'

'Yeah, it's all too like that for my liking. Everyone I've spoken to couldn't wait for me to shut up so they could begin talking at me,' she said. 'Too bloody full of themselves if you ask me. C'mon, let's go back and find her.'

They left the gallery room and took the thickly carpeted curved stairway up to the first floor.

As they reached the landing, Frankie Gray came towards them. 'If you need a bedroom, you can use any on this floor - he doesn't use them.' He laughed and trotted downstairs.

Nick looked at Julie. 'Urghh. Is he sleazy, or what?'

She mimed putting her finger down her throat. 'Come on, she was down here.'

They walked past a white tiled toilet beyond which a bedroom door was open. A large bed covered in a white cotton quilt was visible.

'She was sitting on the edge of the bed here,' said Julie as they went in. There was still an indentation where she'd sat and a scrunched-up tissue on the floor, but she'd gone.

They walked back to the landing and looked in other rooms but they were empty. Immaculate but empty.

They had a quick look around the rest of the house. No sign of her.

'She must have left,' said Nick. Julie let out a sigh.

'I hope she's okay. I bet she's gone home to Maggie's,' said Julie. 'Shall we make our excuses and go? There's something really soulless about this place. There's no warmth in it, nothing that makes you feel as though people actually live their lives here. It's all a bit depressing and I think being around so much money is basically getting on my wick.'

'You know what it looks like? It looks like the set of an early 80s soft porn movie. All we need is some saxophone music and big hair. I'd much rather live in our scruffy run-down farmhouse. Yeah let's do the polite stuff and get going.'

They went back through to the kitchen and spotted Jimmy out by the pool talking to Macca and Frankie. They all stopped talking and turned to look at them as they approached. Frankie glanced at Julie, said something in Macca's ear and he nodded with a sly smile on his lips. It was irritating and felt like being back at school, somehow.

'We've got to get going, Jimmy...thanks for inviting us, I hope your gallery does well,' said Nick, holding his hand out. Jimmy shook it with a smile.

'No problem guys...thanks for coming over. I hope you'll come to the opening. I'll send you an invitation, okay?'

'Thank you,' said Julie with a polite smile. 'I don't know if you know but Pinky seems to have left, she was very upset, she was crying...well...err...I thought you should know.'

She looked from one of them to the other. No response. Not a flicker of concern or sympathy from any of them. Jimmy didn't even stop smiling. He nodded and then shrugged. 'Oh yeah, well she gets like that, you know, a little crazy...she'll be fine...she'll probably have gone to her mother's. You guys know your way out, don't you? Straight through to the front door.'

'Okay guys, nice to meet you all,' said Nick as the two other men waved a hand each.

As Nick and Julie walked back through the house and out of the front door, she took his hand and said: 'Well that was creepy.'

'Agreed. Didn't like that at all. Bad vibes, man.'

'Something is wrong there. That Macca sets my 'rapey' alarm off, for a start. And now I'm bloody worried about that poor girl too. I hope something hasn't been going on...y'know...something seedy. You know what footballers are like...roasting girls in hotels and all that. They seem to think sex is a competitive group sport.'

'I don't think Jimmy is like that and there are no other players here.'

'No. Not him maybe but the others and that Yashie guy - he was just downright odd.'

'Have you really got a rapey alarm?' he said as they got in the car.

'Most women have got a rapey alarm. Ask anyone. Some men just give off that vibe.'

'I suppose it's the same as that sixth sense that you had when going to the football in the 70s which told you when it was all about to kick off. Intuitively, somehow you just knew when a fight was about to break out.'

'Yeah it's exactly like that. I might go round to her mam's tomorrow morning to see if Pinky's there and make sure she's okay.'

'That's bloody good of you but you can't take other people's problems to your heart too much. She's probably a tough kid, like you were.'

'I know...I know... it's just...I don't know...maybe somehow she reminded me of myself at the age.'

'You never shacked up with a footballer, did you?'

'Of course not, I couldn't have lived with a man who had a bubble perm, very unsexy...but seriously man, lots of things push and pull you around and you just don't know how to cope with the pressures. I made some terrible relationship decisions, especially when I was in my 20s. You con yourself into thinking you're being clever and in control but you're really not. In fact you're often being manipulated and then end up being very vulnerable and isolated.'

'Well, being born into sod all and growing up with the idea that nothing is down for you and that you're just cannon fodder weighs us all down, doesn't it? You fight it but it's bloody hard work to break the attitudes you've been spoon fed since you were a kid. I know I've still got a massive chip on my shoulder about it. Okay, we'll go and see if Pinky is with her mam. Does that mean we have to visit your mother?'

'Fraid so...if she hears I've been three doors down and not said hello she'll give me grief. This is what I hate about family – the pointless bloody obligation. She doesn't really want to see me, she just feels that I should see her because I'm her daughter and that's what daughters do. If I wasn't her daughter she'd want nowt to do with me. In fact she'd probably hate someone like me. She'd think I'm jumped-up. In fact I'm sure she does think I'm jumped-up.'

'Why is that such a crime?'

'She thinks it means you're getting up above your station in life, being pretentious and all that.'

'You mean because you eat watercress, read The Guardian and collect Sara Paretsky books?'

'Exactly that...and so much more,' she let out a sigh and cursed under her breath, '...and now I'm all cross and upset and drunk.'

Nick reached out and patted her on the thigh.

'Don't fret about it - I'll be with you, that'll take some of the heat off. She can't be as nasty to you when I'm there, it'd be like giving away the family secret.'

'That's true. She likes to maintain the illusion that we get on to visitors even though she knows it's a façade.'

He turned off the road and up the track to their farmhouse in the pitch black. It was still a mild evening as he parked outside the house, and looked up at the starry sky with the orange glow of Yarm's lights glowing to the north. She put her arms around his waist and looked up at the sky.

'What a lovely night,' he said. 'People don't realise that it can be so quiet and beautiful on Teesside. I think I'd forgotten it as well y'know, after living away for so long. Really glad I came back, even if it does mean I have to occasionally meet your mother.'

Nick woke before seven as usual. Since quitting drinking he woke up earlier, needed less sleep and slept much better. It was some compensation for being sober. Julie was still asleep, mouth open and snoring slightly. He put the kettle on and then walked out into the front garden. Blackbirds scurried to and fro feeding newly fledged youngsters. A lesser-spotted woodpecker worked on a dead tree, filling the air with the sound of hammering. It was cool, the skies were clear and a low mist sat over the fields, the air smelling sweet of earth and growing nature. The life force was doing its thing. He stood breathing it all in. There was a mystery to nature that invigorated your soul. It was all just happening without man's intervention, a passion play full of drama. Life, death and copulation was in the air.

He went back in to make green tea and took his shower while it brewed. The tiles on the bathroom floor were old and cracked and needed replacing. The shower was probably modern in 1972 and there was damp in the corner on which flecks of black mould grew. The walls were painted a hospital green and the sink cracked from top to bottom. Even the bathroom mirror was worn out. How did you wear out a mirror? Did your face rub it all away? What the hell was a mirror anyway?

As he got dried Julie came in and sat on the toilet.

'Morning gorgeous,' he said as she plonked herself down.

'Don't be too perky, please.'

'You passed out as soon as you got into bed.'

'My head feels like a head that has recently passed out. I don't know why I do it really. Look at you, all fit and healthy. It's enough to make a girl sick.'

She aimed to slap him on the bare buttocks with her hand but he turned around just as she did so, taking the blow full in the balls.

'Ha ha…sorry love. Serves you right for having such a big target to hit, doesn't it?'

'I think you may have knocked one of my bollocks up into my rib cage,' he said, bent double, a dull, hollow ache in his groin.

She got up, flushed the toilet, washed her hands and looked at him.

'I suppose you want me to kiss it better now?'

'Well it'd be rude not to, Jules. And sex endorphins are good for curing hangovers, it's well-proven.'

She laughed. 'I'll take your word for it. Come on then, as long as you're quick, I don't want my tea to get cold. Fizzin' hell, it can't have hurt that much. Is this what they mean by being up early in the morning?'

CHAPTER 3

'Oh Christ, I get a feeling of utter dread as soon as I reach Hardwick.'

'I don't know Jules, it's not that bad. They're knocking down some of the worst bits. It's just a classic massive old-school council estate, isn't it? Mind, all the hard kids at our school lived here. Just the word Hardwick had real power. If someone was a Hardwick kid, you took a step back.'

'Sometimes I just feel like it's got hold of my foot and won't let me go, like I can't get away. Like a man trap, or a woman trap in this case. Somehow, no matter where you go or what you do, you never really move off the estate, or you certainly always leave a bit of yourself here.' She sighed, exasperated. 'I know it's stupid, I'm in my 40s, I've not lived here since I was 18, but I can't shake the idea that somehow I'm going to end up back here. Nice try Julie, you thought you could get away but here youse are back again, like a bad penny.'

He laughed. 'It's just some houses Jules, it isn't a malevolent entity.'

'I wouldn't be so bloody sure.'

He drove down High Newham Road, taking a left up the street where Julie's old family home was situated. It was a small semi-detached house. Like most of the houses on the estate, it had a shallow bay window and a metal support pole by the door which held up a concrete porch. The window frames had recently been replaced, swapping the old white wood for new white plastic. The door was also new and plastic, set into a thick-lipped frame. The front garden was no more than six or seven foot long, mostly a concrete drive with a strip of grass to one side, rather incongruously. The estate was part of a huge post-war social housing building scheme which at one point had been home to up to 7,000 people, all working in local industries. But with the collapse of the economy in the 80s, it had struggled to recover and, by the late 90s, the Hardwick ward was one of the ten poorest in the whole country. Plans were afoot to knock down long-empty properties and build some smarter new homes as part of a large-scale upgrade. The area certainly needed it.

'That's Pinky's house,' said Julie, pointing at a door three houses up the street. Outside stood a huge black four-wheel drive SUV with blacked-out windows, squatting like a giant animal outside a small house, the proportions of the car out of whack with the architecture.

'Look at that thing, must be a 70 grand car,' said Julie. 'There's no way Maggie could afford that.'

'Crumbs from the footballer's table,' said Nick, looking around at the empty streets and expanses of wasteland. Where were all the kids? The place was choked with children messing about and getting up to no good when he was young.

'We'd better go and see my mam first; she'll be nosing out the window at us if we don't.'

They walked up the front path, Julie pushed her hair behind her ears, pressed the doorbell and opened the front door.

'Mam! It's me!' she called out.

Her mother, a woman in her late 60s, appeared out of the kitchen. 'Eeee it's our Julie. What are you doing here? Is everything alright? Are you on the cadge or something?'

'No, we're not on the cadge. I'm never on the cadge mam, am I? When was I ever on the cadge? Yeah, I'm fine. I've brought Nick with me.'

He waved and smiled. 'Hello Jackie. How are you?'

'I'm all right I suppose, for an old cow,' she said. 'Come in then, the pair of youse.'

The house was imbued with the acrid stink of a million cigarettes mixed with the smell of stale chip fat and dogs.

'Where's the mutt?' said Julie, walking after her mother into the kitchen.

'She's out the back in the garden. I'll put the kettle on, eh.'

She opened a window and called the dog, which dutifully came trotting up the small garden path to the back door and pushed its way in. On seeing Julie, she barked and wagged her tail.

'Hello Bessie, darlin',' said Julie, ruffling the dog's ears. Nick made a fuss of her too. She was a border collie with a lot of sheepdog and some other less definable breeds thrown in.

Nick had always found Julie's mother to be a slightly scary woman. Blunt to the point of rudeness and not one to suffer fools gladly, her daughter had inherited her fearlessness but not her lack of social grace. She was a classic old-school working-class woman who had grafted for low wages most of her life and who now considered it almost a badge of honour.

She lit a fag, held it between index and middle finger of her right hand, rested her right elbow on her left arm and peered through the blue smoke at them with squinting eyes. Her skin looked like it was made of old leather and didn't really fit her face anymore, her top lip heavily creased with over 50 years of sucking on strong cigarettes.

'So how's that new place of yours?'

'It's great. We love it,' said Nick, still stroking the dog. 'Very quiet and dark at night.'

'I couldn't stand living in the countryside, me. Too quiet and isolated, like. '

'We actually came over to go and see Maggie Gull, three doors down.'

'So you didn't really come to see us then?'

'I didn't say that mam, don't try and pick a fight with me,' admonished Julie, folding her arms across her chest and setting her jaw against her mother.

'And why do you want to see Maggie Gull?' asked Jackie defensively, setting her jaw against her daughter in turn. The old cliché that you should look at the mother to see the future incarnation of the daughter was to a degree true of Julie. She was her mother's daughter in so many ways. Same chin, same intense turquoise blue eyes and capable of the same defiant, who-the-fuck-do-you-think-you're-talking-to glare.

'We saw Pinky at a party at Jimmy Repp's house.'

'Pinky? That one, eh. We don't see her round here much since she hooked up with him.'

'Did he buy Maggie that big four-wheel drive car?'

'Of course he did. It turned up a month ago. You can't buy one of those when you're a dinner lady, can you? She's always been a proper scunner that one.'

'Pinky, you mean?' asked Julie.

'No. Maggie. Pinky's a nice lass. God knows how. You used to babysit her sometimes; you know what she's like.'

'Yeah but the last time was when she was 12 or 13. I've only really seen her at a distance since then or just to talk to briefly when me and you go in the North-Easterner. She's grown into a very pretty girl, glamorous, like.'

'She's got the looks, I'll give her that,' said Jackie. 'They say the apple doesn't fall far from the tree but I reckon it did with her and Maggie 'cos she's got a face like an angry ferret, that one.'

Nick burst out laughing. 'Nice expression Mrs W.'

'Don't be so rude about her, mam. She's a good-looking woman is Maggie. Under all the make-up, anyway. She's must be a couple of years younger than me.'

'Aye well, she got knocked-up at 16, didn't she? Thank God you never did that our Jules. I'd have bloody murdered you.'

'No you wouldn't. You'd have liked to have a grandkid to fuss over even if I'd dropped one at 16,' said Julie, shaking her head, 'but I didn't because you'd told me how to avoid getting pregnant, remember?'

'Did I? How did I do that?'

She adopted her mother's rasping tone: 'Don't let him put his willy in you. You can do owt else you want but don't let him do that and you'll be alright.'

Jackie snorted a coarse laugh.

'See, I'm not such a bad mother, am I? Kids want to have sex, don't they? It's just natural but you don't have to go all the way, do you? Kids need to be told that today, if you ask me. Too many lasses getting knocked up before they're even 16.'

'So is Pinky not back that often now then?' asked Julie.

'I don't know, do I? I don't keep check on them. I've not seen her for a while anyway. What's it to you like, our Jules?'

'She was upset last night - she had a big fight with Jimmy and stormed out and I was worried about her.'

Julie's mother shook her head. 'Honestly, what are you like? You can't go around worrying about everyone and fighting their battles for them...'

'...I'm not fighting her battles, mam, I'm just concerned. She's only a young girl...'

'...she's not a young girl...she's a young woman and as you well know, lasses grow up quick on this estate. You don't grow up here and not learn what's what. You should know that better than most. You were a proper little madam by the time you were 21. Couldn't tell you owt about owt. She's got her head screwed on that one, don't you worry about that.'

'What do you mean?' asked Nick.

'I mean she knows what's what.'

This didn't seem to cast any more light on matters.

'Well we'll just nip round and see if Pinky's there,' said Julie. 'We won't be long.'

They walked three doors down.

'I could bloody strangle my mother sometimes,' said Julie as soon as they were out of the door.

'You're doing fine,' said Nick, but then parents were less annoying when they weren't your own.

She knocked on the door and stood back. The curtain twitched and a face peered at them. Julie waved. It was Maggie Gull and she wasn't ferret-faced at all. She was much younger-looking than he'd thought with nice pale blue almond eyes that Pinky had inherited.

She was short but, like her daughter, perfectly formed only with shorter, fair hair. She wore an expensive-looking Versace shirt with pearl buttons in a garish green and red pattern.

'Hello Julie. I've not seen you for ages. How are you?' she said, standing in the doorway.

'I'm great thanks Maggie. You look well. This is my partner, Nick. We were just wondering if Pinky was around.'

'Pinky?' As she said it, her eyes flicked from side to side quickly, just once. There was a moment's doubt or worry in her eyes.

'Why do you want to see Pinky?'

She ran her fingers through her hair, squinted and then began fidgeting with a ring on her finger. She was definitely jumpy.

'We met her last night at a party at Jimmy's, y'see, Nick is a football writer and he got an invite from Jimmy to this party and...well, to be honest Maggie, there was a big row between her and Jimmy and she was quite upset when she left. I was just a bit worried about her, so I thought I'd just check to see if she was okay. I assumed she'd come here.'

As she talked Maggie couldn't stand still, wobbling her right leg in an agitated fashion, at times almost violently.

'Well...I've not seen her. She's not been here.' She shook her head, leaned over to a small table, took a cigarette out of a packet of Marlboro and lit it.

'Are you okay Maggie?' asked Julie, clearly concerned.

'Me? Yeah, I'm fine,' she said. Nick didn't think so. She was clearly on edge.

'Look, Pinky doesn't come home much these days. Not for long anyway.'

'Oh, right. Where might she have gone then, do you know?'

Maggie Gull shrugged and went silent for ten seconds or more. It was awkward. She seemed to drift off almost, as if distracted by her own thoughts. Then she came back to life and said: 'I don't know where she is most of the time.'

She was obviously not telling the truth. She was hesitant, clearly trying to sort out a story in her mind, trying to say the right thing.

'She might be at a friend's, or she'll have just gone back to Jimmy's. Why don't you ask Siobhan?' She looked at her watch. 'She'll be behind the bar at the North-Easterner in half an hour.'

'Is that Siobhan Rodgers?' asked Julie.

'Aye, you know her mam and dad don't you? She's always been Pinky's best friend. She'll know where she is.'

She looked pleased with herself for coming up with a strategy to get rid of them. Nick doubted that Siobhan would know anything but it was a way to get them off her doorstep.

'I'm sure she's fine. There's nothing to worry about, though it's nice of you to be worried, like.' She had the door closed before they had even turned around.

'She was odd,' said Nick as they returned to her mother's house. 'She seemed agitated and nervous. Is she on drugs?'

'She might be. I don't remember her being like that at all.'

'She's not there is she?' asked Jackie as they went back in.

'No. Well, Maggie says she's not. She was a bit shifty though,' said Julie. 'Is she alright, mam? She seemed a bit weird, edgy like.'

'Alright? I don't know. I don't talk much to her if I can help it. She's always been a sly one her though. I always felt she was hiding something ever since she came here 20-odd years ago. I wouldn't trust her.'

'Don't be daft, mam. She can't have been hiding something for 20 years. She seemed a bit jittery to us, nervous, like. Will you keep an eye open for Pinky though? Let me know if she turns up?'

'Okay, but I think you're sticking your nose in where it's not wanted or needed. She's nobody's fool, that girl.'

'Thanks for the tea Mrs W,' said Nick.

'You're welcome, son. I don't suppose you're planning to propose to my daughter, are you? I'd like to go to at least one family wedding before I die.'

'Mam, shut up. I've told you, we're not getting married. It's all bullshit; you should know that given the way dad went on.'

'Eeee and you'd look lovely in a big dress, our Julie. Not white, of course, not at your age. Winter white or maybe black would be more appropriate, like.' She rasped a laugh.

'Bye mam,' shouted Julie, walking away quickly to disengage from the wedding talk.

The North-Easterner was a large pub, purpose-built to service the estate. It had held a fearsome reputation when they were kids. If you wanted a fight on a Friday night or pretty much any other night of the week, you could guarantee one in the North-Easterner. These days it was a bit nicer. They'd put carpets down, though not very nice carpets, and now they served food and wine, though not very nice food or wine.

Nick stood outside looking at the menu, which was a litany of microwaved and deep-fried bought-in meals pretending to be made on the premises.

'You shouldn't be allowed to call something home cooking when you've bought it in frozen from a wholesaler, should you? Home-heated would be a better expression. I remember when they first started doing toasties in here in 1978 - we thought it was very fancy and modern to sell food in a pub. They put them under a grill in a weird crinkly plastic bag that went all brittle, and out of it emerged your toastie, now at the same temperature as the core of the sun. Many a drinker had their lips burned on the molten hot cheese toastie, y'know. Never mind all the fuss about the fighting, more people got hurt by their toasties than anything else in here.'

'This was the first pub I ever got served in,' said Julie. '1980. I was 15 and had put on loads of make-up, which was bloody daft because they all knew who I was and how old I was. No-one cared about under-age drinking though really, did they? Not back then.'

'Nah, as long as you sat in a corner and didn't piss off the old regulars with your youthful ways or by putting Black Sabbath B-sides on the jukebox, they were quite happy to take your money. You couldn't get out of line or misbehave because one of the old lads would just put his fist in your face with the full approval of the coppers. Happy days, eh?'

'Pffft. Maybe. Funnily enough, I was going out with Freddie Rodgers, this lass Siobhan's dad, at the time. He was a year or two older and had a second-hand Capri which I considered to be very glamorous.'

'Rightly so. But it wasn't enough to keep you in his arms for long?'

'Nah. He was an arrogant sod really. And he had a weird wanger.' Nick laughed loudly. 'Weird? In what way?'

'It was a funny shape, sort of twisted like a corkscrew. I think he needed an operation or something. It wasn't right. It looked like something a butcher would cut off and throw out.'

Nick laughed. 'Good God. Mind you, a corkscrew cock could come in useful at parties if you've turned up without a bottle opener.'

'Call me old-fashioned if you like, but even aged 15, I liked a traditional-shaped nadger.'

They went inside. As the smoking ban was now in operation, it seemed odd that the place was clean and not enveloped in a fug of blue smoke. A fat girl was pulling a pint behind the bar.

'That's her,' said Julie.

'My God, you wouldn't get many of her in a Mini. Maybe this is the sort of kid you get out of a wonky willy.'

Julie made a low, gurgling laugh and they took a bar stool each.

'Hiya, what can I get you?' asked Siobhan, not recognising Julie.

'It's Siobhan, isn't it?' said Julie.

The girl looked shifty. Anyone asking for you by name was generally a bad thing on the estate. It usually meant some form of authority was looking for you - the coppers, the social services, CSA, teachers or whoever. They brought only bad news.

'Who's askin', like?' came the standard response.

'Don't you remember me? I'm Julie Wells, you know, off the estate. I used to babysit you and Pinky.'

Her face visibly relaxed along with her suspicion of these

strangers.

'Eeee. Aye, course I do...how's your Terry? He's just got out of Durham, hasn't he?'

'Yeah, about six months ago. He's alright thanks. He's got a job working on the bins. Says he's going to go straight...but y'know...he always says that. He's got a flat over in Roseworth now.'

Terry was Julie's youngest brother. At just 28, he was 14 years her junior and the result of a last burst of passion before their father had left to work abroad, never to return.

'Well if you see him, tell him I said hello. I always thought he was lush,' she said, her thick, fatty, blushed pink arms resting on the bar.

'Have you seen Pinky recently?' asked Julie.

'Yeah I saw her a couple of days ago. I was supposed to go to a party she was having at Jimmy's place; they reckon it's brill out there, like. But I couldn't go 'cos I was working. Why, like?'

'We were at that party...,' said Nick,

'...and she left in tears. She'd had a big row with Jimmy and we were worried about her. We thought she might have come home to her mam's but Maggie says she didn't,' said Julie.

'Eeee well it's the first I've heard of it. I'll give her a ring. Just a minute, I'll just get this...yes mate, pint of bitter?'

She pulled a pint for an old man, pushed it across the bar and then went to her handbag, took out her phone and dialled. 'I've got the voice mail,' she said with a tut.

'Hiya Pinks, it's me, are you alright? It's just that I've got Julie Wells here and she said you'd left the party in tears, like...what happened babe? Give us a ring. Ta ra.'

'Do you want me to ring you when she calls back?' asked Siobhan.

'Yeah, if you could, thanks,' said Julie, writing her number onto a beer mat, though it seemed unlikely Siobhan would make the effort to call.

'How long has she been living with Jimmy Repp?' asked Nick.

'Eeee it must be eight or nine month now. She moved in with him sharpish, like. They'd not even been going out long. They lived at the Teesside International. Eeee God, fancy living in a five-star hotel, eh. Finlay wasn't best pleased, mind.'

'Who's Finlay?' asked Julie.

'Finlay? He was Pinky's last boyfriend before she met Jimmy. She went out with both of them for about a month or two and then she dumped him when Jimmy asked her to move into the hotel.'

'That was all very quick, wasn't it?' said Julie. 'Had she been going out with Finlay long?'

'Yeah, nearly two years – she was really keen on him for a while but well...you know...a footballer and all his money and that...it's hard to resist, isn't it? I bloody wouldn't resist and he's a nice fella is Jimmy. I met him a couple of times, like. '

'Is Finlay off the estate then?' asked Julie.

'No, he's a Billingham lad...works at the Boro in the ticket office. I feel dead sorry for him. He must see Jimmy coming in and it must piss him off, like. But there's not much he can do is there? He can't compete with a footballer's money.'

Siobhan went to the far end of the bar to serve an old couple who had just come in, leaving her phone in front of Nick, He spun it around with his index finger and pressed a button to see the last number dialled. Julie took out a pen and wrote it on another beer mat while Nick spun it around and back to its original position.

'Good work James Bond,' said Julie with a smile.

'We'll get off then,' she said to the fat barmaid. 'Thanks for your help Siobhan. I'll see you around, eh, tell your mam and dad I said hello.'

'Alright Julie, nice to see you again. Ta ra now. Don't forget to say hello to your Terry for me.'

They walked back out into the bright sunshine. 'Do you fancy having her as a sister-in-law? She seems keen on your Terry.'

'She's nice enough really, thick as a pit pony's leg, like, but she's probably too young for him. He's nearly 29 now. She can't be more

45

than 20 or 21.'

Nick laughed. 'That's nowt man. I'd be more inclined to worry about how much she'd cost to feed. Right, so what now? Home? It sounds like Pinky's okay. She's probably spending Jimmy's money in some fancy hotel.'

'Yeah, maybe I was over-thinking this.'

He took the Durham Road down to Oxbridge Avenue, onto Hartburn Avenue, then picking up Yarm Lane and heading south on the A135 to Yarm and home. Maybe they had over-reacted to Pinky's tears and maybe Jackie Wells had been right about not sticking their noses into her business. It could all have been nothing, but then maybe it was something. Maybe it was a big something.

CHAPTER 4

The next day Nick was reporting on an evening pre-season friendly at Leeds and also had a session booked with his therapist, so he drove down in the afternoon and stopped off in Harrogate to see his oldest mate, Jeff Evans, who ran a second-hand record shop in the town. He and Jeff had gone to the same school and had been friends since their teens. Until Nick had moved back to Teesside to live with Julie, they had both lived in Harrogate since the early 90s.

Jeff was a massive bloke. At over 6'3", 20 stone and with long, greying hair down his back matched with a huge beard, he was a big presence even in the largest of rooms. Like Nick, he was over-focused on vinyl records to the exclusion of almost everything else and, like Nick, was widely regarded as a bit odd. For years he'd almost been Nick's only true friend.

'Ah here he is, the farm boy,' said Jeff as Nick walked into his shop on Commercial Street.

'Now then...how are we?'

'We are both hunky and dory aren't we Lukey?'

Luke was the 20-year-old lad who helped out Jeff three days a week.

'Aye, we're a pair of diamond dogs, if we're keeping the Bowie thing going,' he said, while looking through a big box of old seven-inch singles.

'How's life in the country?'

'I bloody love it man, it's great,' said Nick.

'Aye, all that nude badger-watching, you can't beat it.'

'Yeah, we love the nude badger-watching...obviously that's why we moved out there.'

'Right then, let's go and get some oral lubrication. Will you lock up Lukey? We'll just be down the road if you want to join us later.'

They walked up to Jack & Danny's, their old, familiar watering-hole.

'It's weird, I've only been moved out for a month but life in

Harrogate already seems a long time ago,' Nick said, buying Jeff a pint of lager and himself a mineral water.

'And you're still off the drink, I see...'

'Aye.'

'...you reckon it's really made a massive difference to your old...,' he made a loopy sign to his head.

'To the depression and all that? Yeah I think it's helped keep it away. I still get a bit moody, like...but the worst patches have eased. Considering how bad things had got, I'm in a pretty good place.'

He held up the palms of his hands.

'Ah, not digging your nails in anymore. No depression stigmata...you must be a happy bunny.'

'Yeah. It's some sort of progress anyway.'

'Julie loving it in the country as well?'

'Totally yeah.'

'I can see her as country wench in a nice gingham frock with those big, unfettered breasts jiggling around like two well-set blancmanges.'

'Ha ha...I'll tell her that...she hates gingham but she is mostly unfettered. Not sure about them being like blancmanges though. I've not had blancmange since 1977.'

'No-one has. Where would you get one from?'

Nick shrugged. 'There are no blancmange shops, are there?'

'There should be. I might open one. Or, on the other hand, I might not. Anyway, don't get me thinking about her breasts, 'cos I might get aroused and no-one wants to see that. Hey, I've put a few records to one side for you, so you've got first dibs on them, like. Mostly west coast stuff. Got a beautiful original UK first pressing of the Grateful Dead's first album on green Warner.'

Nick pulled a face. 'Oooh, very nice. How much is that?'

'It should be about 75 but I only paid 25 so you can have it for that.'

'Ah, thanks man.'

Nick's love of record-collecting matched Jeff's and one of the stipulations he'd made before moving to the farmhouse was that there was enough room for his 10,000-strong record collection.

For half an hour, as usual, they talked about almost nothing except music and records and gigs and that was exactly how both of them liked it.

'Hiya stranger,' said a familiar Yorkshire voice.

Leaning over him was Lisa Lambert, a local painter who he'd seen a couple of times before getting back together with Julie. They'd always got on really well. She was in her mid-30s and, as usual, had her unruly dark hair wrapped in a headscarf and wore a pair of loose-fitting, white, paint-splattered dungarees.

'Hey Lisa,' he said, getting to his feet to give her a hug. She gripped his buttocks and pulled her to him, kissing him on the lips.

'Where did you get to? I've not seen you for ages,' she said, nose to nose with him.

'I moved up to Teesside with Julie. You remember Julie?'

She certainly should - they'd had a massive stand-up drunken row in a wine bar the year before. This wasn't unusual for Lisa, who liked drinking the way bees like nectar, and she liked arguing almost as much.

'We got an old farmhouse up near Yarm...loving it up there. Sad to leave Harrogate but...well...y'know...life moves on and all that.'

Lisa looked him up and down and shook her head. 'What a waste of good meat you are,' she said and then laughed it off. 'Ah well, fair fucks to you. If you ever need any art for the walls of your house, you know where to come - I know Julie likes all that naturalistic crap but don't put up with that whatever you do, you'll die inside one day at a time if you're surrounded by shitty fucking watercolours of the Lake District or cutesy cats. It'll infect your brain with convention and then you'll be voting Tory and only having it off on your birthday and you'll settle into neat and tidy domesticity. Keep room for some abstract impressionism, I beg you, purleeeeaaase,' she implored, bending at the knees in mock prayer.

'I'll bear that in mind, but don't worry, the house won't become a temple to cute.'

She slapped him lightly on the cheek. 'Good man...and if you ever feel the urge to have a wild, passionate affair, you know where I am. I have good drugs and a notoriously fabulous vagina,' she said, looking him right in the eyes.

'If I feel that urge, I'll certainly let you know,' he laughed.

Jeff raised his hand. 'Please miss, I'd like some drugs and access to a fabulous vagina.'

Lisa squatted down on her hunkers and took his big hairy head in her hands. 'Jeffrey, my dear, I couldn't stand that much fucking pleasure and you know it! The rush of endorphins after sex with you would kill me.'

Jeff blushed and laughed. Just as he did so, an older woman, dressed neatly in a lightweight earth-coloured linen suit, came over. She had close-cut short, dark hair with a white streak from front to back, fine silver-rimmed glasses and silver bangles on her wrists. Her blouse was fine cream silk with pearl buttons. It was the tanned look of the wealthy and arty middle-class.

'Hello Lisa. Are you causing trouble as usual?'

'Emmy - there you are - no, I'm just offering these boys my body for their pleasure. Is that wrong, darling? This is Emmy Green, she's my agent. She makes me rich and in return I have to perform acts of gross lesbianism upon her naked body. She wears my tongue out!'

Emmy rolled her grey eyes at Nick and laughed. 'As I'm sure you know, that's just Lisa being Lisa,' she said in an accent-less, well-spoken voice.

'Why don't I get us all a drink?' said Lisa.

'Mine's a pint of Stella,' said Jeff.

'Just mineral water for me, Lisa. I've given up drinking.'

'Oh fucking hell Nick, what's wrong with you, man? Don't turn into a pussy, please.'

'I've chosen being a pussy over being depressed.'

'Look, being depressed is the artist's lot. It's what separates us from the grunt labour. We work from inside our dark, twisted souls. Being mentally fucked-up is a blessing for an artist.'

He could feel little flecks of spit land on his cheek as she spoke.

'That sounds great but I was miserable and, controversially, I'd rather not be miserable.'

Lisa went to the bar.

'Good for you,' said Emmy, taking two seats and arranging them around Nick and Jeff's table. 'Depression is a terrible thing. Have you found not drinking helps?'

'Yeah and being low-carb as well. Anything that stops my blood sugar levels going high and low seems to help.'

'Good for you,' she said again. 'Ignore what Lisa says, she doesn't mean it...well...I'm sure you know that.'

'I know. It's mostly for effect but if you tell her that she goes crazy.'

Lisa returned with two drinks. 'Stop talking about me, I don't want to know how much you hate me,' she said, and returned to the bar for the other glasses.

Jeff laughed, thanked her for the lager and turned to Emmy Green.

'So you're Lisa's agent - what does that entail, like?'

'Basically I arrange for her art to be exhibited, sold, used in advertising or whatever. It's my job to maximise her income from her work.'

'That sounds like a game that's all about contacts,' said Jeff. 'All about who you know, like.'

'Absolutely. Private sales are what we're working on at the moment. Collectors and so on.'

'I know a footballer called Jimmy Repp and he collects art.'

As soon as Nick said the Dutchman's name she broke into a smile.

'Oh I know Jimmy. He's a great collector. I have quite a few clients whose work he buys. He has some of Lisa's work, in fact.'

'Who does?' asked Lisa, coming back with two glasses of wine for herself and one for Emmy.

'Jimmy Repp. He's a Dutch footballer.'

'Footballers are all evil wankers with shit for brains,' she said, dismissively. Jeff laughed again.

'Jimmy is different to normal footballers. He's quite the renaissance man,' said Emmy.

'I was at his house the other night actually. He's opening his own place...and he's got a gallery in his house. He was showing us his Phyllis Plant collection.'

'I bloody love PP. What a woman she was,' said Lisa, taking two big gulps of wine.

'Yes indeed, well I actually secured some of those for him,' said Emmy. Her eyes twinkled. 'He's really putting together a substantial collection. He was telling me about this new gallery project.'

'He must have invested a lot of money,' said Nick.

'Yeah, how much does a PP go for, Emmy?' said Lisa. 'I bet it's a fucking big sackful of cash - a bigger sack than even your scrotum Jeffrey.'

'Surely nothing is that big,' said Jeff.

Lisa roared with laughter and scratched his beard as though he were a dog.

'Depends on the size, the quality and the age. Large early ones fetch over £300,000, small ones perhaps 50 or 60,000. Her best sculptures are worth half a million now. She had a Russian father and it's the Russians who are paying big money. Anything with a Russian connection goes through the roof.'

'Christ, Jimmy had 50 or 60 in his house. A dozen of them were big paintings too, so they must have been worth top dollar. And he had four sculptures,' said Nick.

'Oh yes, he's got *Woman Heart* - on the open market today that would fetch at least 500, 600 thousand pounds...he's spent a lot...a remarkable amount really but footballers are paid handsomely these days aren't they?' said Emmy.

Nick didn't answer but he knew Jimmy couldn't be on more than a million a year at Boro, and that was before tax - a fortune just for playing football but probably nowhere near enough to amass such a collection. Maybe he'd been on better money in Spain. Even so, this seemed like a phenomenal investment. He made a mental note to call a Madrid-based journalist he knew to find out what he was paid out there.

'Is he the only footballer who collects art?' asked Jeff.

'Yes, pretty much. There are one or two managers who dabble and David James paints...not very well...but that's about it. It's not a culture conducive to the arts, is it?'

'Footballers think an interest in the arts means you're gay. They think if you watch BBC2 that means you're gay, as well. Read the *Guardian*? Gay. Read at all? Gay. Only want to have sex with one woman at a time without your mates watching? Gay. They're all such cultural and sexual Neanderthals,' said Lisa, finishing her first glass.

'Footballers always have dodgy taste...remember those curly perms and the love of Phil Collins solo albums? Bizarre,' said Jeff.

Lisa laughed and said: 'One is an expression of the other somehow. Now it's all massive headphones and lame R and fucking B sung by hysterical women and sexist pig-men. Like I said, they're all wankers.

'Have you heard of Myra LeFevre? She's my best friend. Emmy tries to sell her stuff, don't you? She's absolutely fucking brilliant but can hardly sell anything. She's always saying how people like rich footballers or businessmen who buy art - it's always business*men* - they're just acquiring an asset. It could be a car or a vase or a painting. They're not bothered. That's the worst sort of philistinism to me, buying art because it'll accrue value not because you feel it in your heart.' She thumped her chest to make the point.

'I think she was exaggerating,' said Emmy, defensively. 'She's like you Lisa, she says things she doesn't mean. I've always found most footballers and business buyers to be very nice. Myra's type of work is just not the fashion right now, her time will come. She has a great talent.'

'Well I'm glad I don't have to fucking meet people like this Repp guy because I'd have to fuck him up if he was uncool to me or to any of my friends and I'd expect any of you to do the same. You'd fuck him up for me wouldn't you, Nick?'

She thumped the table with her clenched fist.

'I'm the go-to man for fucking people up, Lisa, you know that,' said Nick with a smile.

'You and me brother,' she said, bumping knuckles with him.

'Have you met his girlfriend, Emmy? She's called Pinky. Short-ish blonde girl,' asked Nick.

'Oh yes, I've met Pinky. Nice girl. A bit...footballer's wife maybe...'

'...what does that mean?' interjected Lisa with a look of horror on her face.

'Well...you know...she had that air about her.'

'You bloody snob. What you mean is she's working-class and dresses flash and probably isn't highly educated. Getting in a footballer's pants is sometimes the only bloody way to get out of the hellholes they grow up in. Don't be so bloody judgemental.'

'Judgemental? Me?! Don't be so bloody hypocritical. You're the one who says footballers are all wankers,' said Emmy, flushed with annoyance, her tone switching from placation to admonishment like a parent. 'That's a very sweeping assumption and hardly a fair one either, I might add. You do that all the time, Lisa. You're forever making generalisations and value judgements, often about people and things you know nothing about.' She was clearly angry.

Lisa just ignored her and carried on, 'If she's creaming up a footballer for money to better her chances in life then good on her, I say. When you're born into shit the whole fucking world is against you, so you take your chances where and when you can. I hope she drains every last fucking penny out of him.'

Sometimes Lisa reminded Nick of Julie so much it was scary.

'I wasn't being unpleasant...or it wasn't my intention anyway. She just wasn't actually that interested in the art he was collecting, but I liked her,' said Emmy, still angry.

Surely she must have been used to this by now. If you spent any amount of time with Lisa, you would at some point suffer the sharp edge of her tongue. She seemed to have no filter between her brain and her mouth, just blurting out whatever she thought without consideration. It was often hard to know if she actually meant what she said or it was all bluster.

'Myra says that it's the signature that's worth the big money and not the art itself. She can paint just like me, she could copy my style easily and put my signature on it and because I'm fashionable or whatever, it'd sell for tens of thousands, but if she signed it, it would go for next to nothing. Now if that's not total bullshit I don't know what is.'

They talked all afternoon, by which time Lisa was onto her third bottle of wine. Nick got up to go to his therapy session.

'Right, lovely to see you all. I'll be in touch Jeff – come up and stay with us soon, right?'

'Will do, captain,' said Jeff, saluting.

'Nice to meet you Emmy...and you too Lisa.'

She got up, threw her arms round his shoulders and squinted at him.

'Are you sure you don't want to come back to my flat for a really, really good big fat fuck?' she whispered in his ear, her breath hot and boozy, her eyes glazed over, her pupils dilated.

'What and miss a Leeds pre-season friendly?' he said and kissed her on the cheek. 'Look after yourself and that fabulous vagina, Lisa.'

After an hour of therapy, the match was a lame, inconsequential affair, like most pre-season games. He was incredibly glad to get back to the farmhouse.

'Hey Jules. I'm home,' said Nick, putting his laptop down on the kitchen table. 'Something smells good...roast pork?'

'I thought I'd do my housewife impression and cook you a dinner even though you're much better at it than I am, so I roasted a joint. You look tired, was the traffic bad?'

'Yeah...hard work. It was lashing it down in Yorkshire. Proper big summer storm. It's nice to be home.'

He gave her a hug and a kiss.

'What have you been up to today?'

'Just working on my dissertation.'

She sat down on a kitchen chair and pulled her feet up underneath her so she was sitting cross-legged.

'I had an odd phone call earlier though.'

'Odd?'

'It was from Maggie Gull.'

'Pinky's mam? What did she want?' He kicked off his boots, washed his hands, took the pork out of the oven and cut off some succulent slices.

'She was asking if we'd found or spoken to Pinky, so I told her I hadn't. She said she'd been trying to get hold of her since we'd been round there but she wasn't answering her phone.'

Nick flopped down on a chair with his plate. 'Well a kid ignoring her mother's phone calls is normal enough, isn't it?'

'I'd have thought so but Maggie seemed concerned. She reckons she speaks to her almost every day and she said she hadn't heard from her since the morning of the party.'

'Still, it's not that long, is it? Maybe her phone is knackered or something.'

Julie nodded and fastened her hair back into a ponytail.

'That's what I said to her. I told her to call Jimmy and she said she'd tried but got no reply.'

'She should try calling her phone but disguising her number. Everyone knows who's ringing these days so they filter their calls.'

He yawned. 'This meat is lovely, you'll make someone a good wife, you.'

'Yer bollocks I will, there's a bit of salad in the fridge if you want it...anyway, I was wondering if we should try calling her?'

'It's none of our business really is it?' he said, putting some greenery and a tomato on his plate. 'I mean, fair enough if she's missing for a few weeks, but not a few days. This era of mass communication makes everyone panic if someone drops off the radar for a few days; it's a form of insanity if you ask me. Maybe she just doesn't want to talk to anyone. That's not that mental.'

'Yeah...of course...you're right. So what were Leeds like?'

'Poor. Hey, I dropped in to see Jeff before the game and took him for a drink.'

'How is he?'

'His usual self. Anyway, while we were in Jack & Danny's, Lisa Lambert and her agent Emmy Green came in. You remember her, don't you?'

'How could I bloody forget?' she asked with a snort.

'She wasn't massively drunk at first so she was on good form. Anyway, it turned out that her agent, this Emmy Green woman, knew Jimmy and Pinky. She sells art to him - not just Lisa's but other stuff too. She sold him that Phyllis Plant collection and it cost a bloody fortune, man. They're worth 50 or 60 grand each and the big ones three or four times that. The four sculptures are probably two million quid in total. Add in all his other art and his collection runs into tens of millions.'

'Blimey. That house can't have been cheap, either.'

'The thing is right, I don't see how he's afforded that on Boro's wages.'

'Maybe he was on a big contract in Spain?'

'That was my thought so I e-mailed my old pal Alf Porter in Spain. He's covered Spanish football for decades and he reckons he wasn't on any more at Seville than at Boro, probably a lot less in fact, maybe 60 grand a month. If he's getting more than 120 a month at Boro, I'd be surprised. So he just doesn't earn that sort of money - big money by normal standards but nowhere near big enough to fund an art collection like that.'

'What are you saying, like?' she said, pulled her legs up under her again and sitting cross-legged on a kitchen chair.

'I'd like to know how he's afforded it all.'

'Maybe he was left a lot of money by his family?'

Nick shrugged. 'Maybe, but who gets left that much money? It'd take millions to collect what he's got. I know from an interview I did with him when he came over here that he grew up in Holland with just his mother. She was a single parent. Gambling is the only thing I can think of that would raise so much money in just a few years, well that and getting paid to match-fix...and even then...it's a lot of money.'

He pushed his empty plate away and drank some tea.

'Do you think he's dodgy, like?' she said.

'It looks wrong doesn't it? I'd like to find out more.'

He had a bath before going to bed. It was small, chipped and old. He couldn't even lie down fully but the hot water was relaxing.

Julie brought him another mug of tea and sat down on a bathroom chair opposite him.

'I just looked up Jimmy's house – it's still on the Oak Properties website – it was sold for just under three million quid, which must make it one of the most expensive on Teesside,' she said.

'Bloody hell. Three mill, eh. Maybe he buys and sells the art at a massive profit.'

'But at the party he said he'd only been collecting for five or six years - surely it couldn't have gone up in value that much in such a short space of time. Not enough to make tens of millions anyway.'

'True. God, I feel like a very large chicken that's been put in a very small pan in this thing. We've got to get a nice big bath, Jules. I swear when I try to get out I'll have it stuck on my arse.'

She handed him a bath towel.

'Seriously though, I think there's something in this Jimmy Repp thing. I might do a bit of the old investigative journalism to see what I can drag up,' said Nick as he got dried. 'You never know, I might be able to sell it to one of the few newspapers who still pay for a big scoop and buy a new bath.'

She put her hands on his chest.

'That's all very well mister, but now that you're all clean, I need you to do a thorough investigation into me.'

'What is this, *Carry On Spying* or something? Do you want me to take down your particulars?'

She shook her head and put her hand on his groin.

'Nah, just my knickers.'

CHAPTER 5

Nick was making breakfast when his phone rang. The display showed the number was withheld so he rejected the call and went back to frying bacon.

'God, could anyone actually sleep through the smell of hot lard,' said Julie, coming into the kitchen in her pyjamas.

'Two rashers or three?'

'Three please, I'm starving. Who was that on the phone this early?'

'I dunno, a chef can't be interrupted you know. I'm having fried chicory, you want some?'

'You're a mad sod. Chicory for breakfast? Have I ever eaten chicory? Do I like it?'

'It goes well with bacon.'

'Go on then. Lots of eggs too if you made plenty.'

'I used six eggs for the scramble, threw in some cream and cheese as well.'

She sat down at the table, picked up her knife and fork and banged them on the table. 'Give me foooood,' she shouted, laughing. He put a big plate in front of her.

'Oh God, that looks brill. I bloody love a big breakfast. All those stupid years of trying to get through till one o'clock on two Ryvitas, what the hell was I thinking?'

'Madness, you need a big feed to get your engine running. Looks like another lovely day,' he said as sun streamed in from the east-facing kitchen window. 'What a summer, eh. I was walking out the back earlier, not a sound except birdsong. Fantastic...no neighbours for half a mile. It's brilliant.'

'It's just as well we've no neighbours given the racket we made in bed last night.'

'They'd have just thought it was foxes mating.'

'It was! Good God, I've never known the like,' she said, gurgling a laugh as she ate. 'I'm amazed that bed hasn't broken in half - you've been going at it like a well-oiled piston engine. You didn't used to have that sort of stamina; you're an unstoppable love machine, Guymer.'

'Sorry. I'm just a very horny sod at the moment. Even the thought of you naked sets me off.'

'Don't apologise man, I bloody love it. We're making up for lost time, aren't we? If you can keep it up baby, I can take it all night long...all day too if you want. In fact, it's been about six hours since we've done it, surely it's time for another go?'

He sat down to eat.

'It has to be said, you're just as randy as I am, more so if anything. I thought you'd eat me alive at one point last night and the dirty mouth on you...if your mam could hear you...'

'...she'd not be surprised at all. God I thought I could orgasm all night. The more we have it off, the more we seem to want to have it off. I can't stop thinking about doing it with you. It's like I'm 17 all over again.'

'Me too. In fact, this sex talk is making me horny again.'

She finished her last mouthful of bacon.

'Come on then...'

They got up and put their arms around each other, kissing. The phone rang again. Nick glanced and again it said 'withheld'.

'Hold that thought...I'll just take this,' he said as she was unbuttoning her pyjama jacket.

He heard a male voice, quite light in tone and with a Teesside accent.

'We've kidnapped Pinky Gull. Tell Jimmy Repp that if he wants to see his girlfriend again, it'll cost him a million pounds. Tell him we need it by tomorrow. If he doesn't give us it, we'll kill her. Any police presence, we kill her. If you tell anyone except Repp, we'll kill Julie Wells. We know where you live. I'll call tonight at 8pm to give you instructions.'

Nick scrambled for a pen and paper as he listened. Then the line when dead.

'What is it?' asked Julie, pulling her clothes back on, seeing the concern on his face.

He wrote the words down exactly as they were spoken, heart pounding. Just before the phone went dead, there was a half-second of noise in the background that he couldn't identify.

'What's wrong? You've gone white. We've not re-signed Juninho again have we?'

'Someone has kidnapped Pinky.'

'They've what?!'

'Repp has to give them a million quid or they'll kill her.'

His mouth had gone totally dry. He filled a glass with water.

'I...I...I can't believe it...are you sure it's not a practical joke someone's playing?' asked Julie, just staring at him in disbelief.

'No. It wasn't a joke.' He felt cold. 'They said if I told anyone except Repp they'd kill her and you.'

'They said what? Bollocks they will. They can fuck right off! Hold on, hold on...why are they telling you? Why not tell him directly? It makes no sense. No-one makes a vicarious threat.'

That hadn't occurred to him. She was right. Why go through him? There had to be a reason.

'I don't know Jules...shall I ring the police or Jimmy? Fuck, one minute you're having your breakfast and the next everything's been turned upside down.'

'What did they say exactly? Was it a man or a woman?

'A man...not a big aggressive voice but firm.'

'Any accent?'

'Teesside. Wish I had a recording to play back. I was concentrating on what he was saying. If we tell the police, they said they'd kill her and you. I was to tell Jimmy they wanted a million quid tomorrow and that they'd call tonight at eight with instructions.'

'We have to tell Jimmy. It's his decision to make. Fucking hell. Christ, poor Pinky. That's why Maggie couldn't get hold of her.'

'I've heard of this happening a lot to African footballers' families, but not so much to anyone on Teesside.'

'They must have rung you for a reason and not Jimmy...they didn't want to speak to Jimmy...but why?'

Nick stood up and drank some more water.

'It's obvious isn't it? They didn't want him to recognise their voice. It must be someone he knows. So they needed to use a go-between and I bet Pinky gave them my number. I gave it to her at the party so she'll have had it on her. We'd better get over to Jimmy's and tell him what's happened. I'm not breaking news like this over the phone.'

It was just before 9am when they pulled up to the gates of Jimmy's house. Nick pressed the intercom.

'Yeah?' It was Jimmy's voice.

'Jimmy, it's Nick Guymer, I need to see you.'

He was buzzed in, drove up the driveway and parked. He took a deep breath as he got out of the car. Jimmy was already at the door, a smile on his face.

'Hey Nick, Julie, what brings you around here at such an early hour? What's up? You look worried.'

They went in and walked through to the kitchen, the aroma of coffee in the air. Frankie Gray was perched on a stool eating a bowl of cornflakes, dressed immaculately in what looked like a hand-tailored dress shirt with cuff links and expensive mother of pearl buttons. Smooth.

'Alright there,' he said with a smile.

Nick thought it best to just get to the point.

'Look Jimmy, I got a phone call just after 8am and it was from someone who said they had Pinky...and...'

'...they *had* Pinky? What does that mean?' asked Jimmy, his dark eyebrows knitted together.

Frankie Gray stopped eating and stared at him.

'That they were holding her - had kidnapped her - and they want...'

'...what? Who? Come on, this is a joke...,' Jimmy said, running his long fingers through his floppy hair, his face contorted.

'I don't think it is. They said they want a million pounds tomorrow or they'll kill her.'

He went over all the details again and read out the transcription he'd made of the conversation. Frankie Gray took out his phone, started skimming through his address book, found a number and walked out of the kitchen and onto the patio.

Jimmy looked visibly scared.

'What the hell do we do? We can't go to the police. Shit shit shit...where's Frankie? Frankie! Fuck, why did they call you? Why not call me?'

'We thought it must be because you know someone involved - you'd recognise their voice, perhaps,' said Julie, sympathetically.

He was hyper now, walking in little bursts, stopping then turning around, eyes flashing from side to side, his brain a jumble of thoughts. 'Frankie!' he shouted again.

His business manager came back in and spoke in his deep baritone voice.

'No police. We say nothing to the police and neither do you Nick, Julie. Right? Nothing. We don't want them all over this. If word gets out, this sort of thing will just keep happening. We'll sort it out ourselves. Calm down. Don't panic, Jimmy,' he put out the palms of his hands downwards, 'we can sort this out. We'll give them the money and then we'll find out who the fuck has done this and we'll sort them out and get the money back, right?' He spoke firmly but evenly. 'I've already got someone on it. We'll have the cash by tomorrow morning, right? No panicking. These things happen. We'll sort it, okay? We all keep calm and keep quiet. This will be our secret. No stories in the press, right?' His tone was smooth, mellow and reassuring.

He was good under fire, no doubt about that.

'Yeah, yeah...thanks Frankie,' said Jimmy.

'Have you any idea who might do this?' said Nick. 'Any idea at all?'

Jimmy looked around himself wildly. 'No...no...no idea...who could it be Frankie?'

Frankie shrugged and picked up his bowl of cornflakes again. 'It could be anyone. It happens in football. I'll sort it out.'

He said this in the firm, certain manner of a Mafia boss who knew he would enact his revenge sooner or later. It was genuinely scary. Nick glanced at Julie and could see by her wary expression that she was thinking the same thing. Frankie's stance was almost one of nonchalance. Jimmy, on the other hand, was a wreck. His hands were shaking and he couldn't settle.

'So they're calling you tonight to confirm the arrangements, yes?' asked Frankie.

Nick nodded. 'Do you want me to say anything?'

'No. When they call just tell them the money will be wherever they want it to be and that we want the girl released immediately. If they don't release her as soon as they get the money, tell them there will be trouble.'

'Trouble? What sort of trouble?' asked Nick.

'Just say trouble. Big trouble. I don't fuck around, they'll know that.'

Nick nodded, noting that he hadn't used Pinky's name once yet. It was as if she was an object or even just a concept rather than a person.

'Okay, as soon as I hear from them, I'll let you know. Sorry to have to be the bearer of such bad news Jimmy.'

They left the big house and Nick blew out air as he drove back home. 'That was pretty heavy, eh.'

'Weird is what it was. Neither of those men reacted normally. If I heard you'd been kidnapped, my first thought would be for your welfare, but they didn't seem in the slightest bit bothered about Pinky. They were both bothered about the kidnapping but not about her as a person. That's not right. It was like the other night. I don't bloody like it.'

'And it took Frankie Gray about four minutes to come up with a million quid - not many could do that so easily.'

'You know, I think you should definitely do that investigation into Jimmy Repp - he's dodgy, Nick. He bloody is, I'm sure of it, and so is Frankie Gray. There's something....,' she waved her hands in the air grasping for words, '...something wrong about that house and those people.'

'Yeah, I agree. Let's see what we can find out about them when we get home.'

The sun was already burning in a clear blue sky when they got back to the farmhouse. Julie made tea while Nick began to go through his contact files and do some research. First he looked up Jimmy Repp's career details. He had begun his career in the Ajax academy but had been moved on at 16 to FC Groningen, where he'd broken into the first team in 1995 aged just 18 and was picked for Holland Under 21s ten times. After four seasons he was transferred out to Lyon, where he'd kept Gregory Coupet out of the first team for a couple of seasons. Lyon had won the French league seven seasons on the bounce but in his last year there in 2004, injury and poor form had seen him lose his place and he was moved onto Seville. And then a year ago he'd transferred to Middlesbrough after winning the UEFA Cup by beating the Boro 4-0 in the final at the conclusion of their epic UEFA Cup campaign. Why did clubs always sign players who had played well against them? It so often seemed to be the deciding factor almost regardless of their form against anyone else.

Injury had meant he was in and out for much of last season and, as back-up to Mark Schwarzer, he made only six first-team appearances, though he had done well in the reserves.

Nick did a search for news stories going back to the mid-90s. There were pages and pages of match reports.

Julie put a mug of green tea in front of him. 'Found anything interesting?'

'Not really. Then again, I don't know what I'm looking for really.'

'Any hint of scandal, financial or sexual...anything to suggest there has been suspicions about him.'

He looked out of the window at a thrush hopping around the garden.

'If there was anything well-known, the Boro probably wouldn't have signed him. He looks clean as far as I can tell. He went through a bad spell of form in 2003 and 2004 at Lyon and became a bit of a hate figure there but that's normal in football, isn't it? Yesterday's hero is tomorrow's zero. Hang on, oh God, he threw one in in a cup game in 2003 look, here's a video clip...ha ha...a touch of the Gary Sprakes there, son. That won't endear you to fans.'

The blurry clip showed Repp collecting the ball and looking to quickly launch a counter-attack by throwing it long to a team-mate standing on the left touchline but, as he was in mid-throw, he seemed to lose his balance, releasing the ball too late and letting it roll behind him into his own net.

'God that's embarrassing.' said Julie, looking over his shoulder.

'Aye...shit...look...he did another one a couple of months later against Saint Etienne...'

'...that's their big rivals.'

Nick played another 30-second video clip. This time Repp went up to catch a corner on the edge of his own six-yard box. He caught it but seemed to land awkwardly and dropped it into the net.

'That is shit,' said Julie. 'I'd be bloody furious if he did that for us. He wasn't even under pressure there.'

Nick replayed it. 'The ball just squirts out of his grasp...weird one that.'

'Play it again and stop it just before he loses grip on the ball,' she said.

He froze it just as the big goalie landed back on his feet.

'See, he's got hold of it cleanly there, a hand either side of the ball. Now roll it on...now stop it! Look, he's rolled his right hand over the ball and pushed it behind him into the goal.'

He rewound and played it again and then again.

'You're right...weird. I don't see how that could happen. He'd already landed after the jump. If he'd done that in mid-air you could have understood it slipping but ...I just don't see how that's happened.'

Julie pointed at the screen. 'He's done that deliberately. He's thrown it in on purpose. I'm telling you, no proper goalkeeper makes a mistake like that...actually, it's not the sort of mistake anyone would make.'

She went onto the back porch and picked up a plastic football they kicked around the back garden.

'He's gone like this...,' she held it in her hands firmly, rolled her right hand over the top of the ball and swiped at the back of the ball to propel it behind her.

'You can't do that by accident,' she said.

'Yeah...yeah that looks bad. So, what? You're thinking betting scam?'

'Of course – that'd explain where he's got at least some of his money. Hasn't anyone ever accused him? Do a search.'

Nick tried several phrases but it produced nothing except a few old message board comments laughing at one of his cock-ups. There were a couple of jokes suggesting it was all part of a betting scam but no serious accusations.

'I suppose it could just have been an accident. I saw Gary Sprake make errors like that in the 60s and 70s and he was capable of being utterly brilliant as well. Thing is Jules, it's hard to rig a football match even as a goalie. You still can't guarantee a result even if you want to lose. Your striker might hit a 35-yard volley into the net in injury-time.'

'Yeah but it won't be betting on a result, it'll be on a goal being scored in a set time frame or something precise like that. Spot betting, isn't that what they call it?'

'Even so, say you've been told to let one in between the 50th and 55th minutes, what if the ball doesn't even come near you at the allotted time?'

'I suppose what you need is to be able to be influenced by in-match betting. So you get the nod that your team has to concede the next goal...something like that...okay it's not fool-proof but most goalies get something to do every few minutes.'

'Yeah...yeah I can see that working.'

He continued to look through match statistics from his time at Lyon and Seville while Julie watched more footage

'When he was at Seville he gave away three penalties in seven games, though they won five of them and drew one, so it wasn't too bad for them results-wise. But it's why he was dropped for a couple of months and he only came back due to injury,' said Nick. 'See if you can find these games.'

He wrote them out on a piece of paper and she began searching.

'Here's a mention of him from 2005 being seen at the Cannes Film Festival with that kid Ami Pirlo, the actress.

Ami Pirlo had starred in an art-house movie which had received a lot of acclaim. She wasn't much more than 17 at the time and looked stunning with high cheekbones and big blue eyes.

'Never mind that...look at this...this is the first of those penalties you listed, it's against Atletico Madrid. Watch.'

A back-pass was made to him but it was a bit short and a striker chased it down. Instead of just sprinting to the ball and hoofing it clear, he backed off, allowed the striker to collect and then, as he attempted to go round him, scythed him down with a long leg. A clear penalty.

'Now look at this one, two games later,' she said, clicking again.

This time a striker hit a dipping volley from 25 yards, Repp leapt athletically to his top left corner and clawed away the ball with his fingertips. It was a fantastic save at full stretch, one of those saves where it briefly appears the goalkeeper has telescopic arms. But his one-handed parry pushed the ball back into play at the feet of an advancing striker. Repp was up quickly and advanced towards the player to seemingly block his shot but inexplicably, instead of trying to smother the ball, he lashed out a leg and hacked down the striker. Another clear penalty.

'That is two terrible decisions...'

'He's given them away on purpose if you ask me. He's a bloody good keeper...look at that save man, no-one can do that and then just clog a player down. The thing is, he makes so many world-class saves that it hides these mistakes – or at least – he's forgiven for them. There's some amazing stuff here...in one Copa Del Rey game against Malaga he wins it single-handedly for them with at least three, like, really incredible saves...look at this...look at the ground he covers...'

She showed him diving to the right corner of his net to push the ball wide of the goal, which was then collected by a winger who crossed at pace onto the head of striker who placed it in the left-hand corner. In the meantime Repp had jumped to his feet, sprinted across his goal and, with one last leap which kept him hanging in the air, tipped the ball over the bar. A stunning save.

'So what you're saying is, if he can do this, there's no way he'd make these other clumsy errors.'

'Exactly. I mean, we can't prove it just from the footage but it's very suspicious. I bet if we went through his whole career we'd find more of this sort of thing. He got the 'Dutch Diver' nickname because of his agility but some of these clips look like he's a total donkey.'

'Okay, well let's see if we can find out when Frankie Gray came into the picture because if he's been taking money for match-fixing then he'll be involved somehow, I'm sure of it. Pity he doesn't have a more distinctive name. Why can't he be called Frankie Fellatio or something? All I'm getting here is the ex-Leeds man Frank Gray....loads of Yanks...lawyers…can't see anything obviously him.'

'Try doing an image search. I bet he's done charity functions and those sorts of pics always appear in local newspapers. Local dignitary with glassy-eyed special guest who's been on the free wine all night,' said Julie.

'Aye....ah...gotcha...here we go...here he is on the *Gazette* website with our boy Jimmy at a charity do in the Swallow Hotel, Stockton....let's have a look...Jimmy Repp with his business associate Frankie Gray. Nothing more. I wonder when he started working for Jimmy?'

'Well, he's English so maybe he only came on the scene when he came to the Boro?'

'There are other images of him in Monte Carlo in 2004 with another model, Cara Rennington,' said Nick, 'and another here, Miranda Kelly. All legs and teeth, both of them younger than Pinky it has to be said and all of them stunners. Doesn't it strike you as odd that in Europe he was going out with models and then he moves to England and hooks up with a local Teesside lass?' said Nick.

She frowned at him. 'Why?'

'Well...you know...nothing against the kid but she's not a supermodel in this class, is she?'

'She's really good-looking.'

'Yeah but...I dunno...maybe I'm being unfair.'

'Yeah you are. These women – I say women but they're barely women really are they? – these girls just seem more glamorous because you don't know where they're from. 'Cos Pinky is from Stockton you can't think of her as glamorous. Most men would fancy her if you put her on a red carpet in Cannes.'

Nick scanned the pictures again. 'Ah ha. Here he is at the Monte Carlo Grand Prix in 1999 and he's got another model on his arm...err...not sure what her name is...but right behind him, with more hair than he's got now, is Frankie Gray.'

'So they go a way back then.'

'Yeah, but there's no scandal online at all. Not that I can find, anyway. No 'my night of passion' type scandals. Nothing in fact. It seems he's a good clean boy. You know, even if he has been doing match-fixing of some sort over the years, as you said, we'd never be able to prove it, not unless we could get our hands on some hard evidence – an e-mail or a letter or something telling him to do something at a specific time, which he subsequently does. Just making a bad decision during a football match proves nothing. If I'm going to put together a story, I need something substantial to stand it all up. Otherwise it's just gossip, isn't it?'

Nick was worried all day, fretting about taking the kidnappers' call. He set the phone down by a notepad and made sure it was fully charged. He didn't want to get anything wrong. Pinky's life might depend on him writing it all down correctly and that thought made him break out in a sweat. Christ, why did this have to happen? He bloody well resented its intrusion into their happy little world in the countryside and so alternated between anger and fear all day.

Bang on 8pm, his phone rang, the number showing as 'withheld'. Julie sat opposite him at the large pine kitchen table. She crossed her fingers as he picked up.

'Hello?'

'Have you got the cash?' It was the same voice as before.

'I haven't but Jimmy's manager says he'll have it for you tomorrow. He wants Pinky released as soon as you've picked it up or he says there'll be trouble.' Nick listened intently, pen in hand. There was background noise again - a whooshing, hissing sound - but he still couldn't discern what it was.

'Tell him to leave it in the bin beside Middlesbrough Town Hall steps on Albert Road, opposite the entrance to the Centre North East building. Got that?'

Nick wrote it down word for word. 'Got it, yeah. What time?'

'Two in the afternoon. Tell him to put the money in one of those tartan holdalls.'

'Does it have to be tartan?' he asked in all seriousness.

' 'Yeah...err...tartan.'

'Any particular type of tartan? Black Watch? Campbell? Stewart?'

'Shut up. Don't try and be clever.'

That annoyed Nick. 'I'm not...just tell me what you want.'

'Any tartan. We'll be watching. Any police and she dies.'

'He said there'll be no police. Where will Pinky be?'

'As soon as we have the money she'll be released. 2pm, make sure he does it or we'll come round there and kill Julie Wells as well, got that?'

That instantly angered him. Hot blood rose in his throat. He didn't take well to threats and bullying. Not well at all. He hissed into the phone, fury burning behind his eyes.

'The fuck you will, son! You harm one hair on her head and I'll hunt you down and kill you. I'm not threatening you, I'm telling you and don't fucking doubt it for a millisecond. I don't give a fuck who you are...I'll fuck you up, son. And don't try and play the fucking hard man with me, I'm not impressed and remember, I'm helping you here. You need me so don't piss me off again or I might just fucking come and kill you. Don't think I can't work out who the fuck you are...you're not that clever, son. I'll come for you so don't you dare make these fucking threats...you fucker!'

Julie was making 'calm down' gestures to him. He could see her but he couldn't register them in his brain. The man on the other end of the phone didn't respond. Nick expected a counter-threat or for the phone to be banged down but there was nothing. He could hear breathing.

'Yeah...well…just...just do what we say and no-one gets hurt,' the man said after a couple of seconds too long. His tone was not quite so firm now, more shaky and breathy. 'So...2pm then, right?' He now sounded more like someone making a date.

'2pm it is.'

Nick put down the phone and held his hands up immediately.

'I told you to keep calm - you can't go losing your bloody nut at a time like this! God man, this isn't a game. What did he say?' She sat back with her arms crossed over her chest, annoyed but worried.

Nick sat back and took a drink of water.

'Sorry man, he just threatened you, it made me mad, I mean who the fuck does he think he is? We've done nowt to him, but to be honest, I think I scared the shit out of him actually, he went all stuttering and wimpy.'

'Getaway....are you sure?'

'Yeah, he was trying to be all tough with me and then when I blew up, he lost his bottle. Dunno what I was thinking really, it all just came out like a primal defence thing...I meant it too...you can't fake that sort of shit and maybe that's what the bloke picked up on...fuck, we've got a crazy one here...or something.'

She shook her head. 'What are you like?' she said, a hint of admiration in her voice now. 'So when's the drop?'

'2pm outside Middlesbrough Town Hall.'

'In a tartan holdall? That was funny.'

'Well I thought he might want it in a specific tartan but it didn't seem to have occurred to him. He probably just wanted it to look distinctive and I took it very literally. Ha ha...shit, I'm sweating bullets...I'd better ring Jimmy and tell him.'

He punched in the footballer's number.

'Jimmy, it's Nick. I've had the call.'

'Shit...okay, okay...I'll put Frankie on. He's organising it all.'

There was a brief pause and Frankie's deep baritone came on the line.

'Nick. How goes it, my friend?'

People who say 'my friend' are never your friend; usually it's a subconscious expression of the absolute opposite. Nick let it slide.

'Hi Frankie, I just got the call. They want the money put in a tartan holdall and left in the bin that's beside the steps at Middlesbrough Town Hall, on Albert Road, opposite the Centre North East building entrance. Do you know where that is?'

'Yeah yeah...of course...it's a very public place...as I expected.'

'He repeated his threat about there being no police or Pinky dies. He also threatened Julie if you don't go through with this. I wasn't best pleased about that, as you can imagine.'

'Yup, yup. All cool,' he said almost happily, as though he was arranging a social occasion.

'The drop must be done by 2pm tomorrow and they'll release Pinky after they've got the money.'

'2pm, right, right. That's fine.'

'Are you going to try and follow them?'

'Thanks for your help Nick, leave this to me now. It will all be sorted. You don't need to worry about it and don't worry about Julie either. She'll not be hurt. I'll get this whole thing shut down. Thanks again.'

The line went dead. Weirdly, Frankie Gray was both reassuringly cool and firm but also sinister.

Julie was typing at her computer as he put down the phone.

'That's one strange bloke. What are you writing?'

'I'm mailing my friend Karen Compton. She works in the Centre North East building.'

'I still think of it as Corporation House. Tallest building in Middlesbrough that, y'know. You'd think someone would have built a bigger one since 1974, especially as it's not exactly massive. Why are you mailing her?'

'Because her office looks out onto Albert Road. We can drop by and watch what happens from the perfect vantage point. What? Don't look at me like that, we're not missing this. If someone's threatening to kill me if they don't get the money, I want to make sure they get it, don't I? And I'd like to see Pinky safe as well. I don't take kindly to weasels making death threats on the phone. If they want to threaten me they can do it to my bloody face.'

The 'no retreat, no surrender' culture engendered on the estate was never far below the surface.

'Of course, why did I even think for a second that we'd stay away?' He laughed. 'Something about all of this is odd though. Obviously I'm not an expert on the politics of a hostage crisis, but the bloke on the phone seemed too...I know this sounds stupid, right, but he sounded too nice. He was trying to come across all tough but he wasn't. Like when a soft kid at school is trying to be the hard kid but you know it's an act. And the more I think about it, the more I'm sure he crapped himself when I lost my rag.'

'Well you can be a bit scary when you lose your shit, kidda,' said Julie, biting into an apple.

'Yeah but does someone who is a bit of a pussy really do kidnapping? I dunno. I guess he might not be the kidnapper; he could just be doing the phone work. Do kidnappers employ customer service people?'

Julie laughed and shook her head. 'Nah...it must be him that's done it. In fact it must be a lone man because remember, he's only calling you because he knows Jimmy would recognise his voice. If there was a gang of them, chances are at least one wouldn't be known to Jimmy, so he must be a solo act.'

She grinned. 'I'm like Cagney and Lacey all rolled into one. Always loved Sharon Gless, me.'

'Aye, that's good thinking. You're right. Okay, so we'll watch it go down.'

'As long as Pinky gets out okay, that's the only important thing,' she said. 'I'm worried sick about her. I hope they're treating her well and not being weird or pervy.'

'Yeah but I'm left with the feeling that both sides are as bad as each other, somehow. And I'll tell you another thing, of the two sides, I think it's Frankie Gray who actually scares me the most.

CHAPTER 6

The day dawned overcast, muggy and nearly 70 degrees. Nick and Julie had scrambled eggs and salmon for a late breakfast and set off for Middlesbrough just after one.

'Have you told your friend Karen what this is all about?' asked Nick as he took the A66 into Middlesbrough, parking in the Cleveland Centre multi-storey.

'I said we wanted to spy on someone, that's all. She was quite amused. I think she thinks it's some sort of romantic tryst.'

'My nerves are giving me terrible wind,' said Nick, letting out a huge fart as they got out of his BMW.

'You should use your wind as a defence mechanism if anyone ever kidnaps you. A few expulsions of Guymer gas will ensure they release you immediately.'

They walked out of the car park, onto Albert Road and down to the 232-foot, 19-storey Centre North East building. An unlovely glass and steel office block, it had been built in 1974 but had been through various hands with one owner after another going bust or selling up. It stood across the road from Middlesbrough Town Hall, a relic of the grand days of Victorian civic architecture. Constructed in the 1880s, it was now a Grade II listed building. It was a large, impressive, gothic building and reflected the ambition and money in the town during the boom years of the industrial revolution.

Nine steps led up from the pavement to a large double wooden door. Alongside the steps was a metal waste bin just about big enough to place a holdall. Nick pointed it out as they walked past.

'There's the star of the show.'

They stopped and looked up at the tower block and then went into the foyer and looked at a list of companies occupying the building.

'Most of this place is empty, look, floor after floor is available, I wonder if we can get access to one of the empty floors so we don't have to explain what we're doing. Christ, I'd have thought this was primo office space. Amazed it's so unwanted. Is it floor four that Karen's on?' asked Nick, pressing the lift button.

'Yeah, four. Probably asking too much money. Rents in town are still stupidly high,' said Julie.

The fourth floor was used by the council for their rent department. Karen Smith was an ex-colleague of Julie's from her days as a legal PA who had since taken up a management position. They met beside a vending machine in a corridor. She was a fleshy woman in her 50s dressed in a black suit and an eye-watering acid green top.

'Now then, Julie. You look great, pet,' she said, giving her a little hug.

'So do you. This is Nick.'

'Ah this is Nick is it? She used to talk about you a lot when you first started going out.'

'Did she? Oh dear. Not all bad I hope.'

'Oh no. Quite the opposite,' she burst into a rolling laugh and touched Julie on the arm.

'I used to extol your virtues,' said Julie, laughing along with her.

'Yes, she said you had very impressive virtues,' she went off on a rolling laugh again.

Nick looked at his watch, feeling a little embarrassed. It was 1.40pm. He wanted to get in place to see the afternoon's events unfold.

'Hey Karen, is there an empty floor of offices we could get access to?'

'So what's this all about?' she asked, finally stopping laughing.

'I'll tell you all about it over a quick hot chocolate,' said Julie, pressing the buttons on the vending machine.

'I hope it's juicy. The next floor up is empty if you want to use it, Nick. In fact, almost all the floors are empty these days. It used to be a council floor as well but they moved it last year. The doors are open - we got a couple of tables from there last week.'

'Great. Thanks,' he said and took off up the stairs.

The whole floor was open-plan - a soulless mix of limitless glass windows and cheap blue floor tiles. Wires hung from the ceiling tiles where strip lights had been taken out. Sheets of paper, a few cardboard boxes and waste bins littered the floor. If tumbleweed had blown across the floor it would only have been appropriate. It was a space, not a room, not a building but a void, a facility utterly without character or feeling.

He walked to the right-hand side and looked down at the town hall below. He was directly in front of the steps and the waste bin. With a small pair of binoculars he focused on the bin. There was nothing in there. Corporation Road, which ran at a right angle to Albert Road and intersected it right beside the town hall, was busy with traffic. Plenty of people were milling around on foot during their lunch hour. Although Middlesbrough was almost permanently an economically deprived, some said devastated, town, it was still a lively place full of lively people who were determined, come boom or bust, to have a good time if at all possible. It was the only way to survive the long bouts of unemployment and low-paid work. It was also true that, contrary to outsiders' beliefs, some people in town actually had a few quid. Not everyone lived huddled under a tarpaulin on Linthorpe Road eating gravel.

Nick took a video camera from his bag and watched as people came up and down, in and out and side to side, a shapeless constantly shifting assembly of people. The clock tower which loomed over the town hall showed it was 1.52. How would this happen? Would the money be dropped off at 2pm and then immediately picked up by someone or would it sit there for a while? Surely not. Who would do the drop? It wouldn't be Jimmy surely, he'd be too well known. He looked up the street to where the railway station sat at the top end of Albert Road. A train must have come in as a steady stream of people pulling luggage and suitcases were filing down towards him.

1.55: A man in a blue suit stopped alongside the bin, lit a cigarette, brushed hair off his face and wandered on. False alarm.

1.56: A couple hugged each other beside the town hall steps. They laughed, held hands and then moved away.

1.57: A dog with a collar but not on a lead came trotting up the road sniffing at lamp-posts. It stopped at the metal waste bin, cocked its leg and released a squirt of piss before trotting off pleased with itself.

1.58: He heard the doors open. He turned quickly to see who it was. Julie.

'Hiya...anything happened yet...?' she said, standing alongside him. 'Great view from here.'

'Nothing yet, except a nice dog having a piss.'

The sky darkened as a blue-black summer storm cloud began to release its payload.

Nick focused the video camera on the waste bin and began to film.

1.59: A bin wagon stopped on Corporation Road and two men in orange overalls got out and emptied a waste bin that was full to the brim with cans and paper. Julie nudged him and pointed at them. 'Do you reckon this lot are in on it? The binnies?'

'I doubt it...hang on...isn't that....look at the bloke who has just put that wheelie bin on the machine....I'd swear that's your brother Terry.'

Julie leaned right up to the glass.

'Bloody hell, it is, aye...it's our Terry. I didn't know this was his round. Christ almighty, I'd better ring him. I don't want him getting caught up in this.' She dialled his number but there was no reply.

2.00: The Town Hall clock struck the hour.

'Look, look…,' urged Julie, 'Frankie Gray.'

Nick filmed as the business manager came out of a coffee shop underneath the Centre North East building carrying a tartan canvas bag. It looked heavy and it weighed him down on his right side. He didn't pause as he crossed the road and, without looking around, placed the bag in the bin. It slipped out of view under the lip. Then he walked up Albert Road, turned right on Corporation Road and disappeared from sight.

Meanwhile, the bin wagon turned left onto Albert Road and stopped outside the town hall.

'Shit...he's going to empty the fucking bin with the bag in,' shouted Julie, dialling his number again. 'A million fucking quid is about to end up in the back of a bin wagon.'

Nick kept filming as Terry and his co-worker, dressed in orange overalls and fluorescent yellow high-viz jackets, advanced towards the metal bin. Terry yanked at it once, then, feeling its weight, took a better hold and hoisted it up and out of its container and into the back of the wagon. The vehicle moved away and Terry took the empty liner back to its holder and walked off down the road with his colleague. As the back of the wagon became visible, the tartan holdall was clearly wedged in the back of the truck. The large grinding mechanism that sucked trash into the void behind had not been turned on yet.

'He's still not answering. He's probably not even allowed it at work,' said Julie.

Nick and Julie watched as the they continued to collect rubbish from waste bins on either side of the road. Nick's camera rolled on.

'Who the fuck was supposed to collect that then? I keep expecting to see someone come up and look into the empty bin,' said Nick. 'Keep your eyes on the bin while I film the wagon.'

She kept up a commentary. 'There's no-one around. A group of three people walking together...but they've just walked past. Now there's someone from the station pulling a suitcase on wheels but he's not stopped or looked at it. Wait, there's a big bloke in a checked shirt. He's stopped right in front of the bin....hang on...no, he's lighting a fag and he's away again.'

A bus came down Corporation Road and turned onto Albert Road and was immediately held up by the bin wagon. Nick looked up from his camera.

'Any sign of anyone looking for the money?'

'Nope. No-one. I can't believe Terry is in the middle of all this.'

'It's probably as well he doesn't know anything about it,' said Nick. 'Look, the traffic has ground to a halt behind him. '

They watched as the bus eventually overtook the wagon and other cars filed past as they moved slowly down the street clearing rubbish. Nick was just about to stop filming when he noticed something.

'Jules! Get the binoculars. Quick! Look in the back of wagon.'

She focused the lens on the vehicle. 'Okay, got it.'

'Can you see the tartan holdall?'

She paused for a moment.

'No! It's not there. Fuck. Have they turned the machine on and chewed it up?'

'No. Look, there's a big box sitting at the front, they threw that in before they came onto Albert Road. If they'd turned it on, that'd have been pulled in too.'

'The bag isn't there. I can see the back of the wagon really clearly and it's not there.'

'Fucking hell, someone must have grabbed it but I never saw them.' He stopped filming and looked up and down the street but nobody was carrying a tartan holdall.

'Terry must have seen what happened. He must have,' said Julie. 'I'm going down there to see him, come on...we need to know if it was collected, stolen or whatever...if the kidnappers haven't got the money, they won't release Pinky. Shitting hell man, they might even bloody well kill her.'

They ran down the five flights of stairs rather than wait for the elevator and burst out onto the street. Setting off down Albert Road, the dustbin wagon had just passed Grange Road and was heading to the next block of buildings. As it came to a halt, they finally caught up. Running around to the passenger side of the cab as the two collectors got out, Julie had just about enough breath to cry out, 'Terry! Terry!'

He was tall at nearly six foot and was a strong, broad man with an unruly crop of fair hair and a broken-toothed smile. He looked surprised to see his big sister.

'What are you doing in the Boro, Jules?' he said in a broad Teesside accent. 'Alright Nick, 'ow you doin' mate?'

Nick bent over and put his hands on his knees to get his breath.

'Terry, man, you just picked up a bin outside the town hall, it had a big tartan bag in it, it was heavy...remember?' panted Julie, hands on hips.

'How do you know that, like?'

'I was watching you. But do you remember it?

'Watching me? Where from, like? Why?'

'Never mind, I'll tell you later. Tell me about that holdall.'

'It was no big deal. Just more crap for the wagon. That's all me and Dave do, hoy crap in here.'

Dave was a big beery man in his 30s with greying fag ash stubble and a shaven head.

'Okay but what happened to that bag? It was in the wagon for about two minutes and then it disappeared.'

'Was it? I don't look at the shit, I just throw it in the van, Jules,' he said, puzzled.

'Look, this is important Tez...it was sitting in the front of the wagon, here...,' she walked around the back of the vehicle and pointed to the lip where rubbish sat before being scooped backwards.

'Aye, I saw that,' said Dave. 'What's this about, like? Was there a body in it?'

He seemed delighted by the idea.

'I said I'll tell you later – I just need to know where it went, it's really fucking important,' said Julie, growing exasperated.

The two bin men looked at each other and shrugged.

'I don't know Jules, if you hadn't said, I'd not even have noticed it wasn't here,' said Terry.

'It was on there, like,' said Dave, 'but it's not now, like...and we've not pulled any of the crap in yet so I dunno, maybe it's fallen out or summat.'

He looked back down the road to see if it was lying on the tarmac. The driver sounded his horn.

'Owwee Tez, we've gotta go – we're behind schedule as it is,' said Dave as their driver honked his horn.

'Give us a call later, Jules. Tell us what this is all about,' said Terry.

Nick and Julie stood and watched them go.

'That's the weirdest thing. We didn't imagine that, did we? Someone must have taken it out when they were collecting other rubbish. They must have done, that's why they didn't see anything,' said Nick, wiping sweat from his forehead.

'Yeah someone has, but who? The kidnappers? And what about Pinky? Will they release her?'

'Maybe I'll get a call from the kidnapper again. Come on, there's nowt much more we can do here. Let's go home and look at this film footage; I might have filmed what happened and not even realised. I just hope that the kid is released and nothing bad happens to her. I know it's not our fault but I can't help feeling responsible, somehow,' said Nick as they ran back to the car.

It was still overcast and humid when they got home and the clouds looked a foreboding shade of slate blue and smoke, readying themselves for another summer storm. Nick hooked up the video camera to his computer and they sat down to watch.

'Right, here comes Terry's wagon...round the corner...and he picks up the bin with the bag in,' said Nick, pausing as Terry out lifted the bin. 'Now, look for anyone around watching him.'

The pavement was wide and filled with people now frozen, a little blurred and held at a split-second in time.

'This double denim bloke is watching them - or at least he's turned towards Terry,' said Julie, pointing to the screen at a beefy bloke in a denim shirt and jeans.

'Keep your eye on him then.'

They watched as Terry tipped up the bin and emptied out the bag and a few cans and bits of paper which must have been under the holdall.

'Double Denim just walks off, he wasn't looking at him really, I think he was distracted...but who's this here?'

Nick pointed to a figure walking towards the camera and pulling a big shopping trolley.

'He's stopped and is just watching them both empty the bins. Looking from one to the other and then walking on. He's clocked what they're doing.'

As he played it on, the man with the shopping trolley passed by the bin wagon and went out of view. The tartan bag was still visible as the bus pulled up and then obscured the back of the bin wagon.

'Bugger, I've let it drop a bit there,' said Nick.

The picture blurred and shook as he'd moved the camera around, then re-stabilised.

'Look! Stop it. Go back half a second...look,' said Julie, pointing at the screen.

At the edge of the picture was the man with the shopping trolley - only it wasn't actually a shopping trolley, it was more obviously a large travel bag, strapped onto a trolley, easily big enough to hold the holdall. He was emerging from between the bus and the bin wagon, crossing to the other side of the road.

'He must have the money in that bag. He must do!' she exclaimed. 'He got it out when you let the camera drop.'

He rolled the recording on. The bus overtook the bin wagon followed by the built-up traffic. Terry and Dave each came back with a black bin bag in each hand and threw them in the back. The tartan holdall was now missing.

'It's gone, it's gone...see...see...it must have been the man with the trolley,' she proclaimed triumphantly, pointing. 'He went between the bus and the bin wagon, lifted it out and crossed the road.'

Nick narrowed his eyes and rewound the tape. It didn't look right. He was missing something. He watched again as the bus pulled up, the camera lost its position for about two seconds and, when it refocused, the trolley man emerged from between the bus and bin wagon, crossed the road and went out of the camera's view. Then the bus went around the bin wagon, followed by the cars, revealing the tartan bag had gone. He stopped it again and sat looking at the screen, his chin resting on his hand.

'What are you thinking?' said Julie. 'It's trolley man, isn't it?'

'Maybe, but we can't see what's happening on the pavement on the other side of the bus and bin wagon can we? Anything could be happening there out of view. See here, once the traffic has pulled around to the right of the stationary wagon ...there's a figure here...what's he or she up to there...they're carrying something and there's a blur here but it's out of shot,' he pointed to a rust-coloured trouser leg of someone walking left down the side of the town hall and out of view. 'They could equally have pulled the money out of the wagon and be heading off down the side of the town hall. They must have passed the bus as it pulled up, taken the bag out and walked off without Terry and Dave seeing because they were on the other side of the road and couldn't see him because the view of that side is blocked by the traffic. Look...,' he took it back a few frames, 'look, they're here and can't see what's going on.'

He pointed as the orange figures emerged from out of the camera's view with bin bags.

'Take it back to before the bus comes around the corner. Okay, look for someone with a rust-coloured leg.'

They watched the now-familiar scene again. Nothing.

'Play it again,' said Julie. He did so. Still nothing.

'One last time,' she said.

'Okay but let's not look at the bin at all, look anywhere else but at the bin,' he said and replayed it. This time, just as the bus rounded the corner and advanced towards the stationary bin wagon, Julie let out a yelp and pointed at the bus.

'Look at the reflection in the window of the bus. It's a youngish man with rust-coloured pants and they're those horrible but very fashionable skinny jeans...that must be him. He's standing on our side of the road, out of view of the camera, and must have crossed the road behind the bus when you were filming the dustbin wagon, so you couldn't have caught him on film.'

'Yup...let's just roll it on... look...yes, there he is...through the bus window, just a glimpse of him. Hang on, I'll re-do it...and hold it...there, got him.'

He did a screen grab and blew it up. It was a side-on head shot and a bit blurred as it was captured through the window glass and then both sides of the bus. He was mid-20s with short hair, neatly cut, and a blue polo shirt to go with the rust-coloured skinny jeans.

'Okay so it's either Trolley Man or Skinny Jeans who takes the money. One of them must have taken the bag. It can't have been anyone else because no-one else was in the right position at the time it disappeared,' said Nick, 'and it was taken while Dave and Terry were on our side of the road, which is why they didn't notice.'

'Yup, that sounds right. So what do we do now then?' said Julie with a frown on her brow. 'Has it been stolen or was Skinny Jeans or Trolley Man the kidnapper doing the collection?'

'I think the latter. No-one steals a bag out of a bin lorry, do they? It's just a holdall, it doesn't look worth anything. I think it was planned.'

'How could it be planned?' she asked and looked at him with incredulity. 'How could they have known the bin would be emptied right at that time? They've had to improvise, surely.'

'Ah but...,' Nick held a finger aloft and then quickly put it down as it was exactly what Jeff did when he was inventing one of his madcap conspiracy theories, '...the bins are almost certainly emptied around the same time on set days of the week, aren't they? In Harrogate our bins were emptied at five minutes past eight every other Tuesday, give or take a few minutes. So they could easily have known that and built it into their plan. Y'see, they'll have known that Frankie or Jimmy or someone would be watching the money to see where it went and who collected it. So just taking it out of the bin was too risky. This way it's literally obscured who took it, from this side at least...in fact...yes, yes...', an idea had just dawned on him, '...in fact these two must have been working together. One as a decoy, the other to take it. And it's worked well because we don't know who did take it - it could have been carried off by Skinny Jeans or in Trolley Man's bag and even that was hard to spot with the naked eye. Look how many times we had to watch before we worked it out. They hid it all behind buses, the bin lorry and traffic, which very predictably built up on this very busy road in the middle of the day.'

He quietly punched the air in celebration of his own brainpower.

'Very clever, but what about Pinky?' said Julie.

'Call her. You've still got the beer mat with the number from Siobhan, haven't you?'

She rang the number but it just went to voicemail. 'Pinky, it's Julie Wells, call me when you get this. I just want to make sure you're okay.'

'We've just got to sit and wait then...hopefully the kid will be okay. They've got the money like they wanted.'

'If she has been released surely someone has to tell the cops about it - we can't have gangs of kidnappers just doing what they want...taking people and demanding money.'

'I suppose it'll be up to Pinky and Jimmy if they want to tell the cops. But it seems odd if they don't.'

'Or we could tell them.'

'Yeah we could, but is it our choice to make?'

They sat in silence, the summer birdsong the only noise to be heard until the peace was shattered by Julie's phone ringing. They both visibly jumped in their seats. Julie picked up the phone.

'It's Pinky!' she looked at him with wide eyes.

'Hello? Pinky? Is that you?'

She nodded at him. It was.

'Good grief girl, what's been happening to you? Are you alright?'
She put her thumb up at him.

'Where are you? Where have you been held? Who held you? Oh,

okay. We were really worried about you. The kidnappers rang Nick so we think they must be known to Jimmy. Didn't you recognise them? Well I'm so glad that you're safe. Are you calling your mam, she's been worried about you? Good. No we won't. Take care of yourself.'

She rang off and let out a huge sigh of relief.

'That girl has balls of steel. She's only been let go half an hour ago and she was so calm and together.'

'And she's alright?' he asked.

'Yeah, she said she's fine. She hadn't seen who had grabbed her but they didn't hurt her. They kept her in a house somewhere. She didn't want us to tell anyone, Jimmy said not to let it get out in case it encourages more people to have a go. He says the police will leak it to the press, they always do when it involves footballers.'

'That does make sense, actually.'

He was so relieved. It was impossible to know whether the kidnappers were serious nutters and would have killed her or whether they were just chancers. The man who had called him was way too easily put off his stride to be a serious criminal hard man but then again, even the most accomplished kidnappers have to start somewhere.

Julie let out a big sigh again, 'God this whole thing has made me so tense...so glad it's over.'

He reached across the table and took her hand.

'You did good, man...now, can we get back to our normal life?'

She pushed her hair back over her ears. 'I bloody hope so...but, I don't know, man...I've got a feeling in my water.'

'Cystitis?'

She shook her head and looked out of the window. 'I've got a feeling this isn't the end of something, it's just the start.'

CHAPTER 7

A day later, Nick was sitting in the garden enjoying the afternoon sun, writing on his laptop. Julie lay stretched out on a towel, sunbathing in shorts and a white vest. It was another hot, sunny day in the high 70s and the only sound in the air had been the buzzing of the bees on their large overgrown purple buddleia until his phone chirped into life.

'Hello?'

'Nick old boy, is that you?'

'I recognise that velvet fog voice. Alf Porter, how are you? Still enjoying the Spanish sunshine?'

'Ah yes indeed, old boy. Nothing like it. Beats sitting in a sordid grief hole in an over-priced suburb of London, staring at the rain, that's for sure. And how do I find you?'

'I'm great. Just moved into an old farmhouse in the countryside with Julie...you remember Julie, don't you?'

'Ah yes indeed, a fine filly, as I recall. And which part of the countryside is this?'

'Teesside, just south of Yarm.'

'Teesside and countryside. These are not words which I normally put together, old boy. Don't tell me there that bucolic nature interrupts the bleak industrial misery.'

He laughed. 'Yeah it surprises a lot of people but Teesside is surrounded by some magnificent countryside and it's sunny here too...only occasionally but it does happen.'

'Now that I do find hard to believe.'

'Aye we do get summers here Alf, believe it or not.'

'Well it all sounds marvellous. I'm actually calling you because of your e-mail the other day. I know I replied but since then I've been doing a bit of work on this and I may have understated the degree to which Jimmy Repp had been under scrutiny while at Seville.'

Nick sat up.

'Really? Now, that is interesting. So suspicions were raised by his goalkeeping howlers?'

'Not that, no. More because of the company he was said to be keeping. I spoke to a couple of Spanish journalists from the south about him. I think the strange goals and penalties he gave away had been largely disregarded as the silly things that sometimes happen but then a few months before his move he was seen in Guido Malaga's restaurant in Milan, a famous place for criminals to do their business over a decent seafood platter. He was seen with three other men, all of whom are known to have connections to organised crime in Spain and in Italy and there was a chappie from Singapore there too who, it's rumoured, is one of Europe's top match-fixers.'

'Bad company to keep, huh,' said Nick, writing notes as Alf spoke. That had to be the weird man Yashie, didn't it?

'Indeed, old boy. Nothing was written because there was no proof and a fellow can meet who he wants but a few alarm bells had started ringing and when you connect the goalkeeping errors with these unsavoury types, well...as you know, match-fixing is a way of life in Italy. When he was transferred to the glorious Middlesbrough FC it seems to have put an end to it all anyway. Thought you might like to know if you're doing a bit of sniffing around.'

'Indeed, thanks Alf...I really appreciate that.'

'No problem at all. From what the local press boys tells me, he was a popular chap, always very accommodating and I think that might have led to many giving him the benefit of the doubt.'

'Did anyone mention his girlfriend? She's a good-looking kid called Pinky.'

'Pinky? No. I never heard the name and I'm pretty sure I'd have remembered.'

'How about his business manager. Frankie Gray? Heard of him?'

'Well it's a common enough name but, no. Sorry. However, there is one final thing.'

'Yeah?'

'A suicide.'

'A suicide? Who? A footballer?'

'No. A girl. In Amsterdam in January.'

'Okay. How does this relate?'

'Jimmy Repp was very briefly interviewed by the police in connection with it.'

'Really? Do you know why?'

'Apparently the girl was found in an apartment he owned.'

'Christ. Who was she?'

'The boys I spoke to said it was an English street girl with drug problems. Young. About 14 as it turned out; though I'm told she looked older. He seems to have been letting her stay there. He was in England when it happened. It didn't make much of a splash in the media because it was just a small, sad story and I get the impression palms were greased by Repp's people to make sure it was all kept low-key, though that's just my speculation based on being an old, cynical man who knows the way this world of sin works.'

'I might ask him about that. He's quite a generous guy - letting someone stay in his place sounds quite typical of him.'

'Indeed, that's what my contact said. He was quite affected by it apparently and made some large donations to homeless and drug charities as a result.'

'Okay, thanks Alf. If you hear anything else, do let me know and if there's anything I can do for you, just shout.'

'Okay Nick, nice to speak to you.'

'What was that about?' said Julie, sitting up.

Nick made some quick notes and outlined what Alf had said.

'He made large donations to charity? I wonder how large 'large' is? Where *does* all this money come from? I don't know…dodgy friends, a young girl killing herself…this is why my water is playing up and telling me something is weird over at the House of Goalkeeping Errors.'

'The thing is, I've had dinner with criminals and not known it at the time. From the outside it might look like you're dodgy too, but in fact you've innocently been introduced to someone who is a big drug dealer or something and you don't have a clue,' said Nick.

'I once had dinner in New York with a man who was later arrested for bringing ten million dollars' worth of cocaine into Florida.'

'Did you? That sounds quite glamorous.'

'Yeah, he was nice enough. Smart but nothing special. It was when I was working out there for Watson's just after college. He asked me out and paid for champagne and everything. I just thought he was well-off and had a good job. It never occurred to me for a second that he might be a major drug dude.'

'He didn't offer you a toot of something?'

'Nope. He asked if I wanted to go to his flat for coffee but I said no.'

'Because coffee is never coffee, coffee is sex?'

'That's probably what I assumed and I didn't really fancy him so I gave him the red card.'

'Well there you go. So the fact Jimmy was seen in these people's company isn't necessarily incriminating but it's odder that he let a young girl stay at his flat. That's not something most people would do.'

'Like you said, maybe he was just being kind. He is a generous bloke. But letting a girl stay in your flat, especially one who's into drugs, is pretty dangerous. People would get the wrong idea.'

'Maybe they'd be right to get the wrong idea.' said Nick, raising his eyebrows.

'Jimmy? Nah. He's not that sort.'

'He doesn't set off your rapey alarm then?'

'No way. But he does set off my dodgy keeper alarm.'

'Yeah, me too, let's go and look at his bloopers again.'

They went inside and re-ran the videos. Some of them were ridiculous - they were cartoon mistakes, so blatant and rank amateur that it was almost hard to believe they were deliberate. Surely you'd try and make your mistakes look more like typical errors if you wanted to get away with them. If they were deliberate, it was like he was hiding in clear view. If you made a bad enough error, no-one could seriously think you were match-fixing because everyone would assume it'd be harder to spot. When you added in the fact that he was capable of world-class, remarkable saves, it somehow made the mistakes look like the work of an eccentric rather than a criminal.

He searched for some more videos of 'Repp gaffs' and 'goalkeeping howlers' and found a couple more, including one he'd forgotten from his début for the Boro in a League Cup game against Swindon Town. He'd come out to collect a cross and, even though he wasn't under pressure, he dropped the ball, which bounced loose and was put in by a striker. Slowing it down and playing it back again, it was clear he had rolled his right hand over the ball, just as he had when playing for Seville. It wasn't a mere slip. It would be hard to do if it wasn't deliberate. But how much money was really to be made from throwing one in against Swindon in the early rounds of the League Cup? The clip played on after the goal, showing Repp picking the ball out of the net. As he stood up, there was a man behind the goal in a bright orange wool hat. That was odd. It was late August and hardly freezing cold, not even in Middlesbrough.

Another clip from the following month, also in the League Cup, showed two great saves from Repp. There were no glaring errors this time but the orange hat was behind the goal again.

He cross-referenced the games he'd played and the goals he'd conceded and tried to find as many clips as possible on YouTube. As he'd been injured for much of the season there weren't many, but there was one other big mistake, this time in a midweek game against Everton in which he gave away a penalty by simply barging into a striker as he tried to round him. It was clumsy and poor goalkeeping but not especially suspicious. He had no chance with the penalty as it was placed out of reach at pace into the right-hand corner. But as he picked the ball out of the net, there was the orange hat behind the goal again. Was it the same fan? It was hard to make out clearly.

He went back to the bookmarked Seville games and re-ran them. He let out a yelp and called Julie. There was the orange hat again and again and again. Sometimes, if the clip was filmed at a distance, it was little more than a small blob on the screen but it was always somewhere behind his goal, always visible even on wobbly, distant, blurred phone footage.

He went back and looked at the clips from his time at Lyon. For most of his first season there seemed to be no hat there at all, but it appeared early in his second season and it was there in every clip afterwards, regardless of whether he made an error.

Making out any features on the hat-wearer was almost impossible in most of the clips but, when visible, it looked like the same person. One time in Seville it was obviously a man with a grey beard and he reappeared on three more occasions, but at the Middlesbrough games it was a different person with a different-shaped face and no beard. Either way, he'd never seen them before.

'That's really weird,' said Julie. 'He must walk from one end to the other at half-time.'

'Or it's two different people at each game. I can't see someone walking from end to end, especially in big, sold-out games.'

She stood up, took a drink of water and paced around the living room.

'Orange hat...think about it...it's very easy to spot in a crowd - that's why you've noticed it, so someone on the pitch could spot him as well.'

'Exactly what I was thinking. Is he giving signals to Jimmy? Jimmy is in the goal, turns around, Orange Hat makes a pre-arranged gesture and Jimmy does whatever is needed to make a big bet pay off. But the thing is Jules, he's there whether there's a goal let in or not. It's not like he's only there when Jimmy makes a massive rick.'

She sucked her bottom lip and thought for a moment.

'Yeah, but that could be for the sake of consistency in case anyone notices. If you're there when nothing happens it deflects suspicion for when it does. But also, we don't know what the bet is for each time. It might be related to anything and not just goals or results. It could be number of free-kicks, throw-ins, fouls, distance of goal-kicks. I mean, people will gamble on anything. The in-play markets are the big thing, so to properly rig those you need someone live on the spot to make the call to the goalie to drop the ball, kick it out or whatever. When he kicks a dead ball into touch, that could be a bet paying off right there, but it looks totally innocuous.'

He nodded. 'I can't see any sign of him making a gesture or a signal but then, the camera isn't on him for long and I'm sure he'd only make a signal when the action was elsewhere anyway. And even then it might just be a scratch of the head or something innocent-looking.'

'Yeah...but...I dunno, maybe we're letting our imagination run away with us.'

He thought for a moment.

'Nah, I'm not having that...there's no way some bloke is behind the goal at each end in a bright hat without it being dodgy.'

'It's another piece in the Jimmy Repp jigsaw, isn't it? I'm just not sure what picture it's going to make. Shit, I'm sweating like a pig in this humidity; I'm just going to have a quick shower,' said Julie.

She'd just gone upstairs when Nick's phone rang. He looked at the display. Lisa Lambert. Lisa? What the hell was she calling for? She never called. In fact, she'd only called him once before, when he lived in Harrogate. She had been pissed.

'Hello Lisa. How nice to hear from you.'

'Nick. You old bastard. How's life?'

'Good. Loving the hot weather. It was good to see you the other day. How's Harrogate?'

'As middle-class and repressed as ever. Look, I won't piss you around. I'm worried something has happened to my friend Myra LeFevre. Remember I told you about her? She's a painter. She told me something really weird the other night and now I can't find her and I can't get hold of her and I'm worried. I'll be in York tonight. Are you around?'

'I can be. It's only a 40-minute drive from here.'

'Right, well how about I meet you outside Betty's at seven?'

'What's this all about Lisa?'

'Basically it's about your man, Jimmy Repp. I really need your help.'

'Jimmy?'

'Yeah. I'll explain everything later; it's complicated. I wouldn't ask if it wasn't very fucking serious, you know that.'

Lisa was prone to be more than a little crazy but for her to call him like this definitely meant something wasn't right.

He went upstairs. Julie was dressing after her shower, pulling on a loose white t-shirt and a baggy pair of linen trousers.

'Just had a weird call.'

'Oh yeah? That makes two of us.'

'Eh?'

'Mam just called me.'

'Your mother? What did she want?'

She frowned and rubbed her hair with a towel. 'Not sure. She wouldn't say. Said she needed to speak to me about Maggie.'

'Pinky's mam?'

'Yeah...it's probably nothing important, She's just a nosey cow.'

'Yeah but she'd just do that on the phone, She'd not demand to see you just to pass on some gossip about who she's shagging or something.'

'That's the weird thing, but she might just want some company for an hour. She won't admit to getting lonely but I know she does. So I said I'd go over tonight and be a good dutiful daughter, even though she'll spend most of the time picking on me. Who was your call from?'

'Lisa Lambert.'

'What did she want, apart from to get in your pants?'

'She never calls me. She said a friend of hers has disappeared and she said it's something to do with Repp.'

Julie raised her eyebrows. 'Repp? The man of the moment, eh. What could she know about him? Is she just being nutty?'

'He buys her art, I know that much, and her agent Emmy Green knows him. Beyond that I can't guess. She wouldn't call if it wasn't important though. She wanted to meet up in York at seven. Is that okay?'

'Okay?'

'You don't mind, do you?'

'Why would I mind?'

'I dunno...'

She laughed. 'I know you fancied her, you big pillock, but I also know you're not going to jump into bed with her, though I've no doubt she'll try.'

'Nah she won't.'

'Well she bloody should, she doesn't know what she's missing,' she laughed again, 'but she might have something you can use in your story. This whole Jimmy Repp thing...he's like a planet around which a lot of weird stuff is orbiting.'

'Yeah, that's what I thought.'

'Well I'll go to mam's and you go to York then.' She kissed him on the lips briefly. She smelled of Calvin Klein's 'Escape for Women'. He held her as she pulled away from the kiss, slipping his hands down the back of her pants so they rested on her bare buttocks, holding her close.

'I've got a funny feeling.'

'I know, I can feel it pressing against my crotch,' she said, grinning.

'Sorry, I just can't stop that happening.'

'As long as you don't expect me to do anything about it right now.'

'No, I mean, like you, I've got a funny feeling about this Repp business. His girlfriend was kidnapped, a young girl dies in his apartment, he's got more art than he could possibly afford, he meets gangsters, he's probably doing match-fixing and now he's connected to an artist who seems to have gone missing. That is one weird life.'

'But when you meet him, he seems so nice and friendly. Some people give off a dodgy vibe, like that Macca bloke. But Jimmy just doesn't, he seems like one of the good guys, and I pride myself on being a good judge of character.'

'I'm a notoriously terrible judge of character but even I know something's not right.'

Nick drove down the A19 towards York as the sun began to sink in the western sky, feeling the glorious nature of the north. Even if you're not actually in wild country, you're never far away from somewhere that is open, windswept and epic. To the east, the sky was wide and clear and sapphire blue, to the west it was turning gold and dark navy over the Pennines.

He listened to Neil Young's *Everybody Knows This is Nowhere* album as he drove into York and parked in a car park next to the remains of the castle.

York was one of his favourite places, being part modern urban town and part open-air museum. Two thousand years of history is laid out under your feet all across the city from Roman to Anglo-Saxon, Viking, medieval and beyond. It's not a pretty town and there is nothing delicate about York. Long the major seat of power in the north, its architecture, from the breath-taking Minster to the still-solid city walls which, in parts, are 2000 years old, it has real muscle and sinew.

As he walked through the streets towards Betty's tea rooms, he took it all in with real pleasure. The fine summer's evening had brought out tourists and locals alike, sitting outside pubs drinking, and it made him lust for a long chilled glass of wine. Since quitting alcohol, the urge to drink had rarely been a problem but, on days such as these, the pleasures of a cold glass of a good *Gewürztraminer* were all-too obvious.

He could already see Lisa in the distance in St. Helen's Square standing outside Betty's in loose white dungarees worn with a white t-shirt, red baseball boots and a vibrant, multi-coloured head scarf in which her raggy, raven-coloured hair was wrapped.

At nearly six feet tall and broad in the shoulder, she was a very striking figure. Though not conventionally good-looking, he'd always found her attractive. She had such energy and life.

He waved as he approached and she turned and acknowledged him.

'Hey Lisa.'

'Can we go for a fucking drink please and hello again Nick,' she said, ruffling his hair, kissing him on the forehead and pointing to a bar opposite that was housed in a grand ex-bank building.

He bought her a glass of Chardonnay and himself a mineral water.

'You not drinking just doesn't seem natural,' she said as he put down the glasses.

'Yeah to me as well...but...it's for the best, I reckon.'

'Yeah well, I really...y'know I admire you for it...breaking any habit or routine is good for the creative soul...even if you're a pisshead like me. I know that I should rebel against myself more often. Being a pisshead is no more radical than being sober when it's all you do.'

She picked at some paint splashes on her nails, more introverted and self-analytical than she was normally inclined to be.

'So what's this all about?' asked Nick.

She took a big gulp of wine, her black eyebrows knitted together in a frown.

'What I'm about to tell you is...well...it's a bit weird and I don't really know what to do about it. I can't tell the police, that's for sure.'

He gestured towards her to spill the beans.

'As I said on the phone, my best mate Myra LeFevre, I told you about her...she's a brilliant artist but never sells anything and so she's always skint. I went to see her and she was sitting on a new sofa, had a big new TV, loads of other stuff. I asked her where this lot had come from...long story short...,' she took another drink,'...she's been doing fakes.'

She looked at him intensely.

'Fakes? Fakes of what?'

'Fake pictures.'

'Forgeries of famous paintings, is that what you mean?'

'She's been asked to copy existing pictures in an artist's style, signature and everything.'

'Ah yeah, I've heard of this. There was that bloke ...what was his name...Eric Hebborn, wasn't it? The authorities hated him because they couldn't tell how many he'd done, what was real or what was fake.'

She nodded vigorously. 'It's happened forever going back hundreds of fucking years. People have been forging art for as long as there's been money in art. The thing is, she told me she'd been doing a lot of Phyllis Plant work which had been bought by your man Jimmy Repp. She said she'd been asked to copy existing pieces and do a few fake new ones too and had just got ten grand for the first batch.'

Nick sat back and let this news sink in. So his precious collection wasn't so precious after all.

'Does Jimmy know they're fakes?'

'No of course not, man. He thinks they're for real. He thinks he's bought a private collection. Some of it may well be real but a lot of it is Myra's fakes. Now here's the weirder shit. She told me that she'd been asked to do this by Emmy Green, who you also met.'

'Your agent? Wow. That's very naughty of her. So she's been getting fakes painted and has then sold them on, no doubt taking her 15% of the full price. But hang on, if they're copies of existing Plant pictures, then where are the originals?'

'I don't know. I don't understand any of it. If they're not real, then surely he'd soon find out that the real ones are in someone else's hands, especially with someone as high profile as PP?'

Nick frowned. It didn't make any sense to him either.

Lisa was unusually quiet, her lips pursed in contemplation.

'But it doesn't stop there...she told me all this two nights ago, right? And now she's just disappeared. I'm not being over-dramatic here. She's not at home, she's not answering her phone and no-one knows where she's gone. She would have told me if she was going anywhere for any length of time. She just would. She always does.'

'And so you think this is somehow, like, sinister?'

She nodded. 'Look, I understand Myra's position. I dig it in fact. To be honest, I like the idea of ripping off stupid footballers or anyone else who doesn't appreciate art as anything other than an investment. That's really fucking rock 'n' roll, y'know...but on the other hand, it's pretty damn go-straight-to-jail illegal, which is why I don't want to tell the police about her going missing. If I do that, the whole story will come out and then she'll be in massive fucking trouble.'

She picked at her nails again and looked at him with real worry in her eyes. He reached out, put a hand on her arm and patted her a couple of times.

'And that's why you called me?'

'I didn't know what the fuck to do or who to tell. You know Repp and I know you've got balls because of all that shit you went through in the last year with your dad and then with that old girl's death. And I know you're loyal; you stick by your mates. So that's why I thought of you. I want to find Myra.'

'So your agent is corrupt? She's a criminal?'

'Looks that way, yeah.' She shrugged and turned down her mouth.

'Christ, she seemed such a straight, middle-class woman. I'd never have thought that she was bent.'

Lisa shrugged. 'You can't trust anyone, middle-class or not. They're the fucking worst if you ask me. Fucking people who run art galleries, they dress it all up like they're doing you a favour but half of them are venal bastards and the other half are brown-nosers and creeps who you wouldn't trust as far as you could shit them. I'm really, really worried about Myra though. She never goes off the radar. I know her really well. She would get in touch with me if she could. Something's happened.'

'Something as in...you think she's been killed?'

'Killed or taken and held against her will, yes. I'm not fucking around Nick. This is for real.'

'Okay, let's just think about this. So she told you about the forgeries for the first time two days ago?'

'I was at her place and we were hammered and she was laughing about all the money she was making. She'd got the first wedge last week. Ten grand but with what she called 'a really big shitload' more to come. I was shocked but I sort of admired her, like I said.'

'Was she afraid of anyone? Did she sound like there was a problem?'

Lisa shook her head. 'No, she was laughing about it. She was taking the piss out of Emmy saying, 'yeah, you can't sell my own art but put the PP initials on and every fucker wants them'. She was bitter, but laughing, if you know what I mean. She'd had been out on the lash a couple of times, mouthing off about it, bragging about it. I've been thinking about what we talked about that night and I think part of her wanted to get Emmy into trouble as payback for not being able to sell her work. She certainly didn't care who knew what she'd done, put it that way. I thought she was taking a massive risk by being so open about it...but she didn't care. She is a ballsy sort of woman though.'

He nodded and took a drink of water.

'So the word that she was mouthing off about it might have got back to Emmy?'

'It might have. I've not seen or spoken to her since though.'

'Does Myra have any money or does her family have any money?'

'For a ransom you mean? No. She doesn't have any family or not any she's been in touch with since she was 16. She's a loner but she's not crazy like me. She doesn't go wild and mess with people.'

'Maybe she got wasted and passed out somewhere or fell in the river.'

'Nah, not going to happen. She's careful. Not like me. She doesn't go around town out of her brain. She sits at home, hunkers down, drinks and paints. I wish I was more like that. '

'Did she say what she was planning to do after you'd left her?'

'Yeah, she was meeting someone in Middlesbrough from a new gallery up there. She'd got a call about it the night I was there and was going up on the train when I left her.'

'Is Myra a Teessider?'

'Originally, yeah. She was brought up in Middlesbrough, I think, or somewhere near there. She's one of your mob, though she'd lost her accent.

'But she lives in York?'

'Aye, on Clifton Road. I've been round to her flat. It's locked up. The curtains are drawn. Her studio is a converted garage around the corner and that's locked up too.'

'Come on then, let's go round there and check it out, see if we can find anything that might give us a clue what's happened.'

It was only a 15-minute walk to Myra's flat, which was on the top floor of a Victorian villa. As they walked he couldn't help wondering if this was a second kidnapping and what that might mean. Was it the same people involved? Would there be another ransom demand? Surely not. Okay, her forged art was bought by Jimmy Repp, but that's not much of a connection. Why would anyone kidnap her?

They rang the illuminated doorbell but there was no reply.

'Let's check out her studio,' he said. Lisa led him around the corner to a row of old 1950s garages which had been converted into workshops. The end one of four was Myra's. The old wooden side door was locked.

'Is this alarmed do you know?' said Nick.

'No. I'm sure it isn't. That'd be too much expense and hassle. No-one wants to steal paint and canvas anyway, do they?'

There was no-one around. It was a quiet cul-de-sac at the back of a residential area. He leaned on the wooden door and with one swift, hard kick beside the Yale lock, popped it open.

Lisa laughed a little. 'Done a lot of burgling have you Nick?'

'Missed my vocation, maybe. Actually, a couple of Julie's brothers were thieves and they told me some of the tricks of the trade. Mind, they've both done time so I'm not sure they're any good.'

They went in. Nick closed the door. The lock catch had splintered away from the door frame but that could easily be reattached.

The studio was an airy space with glass across half of the roof. The whole place carried the smell of paint and turpentine. The summer evening light cast long shadows across the floor. It was tidy with blank and painted canvases stacked in racks in one corner, three easels of uncompleted work standing centrally and drawers of paints all neatly arranged along one wall. None of the work looked like it was done in the style of Phyllis Plant.

He pulled open a wide, flat drawer to reveal sheets of white paper. Lisa looked over his shoulder, picked up a sheet and inspected it. 'This is old paper...I bet that's what she used to do the fakes. She said she'd got a source of paper from the 40s and 50s. Obviously you get spotted in an instant if you use modern paper.'

'When was the last time you heard from her?'

'The last time I saw her was when I left her flat and got the train home at half-past ten.'

'And you'd slept over at her place?'

'Yeah.'

'And everything was normal?'

'Totally, yeah.'

'Okay so we know she was there until half-past ten and was planning to go to Middlesbrough. On the train?'

'Yeah, she doesn't have a car.'

'And she hasn't answered your calls since?'

'No. It goes straight to voicemail. She was going to get the train at one, so she'd have been on Teesside by two-ish.'

On a table stood a large jar of brushes soaking in white spirit. Next to the jar was a large sheet of thick paper stuck onto a board with brown gummed tape, marked with sweeping black brush strokes. He stood back and took in the scene as a shaft of light shone underneath a desk and illuminated a rogue brush.

He squatted down, picked up the brush and sniffed. Black oil paint. The same black oil paint that had been used on the canvas. He dabbed at it with his finger - it was still damp. The paint on the paper was also still a little wet in the thickest parts.

'What are you looking at?' asked Lisa, who had been inspecting the art resting in the racks and on shelves.

'It's a paintbrush and I think it was used on this paper. Everything else is so neat, but this was just under this desk.'

He stood at the easel with the brush. His back was to the door.

'Is she left or right-handed?'

'She's a lefty.'

'Ah, like me. Okay so imagine if I was Myra painting here, then someone comes in the door, I turn to my left, look at the door and see who it is. It's someone I'm scared of or I'm shocked to see, so I drop my brush and it rolls under this desk. See?'

He recreated the potential scene.

'How old would you say the paint on this brush and canvas is?' he said, handing her the long, thick brush.

She flicked at the bristles. 'Easily two days...not much longer though because it's only now starting to go stiff...if it was, like, a week old it'd be harder. So you could be right.'

'Was she up and about when you left at half-ten that morning?'

'Yeah she was. Just...she'd not eaten though. So if she had some toast and a coffee and then left for her studio, she'd probably not have been in here much before midday and then she had a train to catch at one so she couldn't have got much done.'

He re-enacted turning around, dropping the paint brush and then rotating fully to confront a visitor. She would have had to move either to the left as she turned around or forward towards them because the easel prevented her going backwards and the desk blocked her on one side.

It was about ten paces to the door. He walked forward two steps and looked around him for any indication of a struggle. He squatted onto his haunches and looked at the floor. It was paint-splattered and dusty with little rolls of fluff blown into nooks and crannies. The floor was old concrete and was cracked and chipped from its years as a garage. He stood up and walked two more steps and looked closely at the floor again. Sitting in one of the cracks was a button. He picked it out. It was a small mother of pearl button from a shirt. A small clump of cotton was still attached.

'What's that?' asked Lisa.

'It's a button which I think must have been torn off a shirt because there's a bit of material attached.'

'That's not from anything Myra would wear. It looks too expensive for a start.'

'Are you sure?'

'Totally. She doesn't wear shirts...she works in overalls and lives in t-shirts and baggy pants and jumpers.'

'I do think this is expensive you know.'

'I'm no expert - I'll take your word for it. So there was a struggle here and Myra rips this bloke's shirt?'

'We don't know it was a bloke. Could have been on a woman's shirt or blouse.'

He walked slowly to the door. The back was originally painted white but had flaked off to reveal the wood underneath. But at about knee height was a muddy print of the sole of a shoe. Someone had kicked the door open and it had left half a print of thick, wavy lines.

He went outside and looked around. There was a muddy verge right beside the end garage with a path which people had clearly used for a shortcut. Anyone parking a car for a quick get-away would have pulled up alongside so they could zoom out of the cul-de-sac and back out onto the main road without having to turn around. But you could only get muddy from the verge if you'd got out of the driver's side.

There were two prints that, though broken and distorted, looked very like that on the door inside the studio.

'I think what's happened is that someone's pulled up here, got out of the car and gone into the studio. There's been a struggle and they've dragged Myra out, kicking the door open because both hands were holding her. How big is she?'

'About five four and eight stone. There's nowt on her. My fucking nipples weigh more than that.'

Nick laughed loudly. 'Four stone per nipple, eh. Are they made of gold?'

'I'll show you if you like,' she said, feigning to open her shirt.

'This is no time for a nipple inspection, Lisa.'

She shrugged, looked around and said: 'Someone who lives in a top-floor flat up there might have seen something.' She pointed to the back of a row of houses on Clifton Road. 'The lower-floor flats wouldn't be able to see over the trees at the back.'

Nick went back inside, found a knife and screwed the lock catch back on well enough to hold it shut, closed the door and walked back onto the main road after noting which three buildings would have had the best view.

They were all three stories high and had been converted from large houses into three flats. The first one they rang was empty and no-one replied. As they walked up the path to the second, a young woman was coming out of the front door. She looked like a student.

'Hi there,' said Nick.

'Hiya,' she said cheerfully, pushing a long strand of brown hair off her face.

'Do you know who lives on the top floor?'

'Me. I do,' she said, bouncing on her toes a little.

'Ah good...our friend has an art studio at the back, in those old garages, do you know them?'

'Yes...you can see them from my flat.'

'Myra...that is, my friend, has the end one and she's gone missing. We're trying to find out what has happened to her,' said Lisa. 'Did you see anything a couple of afternoons ago between about noon and one?'

The girl frowned and then widened her eyes.

'I leave at around half-twelve every day. But yeah, actually I heard a screech of tyres at the back, which was unusual as it's always really quiet – I spend most of my time in the back room 'cos Clifton Road is so busy.'

'Did you see anything?' asked Nick.

'Not really. I looked out when I heard the noise and a car was pulling away...I thought nothing more of it. Is that any help?'

'What sort of car was it?'

'Silver...big...like a Mercedes or something, maybe a Jag...I'm not good with cars.'

'But it was a big posh car?' asked Lisa.

'Yeah definitely. I think it was a woman with short-ish hair driving but it's hard to see properly from up here. There was someone in the passenger seat though.'

'What did they look like?' asked Nick. The girl narrowed her eyes in an effort to recall.

'All I can think is she had dark hair.'

'It was a she?' said Lisa.

'Yes. I'm pretty sure it was two women in the car. Sorry I can't be of more help.'

Nick thanked her and gave her his number in case she thought of anything else.

'That sounds to me like Emmy and Myra,' said Nick. 'She'd also wear a blouse with pearl buttons wouldn't she?'

'Damn right she would,' said Lisa. 'She's also bigger and stronger than Myra.'

As they walked back into York city centre, she tried calling Myra's number again.

'It's now saying the voicemail is full,' she said, ringing off, 'which is a bad sign. Means everyone's left her messages and she's not picked them up. I'm really fucking worried now.'

'Would it be worth calling Emmy and asking her what she was doing there?'

'I dunno. She's clearly slap bang in the middle of this, isn't she? And we already know she's dodgy - dodgy is as dodgy does. Maybe I should go to the police and just not mention the fakes, just say she's gone missing.'

'Yeah, maybe you should. What more can we do? It looks very much like something happened in her studio before she even took off for Middlesbrough but we don't know why and I can't think how we could find out without breaking into her flat and searching her computer and that would make us look a bit dodgy ourselves if the cops got involved.'

'I'm not sure they'll think she's even a missing person after just two days,' said Lisa. 'I just want to do something but I don't know what. Fuck.'

The sun was almost down and the sky was turning to navy blue night. He was desperately trying to think of a way he could help.

'Lisa, if Jimmy Repp found out his pictures were fakes, what would he do?'

'Do? Be fucking furious, I should think. Then go to the police.'

'A collector would go to the police in those circumstances, would he?'

'Yes. It's fraud innit?'

'So if he knew and didn't do that, that'd be weird wouldn't it?'

'Very weird. He'd only do that if he'd bought them with dodgy money, some sort of money-laundering thing. People say art is used all the time for that kind of racket.'

'So we have to assume he's either dodgy or ignorant or the cops would already be on Myra's case. So maybe only you, Myra, Emmy and now me know about them.'

'Are you saying I might be in danger because of that?'

That was exactly what his instinct said but he didn't want to alarm her.

'No, of course not. We don't know if Myra's disappearance is even anything to do with the fakes, do we? Was she into drugs, do you know?'

'Not really. Some dope but nothing proper. She's just a boozer.'

'Any old boyfriends who might want to hurt her?'

'Girlfriends would be more accurate. She had a couple of crazies. Most lasses do at some point, but nothing recently.'

They reached his car.

'Can I give you a lift home?'

'I'll get the last train.'

He drove around to the front of York station and parked briefly to let her out.

'Sorry to have brought you down here on a wild goose chase,' she said, putting her hand on his shoulder, 'I just didn't know what to do.'

'Look Lisa, I already know that there's some strange shit going on around Jimmy Repp and his life. All sorts of odd things. This thing about the pictures is just another thing to add to the weird pile. Go to the police tomorrow if you've not heard anything from her - that's all you can do. Even if it does get her into trouble later, you might be saving her life now.'

She nodded and let out a deep, boozy breath.

'If someone has hurt her, if something has happened to her, I'll fuck up whoever has done it and I swear to God I'll fuck them up bad. They won't get away with it. She's my best mate - I'll not let it go until I've found her, alive or...whatever. She'd expect nothing less of me.'

'And rightly so.'

She chewed at her cheek nervously, gave his hand a squeeze and got out.

Half an hour later he was on the A19 travelling north when his phone rang. It was Julie.

'Hey lady,' he said.

'Where are you?' she said without introduction.

'About 20 minutes from home. How did it go at your mam's?'

'Never mind that now. What was the name of that artist friend of Lisa Lambert?'

'Myra LeFevre. Why?'

'They found her body this afternoon. It's just been on the late local news.'

'Oh Christ. Fucking hell. Where was she?'

'They found her on the breakwater at South Gare right at the mouth of the Tees.'

'What the fuck? What was she doing there?'

He blew out air, his head swimming slightly with the news.

'Any news on cause of death?'

'It's too early for that.'

'Fuck. Me and Lisa were just trying to find her this evening, man.'

'You were what?'

'I'll explain when I get home.'

He rang off. Should he call Lisa and tell her? She should know. It probably wouldn't be on the Harrogate local news and even if it was, he should tell her. It should come from him. Shit. What a call to have to make.

He pulled over in a lay-by after the Northallerton turn-off, took a deep breath and, with his guts turning over, called Lisa. She answered after three rings. It sounded like she was walking, probably still on the way home.

'Hello Nick.'

'Lisa...look, I've err...I've just had some news about Myra.'

'Really? What?'

He paused for too long.

'It's not good, is it?' she said.

'Julie just called me - it was on the local Teesside news tonight. I'm sorry Lisa, they found her body at the entrance to the Tees at a place called South Gare. A fucking bleak, desolate place it is as well...it's just this spit of land that juts out into the river.'

All he could hear was her breath, distorting the phone.

'Are you still there?'

There was a retching sound as she threw up. Nick looked out at the blackness of the North Yorkshire night. The bright lights of a car approached, blinding him, and he turned away as it sped past, oblivious to this tragedy.

'Lisa?'

He heard her spit. 'Yes. Fucking hell.' She groaned. 'I sort of expected it so part of my brain was ready for it but the shock of hearing it....fuck. Myra, what the fuck's happened to you? Did they say?'

'No. Not yet. You need to tell the police what we found out, Lisa. The whole fakes business doesn't matter now that she's dead. In fact, it's probably the reason she's dead.'

'Damn right. I just fucking know this isn't an accident. Someone has taken her from her studio and killed her. I don't think she ever got that train to Middlesbrough. I think she was taken from her studio by Emmy, like the girl from the flat said.'

'Aye. So you've got to go to the police, Lisa. I'll help you as much as I can but you can't keep it from the cops. Not now.'

'But Emmy wouldn't kill someone. She wouldn't...I need to speak to her first...'

'No, don't do that. Don't let her know anything. It...I dunno...it might be dangerous. Tell the cops first, right?'

'Fuck, I'm so confused. Yeah...okay...I've got to find out who the fuck killed Myra.'

'Of course, yeah. Call the police though, Lisa. Just tell them about the money and what she said...that's all you can do.'

'Okay.'

She rang off. He rubbed his face with the palms of his hand.

By the time he got home it was after midnight.

He turned off the engine, got out of the car and looked up at the night sky with the orange glow of Yarm to the north. It was deliciously quiet. He stood, drinking it all in, trying to let the calm of nature wash into his disturbed mind.

Julie opened the front door and walked out to greet him. A shaft of light poured out onto the track like silver on black.

He took her in his arms and squeezed her. She was warm and so alive.

Over a chicken salad, he recounted his evening.

'Is it not possible that she just committed suicide? We don't know it was murder,' she said, taking his plate and washing it under the tap.

'Lisa reckons she was a happy-go-lucky sort of person. Pissed off that her career was going nowhere but not suicidal. The thing I keep coming back to is this Jimmy Repp connection. Has he just been conned by Emmy Green into buying expensive fakes or was he conspiring with her to buy them in and then sell them on at an inflated price through his gallery? And does Frankie Gray know about it? He must do, surely.'

'Yeah and when you add in the kidnapping and the match-fixing thing, it's like he's a magnet for dodgy, isn't it? But I mean, you can't sell copies of significant art without someone finding out sooner or later, can you? The real ones still exist to disprove the fakes. I don't get it at all.'

'No. I don't either.'

'So what happened at your mam's?'

Julie rolled her eyes and poured another cup of tea.

'Because we'd been around the other day to see if Pinky was at her mam's, my mam has started taking an interest in what Maggie is up to.'

'She's being a nosey old bag you mean.'

'Exactly. Apparently Pinky stayed there last night and left early in morning. And mam thinks she had Finlay with her.'

'...the old boyfriend?'

'Yeah. Mam has, of course, constructed an entire story about what's been going on which is basically that Pinky has left Jimmy to go back to the man she really loves. There was also a woman knocking on Maggie's door a few days ago. Mam, as is her way, stuck her head out and asked her what she wanted. She said she was posh and wore a baggy suit, was middle-aged, with a grey streak in her hair. She called it a Mallen Streak because she reads all those Catherine Cookson books. But you know my mam, everyone seems posh to her. She was asking for Pinky. Mam thinks it's suspicious and that someone is after her.'

'Does she always think that when anyone who looks like they're posh turns up on the estate?'

'Yeah, of course. And she's usually right because there's no reason for anyone posh to be there if they're not chasing someone, is there?'

'So what did you make of it all? Just Jackie turning life into a soap opera?'

'Yeah, I'm sure that's what it is, though if she has been seeing her old boyfriend it might mean something about her relationship with Repp, mightn't it?'

Nick said, 'I feel cynical about everything to do with Repp right now, including Pinky's kidnapping and the collection of the money. Like Lisa said, dodgy is as dodgy does. If he's a match-fixer, and I'm almost certain he is, he'll be bent in other areas of his life. You cross the Rubicon, don't you? It's like losing your virginity - once you've had sex once, it's much easier to do it again and again. What was once special, sacred almost, becomes routine after four pints of cider.'

She chuckled. 'You might be right, I couldn't possibly comment.'

'Here's a really mad idea that I came up with on the way home, Jules,' he said, getting up and locking the back door and putting out the kitchen light. 'What if somehow it was Pinky who staged that kidnapping? We have no evidence of any kidnappers other than that phone call and that could have been anyone. There was no proof anyone was actually holding her, no photo of her holding up a newspaper or anything. And when you think about it, Frankie Gray just conjured up that money without even asking for proof that Pinky had been taken. You said she was very cool on the phone after being released. Well, who'd be like that? You'd be upset, wouldn't you?'

'Yeah but she's a tough kid. Really tough. You'd have to be with Maggie as your mam. She was a fighter and would thump anyone after she'd been on the drink down the club. So she's conditioned to be resilient and not show weakness. But I agree - the speed Frankie accepted it had happened was odd. Could Pinky and Gray have cooked it up to screw the money out of Jimmy?'

'They certainly could, yeah. Jimmy was shitting himself about it; that was no act. Though weirdly, he didn't seem over-worried about her safety, if you remember. He never once even said that he hoped she was okay.'

As he spoke, a memory seeped into his brain.

'...hold on, hold on...'

A surge of adrenalin shot up his spine.

'That woman knocking on Maggie's door had a Mallen Streak, did you say?'

'Yeah, that's right.'

'Emmy Green has a Mallen Streak, a wide strip of grey from her left temple. It's really distinctive. It couldn't be her, could it?'

'How could it be her? How could she know where Pinky's mam's house would be? And why?'

'God knows,' he paused to think, 'but she said she'd met Pinky with Jimmy a couple of times. I bet it's something to do with those fake pictures but my brain is too tired to work it out. I might ring Jeff tomorrow and ask him - he's always good for a wild theory or two.'

'Jeff is actually disconnected from reality though,' she said as they climbed the stairs to the bedroom.

'Yeah, but sometimes you've got to get outside to see inside, you know.'

'Very philosophical.'

116

She kissed him at the top of the stairs.

'Fancy a quickie?'

'Do you mind if we don't? I'm not really in the mood after all this.'

'I'm glad you said that. I don't fancy it either. It feels like a big black cloud has blown over us.'

CHAPTER 8

Nick couldn't sleep. He lay staring into the pitch-black silence long after Julie had dropped off, mulling over everything that had happened. He was sure that Myra had been murdered. Killing the artist meant the secret of the forgeries was preserved, or at least it would if he and Lisa didn't know. As far as he could tell, the only person who obviously stood to benefit from the scam was Emmy Green. She apparently delivered the fakes to Jimmy, who paid her thinking they were real. She in turn pays Myra and pockets the difference. Was that how it worked? Surely there had to be more checks than that, if only for insurance. What if Jimmy realised he'd been conned? Would Frankie send out a hit man to get revenge? Was that what happened? Frankie definitely seemed capable of that. But surely Emmy Green would know that the fakes would be exposed sooner or later when the originals were found to be in someone else's possession. What if Jimmy knew they were fakes? Why would he buy fake paintings? Was he trying to con someone? Or was Frankie trying to con Jimmy? Was Lisa in danger? Did anyone know that she knew? All these questions went around and around in his mind.

Eventually, he drifted into an awkward sleep, constantly rising to the surface of consciousness. By 6.30am he was wide awake. The early-morning sun was already casting shafts of light around their curtains. He got up, put the kettle on and then picked up his phone to dial Lisa's number.

To his surprise she answered almost immediately.

'Nick? Why are you calling this early?'

'I couldn't sleep. Have you called the police?'

'Not yet. I was going to do that this morning.'

'Don't tell anyone else at all about the fake pictures, right. Not just Emmy...but anyone...we don't want it to get out that we know about them. Have you told anyone else?'

'No...but her death must have been something to do with them.

Why else would someone grab her from her studio to...to....where they found her...that's not just a random act, is it?'

She sounded sober and upset.

'No it's not. It can't be.'

Julie wandered into the kitchen in her pale blue pyjamas, her hair all ruffled. Lisa was still talking.

'Listen, I found the number of that gallery owner she was going to meet in my sketchpad. I forgot that she'd jotted it down on my pad because it was the nearest thing to hand when the woman called. She reckoned this woman has got big money to spend. I'm going to call her and see if Myra ever made it up there to see her,' she said.

'What's her name?'

'Grace Edwards.'

'And where is her gallery going to be?'

'I don't know.'

'Well be careful Lisa. You don't know anything about her. This Grace Edwards could be anyone. She could be the killer.'

'I will be.'

'I hate to say this but I think Emmy might be behind Myra's death, you know. I think she was asking for Pinky at her mother's house in Stockton; Pinky is Jimmy Repp's girlfriend. That seems very weird to me.'

'That makes no sense.'

'No. I know it doesn't. Where does Emmy live?'

'Northallerton.'

'That's close enough to Teesside.'

'Fuck. Emmy can't have killed Myra. She can't have. She's not that sort of person. She's not a killer. I've worked with her for three years, I know her.'

'She might not have, she might have paid someone to do it to shut her up.'

'Nick?'

'Yeah?'

'If something happens to me, promise me something...'

'I'm sure nothing is going to...'

'...promise me you'll fuck them up. Somehow, some way, fuck them up, Nick, fuck them up.'

'Yeah, you keep saying that Lisa, but nothing's going to happen, I'm sure.'

'Yeah but if you're right and if Emmy knows Myra told me about the fakes, then I'm next aren't I?'

'We don't even know how Myra died yet. We're getting ahead of ourselves. When you've spoken to Grace Edwards, call the police and tell them everything you know. Right?'

'Yes, that's what I'm going to do.'

She rang off.

'Was that Lisa?' asked Julie, scratching her left buttock as she re-boiled the kettle.

'Yeah. I called her to tell her not to tell anyone else about the fake pictures. It's best no-one else knows what we know.'

He put his arm around her and pulled her in for a hug.

'Are you alright?' she asked, brushing his hair off his eyes.

'I never knew this Myra woman but...I don't know...I was in her studio and when you see someone's art, it's like you're seeing a part of them, a big part in fact. Ending your days slumped on South Gare…it's just so fucking bleak, isn't it?'

She rested her hands on his shoulders.

'You said Myra had told Lisa she'd been doing these forgeries, but maybe she was just taking the piss, spinning her a line, like. You've both assumed that it was the truth but if you stand back for a minute, we don't actually know that. You saw a picture on an easel in the studio but you didn't see a big stack of pictures all signed 'Phyllis Plant', did you?'

That sent a jolt through him. He pulled away from her and paced around the kitchen.

'No, you're right Jules, totally right. I just assumed the black outlines on the paper were another forgery, but I have no proof, do I? The other canvases I saw were all her own work and signed by her. Now I think on, Lisa said she had a new TV and sofa and basically invited her around to celebrate her windfall but...that's the only proof we have she was paid to do fakes – which is actually no proof at all. So her death could be related to something else altogether.'

'She got money from somewhere but not necessarily from forgeries. She might have made that up to protect the truth, to hide behind it, like. Maybe the truth of where she got the money would tell us why she got killed. Maybe it was a drug deal or something like that.'

Nick nodded. 'You're a clever lass you. Must be why I fell in love with you.'

He kissed her on the forehead.

She lifted up her pyjama top to flash her bare breasts,

'Eeee and I thought it was because of these!'

After breakfast, Nick turned on his computer to check the local news. The headline story was 'South Gare Murder'. The story didn't say how Myra had died, only that it was being now being treated as murder. He then did a search and found a picture of Emmy Green. She was posed in a headshot for her website advertising her services as an agent specialising in art. He printed it out and showed Julie.

'This is Lisa's dodgy agent. I'm going to show it to your mam to see if it was the woman looking for Pinky. She's got the Mallen Streak. Are you coming with me?'

'No. I've seen enough of my mother recently. If it was her...what does it mean?'

He shrugged. 'I don't really know for sure but it means something, that much I do know. Somehow all these things fit together. I just want to make sure it was her and not just some other random posh woman.'

He drove to the Hardwick estate and parked up outside Jackie Wells' house.

'Hey Jackie,' he said as she opened the door in three-quarter-length white pants and a purple top.

She narrowed her eyes at him.

'What are you doing here? Is our Julie alright?' Her first thought was usually a negative one.

'Yeah, she's fine. She's busy on some coursework. I just dropped by to ask you something.'

'Ask me something? What, like?' she said, ushering him into the house.

He took out the picture and gave it to her.

'You said to Jules that some woman had been asking for Pinky the other day. Is this her?'

Her glasses were on a cord around her neck. She perched them on her nose and tapped the picture with a nicotine-stained finger.

'Eeee, yeah, that's her. That's definitely her. She had the Mallen Streak. Who is she?'

'A woman called Emmy Green.'

'Emmy? Aye, that'll be right, she looked like an Emmy in that linen suit and everything. Is she the police?' she asked, filling the kettle then lighting up a cigarette, sucking on it deeply and only reluctantly releasing the stream of blue, drifting smoke.

'No, she's an art agent.'

'An art agent? What the hell does an art agent do?' she said, almost indignant, as though their very existence was an insult.

'She sells artists' paintings and stuff...you know....to people, or corporations or galleries...basically she makes money for the artist and keeps 15%.'

'Does she now? Uh huh,' Jackie said, 'well she was very lah-de-dah with me, I must say.'

'She was knocking at Maggie's?'

She nodded. 'I went out and told her that Maggie had gone out and that no-one was at home. She said she was looking for Pinky. I said I didn't know where she was and then she asked me if I'd seen her recently.'

'And had you seen her recently?'

'Yeah, but I wasn't going to tell her that, like. Obviously. '

Nick laughed. 'When any stranger wants to know where anyone on the estate is, is the answer always 'I don't know'?'

'Of course it is. Unless you're an idiot, like.'

'So did you ask her what she wanted?'

'Of course I did. She said someone wanted to use Pinky as a model for some paintings, which sounded made-up to me. Anyway, how did she know where she lived?'

'Well, she did know her a bit because she sells art to Jimmy and she met Pinky through him. But it is odd that she went to Maggie's instead of Jimmy's to look for her.'

'She was lying if you ask me.'

'Jules said you'd seen Pinky's old boyfriend around. Do you reckon they're together again?'

She stubbed out the cigarette on the edge of a glass ashtray that was only slightly smaller than a hub cap and full to the brim of old dog-ends and a mountain of ash, and then lit another.

'Aye, I reckon, like. Mind, he's always gone round to Maggie's even after the break-up. He's the son she never had and she's the mam he never had. She was devastated when Pinky broke up with him. She thought he was son-in-law material. He's probably round there having his dinner as we speak.'

'He goes there for his dinner? Isn't that weird?'

'He's got no-one else. No mam or dad. He grew up in that kids' home in Billingham, didn't he?'

'What's he like then? Hard knock?'

She sucked deeply on the cigarette again and blew out smoke at speed from the corner of her mouth.

'No. Not hard. He's alright. I like him. He's not a bad lad. He looks and dresses like a skinhead but there's not a nasty bone in him which, considering where he grew up, is bloody amazing 'cos those homes are terrible places where God knows what goes on. He was totally under Pinky's thumb of course, but I don't think he minded. Quite the opposite, like.'

Nick nodded and took out a small notepad.

Jackie went on: 'So why would this Emmy Green want to speak to a lass like Pinky, I mean, she's not a model is she? That's a load of rubbish she told me. Alright, she's good-looking but she's too short, her arse is too big and her tits aren't big enough to be a model.'

No-one escaped her acid tongue.

'Well, she probably didn't mean that kind of model. Artists' models can be all shapes and sizes.'

'Art? She knows sod all about art, that one. There's something funny going on in that house, you mark my words. They're all up to something.'

He smiled inwardly. She took pleasure in conspiracy and speculation. It made life more exciting to think that a neighbour was up to no good. Of course, some of them were, not least Jackie's own three sons.

'I'm actually doing a piece on Jimmy, so I'm trying to dig into his past to see if there's any scandal or skeletons.'

'He's as soft as clarts that one.'

'Jimmy?'

'Aye. Big soft get if you ask me. I've seen him over here a few times and on the TV. Wet behind the ears. I've always thought that if I know Maggie Gull's kid, and mind, I do, she'll be the boss of him every hour of the day.'

'But she's only a girl really, isn't she? Pinky, I mean. She's only 21 and she's hardly a big lass.'

Jackie folded her arms across her chest. 'Makes no difference. She'll not stand being bossed by anyone, just like our Jules, in fact. And that Jimmy, he's a foot taller but a foot smaller than her, if you know what I mean.'

Nick nodded. He knew exactly what she meant.

'Julie thinks he's a nice bloke.'

'Does she? Well, I didn't say he wasn't a nice fella, he probably is and if our Jules thinks he's alright then he probably is...but I don't know...he looks to me like one of those men who you could twist around your finger. Always wants to say or do the right thing and can't say no, y'know...sort of weak. Pinky will be milking him for all he's worth, I should think.'

'So you don't think it's love?'

She laughed bitterly. 'Don't be stupid, son. That Finlay kid was the one for her, still is if you ask me. He's still in the picture, mark my words.' She wagged a finger at him.

She was always wanting her words marked and said everything with such certainty - even when it was just speculation, rumour or her own fabrication - that it sounded like the truth.

'In fact there are some on the estate who say Jimmy Repp is a queer,' she said with a sour little grin.

'Jimmy Repp is gay? Nah. He's not is he? What do you reckon?'

She burst out laughing. 'No, he hasn't got it in him,' she said and laughed again, 'or he hasn't had it in him,' she laughed another rasping laugh. Her lined and heavily creased face broke into the broad grin that her daughter had inherited. It made Jackie seem a nicer person when she smiled. Most of the time her face was set in a look that was somewhere between a sneer and a scowl. She looked out of the kitchen window and then turned back to him. 'You know what I mean though son...he's not that....you know... he's not queer, that's for sure. You just have to look at him.'

'Why? Because of Pinky, you mean. Sometimes, you know, that doesn't mean anything.'

She held her hands up.

'I might be sixty bloody eight years old Nick but I don't need telling about how married blokes can be secretly queer. I'm not naïve, son. That's been going on forever. Your bloody generation think they invented homo-bloody-sexuality. I'm telling you he's not a nancy boy. You can tell. Lads who are like that have got more gumption than he has. They've had to fight against everyone who hates queers for a start so it makes them tougher, makes them have a bit of grit about them. He's just a soft sod who can play football.

People round here only said he's gay because he's not the macho type.'

There was no room for obfuscation, sensitivity or politeness in Jackie Wells' language - you called a spade a fucking spade and if you didn't like it you could sod off. She wouldn't win any prizes for diplomacy but at her time in life there was neither need nor point in beating around the bush.

'Right, I'm off...thanks for your help, Jackie.'

'I can make you some dinner if you want.'

'No thanks, I'd better get off.'

She patted him on the back as he turned to leave. 'Alright then, nice to see you kidda. I hope you get your thing written. Give Jules my love....and hey you, am I going to have any grandkids to fuss over from my favourite daughter?'

'You never know, Jackie. It's not something we've planned but I quite fancy it.'

'Planned? Who plans it? You're a big strapping lad, just get in there and get the job done before her tubes dry up, eh.' She cackled the rasping laugh and patted him on the back again.

'Are you giving me permission to have sex with your daughter, Jackie?'

'Aye why not, every other bugger on this estate has!' She laughed even louder.

Although Julie had a long history of butting heads with her mother, he couldn't help but like her. Both women were clearly cut from the same cloth.

He walked back to the car, the stink of thick cigarette smoke clinging to his clothes. He was just about to turn the engine over when a man came out of Maggie Gull's house and got into the black Toyota Hi-Lux. He was quite short, maybe 5'7", had close-cropped blonde hair and wore a red polo shirt and skinny jeans. It had to be Finlay.

Nick watched as he drove away and on a whim decided to follow him.

They left the Hardwick estate and turned right onto Durham Road and took it south to the A1027. The lunchtime traffic was busy and Nick sat in a queue six cars behind Finlay in the left-hand lane to take the road east.

He followed him as he turned off the ring road and onto the A19 south. Was he going to Middlesbrough? It certainly seemed so as he drove south into the heart of Teesside, across the Tees flyover and took the A66 turn-off east. He managed to keep the pick-up in sight the whole way. As ever, the traffic was choked and again he sat in the afternoon sun with the cars moving slowly until the A178 turn-off for Seaton Carew, when the Toyota signalled again.

So he was going to Seaton and not into the Boro. Nick had been taken there many times as a kid. It was only ten miles from his house but back then it seemed a long way away and was always a welcome trip to the seaside. It was a small town set on the wind-blown Teesside coast, just next to Hartlepool's nuclear power station and right at the mouth of the Tees, across the dark water from where Myra's body had been found on South Gare.

Like most seaside towns in Britain, Seaton Carew had a few faint echoes of a wealthier era with a grand art deco bus station and art deco clock. But like much of Teesside, it had been through successive generations of economic travails. A faded, decrepit amusement arcade called, wholly inappropriately, Las Vegas was shuttered up on Tees Road. The Toyota parked outside a three-storey building just opposite the famous bus station and clock. It looked like a typically shabby seaside apartment in a rundown turn-of-the-century building. Nick parked up beyond and watched in his rear-view mirror as Finlay unlocked the door and went into a flat.

Nick strolled over to the clock set onto a tall white column and took a seat on the elegant, curving bus shelter alongside. No ordinary shelter this but a lovely, sinuous white structure on either side of the clock tower. After a minute he saw Finlay peer out from the flat's top-floor window. It would be a cheap place to live, no doubt about that, and he probably needed a cheap place as the Boro would not pay him much to work in the ticket office.

In the distance, probably from somewhere across the Tees, police sirens rang out, blown into the air on a warm, early afternoon breeze. He wondered if it was the police going to or from the crime scene.

Seaton had a part-time career as a local holiday resort: somewhere to go for a day out. On a sunny summer afternoon in July, it didn't seem such a crazy idea as it did in January. Nick, enjoying the sun, stretched out his legs and folded his arms across his chest, feeling a little sleepy. As he'd lived away from Teesside for well over 25 years, he hadn't been to places like Seaton since he was a teenager. They were bleaker in his mind than they were in reality. Not that it was an especially pretty place, but it had an unglamorous but attractive quality. The same could be said for much of Teesside.

Here the golden beaches and the wild mouth of the River Tees rubbed shoulders with a nuclear power station and the chemical and oil industries, nature and man-made industry thrust up against each other; on every skyline, a chimney or industrial plant set against the wild irrepressible North Sea. But that was the essence of Teesside. That was the grit that made its pearl. There was a unique charm to its un-loveliness, to its layers of industrial history and the tough, unpretentious workforce that fuelled it with their labour. Epic grittiness, that was what it had. Epic grittiness.

He smiled to himself as he sat in the bus shelter and didn't immediately notice a cab pull up outside the Las Vegas amusement arcade shutters. Out stepped a woman with short dark hair in a black t-shirt, loose black pants, sneakers and a bright pink bracelet on one wrist which caught his eye. Pink...but it wasn't Pinky. Not with that hair. She leaned into the cab, paid the driver from a black shoulder bag, took out some keys and then rang the top bell of the building Finlay had entered. The top bell had to be the top floor and his flat.

Nick took out his phone and took a photograph as she turned and faced him briefly. He clicked again as she pushed open the door and went in. Maybe she was Finlay's sister or flatmate.

He was wondering whether to take a walk on the beach when Julie called him.

'Hiya. Where are you?' she said. 'Still at mam's?'

'No I'm in glamorous Seaton Carew bus station. It's nice here actually. I just followed Finlay.'

'Pinky's Finlay?'

'Aye. He seems to be living here. I'll tell you about it later. Anyway, what's up?'

'You remember Mr TP? At Jimmy's party?'

'Ah Mr Tiny Penis, or Yashie as he almost certainly prefers to be known. What about him?'

'Alf has just e-mailed you a link to a report published in Marca. I've taken a look and it has a picture of him. I put the article into Google Translate. They say he's one of 20 or 30 main players in European match-fixing. How it works is they make contacts in various countries, often criminals, who then approach refs and players with bribes and other incentives. Once they've got someone in place, they get them to deliver specific results.'

'Scores, you mean?'

'No, not usually an actual result, that's too difficult. Like we thought, usually it's number of yellow or red cards, throw-ins, corners or a specific amount of goals scored or conceded, something the player or ref can massively influence without it looking suspicious.'

'Yeah, Alf mentioned Jimmy had met a top fixer in that restaurant, I assumed it was old TP...so Yashie is over here checking on his investments I should think.'

'Well I looked him up once Alf had sent over his name and he's an international businessman. There are lots of pieces in the business press about him. He runs an IT company specialising in security issues. He seems to be a bit of a globetrotter.'

'Well that'd be good cover for criminal activity, wouldn't it?

There's no way he's just accidentally at Jimmy's is there?'

'Yeah. That's what I thought. It's just more proof, isn't it? Jimmy is up to his neck in corruption. The fact we saw Yashie with that girl in a field below Roseberry Topping is really weird though, don't you think?'

'It's an odd coincidence, yeah.'

'I mean...why's he there with her? He's obvious hugely wealthy. Why get a blow job off a Teesside girl?'

'Because Teesside girls are famously the world's best at blow jobs?'

'Yeah well we got classes at school didn't we?'

'Maybe he's over here a lot and has girlfriends here or whatever.'

'Yeah, maybe. And what did mam have to say?'

'That it definitely was Emmy Green who was asking for Pinky. She recognised her in the picture.'

'I knew it. So she was representing a woman who ended up dead and was looking for Pinky at a time when she had been kidnapped and whose supposed ex-boyfriend lives about 400 yards from where that body was found. That's all too weird. What's she up to?'

'I wish I knew. I'll head back now though Jules, I won't be long unless I get caught in traffic on the A66.'

'Okay gorgeous. See you in a bit.'

Teesside is a small area. Blink and you miss it going north to south on the A19, unless it's rush hour, in which case you'll be stuck on the Tees flyover for enough time to contemplate your own mortality. It really only exists in a cluster either side of the river. So it took Nick just 27 minutes to drive the 18 miles from Seaton Carew on the coast back to the farmhouse outside Yarm which was pretty much on the southern boundary of Teesside, though no official boundaries exist. Yarm is definitely inside, Darlington definitely outside. Some argued Hartlepool wasn't in Teesside at all, but at the very least it was an honorary member. The real heart of Teesside has always been Middlesbrough and Stockton and their respective suburbs. As soon as you get north of Billingham you're pretty much into County Durham proper and as soon as you're south of Middlesbrough you're pretty much into North Yorkshire. Some old-timers liked to think of Middlesbrough as a Yorkshire town, as indeed it was until 1968 when for six years something called the County Borough Of Teesside was invented only to be replaced in 1974 by the never-properly-embraced county of Cleveland. Yorkshire County Cricket was played at Acklam Park until 1996, so the Boro has good Yorkshire credentials, but in recent years it moved in its self-identity from its North Yorkshire past and is now very firmly a Teesside town. In some ways Teesside is fundamentally mythic, existing not on the map but only in the hearts and minds of its natives.

As he was pulling up to the farmhouse, his phone rang. He could see from the display it was Jeff. Julie waved at him from around the side of the house where she was hoeing weeds in a small vegetable bed.

'Now then big man, how's it going?' he said.

'I'm good, like. Aye.'

'Good. I was just thinking about asking you to come up for a few days. I thought we could go and have a sniff around the record fair at the town hall on Sunday along with all the other socially dysfunctional men with poor personal hygiene.'

'Yeah, yeah. Good.'

His speech was halting. Not like him at all.

'What's up, Jeff? Something on your mind?'

'Look, I...I...I just heard this from Sarge...he called me right away because...'

Dave Sargent was a copper that both Nick and Jeff had grown up with in Stockton who worked for the Cleveland Police. He'd quickly become a sergeant so they'd called him Sergeant Sargent or just plain Sarge ever since.

'Sarge? What, like?'

'I'm just going to come out and say it.'

'I wish you would.'

He let out a shaky breath.

'They've just found Lisa Lambert's body. She's dead, Nick. I'm sorry, like...she was a great lass...I can't believe it...she was always so...so alive...sounds stupid that...'

Nick dropped the phone as he heard the news. A wave of numbness spread over him and he couldn't even support his own weight, his muscles briefly ceasing to function. He had to lean against the bonnet of the car. He picked up the phone again, his hand shaking.

'What? How? Was it drinking? Did she go on a bender and get run over or something? I just spoke to her early this morning,'

'They've just found her a couple of hours ago on the beach near South Gare.'

Nick brain felt like it was about to explode. 'South Gare?! Are you sure? South fucking Gare?!'

'Yeah. She was on the sand next to one of those old wartime pill boxes. A dog walker found her.'

'But that can't be far from where Myra was found as well. Surely it must have been crawling with coppers after they'd found one body there?'

'Sarge mentioned that but reckoned they hadn't been able to seal off the whole area. He called me because they identified her quickly and, good copper that he is, he remembered her name from when I'd talked about her a few times, y'know about how sexy she was. You know how we go on about who we fancy and that...so he thought I might know why she was there. I told him everything I knew about her and where she lived.'

'How did she die?'

'I'm not supposed to tell anyone but she was shot once in the head, as was that Myra lass. From a distance too they reckon. Like they were left there and...and someone picked them off.'

'Oh Jesus, oh fucking hell.'

He felt cold and nauseous, a shard of ice stabbing him in his soul.

'I know man. Two murders at the mouth of the Tees. There's some fucking crazy fucker out there, that's for sure.'

'Fuck man, I was just at Seaton Carew today, just across from there...when did she die?'

'Sarge said it was probably around dinner time.'

He closed his eyes.

'Christ, I wasn't that far away. I was in Hardwick. Shit I even heard sirens in the distance when I was in Seaton that must have been Sarge and his mob. Poor Lisa. Oh God...I just can't believe it...I don't want to believe it.'

Julie came over, seeing his distress from a distance.

'What's wrong?' What's the matter?' she asked as she approached.

'Lisa Lambert's been found dead at South Gare. Someone shot her. Myra was shot too.'

He tried to say it calmly but his voice quivered and broke as he spoke.

Julie's mouth fell open, and she put her hand on her head, staring at him with disbelief.

'Sorry mate...I didn't want to have to tell you but I thought you should know, like. I'll come up tomorrow. If I hear anything else from Sarge, I'll let you know.'

Julie put her hand on his arm, concern in her eyes.

'What the hell is going on Nick?'

He stared at a flock of starlings, whirling in the sky like black smoke,

'Only me and Emmy Green are left alive who know about those fake pictures, Jules. It's not me shooting everybody so it must be her, so I must be fucking next!'

She stared at him in horror but then a wave of defiance and determination flooded her face. 'Fucking hell, I'm not having this, no fucking way,' she ran her hands through her hair, stared at the ground and flattened her palms downwards in a calming gesture. 'Okay right, we need some protection. Give us the phone.'

She grabbed it from him and dialled a number.

'Ricky, it's Jules. I need a handgun...never mind why, just get me one...preferably a scary big fuck off handgun. I'll give you the money. Can you get one to me here in the next couple of hours? Yeah? Bring it over as soon as you can and bring Kev with you.'

'What the fuck are you doing?' asked Nick as she rang off.

'Look, calm down, if someone has killed twice they'll do it a third a time and if they're going to come after you, then we're going to have to get fucking hard-core, aren't we? We need to defend ourselves. Ricky's got connections...we'll be okay.'

'Illegal guns? Fuck me, that's a bit over the top, isn't it?'

'Better over the top and alive than sensible and dead,' she said matter-of-factly. She took his face between her hands and stared into his eyes. 'Are you okay? We've just got to be strong. Hard, like.'

'I know. I'm okay. Unlike that poor cow Lisa.'

Less than two hours later, with the sun almost down, Ricky and Kev Wells turned up at the farm in an old Mercedes. In their mid-40s, both stood six foot tall and 15 stone. Both had spent time in jail for various flavours of robbery, Kev with the added spice of aggravated bodily harm. They'd stayed out of jail for the last three years but had spent most of their 20s and 30s doing time.

Their reputation was widespread - the Wells brothers were hard, don't mess with them. He'd heard that since he was 13 and it still wasn't hard to see why. They were not exactly shrinking violets. Both thickset, they looked like men you'd avoid locking eyes with in the pub. They had both inherited their mother's striking turquoise blue eyes and fair hair.

'Now then our Jules...what's going on then?' said Kev as he came in the house, followed by his brother.

Julie told them what had happened, they seemed untroubled by such events.

'Can you talk to your criminal buddies and find out if it's a local gang or some new nutter? We need anything you can find,' she said.

Ricky, the bigger of the two of them, said: 'They'd better not try havin' a pop at youse two or they'll have us to fucking deal with, but those two shootings aren't local are they Kev?'

'Nah. I reckon someone's come up here and brought their gun with them. They've not bought it here. Talking of which…,' he reached inside his bomber jacket and pulled out a pistol, 'there you go Jules. My own personal peacemaker that.'

'Fucking hell Kev, it looks like a toy,' said Julie looking at the gun. In two shades of grey metal and with a short, stubby barrel, it looked like a kid's plaything. 'I was thinking it'd be some huge fucking Clint Eastwood sort of thing.'

'That is a Kel-Tec PF-9mm and will severely burst anyone you shoot. Want a demonstration? This is how you load it. It holds seven rounds.'

Nick felt cold at the sight of the gun. This was all getting so heavy and so quickly. This was wrong. He didn't want this in his life. He got up, walked out the room and into the garden. Their first month in the house had been so good but it had suddenly turned from love to violence. It soured his guts. He kept thinking of Lisa, how she'd been when he last saw her. Her life force, her wit and talent, all snuffed out now. All gone. How could all that energy and experience be extinguished by a single bullet? Where did it all go? All the emotional repression that was second nature to him, or had been until he had undergone therapy, couldn't protect him from his own emotions now.

Tears ran down his cheeks as he thought about her and her big hearted, full-blooded life of art and booze and passion. It hurt inside and he didn't know how to deal with it. But this wasn't like his depression. It didn't feel like that at all. It wasn't an inward blackness or melancholy, it was almost a physical pain, the pain of loss. But there was no changing the facts. Feeling nothing or feeling everything wouldn't change anything. Feelings for the dead were pointless because no matter how powerful those feelings were, it couldn't alter the most basic fact: Lisa was dead and he'd never see her again. But, as he walked around the perimeter of the garden and out into the fields beyond in the gloaming of the day, he realised that wasn't why he was crying. He might never have seen Lisa again anyway; the pain came from knowing that she wasn't in the world anymore. Not there to paint, to kick off, to shout and rant and take the piss. A light had gone out. Was it selfish to cry for the dead? They would never know of your tears.

But then she would have loved the idea that she'd left this existence in such a dramatic way. She loved drama, loved making a scene. He was sure she would have had little or no fear of death. Life was for living; it was all about The Now. Yesterday was gone, and tomorrow, well there's no guarantee about tomorrow, fuck tomorrow, all we have it right here, right now. That was her philosophy and it showed in the passion in her art. That at least was still here in the mortal world - her gift to the living. She would live on brightly in those canvases, her spirit forever transferred from her heart and bones through the brush.

He shook his head slowly, his eyes filled with impotent tears of recollection and loss. He wasn't sure that being better connected to your feelings was really that useful. What would she have said to him about her dying like this? What would have been her response?

The summer night sky was all stars and wisps of low cloud and out of the darkness her words came to him, as clear as the July night. *'Fuck them up, Nick, fuck them up.'* Her words, in her voice, in his brain, like she was there with him.

He shivered, clenched his fists and nodded, one last tear rolling down his cheek and dropping into the thick summer grass. He nodded in agreement. Then he swallowed his emotions deep, deep down into his guts, taking strength from them and strode back to the house, sucking all her energy, all her power and all her sheer fucking spirit into him.

It was time to get serious.

'Are you okay?' said Julie as he returned to the living room, looking at him with worried eyes.

'Fine, yeah. Right, who are we going to shoot with this fucking thing then?' he said, picking up the gun.

Kev and Ricky burst out laughing.

'Look at him, like. He's keen to get some killing done!' roared Ricky.

'There's some ammunition in here,' said Kev, putting a carrier bag on the table. 'Remember to use two hands to shoot this if you can...it's not got a big kick but you're an amateur and you'll never keep it steady otherwise. Jules will show you.'

'How do you know how to shoot a gun?' asked Nick.

'I used to go to a firing range in Darlo, didn't I? It's a bit different to shooting some murderous twat though.'

Kev snorted. 'Not that different. Easier if anything.'

'How much do I owe you?' said Julie.

'Nowt. You've lost that much bail money on us over the years, it wouldn't be fair to charge you,' said Kev and Ricky laughed. 'If you need any muscle, just give us a call.'

'Thanks boys,' said Nick. 'We've got to find out who this killer is, so if you hear anything on the grapevine, let us know.'

'Grapevine? I wish there was a fucking grapevine. It'd make life a lot easier, like,' said Ricky with a hunch of his shoulders.

The late-night local news featured a piece on both shootings. The Chief Superintendent of Cleveland Police had announced at a late news conference that they were now treating both deaths as murder and appealed for witnesses.

Nick downloaded the photos he'd taken earlier that day in Seaton. He stared at the four shots of the woman getting out of the cab and waiting for the door to be opened. He looked and looked again, puzzled at what he was seeing.

'Jules? Take a look at these.'

She came over and squatted alongside him.

'I took these in Seaton. This was the woman who went into Finlay's flat. Am I crazy or is this actually Pinky wearing a short black wig? It looks very like her though I never thought that when I took the shot.'

She narrowed her eyes. 'Blow it up a bit.'

He made the images larger.

She tapped at the photo of her looking directly at him. 'If you'd not said, I don't know that it'd have even occurred to me that it was Pinky because she looks so different with that hair and in loose-fitting clothing as well, but it damn well is her, y'know. You're right. Look, see that mole on her neck. I noticed that the other day. And it's totally her height and body shape, small sticky-out bum, curvy hips, that's her.'

'Yeah, she looks so different because her hair is exactly the opposite of normal. She's got shoulder-length curly blonde hair; this is short, straight and black. That's why it's so disorientating. But if I cut around the hair here…,' he manipulated the image to cut off her hair, 'now, that makes it much more obvious.'

'She's a sly little madam isn't she? Still carrying on with Finlay.'

'But as she's in disguise, presumably she's paranoid and doesn't want to be recognised.'

'Well Teesside is a small place and she's very distinctive. Still got some pink on her wrist there, I see. She can't let that go. You know what? I think it's become a sort of mental problem for her. She has to wear pink or she feels like something is wrong with her or the world. It's freaky.'

'Yeah, that is weird. It's just a colour but it's like it's her self-identity,' said Nick.

'It could be innocent though, I suppose, just stopping by to see an old friend.'

'In a wig? Yeah, right.'

'Yeah…that is pretty incriminating. Well it's her life. Who are we to judge who she does or doesn't have a relationship with?'

'Seems to me that when she said that I shouldn't trust anyone at Jimmy's party, she was including herself. She's pulling the wool over someone's eyes and it just might be us.'

CHAPTER 9

In the morning, over breakfast, Julie said, 'If you're out and about today will you pick up a couple of tickets for the friendly game at the Boro. Feels like ages since we saw any football.'

'Yeah, of course.'

She looked at him as he ate his bacon and eggs.

'What?' he said.

'You've gone all quiet. That's never a good sign with you. Don't go brooding, mister.'

'Jules, a friend has been murdered and we've got a gun in the house to protect ourselves against a fucking killer, which part of that am I not supposed to brood on? It's not....nothing.'

'I know, I know, but I don't want you going off into a depression. You've been doing really well.'

'I won't. It doesn't feel like that. I just want to sort things out. I won't rest until I've found out who killed Lisa and got them fucking strung up for it. I owe it to her. She even said if anything happens to me, promise me you'll fuck them up...I said I would...I have to. That's it.'

'The police will be onto it already. Why don't you give Dave Sargent a call and tell him what you know? The police should have all the information.'

Nick nodded. 'I'm going to try and meet up with him this morning. Are you in all day?'

'Yeah, probably.'

'Okay, well make sure you don't shoot anyone you shouldn't,' he said. 'Jeff won't be here until mid-afternoon.'

'I'll try. Keep in touch with me.' She gave his hand a squeeze and kissed him.

It was just after 9.30am so he decided to go to the Riverside for the tickets. They could have bought them on the day of the match, but getting them in advance meant they could stay in the pub longer. Being drunk was always a superior state to be in when you watched the Boro play football, even in a pre-season friendly. Although he was staying sober, it seemed churlish to deny Julie her lifelong habit of a pre-game piss-up.

There was no-one around the Riverside Stadium as he parked and walked over to the ticket office. Football grounds were odd, ghostly places in the summer and the Riverside was no exception. It felt more like a bleak, abandoned industrial estate than a vibrant Premier League club ground. Although it was a literal improvement on the increasingly decrepit Ayresome Park which the Riverside had replaced in 1995, there was no doubt that in taking the club out of the back streets and putting it by the river they had lost something. It was now a football facility but not so obviously, not so physically, a beating heart of Middlesbrough even though it remained very much a community club.

He went into the ticket office. He recognised Finlay straight away, asked for two tickets for the upcoming friendly game and handed him his debit card.

'Have you sold many tickets?'

Finlay laughed. 'No mate, hardly any. If we sell 500 I'd be surprised and most of them will be on the day, like. We shouldn't charge for it really.'

'That'd be a good idea,' said Nick.

'Oh, our card machines are down this morning, have you got the cash?'

'Yeah, sure.'

'Have you got the cash' whirred around in his mind as he handed over the money and looked Finlay in the eyes. The way he said those words echoed in his brain. That's exactly what the kidnapper had said on the phone. Those words. Exactly those words. He was sure. And it was his voice. It was Finlay's voice. The same light Teesside intonation. It was etched into his brain. The thought released another realisation that his sub-conscious had been keeping secret. The white noise in the background on the phone, that wasn't white noise, it was the sea. He'd called from the beach at Seaton Carew. He'd stepped outside of his flat to make the call and gone down onto the beach. The cheeky little fucker. Now it was clear; in an instant he saw it all.

The whole bloody thing was set up between him and Pinky just as he'd idly speculated. She hadn't been kidnapped at all - that's why she was so calm. She'd gone to stay at Seaton, probably in disguise just like when he'd spotted her, and she'd screwed Jimmy out of a million quid. Jackie was right; she was still with Finlay. They were working together. The kid was even wearing the rust-coloured skinny jeans that they'd spotted in the video. It was him who picked up the tartan bag from the big wagon. What a little fucker. Right, let's put the wind up him.

'Okay Finlay, thanks for my tickets,' he said, looking him directly in the eyes. 'My name's Nick Guymer, by the way.'

He pointed his right index finger at him, winked, turned and left. As he did so, he could see the instant change in expression in Finlay's eyes, swapping everyday boredom for surprise and then a hint of fear. In that moment, he knew that he knew that he knew who he was. Yeah, let the little sod sweat on it. He'd caused him a lot of stress, so let him suck it up. He couldn't call Jimmy with his ransom demands because he worked in the office and Jimmy might have recognised his voice. Yes, it all made sense now.

Nick walked away, a burning feeling of indignation and resentment in his belly for the fear that Julie would be hurt and for drawing him into their little scheme, but it was tempered by the knowledge that, in fairness, it was a bloody good scam. He sat in the car, snorted a laugh and called Julie.

'Jules, I just got our tickets and you know who I met at the ticket office? Pinky's Finlay. And I realised as I was talking to him that he was the voice on the phone – the kidnapper.'

She was silent for a second as the news sank.

'Eeee God, fizzin' hell, he wasn't, was he? Eeee my God...so ...so they did set it up between them just like you said?'

'Well yeah, there was never a kidnap. It's obvious, isn't it? They

141

conspired to get a million quid out of Jimmy and what's more, it bloody well worked like a dream.'

'Eeee my God....Pinky you cheeky little sod.' Her tone was one of shock and almost admiration.

'Yeah, I let him know who I was and I thought he might shit himself because he's not exactly a hard man. No wonder he almost lost his nerve when I lost my rag on the phone.'

'What's he look like?'

'Like a skinny student. Scruffy, all skin and bone. He was the skinny jeans man in our video. I bloody resent him causing us that stress though, I really do.'

'Yeah...but...you've got to admit, there's something a bit good about it. I mean, it's a nice scam.'

'Hmm, well we've got them over a barrel now haven't we? We know what they've done.'

She was silent for a few seconds.

'Aye, but we don't want anything from them, do we? Okay, we could tell the cops but clearly, neither they nor Jimmy wanted that. Jimmy and Frankie seemed very keen to keep the cops out of their business, probably because of the match-fixing. The last thing they need is the police poking into his life.'

'And it says a lot about the state of Pinky's relationship with Jimmy, doesn't it?' he said.

'Ha, just a bit, aye. No-one rips off their lover if they're intending to stick around.'

'Should I tell him?'

She paused. 'I feel like I should say yes, that would be the honest thing to do...but part of me wants Pinky to get away with it...because she grew up with a rough mother and has had no breaks in life, and because everyone at that party treated her like a piece of meat. So because of that I want to say no. Does that make sense?'

'Yeah, I'm annoyed at the kid for putting the shits up me but I can see what you mean, totally.'

As she spoke, he could hear the sound of sirens in the distance.

'You're not on fire are you?' he said, only half-joking.

'I'm out in the garden at the front and it sounds like fire engines coming out of Yarm and going down Aislaby Road - not just one either, sounds like loads of them. The wind is blowing from the north so it's making the sound carry.'

'Probably a chip pan fire, if such a thing still exists. Okay, I'll see you later, Jules.'

He called Dave Sargent's mobile number. It went to voicemail; did no-one ever answer their phone anymore?

'Dave, it's Nick Guymer. Jeff told me about Lisa Lambert. She was a good friend of mine. I might have some information that might help you in the investigation. I'm living on Teesside now so we can meet up if you want.'

He had only just rung off when the policeman called him back. He must have been screening calls.

'Hi Nick, it's Dave Sargent.'

'Now then Sarge. Long time no hear.'

'Yeah, I speak to Jeff quite a bit about records and that, he's mentioned you but it must be ten years since we last met at the school reunion.'

'Oh God, don't remind me. What a depressing night that was.'

'Sad that we talk again in such circumstances. Bad business these Myra LeFevre and Lisa Lambert murders. Very bad. I won't tolerate this sort of thing on my patch. I called Jeff as soon as we identified the second body. The name had stuck with me. I think he was...well...somewhat smitten. So he gave me all the information he could but he mentioned you knew her too.'

He talked in an old-fashioned way, more like something out of Dixon of Dock Green than a modern copper.

'Yeah, we were good friends in a way. We flirted around each other a bit and went out a few times. She was larger than life, Sarge. A great woman, you know.'

'Where are you now, Nick?'

'At the Riverside.'

'Ah perfect. Let's meet up. How about outside Stockton Town Hall in half an hour?'

'No problem. I'll see you there.'

Nick parked in Stockton's Castlegate Shopping Centre car park, a particularly heinous example of brutal modern architecture that had always somehow looked old-fashioned, even when it had first opened in 1972. Renovations, alterations and various superficial enhancements constantly attempted to mitigate the fact that it was a concrete shopping centre squatting on the great, handsomely wide and grand High Street, once reputed, as so many are, to be the longest in the land and playing host to the most pubs. Now it was a shadow of its former self with generations of stores come and gone since Nick was a kid in the 70s. The only constants, as far as he could see, were the post office and a few of the pubs. The Garrick, The Royal Oak and the Castle and Anchor were all his under-age drinking dens and doubtless still served 16-year-old boys with bum-fluff moustaches. For the most part, the High Street was now a series of cheap stores and charity shops but then the area was about as skint and economically deprived as anywhere in the country, so you could hardly expect Fortnum & Mason to open a branch.

As he parked the car and walked out onto the High Street, it all looked familiar in shape and dimension but all the details were different. The old HMV store where he'd bought so many records had long since been replaced by a bank. Finance replacing culture. It seemed symbolic of modern times.

At least the town hall was unchanged, standing in the middle of the High Street as it had since 1735. Even the 60s and 70s passion for knocking seven bells out of grand old architecture hadn't replaced this glorious building with a characterless breezeblock.

He crossed the road and stood outside the front entrance. Yes, Stockton High Street still had a few things in its favour, but like a big beast that had taken a lot of beatings, it wasn't in the best of health and that could be said for many parts of the north-east.

The morning clouds were beginning to disperse, leaving a lovely sunny warm day again and casting shadows onto the shopping centre. Funny how summer sunshine could make even the worst 70s architecture look acceptable.

He only had to wait five minutes before he saw Dave Sargent approaching on foot. He was a tall, dark-haired man in a crisp white shirt, sleeves rolled to the elbow, blue tie and well-cut black trousers, quite handsome in a 1950s movie sort of way, who walked with a slight lope but with shoulders back and chin out. He smiled as he approached and held out his hand.

'Good to see you, Nick,' he said, gripping his hand tightly. 'You have not changed at all.'

'Neither have you Sarge. Still listening to those Jean-Michel Jarre records you used to bring into sixth form for me and Jeff to play in the student lounge?'

He laughed. 'No, I don't get chance to listen to quite as much music as I'd like...work keeps me busy.

'Well that's a blessed relief. I was never that keen on JMJ.'

'Shall we walk down to the riverside?'

They crossed over the road.

'So tell me about Lisa Lambert,' said the policeman.

Nick went over everything he knew about her and that she'd been planning to call a new Middlesbrough gallery owner, Grace Edwards.

'Do you know this Grace Edwards?' asked Sarge.

'No. I've never heard of her.'

'So you don't know if she actually exists?'

Nick shook his head. 'No, it could be anyone.'

'Okay, well hopefully Lisa left the number so we can find out who this Grace Edwards is.'

'She said Myra had written it on her sketchpad. Have you searched Myra's flat in York or Lisa's in Harrogate yet?'

'Myra's yes, but at this stage it's hard to tell what piece of information is the significant piece, which phone number or address.'

'Lisa said that Myra had started doing fake pictures. Or at least claimed to be doing fake pictures.'

'Fake pictures?'

Nick explained.

He nodded. 'I see. That doesn't sound exactly legal. In fact, it sounds very much like fraud to me.'

'Well, exactly. I should make it clear, mind, that I have no proof, only Lisa's word. Myra could have been taking the piss for all we know. Most of the work was supposedly sold to Jimmy Repp...'

'The Dutch footballer?' he interrupted.

'Yes. I saw some of it at his house, actually.'

'Did he know they were not genuine pictures?'

'No. I'm pretty sure he didn't. He paid a lot of money for them too...millions of pounds.'

'And he's still unaware of this?'

'As far as I know, and once Myra was shot, I'm pretty sure no-one else except me and Lisa were alive who did know, apart from Lisa's agent, Emmy Green, who, again, according to Lisa had basically organised the whole thing.'

Sarge nodded slowly as they walked down onto the riverside path.

'I see and what is this Emmy Green like?'

'I've only met her once. She's in her 50s I'd say and an educated middle-class arty type of woman. She's about five-eight and has a grey Mallen Streak in her hair. I think Lisa said she's based in Northallerton. She was also seen at the house of the mother of Jimmy's girlfriend.'

'Is that significant?'

'Well, I don't know Sarge. We think it is but we don't know why. Like I say, she's this middle-class arty type and Pinky's mother's house is on the Hardwick estate.'

'Ah. A bit of a cultural clash?'

'Not just a bit. I doubt many people there buy post-impressionist art for a hundred grand a pop, do they?'

'No. And rightly so, in my opinion. They'd be too sensible.'

Nick laughed a little.

'This is Pinky Gull we're talking about, isn't it?' said Dave.

'Yeah. She's a nice lass or I think she is anyway. Jules reckons so too.'

He wrestled with the idea of telling him about the kidnapping. Should he dump her in the shit?

'What sort of sentence would you get for fraud, Sarge?'

'Depends on how much money is involved. More equals longer. Anything over, say, a million is going to be a long stretch.'

Could he send Pinky down for years? Could he bollocks. It didn't even seem that serious a crime. Yes, he'd initially been scared by Finlay's phone call, but robbing from a rich bloke who was probably only rich because he was match-fixing wasn't a normal crime. Repp wasn't your usual victim. The speed with which Frankie had raised the money suggested his lifestyle wasn't going to be damaged by the loss of a million quid. And to send a kid to jail for years for that? If anything, that seemed more immoral than her kidnapping scan. So he said nothing.

They stopped at a riverside bench seat and sat down. Dave cracked his knuckles.

'I'm asking myself who had the motivation to kill both these women and an easy conclusion would be the woman who set up the whole fraud business, this Emmy Green. She had the most to lose by either woman talking about it. The artist might do a little bit of time for the fraud but it's the agent who has taken receipt of large amounts of money on false pretences and she'd get a decent stretch for that.' Sarge stroked his beard line. 'Obviously I need some evidence before I can arrest her. I'll get someone onto that right away and then get her in for questioning.'

Nick nodded. The river flowed past, thin, brown and swirling like cheap gravy.

'Well, you can find her details on her website. I'm worried though, Sarge. You know, I might be next, or worse still Julie. So the sooner she's in custody the better as far as I'm concerned.'

'Do you know if she's good with a rifle?'

'I have no idea. It doesn't seem likely.'

'She could belong to a gun club. Both women were shot with the same gun; both with a single shot; both to the back of the head, though not from close range. We think they were shot with a high-powered rifle. It would seem both had been taken to South Gare and told to wait there, Myra right on the end of that peninsula, Lisa on the beach. Then the killer has walked away and shot them from some distance. As you know, it's usually pretty deserted out there. They were probably fired at from the cover of a derelict building. It's an odd shooting - the killer had the chance to shoot them at close range but clearly didn't want to. If it's any comfort, I doubt Lisa suffered at all, not even for two seconds. The irony is that we weren't that far away at the time. We just couldn't shut the whole area down...or rather, we could have but didn't, not extensively enough, as it turned out. Bad business all round. You said that some of this fake art was sold to Jimmy Repp...do you know him?'

'Yeah, I've interviewed him a few times. He's not a friend as such but I get on well enough to be invited to a party at his house. I'll be honest Dave, and this can't go any further than between you and me...not yet.'

The policeman nodded.

'I'm working on a piece about Jimmy being involved in match-fixing. See, I couldn't work out how he'd afforded so much expensive art on his wages. He has a history of making errors, bad errors, during games. When I looked at the footage, I noticed there was usually a man wearing a bright orange hat behind the goal. I think he may have been giving him in-game advice on what to do and when to do it.'

Dave Sargent turned his mouth down and shook his head. 'Let me see...he wears orange so that he's easily identified, I suppose. But you don't have any evidence? No hard evidence?'

'No, not yet. It's all supposition, rumour and YouTube footage.

He met some underworld people in a restaurant, I know that, but I know that's not proof of anything in itself. I'm still working on it. Do you know of a man called Frankie Gray? He's Jimmy's business manager. I'm sure he's the muscle behind all of this business.'

'The name is familiar, yes, but he's not a known criminal if that's what you mean. Then again, that doesn't mean he's not a villain...so if I hear you right, you feel there's something a bit iffy about Jimmy Repp and his 'people'?'

'Yeah, that's it.'

'In my experience in this job, if a man is dodgy in one area of his life, he's dodgy in many other areas as well.'

Nick snorted. 'You're not the first to say that.'

'Bearing that in mind, I'd be surprised if he didn't know he was buying fake paintings and my guess is he was buying them in order to sell them on in the future as 'real' paintings – as a con - or he was going to do a big insurance swindle by damaging or destroying fakes, getting a pay-out and keeping the real paintings, which would then be sold after all the fuss has died down. If I was being very suspicious that's what I'd have assumed. Do you know how much he paid for the fakes?'

Nick shook his head.

'So he might have bought them at a low price - the price they're worth.'

Nick felt stupid. He had assumed that Jimmy had paid full price for the copies as though they were genuine, as had Lisa. It hadn't occurred to either of them that this might not be the case at all. He might have paid ten grand for 50 pictures and promised Myra more later. She'd only said there was a 'shitload' more money due. That was a pretty subjective word. One person's shitload is another's pittance.

'I'd have made a rubbish copper, Sarge. That never occurred to me at all.'

The policeman grinned. 'Never be afraid to think the worst of someone, Nick. That's what this job has taught me. These murders have to be my primary concern, mind. I can't have someone running around Teesside shooting people, it's just not on, and so we're throwing all our resources at this. If you get any hard evidence on the Repp match-fixing, let me know as soon as possible. I'm going to try and put together some evidence on Emmy Green. I think she has to be the focus of our investigation.'

They walked back to the High Street, shook hands and went their separate ways. Nick had just returned to the car in the Castlegate Centre when Julie called.

'Nick!' Her voice was urgent. She sounded like she was in her car.

'Are you okay?' he asked urgently, his heart leaping on hearing the emotion in her voice.

'Yeah but those fire engines we heard earlier? They were going to Jimmy Repp's house. I could see the smoke from our place. It's just been on the local radio.'

'Jimmy's? Bloody hell.'

'I'm on my way over there now just to see if I can be of any help, like. I don't know how serious it is yet. More engines went over there after you rang so it might be big.'

Nick stared at the oil-stained patches of concrete on the floor of the car park. It was just as Dave had said - a fire was a great way to get rid of those pictures.

'Be careful Jules and keep your eyes open as well.'

'What do you mean?'

'I mean, look out for anything suspicious and take the gun with you. Someone might have done this to get rid of the fake pictures. Be especially cautious if Emmy Green is there.'

'Okay. I'm just on the Aislaby Road now.'

'Right, I'll meet you there.'

He pulled out of the car park and headed towards the westbound A66. It was another glorious summer's day on Teesside. As he waited at traffic lights a pair of swans flew overhead, their huge wings silhouetted against the blue sky, probably on their way to Billingham Beck Valley, a nature reserve in the heart of the town.

Teesside was changed from the area he knew as a kid; now there was room for nature. For all the problems caused by industrial decline, maybe such places were a sign of progress to a better future, less dependent on the hard industry which had for so long been the lifeblood of the area.

As soon as he turned onto Aislaby Road he could see black smoke rising above trees in the distance. Julie's car was parked at the entrance to a field opposite the walled and fenced grounds of the house. The big black wrought iron gates were wide open. As he pulled in behind her car, the smell of burning wood and plastic was already filling his nostrils. Six fire engines were circled on the huge gravel drive and two police cars were parked up alongside. Great arcs of water from three of the red trucks were being directed into the heart of the blaze. A couple of cars had stopped and local people stood outside to watch the action.

As he ran past them, he stopped suddenly when he saw the house, or what remained of it. The west wing was still flaming, tongues of intense orange and yellow licking up against the blue sky. Thick swirling clouds of black smoke poured from the rest of the house as the fire engines drenched it with water. The roof had fallen in, burnt timbers and joists stuck up at random angles. Firemen scurried around with hoses and ladders and two policewomen stood talking to someone on the fire-fighting team. It was a scene of utter devastation. He'd never seen a big fire up close in real life. Its power to raze a big building like this to the ground was awesome, the heat intense.

The west wing flames grew taller and taller as the inferno took hold and consumed anything and everything flammable in its path, driven on by a stiff breeze from the east.

Suddenly there was more shouting from the fire crew followed by a deep, resonant, earth-shuddering explosion which knocked him back a step. The ground shook underfoot and a small mushroom cloud of black and grey smoke rose from out of the roaring flames. It made him catch his breath in shock. Where the fuck was Julie?

He took off at pace, running the full length of the gravel drive and taking a right-hand arc around the easterly perimeter of the property. This side was burnt to the ground, dripping in water and smouldering, surrounded in a blanket of smoke. The air was peppered with flecks of black carbon embers as he ran past a large grass lawn, now scorched from the heat and littered with incinerated debris. As he reached the back of the house, the full scale of damage to the west wing was evident. All hoses were now being directed at the cacophony of fire.

Running further around the perimeter and towards the swimming pool area where they had stood having drinks at the party, he saw two figures leaning against a timber fence that separated the grounds of the house from the pasture beyond. One of them was Julie, the other was Pinky. She was wearing a bright pink sweatshirt, black jeans and white baseball boots, her blonde hair tied back. She was a small, slight figure compared to Julie. Sprinting as hard as he could, he covered the ground quickly. Their faces were flushed with the heat of the day and the heat of the fire.

'What was that explosion?' he asked as he approached, catching his breath.

'A propane tank,' said Pinky. 'Hello Nick, by the way,' she said with a short grimace, 'Jules said you were on your way.'

'How...how did this start? It's fucking incredible. You can even feel the heat from here.'

Pinky just shook her head.

'They don't know yet,' said Julie. 'We've watched it burning from here and it seems to have moved through the house from east to west.'

'Is Jimmy okay?'

'He's just gone away to do pre-season training; I haven't even been able to get hold of him yet. I came back this morning in a cab to pick up some clothes and found the whole place on fire.'

Aye, back from Seaton Carew, thought Nick.

'So it started over here, the most burnt-out part?' he asked.

He pointed at the area that was destroyed.

'Yeah. That was burning like crazy when I arrived. It must have been burning for quite a while because it spread through the house like, well, wildfire. By the time the fire engines got here it was like bonfire night.'

'Are you okay, though?'

'Fine. Sick. But...what can you do?' she shrugged.

He nodded as he looked at her talking. It was odd knowing a secret about someone when they didn't know that you knew. It wasn't everyone who could claim to have set up their own kidnapping. She was a cool kid. Even now, her house up in flames, she wasn't overly emotional. She stood, arms crossed, an eyebrow raised almost in contempt. He had always thought she had hard eyes, the sort of eyes which were closed off to you somehow, but you had to admire her toughness.

'So what was on that side of the house?' he asked. It was impossible to know now that it was a burnt-out shell.

'The gallery, the sauna and the sports room. My money is on the sauna being defective. It got too hot in there. We had an electrician out to look at it just before the party.'

'I think they're getting on top of it now,' said Julie as the flames from the kitchen died down under the torrent of water.

A senior fireman walked over to them, wiping sweat from his brow, soot smears on his face, looking like an extra from a disaster movie.

'How's it going?' said Nick. The bloke looked exhausted and was dripping in sweat.

'It's under control now. Once it's totally out, then we'll go into damping-down mode to make sure it doesn't flare up anywhere. I'm afraid it's a write-off, miss.'

He gestured at the charred pile of rubble and wood that had been a house.

'I've never seen a house burn with that intensity and it spread so quickly in this wind. I'm just glad this one didn't take any lives.

153

We'll get the investigation team in to look into how and why and where it started but my bet is at the far end there.' He pointed to where the gallery room had been. 'It moved from there through the rest of the house.'

'Thanks for your help, I wish I could offer you a cold drink, you must be exhausted with that heat,' said Pinky with the smile of a polite and friendly waitress.

He smiled back at her. 'No problem, that's why we're here. There's nothing much for you to do now, nothing to rescue really. You can get off if you want to leave a contact number and address with the police,' said the fireman, gesturing at the officers standing by the pool looking at the burning building.

'Yes, I'll do that. Thank you,' said Pinky, politely, again.

'I can give you a lift to your mam's if you're not up to driving,' said Julie.

She smiled. 'Thanks Julie, I'm fine. I'll take my own car. Thank God the garage is separate from the house and hasn't gone up as well. I'll be okay, really. Thanks for coming to see if I was alright. I really appreciate it and it was typically nice of both of youse. I'll speak to Jimmy later. I'm dreading having to tell him what's happened,' she said, letting out a deep sigh.

'Come here,' said Julie, and gave her a big hug. 'These things happen, kidda. At least no-one got hurt.'

'Thanks Jules,' she said and walked away with a confident stride.

Nick and Julie went out onto the road and stood beside their cars.

'Shit, what do you make of it all?' she said, rubbing her face with the palms of her hands.

Nick wobbled his hand from side to side. 'Dodgy if you ask me. Well dodgy. All evidence of those pictures has gone up in smoke and the artist and the artist's best friend are both dead. The whole scam is being wiped off the face of the earth. So that just leaves me to sort out now.'

'Except they might not know you know.'

'I bloody hope they don't but if its anything to do with Emmy

154

Green, she almost certainly will. All it would have taken is one word from Lisa about having met up with me. I just hope Sarge has pulled her in.'

As he spoke, Pinky drove a small black Mazda sports out of the garage and down the driveway before speeding off in the direction of Yarm.

'I was toying with telling Sarge about the kidnapping but decided against it. I couldn't get her into trouble, could I?'

Julie nodded and grinned. 'I'm glad you didn't. I know it's illegal and all that but society would gain nothing by putting a girl like that in jail. She's not innocent but that's not the same thing as being guilty, if you know what I mean.'

'Yeah, I know, and I agree, but then maybe she's taking us all for ride. I mean, what the hell is going on here, Jules? This fire isn't a bloody accident, that's for sure.'

CHAPTER 10

They drove back to the farm and over tea Nick told her about his meeting with Dave Sargent in Stockton. As he was talking, Jeff's old Escort van pulled up outside.

'Hey big man,' said Nick, greeting his old friend, his arms out wide.

'You're not going to hug me are you?' said Jeff, emerging from the car like a bear getting out of a cupboard.

'Of course not. You know our policy: no hugging, no learning.'

'I'm glad to hear it.'

He took a look around, his long hair blowing in the warm summer breeze.

'Mind, you managed to find the one spot on Teesside that isn't a shithole. Well done on that.'

'It is a bit nice, isn't it?'

Jeff scratched his big beard. 'Lovely if you're a boring bastard who gets off on watching sparrows mating, aye.'

'Which fortunately we do.'

'It'd drive me nuts out here. I'd be bored within...actually I'm bored already.'

Julie came out of the house.

'Alright Jeff, I thought I could recognise those distinctive Roseworth tones,' she said.

'Now then Julie. You're looking all tanned and lovely - a proper rural wench.'

'Aye right, I'll put on a gingham frock too shall I?' she said, laughing.

'Well I've brought mine, so it'd be shame not to,' he said.

'Fancy a beer, son?' said Nick.

'I've been here for five minutes so I'm already two pints behind schedule. Of course I bloody well do.'

They'd bought two big boxes of Stella in honour of Jeff's visit.

'We'll go round the back. We've got some chairs and a table back there so we'll get the afternoon sun,' said Nick, leading him to the south of the house around an overgrown garden path.

'There's loads to do here...gardening and that...we've hardly done anything yet. I dug a space for some vegetables, Julie's planted some carrots, but it's a bit late now apparently, so it'll have to be next year when we become proper middle-aged gardeners in corduroy trousers.'

'Or boring bastards as they're more usually known,' said Jeff.

They sat down on cane furniture. Julie brought out a pint of lager and a second can for Jeff, knowing how quickly he would go through the first.

'Look at this...I'm not surprised you fell in love with her...a second pint without even asking, what an angel.'

She brought out iced water for her and Nick.

'No booze. Bloody hell. How do you do it?'

'Sometimes it's not easy. I felt like drinking when I heard about Lisa...but I knew it wouldn't make anything any better, like.'

'...aye, well, here's to you Lisa, eh.' He raised his glass to the sky. 'I was fucking stunned when I heard...still am in fact. Did you speak to Sarge?'

'Yeah I met up with him earlier today, actually. He's not changed much.'

'Is he still tall, dark and handsome?' asked Julie.

'Do you know him?' said Jeff.

'Only because of my brothers getting nicked,' she said.

'Yeah he's very dashing. A bit of the Errol Flynn about him,' said Nick.

'What? You mean he puts cocaine on his knob?' said Julie. 'That's what he used to do isn't it?' Jeff spluttered in laughter

'Yes, he was doing that on Stockton High Street. I had to look the other way,' said Nick. He cleared his throat. 'In all seriousness though, he reckons Lisa and Myra were killed by the same person or at least the same gun. Shot at distance at South Gare.'

'Why though? I know she was a bit of a gobshite and rubbed

people up the wrong way but...you know...so do lots of people and they don't end up murdered,' said Jeff.

'Because of what her and Myra knew - something only me and one other person knows,' said Nick.

'What's that like?'

'I don't want to tell you in case knowing puts you in danger.'

Jeff looked at him with incredulity and then shook his head and said: 'Bollocks to that. Think about it. If someone knows you know and they know you've hung out with me, they'll suspect I know anyway. So just by knowing you I might be in the clarts so I might as well know so that when I get shot it won't be such a mystery.'

Nick looked at Julie. She shrugged.

'And I bet Julie knows,' he added.

'Aye alright.'

He explained about the fake pictures.

Jeff raised his eyebrows.

'I fucking love that. Faking the art market just doesn't even seem like a crime to me. If they can't tell the difference between a real one and a fake, it just shows what bullshit the whole thing is...it's all about the signature and not the artwork itself.'

'That's what I thought,' said Julie, 'I sort of admire her for doing it. It's taking the piss.'

'Myra couldn't sell any pictures of her own for any decent money, so I think it was her sort of revenge,' said Nick, drinking the iced water, 'but like it or not, it is fraud, it is very illegal. I also reckon that she was pretty bolshie about it all.'

'Bolshie?' said Jeff.

'Yeah. I mean she wasn't too bothered who she told. Lisa said she'd been shooting her mouth off. That's probably what got her killed. Someone didn't want it known what had been going on. Probably Emmy Green, that agent we met. Myra said she'd arranged it all.'

'So you think it's this Emmy Green woman who's done the shooting? Couldn't it be some pissed-off punter who has been sold worthless art and is now hell-bent on revenge?' said Jeff.

'Sarge is looking into her. She's his number-one suspect by the looks of it.'

Jeff sank the first lager and opened the second can.

'I only met her for an hour that day when you were down, but she was just a bit of a typical middle-class type wasn't she? Not obvious killer material. Might get blood on her linen suit – terrible to get out of linen is blood - she'd not like that, and Waitrose or John Lewis don't sell guns anyway, do they? I think it's much more likely to be a pissed-off punter who thought they were buying expensive art.'

'Yeah but why kill Lisa too? That doesn't make sense. She was nothing to do with it.'

Jeff pulled at his beard contemplatively as a blackbird landed on an old apple tree and released a volley of melodious twittering. Jeff raised his right index finger, a sign that he had come up with a theory.

'Alright, how about this...someone who has been sold the dodgy paintings is pissed off but can't let it be known that they've been conned. Maybe he's a dealer or someone with a big reputation and they've been totally fooled. If the news gets out their career is over, no-one will trust them again. So they have to kill everyone who knows about it to protect their status. They can't report the crime because it makes them look like amateurs and that ruins their reputation and their career.'

They all paused and looked at each other in silence for a moment.

'What's he like, this fella?' said Nick to Julie. 'He's full of good ideas, isn't he?'

'Sometimes right, sometimes wrong but always certain, that's my, admittedly, unoriginal motto,' said Jeff. 'But here's another idea...what about this? Someone buys the dodgy art at a low price, knowing it's dodgy, then insures it as though it's the real thing, then loses it or has it stolen, and makes a big claim on the insurance and thus makes a tonne of money.'

'That is bloody good...bloody good,' said Julie, sitting forward and pointing at him. 'And I'll tell you why...we know Jimmy Repp bought them and guess what, his house has just gone up in flames this morning, burnt to a fucking cinder along with all the art.'

'Sarge suggested a theory along those lines too. Said Repp was doing an insurance scam. And when you called me about the fire, that was the first thing I thought, that Jimmy or Frankie has torched the place to get rid of evidence of the fakes,' said Nick.

'A fire? Well that's not a coincidence,' said Jeff, sitting up and shaking his head. 'We've got two potential scenarios here - one has Emmy Green as the killer, or someone she's employing as a killer, and the second has Repp or his manager doing the murdering. If it's the latter, Emmy Green must be in the cross-hairs now because she sold the pictures to Jimmy and knows about the fakes because, if Myra is to be believed, she organised it all. So she's got to be silenced as well.' Jeff sat back and took a big drink.

'Which begs the question...why wasn't she the first to get killed?' asked Nick. 'She was surely the first point of contact and it all stemmed from her. I still think Emmy is the killer because if this gets out, she's ruined.'

Julie put on a floppy straw hat to shade her eyes from the bright afternoon sun and said: 'Very good point, that. She'd be the one who went to jail for fraud. Myra would probably get a fine or a short sentence but it was Emmy who made the fraudulent transaction and took millions of Repp's money under false pretences. She was the go-between. She stands to lose most if the news got out, not least because Frankie Gray would come after her.'

'Only if it really was false pretences though,' said Jeff, his finger raised again. 'Can I remind you that we don't actually know she misrepresented the art to Repp, in which case, has any crime actually been committed until the buyers try to pass it on as a genuine Phyllis Plant when they know it's not? The answer, my good-looking friends, is no.'

'But someone has got something to protect or we wouldn't have two murders on our hands,' said Julie.

They went quiet and Jeff sank the second pint. 'Aye, it's not straightforward this is it? Was everything lost in that fire then?'

'Yeah man it was all toast. Huge fire,' said Nick. 'Nothing will be left of his art collection.'

'Well, nothing if he had them stored there,' said Jeff. 'Remember, he may have conveniently stored the real pictures elsewhere recently and just burned the fakes. You saw them at that party didn't you?'

'Yeah.'

'Were they real?'

'I wouldn't have a clue. They were all signed. But they could have been fakes for all we knew.'

'Hiding in plain view, it's an old trick. He hangs a load of fakes and everyone is a witness to them, thinking they're genuine.'

'Good idea man. I never thought of that, I like it,' said Nick.

'That's because you are not fuelled by Stella Artois's finest medicine. It's brain food.'

Julie laughed. 'That's funny because some of the most stupid things I've ever done in my life have been under the influence of Stella.'

'It's not a medicine that works on everyone,' he said, modestly.

'You'd better get another one out of the fridge then because there's another thing we need to work out.'

He soon returned with two more cans.

'Right, what's this other thing?'

'I didn't tell you about this,' said Nick, 'because I didn't want word of it getting out, so you've got to keep it to yourself.'

'I don't know anyone to tell, except Luke in the shop.'

Nick explained about Pinky's kidnap.

Jeff sat back and made no comment.

'Pinky set it up with her old boyfriend Finlay to get a million quid out of Jimmy,' said Julie.

'Do they know that you know?'

'I met Finlay at the Boro shop and he knows I know it was him on the phone. I could see it in his eyes. He knew, alright.'

'Hmmm...seems straightforward then. She's cashing in her chips with Jimmy and preparing to jump ship with as much of his cash in her pockets at possible. Would she benefit from the insurance money from the fire? If so, she might have started the fire herself.'

'I wondered that. She was pretty unemotional, but then they'd just moved in not long since so maybe she wasn't attached to it,' said Julie.

'Yeah and she's a hard kid,' said Nick.

'Hardwick lass, you said? Well there you go then,' said Jeff.

'Hey watch your mouth son, I'm a Hardwick lass, remember.'

'Aye but that's what I mean, you're a tough breed aren't you? Your brothers used to scare the shit out of me when I was a kid.'

'You should have tried living with them,' she said under her breath.

'They were round here the other night. They're still scary,' said Nick with a snort. 'They brought a gun around.'

'A gun? What the fuck for?' said Jeff.

'Protection,' said Julie. 'I'm not having some fucker shooting me or Nick and, lest we forget, someone is out there killing people. We need to be able to defend ourselves and I'm not taking any chances. One thing growing up on the estate taught me was that in times of trouble, you go hard or go home.'

'But what if you're already at home? Can you still go hard?' said Jeff.

'Don't be a smartarse, you know what I mean,' said Julie.

'And lo...we are now tooled up,' said Nick.

'I'd better not upset you then,' said Jeff. 'I don't want you to go hard in my face.'

'We're not going to use it unless we have to,' said Julie, narrowing her eyes in annoyance. 'I don't have bloodlust; I just want to have some protection. I think it's sensible.'

As she spoke Nick heard a car turn off the road and down the track to the farmhouse. It was nearly half a mile away but it was so quiet that any change to the background noise was detectable.

'Sounds like we've got a visitor,' said Nick, getting up.

'Careful,' said Julie, urgency in her voice, 'you don't know who it is.'

Jeff stood up, walked around the side of the house and took a look down the track.

'It's a big silver Merc I reckon. Who do you know drives a Merc?'

'Bollocks to this, I'm not hiding like some fucking scared rabbit every time we get a visitor,' said Nick, following Jeff.

Julie threw off her floppy hat and ran into the house to get the gun.

'Come on big man,' said Nick, gesturing with his head for Jeff to follow him, 'let's see who this is.'

Jeff grabbed his half-full pint glass and followed him.

'A big silver Merc was seen at Myra's studio around the time she disappeared,' said Nick.

'Interesting.'

Nick stood at the front of the house and watched the car approach, his arms folded across his chest. A kestrel swooped in the sky above them as it came to a halt. Now he could see the driver clearly. She was alone. Fucking hell. It was Emmy Green.

'Who is it?' said Jeff out of the corner of his mouth.

'The agent,'

'Fuck. Seriously? I'll glass her in the face if she even looks like she's going to pull a gun on us, right?'

'Gotcha big man. You glass her; I'll kick her fucking head in.'

He rubbed his damp palms on his jeans, adrenaline prickling in his veins. What the hell was she doing here? How did she even know where they lived?

Nick stepped forward as she opened her car door and got out.

'Hello Nick,' she said with a smile, 'sorry to turn up unannounced like this.'

She was wearing an ecru tailored linen jacket, blue jeans and a white t-shirt which, though basic, somehow all looked very expensive. She wore a silver chain with a cross attached and small pearl earrings. All very understated, all very classy.

Nick swallowed hard. This was ridiculous; you can't live your life wondering if someone is going to shoot you. If it bloody happens it bloody happens. Walking side by side with death is the human gig, anyway. He held out his right hand.

'Hello Emmy. Nice to see you. I didn't know I'd given you our address.'

She shut the car door, looked around her and back up the track. Was she checking to see if there was any way for anyone to see what she was about to do? Jeff drained his glass and held it out from his body, ready to use as a weapon. He was one stride from her, ready to smash it into her face. Nick was on his toes and ready for action.

She shook his hand with a soft, dry, weak grip.

'I'm sorry, you didn't give me the address, I picked it up from Jimmy Repp a couple of days ago. I hope you don't mind. I didn't have a contact number or e-mail for you and I really thought we should talk because of what's happened. He couldn't find your number either but he told me where you lived. This is a good spot. So quiet.'

A good spot for what? For shooting someone?

Nick looked at her through narrowed eyes. She was fucking lying. Jimmy had his number and his e-mail address but almost certainly didn't know where they lived, not exactly anyway. His new address was on his business cards – he'd given one to Pinky but not Emmy or Jimmy.

Jeff stood alongside him, turning the glass around in his hand.

'Yeah we like it here. Why don't you come around the back, we were just having a drink. This is my pal Jeff, you remember him from Harrogate?'

'Yes, hello again Jeff. Nice to meet you again,' she said in her accent-less voice. If she was a killer she was a very polite killer.

'Take a seat,' said Nick, gesturing to a chair around the table. Julie was looking out of the kitchen window. He gestured to her to come out. Did Emmy have a gun? Certainly not a rifle. Was a sniper somewhere else? He looked around to see where someone might take cover. Open fields made it almost impossible. There was a track running through some woodland and that would be good cover.

'So where do you live, Emmy?' said Jeff. 'Down in Harrogate?'

'No, I live in on the outskirts of Northallerton. I grew up in North Yorkshire actually. I moved away for 20 years but came back in 2004.'

As she spoke, Julie came out of the house with a tea tray, teapot and cups.

'Hello. I thought you might like some tea,' she said with a nice smile for the visitor. 'I'm Julie, Nick's partner.' She put the tray down and shook hands with her.

'Thanks Jules,' said Nick, looking to see where she was concealing the gun. He couldn't tell.

They sat in silence for fully five seconds. It seemed more like five minutes.

'So what brings you to our door, Emmy?' asked Nick, getting impatient and not enjoying the tension at all.

The kestrel zoomed out of the sky again in a plunging arc, swooping to catch a bird on the wing but missing out.

'Yes...well...obviously you'll be aware of the absolutely terrible...err...things that have happened to Myra and Lisa....poor girls....I can hardly believe it...it's been such a shock...well...I'm worried that I might be next to be honest with you...I mean, I worked with both of them.'

She let out a nervous noise that was half a laugh and half a sigh. Her right hand shook a little as she held her tea mug to her lips.

'Yeah, well, it's shocked all of us,' said Nick.

'I just don't understand it. I don't understand why they were murdered. It doesn't make any sense to me. I know you were friendly with Lisa, did she say anything to you about being in trouble or someone being out to get her, or anything at all like that? The police haven't even called me yet.'

'I'm sure they will soon enough,' said Nick.

'I'm happy to help if I can but I simply don't have a clue about anything like that...I mean...I work in the world of art, it's hardly a rough world, let alone a...a...murderous, violent world. I just want to make sense of it. Both of them were such lovely people and so talented. Have you any idea who might be responsible?'

The lines and creases around her eyes were deep scars into her mottled pink flesh. She looked genuinely distressed. It certainly didn't look fake. As she talked she fiddled with her fingers, intertwining them, rubbing them and then gripping them tightly as though to try and calm her nerves.

Julie looked at her over the rim of her cup with hard eyes, clearly assessing whether she was genuine.

'No. She didn't say anything to me about being in danger,' said Nick, non-committedly. 'Could it be something to do with their art? It's obviously what they have in common.' He saw Jeff raise an eyebrow.

'I have wondered that. But I can't think what.'

'Maybe someone felt they'd been cheated, somehow,' added Julie, 'paid too much for pictures or something.'

Emmy Green looked from side to side as though trying to actually see the answer.

'Well I suppose so....but murder? I mean...really? I can't imagine that. I just can't. And I'd have heard of any dispute. I sold their art. Anyone who was disgruntled would have come to me first and there's been nothing at all.'

Nick rubbed at his beard growth and took a drink of tea from the white china mug. Fuck it. There was no point in skirting around this any longer. What was it Jules had said, go hard or go home? It was time to try going hard.

'Look Emmy, Lisa told me about the fakes Myra had been doing for you so I think it's a bit rich you coming around here pretending otherwise...clearly, someone was disgruntled at your...shall we call it an arrangement? They were killed because of your scam. Either they were murdered because someone was pissed off at being robbed or to keep them quiet. You probably know more than me.'

He sat back with his arms folded across his chest. Julie shifted her weight in her seat, leaning to one side slightly.

Jeff got up and cleared his throat. 'Well this is a bit awkward isn't it? More lager is the answer, I reckon,' he said heading into the kitchen for more cans.

The art agent looked at Nick with an odd expression and let out a nervous laugh.

'I'm sorry...say that again...I don't understand what you mean...w-what do you mean?'

Her mouth was slightly agape, a blank look of apparent incomprehension in her eyes.

Nick glanced at Julie. She opened her eyes wide at him, as though in surprise.

'Myra told Lisa she'd been doing Phyllis Plant fakes for you to sell to people like Jimmy Repp.'

'What? No, no, no, no...that's...that's...just not true. Fakes? No, no, no...I wouldn't do such a thing, no!'

Her confusion was quickly replaced with indignation as the accusation sank in.

'I am not dishonest! I have a long reputation in the art business. I wonder never do that!' Her cheeks were flushed now. 'You must believe me. I have no idea why she would say that...she...she must have been joking.'

'Lisa didn't take it as a joke. I met her after Myra had gone missing and Lisa was really worried because she couldn't get in touch with her. She'd been drinking with her, Myra had bought some new furniture and had money for the first time in a long time and told her all about it. She was supposed to be going to Middlesbrough to see a gallery owner called Grace Edwards the day she disappeared. Do you know a Grace Edwards?'

Emmy Green shook her head.

'After she'd disappeared, me and Lisa went to her studio and talked to neighbours and it seemed like there'd been some sort of struggle and she'd been driven away in a big expensive car, a silver Merc, a neighbour said, a silver Merc like yours, Emmy. I also found a mother of pearl button there – I notice the buttons on your blouse are mother of pearl as well...so you see Emmy, I'm wondering what this is all about.'

He tried to talk calmly and not gabble his words.

She looked at him with her face set in total shock. He was sure she wasn't faking and he was still sure she wasn't faking as she reached into the inside pocket of her jacket and pulled out something small, metallic and silver.

Julie leapt up, kicked over the table and screamed.

'Drop it now or I'll kill you! Don't fuck around, I'll do it. Drop the gun!'

Julie's pistol had been tucked down her trouser band at the back. In one move she had stood up, kicked over the table and drawn the gun, and now stood, arms outstretched, braced to fire the weapon into Emmy Green's head.

Emmy Green screamed and half stood as though to run, but she was so scared her legs wouldn't support her and she fell onto the grass making yelping noises. As she went down, she dropped a lighter from her left hand. It was big enough to look like the handle of a gun, but it wasn't a gun. It was a bloody lighter.

Nick picked it up and showed it to Julie. 'It's a Zippo Jules, calm down and put the gun away, eh.'

'If we're playing at Starsky and Hutch shouldn't someone be wearing a big cardigan?' said Jeff, coming out of the kitchen with two cans of lager and a clean glass and looking with bemusement at the agent on the ground and Julie holding the gun.

Emmy Green burst into tears and was shaking in fear. Nick pulled up the table and the chairs. Two of the mugs were broken and the teapot lay on its side on the grass. Bloody hell. He leaned down to help her up.

'Come on Emmy, calm down. Everything's okay. We were just worried that...well...you understand. Jules, can you get another brew on to settle her down?'

He helped her onto her chair. All colour had drained from her face and her hands were shaking.

'I ...I was just going light a cigarette...that's all,' she said, almost with a whimper. 'I'm not a murderer...honestly, I'm not.'

Jeff sat back down and opened a beer while Julie went into the kitchen.

'Well, well, well... this is all some fun and games, eh, but we can all take some comfort in the fact that no beer was spilt in this fracas...that is the important thing...cheers!' He beamed at them from behind his beard.

After half an hour and a fresh cup of tea, Emmy had recovered her composure enough to talk.

'So what you're telling me is that the art you sold for Myra was her original work and not Phyllis Plant copies?' said Nick.

'Yes. I've only sold a few pieces of hers anyway. She's very talented...she was very talented, rather, but it somehow fell between two stools commercially: a little too literal for modern art lovers but a little too modern for traditionalists. This spring I sold three of a series she did called *Nature Studies* to the corporate headquarters of a flower seed merchant in Spalding for a thousand pounds. I haven't sold anything else, whereas there's always a big demand for Lisa's best work. She was on her way to being a very wealthy woman. I had sold nearly £250,000 of her work this year already and I could have sold more.'

'So when Myra talked about painting fakes for you, was she just taking the piss?' asked Jeff. 'She really didn't get the money from you?'

'Wherever she got it from it wasn't from me, I assure you. The Phyllis Plants I sold Jimmy Repp were from a private collection that was being broken up and sold off. They are 100% genuine. They were all checked and verified by an independent assessor before being insured by Briggs & Sons, as Jimmy's people insisted - rightly so - and that was before any money even changed hands. Those PPs Jimmy Repp bought are all provably genuine. I swear to you. You don't have to rely on my say-so, they were independently assessed. Whatever Myra said, I didn't sell any fakes to Jimmy. I only came here to try and find out if you had any idea who might have killed the girls. I might also say for the record that I did pick her up from her studio that lunchtime, yes...yes I did. But only to take her to the station. I'd dropped in to say hello as I was in town but she was in a rush to leave so I drove her to the station. She was going to Middlesbrough just as you say. But I left her at York station. That was the last time I saw the poor girl and I don't know anything about a button. I suppose it could have been mine.'

'Well, they *were* all genuine works of art, but now they're genuine works of ash,' said Jeff.

'What do you mean?'

'Jimmy Repp had a massive house fire this morning. The whole place was burnt to the ground, including the gallery. So I'm afraid they're no more.'

'Oh good God. What next? How dreadful. Was anyone hurt?'

'Thankfully, no,' said Julie.

'So I hope that insurance was comprehensive - who was it with did you say?' asked Nick.

'Briggs & Sons in Leeds. Good God, what a bloody waste,' said Emmy, shaking her head in disbelief and lighting a cigarette. 'All that art, gone.' She rubbed her face with her hands. 'What caused the fire? Does anyone know?'

'Too early to know,' said Julie.

'Well I don't know what to say. This is all so terrible. Myra, Lisa, the art...what on earth is going on? I can see now why you might have thought I was involved, but do you or the police have any other suspects?'

170

Nick didn't want to discuss any more theories, even though he was now sure she wasn't involved in the murders.

'No, not really Emmy. If I hear anything, I'll let you know. One thing though. You were at Pinky's mother's house recently. Why did you go there and how did you know her address?'

She swallowed and looked a little perturbed at the question, shocked that he knew of the visit.

'One of my artists wanted a nude life model, a small girl, blonde, and I thought of Pinky after meeting her with Jimmy when we did the PP deal. I found the address in the phone book.'

'You didn't think to ring Jimmy and ask to speak to her?'

'Oh well...no...or at least, I sort of had the impression she spent a lot of time at her mother's. I also didn't know how he'd feel about this sort of thing. Not everyone wants their partner to be a nude model. I thought it diplomatic to ask her directly so I found her in the phone book. There is only one Gull family on Teesside.'

It was a plausible enough excuse.

'Are you okay to drive home now?' asked Julie.

She got up. 'Yes, yes, I'm fine now, thank you. Please do keep me up to date. I'm so upset about Myra and Lisa and I want someone to pay for what they've done. I shall tell the police everything I know when they get in touch which, I assume, they will.'

Nick gave her a wave as she drove off.

As he returned to the table at the back of the house, Julie and Jeff were laughing.

'We were just saying, that poor woman nearly shit herself when I pulled out the gun. She actually lost the use of her legs. I'm not that scary, am I?'

'No but the gun is...still, it was the best test. She's clearly not a killer. I think I believed almost everything she said.'

'I don't reckon she could squash a spider, let alone shoot two women she knew,' said Jeff.

'She lied about how she got our address though and she lied about why she was at Maggie's house,' said Julie. 'Her tone changed

171

when she talked about that. She tried to be more casual and relaxed and it sounded like over-compensation to me.'

'Yeah, the big lie is why she really went to the Gull house. I thought she lied about that as well. Must be significant in some way even if only obliquely,' said Jeff.

'She went there to see Pinky and got our address from her, that's what I think.' said Nick.

Julie got up and went inside.

'Well fuck me it's been a hell of a day between meeting Sarge, the house fire, and Emmy Green,' said Nick, puffing out his cheeks.

'Enough to drive you to drink?' said Jeff, pushing a can towards him.

'Very tempting but I'll pass.'

'I'll pass it too in.... about half an hour.' said Jeff, pouring more beer into his glass.

Julie came back out holding a telephone directory.

'Emmy Green might not be a killer but she's definitely a lying cow. She didn't get the Gulls' number out of the phonebook because they're not even listed!'

CHAPTER 11

After midnight, Nick and Julie lay in bed in the darkness. There was a faint rumble from the other side of the house where Jeff was fast asleep and snoring in a spare room.

'I don't want to sound like a snooty cow and I know he's a big bloke but the amount he drinks isn't healthy for anyone,' she said. 'He's had 16 cans of Stella. Sixteen! I looked in the fridge, there's only eight left. He had five of those in the first hour or so. It's incredible. Doesn't he care about his health?'

'There's no telling him. He loves it too much. He could have drunk the lot.'

'God help his liver. I mean really, it's beyond a joke.'

He sighed heavily.

'You sound tense,' she said.

'I am. My mind is racing but I'm too tired to think anymore. My head's gone all woolly. All I can think of is you leaping up and pulling out that gun.'

'Good, wasn't it? I almost wish I'd been able to let a few rounds rip. I was bloody sure she was going to pull out one of those small lady pistols.'

'I'm just glad you didn't shoot her. I'd be no good at prison visits, all that smuggling of drugs and tobacco up my arse, I'd be rubbish at that.'

They went quiet for a couple of minutes.

'I wish Lisa was still alive. I still can't believe she's been murdered. It keeps hitting me. I keep hearing her voice the last time I saw her. She desperately wanted to find out who had killed Myra, she said it was her duty, and now I feel like it's my duty to find out who killed her, you know?'

'Yeah but you're really not obliged. It's the police's job. They'll find out, I'm sure.'

'But I just keep hearing her voice.'

Fuck them up Nick, fuck them up. There it was again, in the silent night.

An owl hooted.

'I can't just wait for the police to do their job, Jules. I can't. I've got to be more proactive than that. I feel like if I don't do this, I'm letting her down. I went down to York to help her find Myra and now I've got to find out who killed her.'

He sat up in bed and ran his hands through his hair.

'It's doing my bloody head in, man. I know it seems stupid...'

He put his head in his hands in an attempt to try and protect himself from his thoughts. She sat up alongside him and put on the bedside light.

'No, it makes sense to me and I'll tell you another thing that makes sense, the sooner we find out who the killer is, the safer I'll feel and we can give the bloody gun back to Ricky.'

'So you're with me?'

'Of course I am. Always.'

She put her hand to his face and lightly kissed him. 'Everything will be alright, luv.'

After a breakfast of kippers and scrambled eggs, Nick called Briggs & Sons. They were a big company based in Leeds who specialised in art insurance.

'Hi there, I have some valuable paintings that I'd like to insure,' he said. He was a good liar when he needed to be. The key was to believe what you said, so now he was a rich man with an art collection to insure. It was a role to play. He sometimes felt he'd missed his vocation on the stage.

He was put through to someone called Greg Phillips who, in calm, measured tones, explained the procedure.

'I understand you have the art independently assessed before insuring,' said Nick.

'Indeed, we will have your collection assessed for authenticity and valued accordingly.'

'I see, and is that done in-house.'

'Where are you located, Mr Guymer?'

'Teesside.'

'Ah well it'd be Simon Harrison. He handles all our Yorkshire and north-east valuations.'

'And he's totally independent?'

'Totally, yes. It's his speciality. He's been doing this for 40 years now. He has his areas of expertise, of course, but he's incredibly knowledgeable in all areas of art. Can I ask the nature of your collection?'

'It's mostly modern art sketches and paintings. I'm a big fan of Phyllis Plant and have a few of hers.'

'Ah yes. Well that is actually Simon's area of interest...mid-20th Century art.'

'Great. Okay, I will be in touch soon to get things underway,' he said, rang off and entered Simon Harrison's name into Google. He had his own website advertising his services as an art valuer. His picture showed an owlish man with bushy eyebrows and fuzzy, thinning hair, the sort of man that appeared to belong to 1907 not 2007. His offices were in Masham in North Yorkshire, a small market town and the home of the Black Sheep brewery.

'Fancy a trip out Jules?'

She nodded. 'Where are we going?'

'Masham.'

'Isn't it Mash-am, like mashed potato, not Mass-am?'

'The locals call it Mass-am. This valuer bloke has his offices there. I want to find out what he made of those Phyllis Plants that Emmy sold to Jimmy. Surely if they were fakes, an expert should have been able to tell.'

'But we already know that they weren't fakes, Emmy said so and I'm pretty certain she wasn't lying, if only because she knew I had a gun in my hand.'

'That's true but all that tells us is that she *thought* they were genuine. She was telling us the truth as she saw it. That doesn't mean it's the actual truth, does it?' said Nick.

'But he obviously thinks they were genuine or he'd not have given

175

them his stamp of approval,' said Julie.

'Aye, but we want to know for sure that he did. We've only her word about that and we know she's prone to lying for reasons unknown. Anyway, he could be in on the insurance scam for a cut of the pay-out after the fire. He'd be the one to get on your side, so I'd like to know when he saw them and how it fits into the timeline of the pictures up to the fire yesterday.'

Jeff appeared in the doorway, a mass of tangled hair dressed in a voluminous tie-dyed Grateful Dead Skullfuck t-shirt.

'Good God you look like a big fucked-up psychedelic bear,' laughed Nick.

'But in a good way, right?' Jeff said, scratching himself.

'There's a bacon sarnie under the grill for you. We're off to Masham to see a man about paintings, do you want to come?'

'Masham? Oh yes, beauty, I can have a drop of Riggwelter at the brewery.'

'Jeff man, haven't you had enough beer for a day or two? You had 16 pints yesterday,' said Julie.

He bit into the sandwich, shaking his head.

'It's all part of my libertine lifestyle. This is bloody lovely by the way. Smoked bacon and mustard. Baby you know what I like.'

'He's been like this since he was 16, there's no changing him now,' said Nick.

She shook her head. 'I know but I don't want him to get ill.'

'He knows what he's doing,' said Nick, who had long since reconciled himself to Jeff's 'everything all the time' lifestyle.

'Hey, hey, I'm still here,' he waved at them. 'I can hear you. And for your information, I am thinking about going on a diet. Only thinking about it, mind. Maybe give this low-carb thing a go, seems to have been good for you.'

'You should. You'll feel much healthier,' said Julie, trying desperately to sound encouraging rather than patronising.

'That means no beer though,' said Nick. 'You'll have to go on the shorts.'

'I can do that. Drop of gin or brandy would go down nicely. You haven't got any, have you? Just joking…it's not ten yet, give it half an hour.'

He finished off the sandwich. 'Right I'm ready. Masham here we come. I'll buy youse two a meal in the King's Head in return for all that lager, since you were counting, like.'

They went south on the A19, taking the A684 through Northallerton and across the A1 to Bedale, first through rolling Yorkshire farmland and later into higher, rougher terrain before dropping into the village of Masham.

'Can't be many villages that have two breweries and two bloody lovely breweries at that,' said Jeff from the back seat of Nick's old BMW.

'Didn't we used to drink Theakston's Old Peculiar in that pub in Hartburn village when we were in the sixth form?' said Nick.

'It was actually called The Masham if you remember…aye, that was out of bottles though, not on draught. Lovely stuff. Mind, Black Sheep is every bit as good.'

They parked in the large, broad, flat marketplace around which the village was built for the 1200 souls who lived there. Masham had an airy, slow-paced vibe. Neither upmarket and snobby nor downmarket and desolate, it had always been one of Nick's favourite Yorkshire villages.

Jeff cracked his knuckles. 'Right, I'm off to the Black Sheep brewery, maybe take their tour. I'll meet you in the King's Head.'

Simon Harrison's offices were in an 18th Century building with small, narrow doors and a low roof. As soon as they were inside, they recognised him from the photo on the website sitting behind a large, green leather-topped desk in one corner. He didn't look up from his computer as they went in; instead they were greeted by a bearded younger man.

'Good morning,' said Nick.

'Hi. How can I help?' said the bearded man.

'We'd like to talk to Simon about assessing some Phyllis Plant works of art.'

As he spoke, Simon Harrison looked up, as though his ears were permanently attuned to the mention of an artist's name. He came over, academic in appearance, short, rotund and well into his 60s.

'Can I help?' he said. 'I'm Simon Harrison.'

They shook hands.

'Hi Simon, yes, as I was saying, we have some art we'd like you to value for insurance purposes,' said Nick.

'Very good. I can arrange to view it at your convenience,' he said, looking from Nick to Julie and then back to Nick.

'Great. You were actually recommended to us by a friend of a friend who said you'd valued the Phyllis Plant pictures Jimmy Repp acquired. For Briggs' insurance.'

'Oh yes indeed. Mr Repp has a fine collection. Very fine indeed.' He smiled.

'Yes, so I understand, though I'm told there was some doubt about the authenticity.'

Harrison frowned. 'Really? I wasn't aware of that. He didn't mention anything of that sort.'

'Yes, that's what I heard. But you were happy with them?'

'Oh yes. Very straightforward. These were well-documented artworks that came from the Thomas Charlesworth collection when it was broken up and sold last year. An agent worked as an intermediary – a Ms Green, as I recall. She brought the relevant parties together. Charlesworth had bought them directly from Phyllis Plant's studio in the 30s and 40s and 50s. Unimpeachable as regards authenticity before one even viewed them and on inspection there was absolutely no doubt at all. Not for a moment.'

He spoke fluently and with the substantial self-confidence of a man well-paid to give his opinion.

'Did you see them in Jimmy's gallery at his house?'

'Yes indeed. First I saw them alongside Ms Green at the Charlesworth estate in Surrey just to check they were worth the substantial money about to be paid. Then I saw them again in Yarm just a couple of weeks ago now and it was there that I made my final valuation for Briggs. No damage had been done in transit and they were hung in a lovely gallery at Mr Repp's house, so it was all fairly routine and straightforward. An impressive and important collection, I must say.'

'Do you come across many fakes Mr Harrison?' asked Julie.

'It does happen, yes,' he nodded, 'but not often. The press always make a big fuss when someone forges something but that's very much the exception. For example, I think I've seen one forged Lowry in the last ten years. More usual are unsigned pictures that have been wrongly assigned to an artist, which is quite a different thing of course.'

'We're quite new to all of this - I must say I did wonder if insurance fraud was commonplace when it came to artwork,' said Nick.

'Fraud?'

'I mean insuring something as though it's an original when you know it's a good copy and then making a claim as though it was an original.'

Harrison shook his head firmly. 'No, it's rather hard to do that, really. Much harder than fiddling general insurance because other professionals, such as myself, a gallery, the seller and an agent, may also be involved, especially if it's highly valued art. It would need to be a conspiracy between all parties and even then, any insurance pay-out on damaged or stolen pictures is exceptionally rigorous. It's not like claiming on your insurance for stolen luggage. They go through it like a dose of salts. Even straightforward cases take a long time to resolve when millions are involved.'

He took out a small appointments diary. 'Now are you local? When would be suitable? I'm free next Wednesday.'

'Oh I'm a bit busy for a few days. Can I call you next week and arrange matters then?' said Nick. 'I just wanted to touch base with you for now.'

'Yes, yes, fine. You have my number? Good '

Outside in the marketplace, Nick took Julie's hand and they walked towards the King's Head pub. It was a glorious blue sky summer morning.

'Well he seemed like a sensible sort of bloke, but more importantly, what he said was right, anything dodgy would have to be co-ordinated across several people or it would be discovered. I hadn't thought of it like that before. That made a lot of sense. It doesn't mean it can't happen but it means it's a lot less likely, I reckon,' said Nick. 'He could be bent and be working with Emmy, but if he was, they'd never have involved the Charlesworth estate in the story because it'd be too easy to check with them if Repp had or hadn't bought the pictures.'

'He smelled weird, that bloke. Like ear wax and mothballs all rolled into one. But yeah, what he said did make sense. And it means we know the paintings Emmy bought were genuine. He checked them before and after they were purchased.'

'You know, the more I think about it, the more I reckon Myra *was* taking the piss when she told Lisa she'd been doing forgeries. We know Emmy and Simon Harrison both think they were genuine pictures with rock-solid provenance. We know Jimmy bought those pictures. There were no fakes in her studio, no pile of work with false signatures or anything like that. So why are we believing she did?'

'Well, because of what Lisa Lambert said - that's the only reason,' said Julie.

'Lisa was convinced by the story, that's true, but she didn't have any proof either. It was all down to Myra's word and nothing else. Even if Emmy was corrupt or stupid or easily conned, this bloke here wouldn't be. He'd ruin his reputation and knacker his business if he didn't spot a whole host of fakes either before or after purchase. I mean, he did his work on this – he didn't just spend ten minutes looking at them. Those pictures Jimmy bought were definitely genuine whether they went up in the fire or not...when he bought them, they were the real deal.'

The King's Head was a fine old Georgian hotel but it was the sort of pub that somehow didn't suit the smoking ban. It still looked and felt like a smoky bar. Perhaps it was simply associative thought. After a lifetime sitting in such old places with your eyes streaming in the thick blue fug, it was impossible to divorce the experience of one from the other.

They ordered coffee and looked at the menu. As it was only 11.30, only one hardened drinker was in, a man who looked older than time sitting at the bar sipping a pint of ruby-coloured bitter.

'I don't really want to start drinking again but you've got to say, sitting in an old bar like this, stocked to the gills with great locally brewed beer, it makes me half-wish I was still a boozer,' said Nick.

'You can have a drink if you want. I can drive us back.'

'Nah I'll pass. But it seems weird drinking coffee in a place like this, don't you think? Okay in a flash modern bar but in here somehow coffee seems a bit fancy and modern and inappropriate and they give you these squat, thick little cups - why can't we have a nice big china mug? Can't they learn from the big coffee chains? It just means adding extra water.'

'This is Yorkshire, remember. They don't give you owt fer nowt,' said Julie in a broad North Riding accent. 'Mind, how middle-class are you complaining about the cups? Menu looks decent though. What you having?'

'Liver and onions should hit the spot.'

'We used to have liver every week when I was a kid.'

'Well it was cheap, wasn't it?'

'It must have been or mam wouldn't have bought it.'

'Trouble is, offal is just another working-class thing that's been co-opted by the middle-class into rustic, artisanal food. It's like duffel coats and names like Alf - all good working-class things which the middle-class have colonised.'

'Class politics and food - you should write about that.'

As he spoke, Jeff came in, gave them an outlandish wave and ordered himself two pints of Theakston's Old Peculiar.

'Now then my pretties, excuse me while I tickle my tonsils with this liquid orgasm.'

'Liquid orgasm? Nicer than orgasm liquid, at least,' said Julie.

'Oh man...oh God that is beer from the God of Beer. Who is the God of Beer?'

'The god of wine is Bacchus so the god of beer must be Vaux,' said Nick.

'Is it?'

'No I made that up.'

'Bastard. Sounded right an' all. So did you find out anything at the boy Harrison's?'

'He seemed straight up and down. Said all the art was bona fide. I was just saying that Myra has to have been bullshitting Lisa about the fakes. We've no actual evidence she ever actually painted any. So the latest theory which we're almost totally sure about until the next time we change our minds is that Jimmy bought genuine pictures.'

Jeff sank the pint in three more gulps.

'I'd better order you a new pancreas for dinner,' said Nick.

'Leave off. I'm a growing boy...largely due to necking so much ale, admittedly. Now what's for dinner?'

'I'm having liver.'

'Pervert. What are you having Jules?'

'The salmon.'

'The lady goes for the pink fishy. Okay. Some sort of roast pig meat will do me....right, so this Myra woman, she's been spinning this line about being a forger. Why would she do that?'

'That's what I don't get,' said Julie. 'If she wasn't doing fakes then why say she was?'

'She was a pisshead,' said Nick, 'there doesn't have to be any logic behind it. She just made it up for a laugh.'

Jeff shook his head and raised his index finger. 'Nah, that wouldn't happen. A decent drunk would come up with something better than that. It's not a big enough lie. Not flash enough, especially as it is basically an admission that you can't get anyone to buy your own work.'

'That was her political statement. That art is all about the signature and not the picture,' said Nick.

'Yeah and it's a great point but really, that's old news isn't it? I know sod all about art but even I know that the signature sells. And she did have an unusual amount of money so she must have got that from somewhere.'

'I'm inclined to agree,' said Julie. 'She told a lie to hide the truth from Lisa.'

'I'd fucking love to have five minutes with the scumbag that killed Lisa, see if I can beat the evil out of him,' said Jeff.

'...or her,' said Julie.

'Eh?'

'...what makes you think it's a bloke that killed her?'

'It's always a bloke, isn't it? There's not many lady killers around, not even on Teesside,' said Jeff.

'No but we don't need many, we only need one. I'm just putting it out there so we don't assume a gender and then end up getting ambushed by a woman.'

The waiter brought their food and Jeff ordered himself more beer.

'Okay, let's just go over everything again, so we can get a few things straight about Myra and Lisa's murders,' said Nick, eating his liver and onions. 'There's the whole issue of the fake paintings, which we now think is a red herring, but Myra got money from something dodgy and that seems to have been what got her and then Lisa killed. We know both of them spoke to this Grace Edwards gallery owner shortly before they died but we don't know who she is or anything about her. From what Emmy said, Myra did go up to Middlesbrough to see her. Maybe Lisa did too. We now think Emmy's innocent of selling Jimmy fakes but she's still a liar and we don't know why. But we know Jimmy was buying more art than he could possibly afford on his wages and that he was probably match-fixing to pay for it.'

'On top of all that is Pinky's fake kidnap,' said Julie.

'Yeah but that's a side issue isn't it?' asked Jeff.

'No, it can't be…or rather, we can't assume it is. Jimmy had to cough up a million quid to her kidnappers and he did it without batting an eyelid so we can't divorce that from Jimmy's money issues, which means we can't divorce them from buying the Plant paintings and thus from Myra's claim that she was painting Plants to order. It's all related, including the fire…which I still think seems very convenient, but maybe I'm just being paranoid about that,' said Nick, finishing a cup of coffee.

'Well if someone started the fire, they'll find evidence of that won't they? I mean the fire people, like,' said Jeff.

'I actually can't see how it all knits together. I don't think it does,' said Julie, getting up to go to the toilet. 'I think it's two or three different threads that have somehow got entangled in our minds but which don't actually belong together.'

'It was a single shot to the head that killed both Myra and Lisa wasn't it?' said Jeff, his arms folded across his chest

'Yeah, though not at close range apparently. They were picked off with a rifle. That is pretty bloody ruthless.'

'And shows some pretty snazzy gun skills too. It's not just pulling out a gun and popping someone in anger. You've got to find your position, take aim and then to do it with a single shot; that's not something an amateur could do. It's also very premeditated. You've got to be tough to do that. Sounds professional,' said Jeff.

'Which makes me think of Frankie Gray. If anyone is a pro killer, it'd be him or someone he knows,' said Nick. 'Everyone else is an amateur in this scenario but he's a bona fide wide boy. He's a fixer.'

They settled the bill and were walking back towards the car when Nick noticed someone in the distance near the church, holding something to his face. As he turned to look more closely, the man seemed to realise he'd been spotted and quickly began walking away towards the churchyard in the corner of the marketplace. From behind he had close-cut grey hair, black jeans and t-shirt.

'Does he look familiar?' he asked, pointing.

They all looked as he disappeared from view.

'I didn't see him,' said Jeff.

'Yeah, hold on. Bloody hell...I think I know who that is,' said Julie. She sprinted off towards the church at speed.

'Bloody hell, she can shift,' said Jeff, watching her go. 'It must be those powerful thighs.'

'They are powerful, like. They've been getting a lot of exercise recently.'

'I bet they have.'

They watched her come to a halt by the churchyard wall and then walk out of view around the corner.

'He was staring at us - just standing there - and then he put something to his face, binoculars or a camera. And when I spotted him he turned and walked away quickly.'

Five minutes later she reappeared and sprinted back to them.

'Guess who it was,' she said between short, quick breaths.

' Was it Zal Cleminson, guitarist from The Sensational Alex Harvey Band?' suggested Jeff.

'Obviously not. No clown make-up,' said Julie, dismissively. 'It was Frankie Gray. I thought it was him right away.'

'Frankie Gray?! Fucking hell, we were just talking about him when you went to the bog. I don't like the sound of that. Did you catch up with him?' asked Nick.

'No, I kept my distance. I don't think he saw me. He was parked further down Millgate. The interesting thing is that he was carrying a camera with a massive lens.'

'Well it's a scenic place Masham, isn't it? People like to come here and take photos,' said Jeff.

'When I first saw him he was holding it up towards us, then as soon he knew I'd clocked him, he legged it,' said Nick.

'He wasn't photographing us, was he? Why would he do that? You're getting paranoid,' said Jeff, waving his hands around to dismiss the idea.

'It does sound paranoid but...I don't know man, it really looked like he was taking pictures of us and when he thought he was spotted he ran off. What do you think, Jules?'

'He wasn't just wandering off the way a tourist would, he was away and gone and had reached his car by the time I got from here to the church gate. But why he'd want to take a photo of us three, I can't imagine.'

Jeff raised his index finger. 'Alright, if you're both so sure, the only reason anyone takes pictures is to show someone else. He's not taking snaps of us for Vogue; it's for someone who doesn't know us. You hand over the photo and say, here you are, these are the people we want shooting...or whatever.'

'Bloody hell Jeff, on that happy fucking note, come on, let's go home,' said Nick.

CHAPTER 12

Early the next morning, Nick called Jimmy Repp's mobile.
'Jimmy?'
'Yeah?'
'It's Nick Guymer. How are you?'
'Hey Nick. Fine thank you.' Surely that wasn't true.
'How's pre-season training going?'
'Ah, it was tough, very tough but I've been given a couple of days off to sort out this fire business.'
'Where are you now?'
'I just got into my old suite at the Teesside International. The house is in ruins.'
'Yeah, that was terrible man. Did Pinky tell you we were there?
'Yes, she told me on the phone. Thanks for trying to help.'
'It was a hell of a fire. Was everything destroyed?'
'Everything...well almost everything but least it was only err...what do you say...err...things that got burnt, not people. Which is good. Such a shock though. I'm still totally amazed by what happened and I'd love to know how it started. All my art has gone, just like that. It's so sickening. All my plans have gone up in flames.'
'But that's why you have insurance, right?'
'Yeah, yeah, of course but you can't replace a one-off piece of art – it's gone forever. I've lost so many – I can't even think of opening the gallery now.'
'You must be gutted.'
'Yes, totally gutted, but what can I do? I've just got to carry on.'
'Yeah, that's the right attitude. Actually Jimmy, I was just wondering if we could meet up. Things are a bit quiet mid-summer so any interviews I can get are much appreciated. Any chance of half an hour of your time to discuss the new season and we could do a bit of human interest on the fire as well?'
'For you Nick, always, yeah. I need something to take my mind of

all this shit. When did you have in mind?'

'Are you free later today?'

'Sure, I'll be back by three. It's suite 112.'

'Thanks Jimmy, I appreciate that.'

Nick put the phone down as Julie poured him a mug of tea.

'He must be the nicest footballer I've ever spoken to. Even if he's up to no good, there's no faulting his manners. Even after a traumatic thing like the fire, he's still so polite,' he said.

'He's the sort of bloke I would have dated, you know. Back in the day, like.'

'Yeah?'

'Yeah, not obviously a big macho bloke but not a mincer either. Quite cultured but not snobby with it. Nice smile and hair.'

'Hmm...and very big hands, and you know what that means?'

'Nah, that's a myth, the big hands, big feet, big cock thing. I once went out with a bloke who had size 14 feet and a tiny cock.'

'I bow to your in-depth research.'

'And you've got quite small, dainty hands and size eight feet and...you know...the opposite downstairs, like.'

'Downstairs? You sound like my grandma.'

'Actually, that might have put me off him. His big hands, I mean. It'd be like getting pawed by a bear. But apart from that, like...he'd have been my kind of meat.'

He took the A66 out of Stockton to the Teesside International Hotel, a huge Georgian country house that had been converted into a posh hotel that specialised in conferences and ceremonies. It also accommodated footballers while they looked for a house to buy or who simply didn't plan on staying around long enough to invest in property.

Nick went straight to Jimmy's room on the first floor, walking up a grand curving staircase carpeted in plush purple red and blue swirling patterns.

'Hey Nick,' said Jimmy, opening the door of his suite with a warm smile. He held out his enormous mitt and dwarfed Nick's dainty fingers in a handshake.

'This is nice isn't it?' said Nick, walking into the high-ceilinged room which faced south across the hotel's grounds, the Pennines on the distant skyline.

'Yeah, they gave me my old room back. Ha. It's like I never left. Would you like a cup of tea or coffee?'

'No I'm okay thanks. Has Pinky moved back in too?' He looked around but could see no sign of anything pink or feminine.

'Ah no. She didn't want to. I think she took the fire badly. It really upset her. She's gone to stay at her mother's. Well, we haven't been getting on really, not since the party, that's the truth. It's sad.'

'Well, it's bound to be upsetting,' said Nick, sitting down on a large cream sofa, wondering if Pinky was actually with Finlay in Seaton and not in Hardwick at all.

'Will you thank Julie for being there for her...she's a great girl, Julie...I should have called you before now to say thank you. I know Pinky appreciated her support.'

Nick nodded. 'I'll pass that on. Did anything survive the fire? It was a hell of a blaze.'

'Well a few things, not much really.'

'Was all your art destroyed?'

'Yeah, I'm afraid so. I had pulled out one from the gallery after the party because I thought it needed a better frame, so it was the only thing that was saved. I just got it back this morning actually.'

He pointed to a picture covered in bubble wrap.

'The sculptures can be cleaned, and they're actually the most valuable items so all is not too...what is it...err...calamitous. But all those lovely PPs have gone...just like that...terrible.'

He clicked his fingers and gave Nick a vacant, shocked look.

'Do they know how it started yet?'

'No, they've got the fire department people doing forensics. I think it was faulty wiring in the sauna, and if it was I'm gonna sue the ass off the company that put that in. I need a full report for the insurance company too - they're going to be very thorough because it's such a big claim.'

'So nothing sinister then? You don't think it was done deliberately?'

Jimmy laughed a little. 'No. Who'd do that? No, I'm pretty sure it was an accident.'

'Julie seemed to think Pinky wasn't too upset about the fire. She was very calm.'

'Ah well, that's the kind of girl she is, you know. She likes to play the tough guy but underneath she's not so tough, not at all. She's been through a lot recently. The kidnapping really scared her. It's been a bad few days to say the least. We must get some good luck soon...maybe a good start to the season?'

'Kidnapping is a pretty bloody traumatic thing to happen to anyone. Has she talked much about it since?'

Jimmy sat down with a bottle of water on a large padded armchair and shook his head.

'No. Not really. I've not, you know...what to say...not pushed her about it. I figured she'd talk when she's ready. I'm just scared it happens again, I mean, they got the money once, what's to stop them doing it again? I wanted to get 24-hour security but she wouldn't hear of it and now she doesn't really want to be around me because, let's face it, shit things keep happening.'

'That's always the problem with paying kidnappers though, isn't it? There's always going to be someone else who sees it as easy money.'

'Frankie didn't want the police involved but I feel we should have told them, you know? But he was great. So cool. He handled it all so well. I didn't get a proper chance to thank you for your help, Nick. It was...well...thank you. I'm only sorry they pulled you into it all.'

He got up and pulled open a drawer.

'I went out earlier, once I knew you were coming...'

The Dutchman handed Nick a small black box with gold

lettering.

'...a little gift for you, just to say thank you. It can't have been easy for you having to talk to those bastards.'

'Ah man, there was no need to do that. It's not like I had a choice in the matter – they rung me and I answered.'

'Yeah I know...why you, I don't know. It must have been someone whose voice I would have recognised - that's what Frankie reckons anyway.'

More than you bloody well know, thought Nick as he opened the box. Inside was a Rolex watch. A bloody Rolex. Fucking hell.

'Jimmy man, this is too much, I can't accept this. It must have cost a fortune.'

'Nonsense, I'd be, you know, offended if you didn't take it. You helped me get my girl back safe. That's a bloody big thing, you know. A token of my...what is the way to say it...of my esteem. Anyway, I shouldn't tell you but I get a discount at the Rolex store in town. They give all the players 20% off because we buy some bloody many.'

Nick didn't have a clue about watches, and didn't even usually wear one, but this looked incredibly expensive with a blushed gold strap and surround and black face.

'It's a rose-gold Daytona, they tell me. Not too bling. I didn't figure you were a bling kind of guy, right?'

'Me and bling have never knowingly been in the same universe, no. This is great though Jimmy. I love it. Thank you. I don't know what to say.'

'Say nothing. I'm a lucky man...you know...with the football and Aunt Mimi, it makes me happy to share it around. Now what about this interview?'

The football and Aunt Mimi? Who was Aunt Mimi? He was being so generous and yet Nick was sitting there knowing the whole kidnapping was a scam and that Jimmy was being betrayed by his girlfriend. Shit, he should tell him really, shouldn't he? He didn't have to reveal everything and get her into serious trouble but he could at least tell him that she was carrying on with her old boyfriend. It was only fair.

'Jimmy, there's something I've got to tell you. It's a bit difficult to say, especially coming on top of everything that's just happened with the fire and that...err...'

'Yeah? What is it? What have you heard? Am I getting transferred or something?'

'No, it's not to do with football.'

'Oh, what, about the fire?'

'No...it's about Pinky.'

'Pinky?'

'Yeah.'

'What about her?'

The big goalkeeper smiled and opened his large palms wide as if to encourage Nick to talk. Better just bloody say it. If it was him being cheated on, he'd want to know.

'Well the thing is, I saw Pinky in Seaton Carew recently. She didn't see me. The thing is Jimmy, she was meeting her old boyfriend, Finlay; he's got a flat there.'

The Dutchman looked blankly at him.

'Is that it? Oh yeah, I know she does.'

He laughed loudly and then pointed at him and nodded.

'Ah I see, you thought she was having an affair, didn't you? Yes, yes, you thought you were going to have to break the news to old Jimmy. Ha ha, well thanks my friend but I know all about it.'

'You do?'

'Yes of course. She goes to see him most weeks. They're still friends but you know...that's as far as it goes. I like him. He's err...what is it...sharp...intelligent.'

'Are you sure?'

'Totally. She's been helping him out with some coursework too. He works in the club ticket office sometimes and goes to college as well. Yeah, he's doing Media Studies and, you know, Pinky was going to go to college and she's helped him with his fees too, you know.'

'You mean you've helped him with his fees.'

'Well, what's mine is hers...if she chooses to use her money like that, I'm okay with it. Education is never wasted, that's what my mother used to say to me.'

Listening to the Dutchman, Nick began to doubt his interpretation of the kidnapping. What if he'd got the Finlay relationship wrong? What if he'd misread the way he'd looked at him in the ticket office? What if Pinky was wearing that black wig as a fashion change rather than a disguise? What if it wasn't Finlay's voice on the phone at all? Oh Christ, maybe it had been a real kidnap and not a set-up, after all.

'Oh okay, I'm really sorry Jimmy. I put two and two together and made 38. It was just that she was wearing a wig when I saw her, a black wig. So I thought that was weird, like she was in disguise or something.'

'Excuse me? She was wearing a wig?'

His expression had changed from a smile to a deep frown. Something was wrong.

'Err...yeah a sort of black bob wig.'

'Now that I don't understand at all; she does not have any wigs, Nick. She has never worn a wig, never even talked about wearing a wig. That is weird.'

'Well, maybe it was just something she fancied doing that day or maybe it was as a joke or something.'

'No she doesn't make the...err...what you say, err...practical jokes. That's not her style and neither is a wig. I shall ask her about this.'

'I'm sure it's nothing to worry about, Jimmy.'

'No, no of course not. Still, it is puzzling. I'll ask her about it.'

'Well, while we're talking about puzzles, did you hear about those two women who were murdered? Their bodies were found out on sand banks at the mouth of the Tees.'

'Yes, I read it in the paper. Both painters that I knew of too...what is the world coming to?'

'Well one of them, Lisa Lambert, was a good friend of mine.'

'She was? Oh fuck. How terrible. When I saw her name I knew it must be the girl whose work I've bought from Emmy Green. She was a good painter. I have...or rather I had some of her work. It was destroyed in the fire.

'Yeah it's...well it's horrible.'

Jimmy shook his head and then leaned forward and slapped Nick on the shoulder as though to comfort him. It was a nice touch.

'I'm so sorry for you, man. Do they have any idea who did it?'

'They're on the case. I actually know one of the officers in charge from school days. The thing is, Jimmy, indirectly it sort of involves you.'

'Yeah? How come?'

'The other woman who was shot was an artist too – Myra LeFevre. Lisa and Myra were really good mates and Myra told her, just before she was killed, that she'd been doing fake paintings in return for cash. She had money for the first time in years, so she was showing off a bit. '

'Wow. Well they say that there are many forged pictures out there.'

'Exactly, but she was faking Phyllis Plant stuff.'

'Wow. Really? Ah, and you think my PPs were fakes? That I was conned?'

'Well no, I don't think that actually because I spoke to Emmy Green, who I sort of knew through Lisa, and she told me the provenance on them was rock solid.'

He decided not to tell him about seeing Simon Harrison. That would look oddly intrusive.

The Dutchman nodded. 'Absolutely. That's what I was told, also.'

'Yeah, I'm sure they're fine, or were fine. They're a pile of ash now, of course.'

'It's worrying though. I do worry about people trying to take advantage of the stupid footballer with too much money. Hey, why don't you take this one,' he pointed at the bubble-wrapped picture, 'and get it checked out for me? I'll pay whatever it costs. A second opinion would put my mind at rest.'

'Well I suppose I could take it to Harrison's in Masham; they're supposed to be good.'

'Yes, yes, take it,' he said, handing it to him. 'Harrison - that was the guy who looked at them for the insurance company. Frankie organised it all. Get him to take a second look and make 100% sure. Thanks for looking out for me, Nick.'

'Well, to be honest Jimmy, I was thinking of Myra. I was wondering if she'd been killed because of what she'd be doing.'

'An angry customer, you mean?'

'Well yeah or because whoever bought them didn't want anyone else to know that they'd bought or sold a bunch of fake paintings. Then Lisa was killed because she'd found out and it all started to look even dodgier.'

Jimmy wiped his big hands across his lips.

'Well, who knows? Now you know and I know. Does that mean we'll be shot? I don't think so, do you?'

'I don't know but I'd like to find out. Lisa was a bright light, man, she was brilliant, and I'd like to get my fucking hands on whoever did this. And I won't rest until I have and I know she'd expect at least that from me.'

As he spoke he could hear her voice as clear as though she was standing behind him.

'Fuck them up Nick, fuck them up.'

'Well that's like err, totally understandable. It's such an awful thing to happen. I tell you what...I'll keep my ears open about these fakes, see if anyone else has heard anything on the art circuit. I'll be in London soon, I'll make some...what's the word...err...discreet enquires. Okay?'

'Okay. Thanks Jimmy. You're a good lad. Right, let's do this interview then...'

'Yeah, let's, as they say, get the bloody ball out!' Jimmy shouted in an imitation of a cockney voice.

'Look at this Jules,' Nick said, tipping his wrist towards her as he walked in the farmhouse after the interview.

'Fizz me, I take it that's a fake Rolex?'

'Nah, it's real, Jimmy bought it for me in town as a thank you for helping him on the kidnapping.'

'You're joking...this is thousands of pounds' worth of watch.'

She took the details of the watch from the box and did an online search.

'You've got yourself a £25,000 quid watch there, mister. He must have more money than sense, you'll only lose it.'

'Yeah, he said it made him happy to spread it around.'

'He's a good friend to have then, eh. Even if he is a match-fixer.'

'Hmm, he mentioned something important though. He said he'd been fortunate and then referred to his Aunt Mimi....don't know what he meant by that.'

'Aunt Mimi? I wonder who she was.'

'Let's try a search for Mimi Repp.'

Julie typed the name into Google. It brought up links to people on MySpace and Facebook. She scoured through the pages.

'Nothing obvious here. I'll add his name, maybe he's talked about her in an interview. Ah here in De Telegraaf...it's on a Dutch website in Dutch of course but look, the word Mimi is there...so he's mentioned her.'

He looked over her shoulder at the extract.

Mijn moeder en vader waren allebei gewone arbeiders, maar mijn tante Mimi, mijn vader's zus, trouwde met een Texaanse oliesjeik die haar na zijn dood een fortuin achterliet. Toen ze overleed in 1990 liet ze een gedeelte daarvan achter voor mij in een trust fund. Ik ben dus echt zeer bevoorrecht.

She cut and pasted the interview text into Google Translate and read it out.

'My mother and father were both ordinary workers, but my aunt

Mimi, my father's sister, married a Texan oil sheik who left her a fortune after his death. When she died in 1990 she left a part of it to me in a trust fund. So I'm really very privileged.'

She did another search for Mimi's name, this time adding the year of her death.

'Look at this obituary archive from a Texas newspaper...,' she tapped the screen, 'Mimi Duke, who died aged 69 in Austin, heir to the Duke Oil fortune believed to be in excess of $500million, was born Mimi Repp in Eindhoven in the Netherlands.'

Nick laughed as a weight fell from his brain.

'Well, that explains that then, doesn't it? He doesn't need money from match-fixing to fund his art collection or anything else. He's richer than Croesus. We must have got all that match-fixing thing wrong. We just made it up in our heads. He doesn't need to do anything like that for money.'

Julie wrinkled her nose. 'You think? I was pretty sure...but a 500 million dollar fortune? Jesus, he must be sodding rich even if he only got half of it. He might still be involved in match-fixing, mind, either for the sheer thrill of it or under pressure from Frankie Gray or someone else, that Yashie guy maybe?'

'I guess so. Whatever, it explains his lavish spending on art and watches, doesn't it? And I can't walk around with this sort of money on my wrist. I'll just lose it, I know I will.'

'Aye well, if you do, you're no worse off are you?'

'Ha true. You're sensible you, aren't you?'

'I prefer the word pragmatic. Sensible sounds like I work in a library and wear massive navy blue knickers.'

'Would that be a bad thing?'

'Not necessarily. But it's not me is it?'

'No. As far as I know you don't own any big navy blue knickers.'

'And I never will.'

The news about the inheritance was actually a relief. He badly wanted Jimmy not to be corrupt or bent or anything other than the nice guy he had always appeared to be.

'I also started to doubt our Pinky kidnap theory, Jules.' He explained why.

'Have we just made all this shit up in our heads? Have we gone stark raving mad?'

She rubbed her face. 'Oh good God in fizzin' hell, I don't know...we haven't made up Myra and Lisa's deaths, that much I do know.'

'Where's Jeff?' asked Nick.

'I took him to the Black Bull. He'll be six pints in now. That lad just does nothing but booze.'

'It keeps him happy.'

'That's the odd thing; it really does, doesn't it? If he's an alkie, at least he's a cheerful one. He seems to drink out of celebration of life and not because he's even the slightest bit depressed.'

Nick called Harrison's and arranged to bring the picture for valuation in the morning.

'Right, that's that sorted. Shall we go into Yarm, pick up the hairy man and maybe get something to eat?'

'Yeah...let's go to that new French place. How long is he staying, has he said? I mean, I don't mind but I liked our lifestyle of wandering around half-naked and spontaneously shagging a lot. It feels like we can't do that when he's here.'

'He'll be away soon - we were going to go to that record fair at the weekend. He won't want Luke to be on his own in the shop for more than a few days.'

'Yeah, I suppose so. But since he's out and can't get back without us giving him a lift...now's a good chance for some mucky-fucky isn't it?' She flashed her turquoise eyes at him.

'Come on then, I'll race you upstairs.'

He jumped in front of her and headed for the door, pulling off his t-shirt as he went. 'Last one naked has to go on top!'

An hour later they strolled into the pub.

'Ah here they are, Darby and Joan,' said Jeff.

'Now then Mr Big, how's the beer?'

'Brown. So what have you been up to?'

'I'll tell you in a bit but we're taking you to dinner now.'

'Ah, that's no more than I deserve. Just as well I put my best suit on.'

'But you're just wearing a checked shirt and jeans.'

'...and your point is?'

'Come on, we're going to this new French place, Henry's.'

Jeff drained his pint.

'Right, I'll see you Stevie,' he said to the man behind the bar. As they walked out of the pub onto Yarm High Street, Jeff stopped and squinted into the distance for a few seconds. The bright summer sun cast long, sharp shadows down the old cobbles.

'What's up?' asked Nick

'Nowt. I just felt a bit dizzy. It's gone off now.'

'That's the drink man, it does that to you, remember?'

'Not after a mere five pints it doesn't.'

'Bloody hell, after five pints I'd be ready for bed,' said Nick.

'Amateur,' scoffed Jeff.

When they got into the restaurant, Nick showed Jeff the watch.

'Give us a look at that. Bloody hell. Where'd this come from?'

'Jimmy gave it to me as a thank you for helping him over the kidnapping.'

He held Nick's wrist and took a photo of the watch with his phone.

'It's worth over 25 grand,' said Julie.

'At least, aye. It's a smashing timepiece that. Do you know for sure it's real?'

Nick tapped it. 'Well it certainly exists.'

'Smartarse. I mean, do you know it's not a fake?'

'No.'

'Well you will soon.'

He sent an e-mail with the picture of the watch attached and 'fake or real?' written underneath.

'Who've you sent that to?' asked Nick.

'Jenny Hanson, sister of Handy Hanson; you remember old Handy?'

'Yeah of course, lovely old bloke. Ran that music shop off Parliament Street in Harrogate.'

'Aye, well his sister is a watch specialist in Leeds.'

'Is she? I never knew that.'

'I didn't until I met her at the party he held when he closed the shop down and retired. I've met her a few times since then. She's a big Beatles fan so comes in now and again to see if we've got any collectibles. She'll know if that's a 25k watch or not.'

Ten minutes later he got an e-mail.

'Ah ha. Here she is.....ha! She says, 'good quality fake. Not many of these around. Ironically, quite collectible. Hope you didn't pay more than £50 for it'.'

Nick's heart sank into his stomach.

'Bloody hell. He said he got it from the Rolex shop in Middlesbrough.'

'Maybe he did. Maybe they ripped him off,' said Julie

'Nah. They don't sell fake Rolex watches, man,' said Jeff. 'He can't have got it there.'

Nick knew he was right. Jimmy had either had been conned himself or not bought it from the shop. Had he known it was a fake?

'I just don't know what to think about him now,' said Nick, exasperated.

Jeff grinned at him. 'I bet that picture is a fake as well. Fake is as fake does.'

'Eh? What do you mean fake is as fake does?'

'I don't know. It sounds good though, doesn't it?'

'I'm totally confused now,' said Julie. 'Is it possible that he's just a pathological liar or something?'

'That or he's just a massive mug who everyone is taking the piss out of by playing 'milk the gullible footballer',' said Jeff with a shake of his head.

The next day dawned warm and damp with long fingers of low lying mist hovering above the fields as Nick and Julie set off for Masham with Jimmy Repp's Phyllis Plant picture, leaving Jeff sleeping off the drink.

As he drove, Nick said: 'Have you ever known a really brilliant liar? Someone who could tell you black is white and you'd believe it, because I'm beginning to wonder if that's what Jimmy Repp really is. Maybe everything he told me is a lie from start to finish.'

'I went out with a bloke in the early 90s for a few months. I had no idea he was married with three kids. He manipulated our relationship so successfully that it never even occurred to me until I was late going on a business trip and went into town for something. He thought I was away and I saw him with his wife on Stockton High Street coming out of Boots.'

'Huh...that must have been a bit vexatious.'

'It was funny. Actually, it makes him seem a bit more interesting than he actually was. It was going nowhere anyway. Mind, he wasn't really a good liar, he was just deceitful, which is probably a different Machiavellian art form.'

'I was never any good at deception. It requires an ability to remember what lies you've told to whom, but the actual lying bit I can do...'

'...you are a very good liar.'

'...but keeping several untruths going at once, that takes real effort.'

They parked in the marketplace again and went into Harrsion's. He was sitting behind his desk and greeted them with a small wave of the hand.

'Hello My Guymer, I didn't expect to see you again so soon...'

'...Nick, please, and Julie....no, well we thought we'd just ask you to take a look at this.'

'Good to see you both. Shall we step into my office?'

They walked around to a small room with a low ceiling. Harrison sat down at his desk and Nick handed him the picture covered in bubble wrap.

'I am a bit of a fan of this lady's work,' he said as he unwrapped, 'and her prices are going up and up and up.'

Nick and Julie sat down and watched as he took the picture, placed it under a bright, angle-poise lamp and took out a comedy-sized magnifying glass.

'Right. Let's see what we have here.'

He peered at it, holding the framed picture at arm's length, and then looked at the signature closely. Air whistled in a high-pitched whine from his nostrils as he inspected the picture, his forehead furrowed into deep lines. After a few minutes' silence he looked up at them.

'I'm very sorry to have to tell you this Nick, but this is clearly a forgery. This is not the work of Phyllis Plant. It's a very good attempt but not authentic. It has been painted on old paper, probably from the early 50s, that's right, but the lines here and here are just wrong, they lack her flow and confidence. The signature is good but deviates a little from what we would normally expect. Basically, the picture just isn't good enough to be a PP. I hope you didn't pay much money for it. You should inform whoever it was you bought it from that it is a fake.'

He tapped the handle of the magnifier on his desk and looked into the middle distance.

'I have seen a PP that is very like this in the collection that Mr Repp bought. It was part of a substantial series she did in St Ives in Cornwall called *The Restless Sea and Other Stories*. If I was to make a guess, I'd say that this is an attempt to copy that or to create a very similar piece which could have been passed off as part of that series.'

Nick looked at Julie and turned his mouth down. He had expected exactly this verdict because his faith in Jimmy was quickly diminishing.

'Okay, well thank you for that,' said Nick, getting up.

'Please send your bill to our address.'

He handed him a business card with his contact details.

'Sorry to be the bearer of bad news.'

'Not at all. It's better to know the truth,' said Julie with a smile.

'Indeed. Yes.'

As they got outside, Nick blew out air and groaned.

'A fake watch and now a fake picture...what's going on Jules? Why is he doing this?'

She took his hand as they walked back to the car.

'But think about it. Why would he ask you to check out a picture he knew was fake? What does he have to gain by doing that? He must surely think that the pictures were kosher. We know he had them checked out by Harrison – including this one presumably, and that he approved them all. He wouldn't give you something that he knew to be a fake and ask you to have it double-checked would he?'

He leaned against the old BMW and folded his arms across his chest.

'Yeah and remember this was on display at the party. Jimmy didn't like how it was framed so afterwards he took it out and sent it to get re-done. If the collection we saw at the party was the real thing, then this couldn't be a fake, could it? But it is.'

Julie clapped her hands together and exclaimed.

'I've got it! The fakes were switched with the real ones at some point between him acquiring the collection, having it assessed and having the party. Myra was telling the truth, she did the fakes under instruction from someone who then swapped the real ones for the fakes before that party, precisely so that when they burnt the house down, they were just burning cheap imitations. All they found was piles of ash. If they do forensics, they'd find the paper was from the right period, and probably the ink too, but they can't inspect the actual artwork. That's smart, that is.'

'So when we saw them at Jimmy's party they were all fakes but he didn't know?'

'Yeah. He had no idea. He thought they were real and none of us know a fake from a real one. We can all swear we saw the collection but what we really saw were Myra's fakes. After the party, without anyone else knowing, Jimmy pulled out this one for re-framing. Unwittingly, he had kept a fake. The rest got burnt. This one should have gone up in flames as well.'

She laughed a little and bounced up and down on her toes.

'Come on...that's a good theory, admit it,' she said, pointing at him and nodding excitedly.

'It's a great theory. It works.'

He unlocked the car; they got in and wound the windows down to let out the heat.

'If Jimmy knows anything at all about this, why would he risk exposing the scam by giving us this picture to check out? He can't know anything at all about it, can he? Nothing. He's innocent.'

'Yeah. He's nothing to gain by this, has he? Except he looks like an idiot. Same goes for the watch. If he knew it was fake, you'd have found out at some point, especially if you were going to insure it.'

'Exactly. I'm coming round to Jeff's idea that he's just a sap who people are taking for a ride and that he's either naïve or a bit dumb.'

They set off for the A1 to return home. The pieces began to fit into a mental jigsaw for Nick.

'There's been two scams here but they're all part of the same thing, the kidnapping and the pictures. We thought Pinky and Finlay pulled off the kidnapping alone but it was Frankie Gray who sorted all that out, remember? He organised the money and everything. So maybe both these scams were his idea. He's the smooth dude in all of this, the fixer, y'know? Maybe he actually arranged to have Pinky kidnapped with her and Finlay's consent,' said Nick. 'He gets to keep a million of Jimmy's money and gives them a few thousand to presumably go off somewhere together. Frankie is already organising the match-fixing and getting a cut of the proceeds, but then he comes up with a scheme to acquire millions of pounds of art. He keeps the real PPs which Jimmy pays for, swaps them for fakes which he's arranged through Emmy Green, and sells them in ten years or whenever when it's all been forgotten about, or he's got a collector who'll pay for black market art. All in all, it's worth tens of millions.'

'Christ, I think we're onto something now, you know, and that news report we found said Jimmy and Frankie met some organised crime people in Spain. So Frankie would know someone who would shoot Myra and Lisa, and that became necessary because Myra was shouting her mouth off about the fakes. She could have brought all of his scams crashing down. Yes. Yes, I like it.'

'Exactly. Which still makes me and you, and now Jeff, targets for the same treatment because we know about it all.'

An icy shard of fear ran the full length of his body.

'And as soon as Jimmy innocently tells Frankie that he gave you that picture, Frankie will be coming after us to close us down,' he said.

'He'll know for sure we know about the fakes, if he didn't know before now,' said Julie. 'We've got one here, for fuck's sake.'

'Close us down? Shoot us dead you mean.'

'We'll be okay,' said Julie, narrowing her eyes.

She seemed calm.

'Yeah but we saw Frankie in Masham with a camera taking pictures of us, Jules. Remember what Jeff said, so he could give someone a photo and say, 'shoot these three'. Fuck. I'd better call Sarge when we get back and tell him all of this. See if we can get some police protection.'

'They won't do that. They can't commit resources to protecting people against whom no threat has been made. Talking of threats, I'd like to get my hands on Pinky. What the hell is she doing getting involved in this? She's just a kid; she's well out of her depth getting mixed up with people like Frankie Gray.'

'Surely she wouldn't condone someone being shot would she, let alone you? I mean, she doesn't know me, but she knows you and your family. '

'No, of course not. I don't think so anyway. She's no beef with me or the family either. She won't even know or suspect Gray is involved in the murders. But one thing she will know for sure is that if anything happens to me, my brothers won't rest until they've had their revenge. Family loyalty is in their blood, hurt one you hurt all of us. Pinky would know that and I'm sure she'd tell Gray that but, like I say, she won't have connected the dots. I'll try and find her this afternoon and get what she knows out of her. Do you think I should bluff her and tell her we know all about the kidnapping?'

'Why not? We need to find out one way or another.'

'Okay but you should go back to see Jimmy unannounced to tell him this theory. Raise the fact we know about the match-fixing as a way to persuade him to tell you everything he knows about Frankie. Say you're not going to do anything about it if he tells you about Gray. We want to bust Gray for the murders and nothing else matters. If he's the nice guy we think he is, as soon as he realises what's been going on, surely he'll jump into bed with us.'

They drove up the track to the farmhouse, the early afternoon sun was hot and the skies a classic summer blue and white.

'God what a beautiful day, I just wish we could sit back and enjoy it,' said Julie as she slammed the BMW door.

'I'm sure Jeff is doing that for both of us.' He looked at his watch. 'It's 12.30, he should have found the lager by now.'

He walked around the side of the house and into the back garden.

'Hey big man,' he shouted.

Jeff was lying on a sun lounger, looking like a beached whale. He looked over as they came around the corner.

'Alright,' he said, quietly.

'Enjoying the sun, eh? Well you'll be glad to know that you were right. The picture is a fake.'

'Told you, didn't I?' he said, his eyes closed.

'Are you alright?' said Julie. 'You look a funny colour.'

'Aye. I'm fine.'

'Are you sure? You do look a bit weird, Jeff. Sort of chewing gum coloured.'

'That's because I'm weird-looking and made of chewing gum.'

'Yeah, but more so than normal. You do look pale.'

'I was feeling a bit sick this morning, as it happens. Dodgy barrel, probably. And I was dizzy again, like yesterday. Just felt a bit short of breath so I came for a lie out here. A bit of sun, like.

'Okay, do you want anything to eat? We're going out to see Jimmy and Pinky this afternoon.'

'No ta.'

Julie followed him into the house and touched Nick's arm once they were inside. He swung around.

'I don't think he's well at all,' she said in a whisper.

'Well, yeah. He said he was feeling a bit off.'

'No. I think it's more serious than food poisoning or a hangover. He looks really bloody terrible.'

She sat down at the kitchen table and opened her laptop.

'Look, look here,' she said, again in a whisper, pointing at a website which had a list of heart attack symptoms.

'See, he's been dizzy, short of breath, feeling sick. He might be having a heart attack.'

Nick looked at her to check if she was joking. She wasn't.

'I thought a heart attack was the old fall-to-the-ground-clutching-your-chest-style affair.'

'Doesn't have to be. I think we should take him to the hospital.'

Nick grunted. 'Well good luck telling him that. He hates anything to do with doctors and hospitals.'

As he spoke, Jeff came in and stood in the doorway for a couple of seconds as though trying to steady himself.

Before Nick could say anything, the big man fell forwards, his 20 stone, 6'3" body crashed onto the old lino and, with a sickening hollow crack, his head hit the floor. He lay motionless, a thin trickle of dark blood running from a head wound.

'Jeff! Fucking hell!' Nick leapt forward and got on his knees to lift Jeff's head.

'Can you hear me, man?'

No reply. He was unconscious.

Julie had grabbed her phone and dialled 999.

Nick kept talking to his comatose friend for want of anything else to do.

'Just take it easy big man, we'll get you an ambulance, Julie's on the case already. Can't have you littering up the kitchen floor can we? The mice will start nibbling you and no-one wants to be eaten by mice, do they?'

Heart racing, he got up, grabbed a hand towel from the sink and put it under Jeff's head. Then he fetched a sponge and wiped away the blood from his temple. His head was already swelling where it had hit the floor under the full force of his huge weight.

'They're on their way now,' said Julie, squatting down beside him and putting her hand on his neck.

'He's not breathing or he's not breathing much. Get him on his back; I'm going to give him CPR.'

Nick didn't even question her. She was in control.

It took both of them to haul him over and lay him flat on his back. She knelt to one side, tore open his plaid shirt and placed the heel of her left hand onto his breastbone, gripped it with her right hand and began pumping on his chest rhythmically.

Nick watched, his mouth dry and his hands sweating. Was his oldest and best friend really going to bloody well die here? Was this it? Was this how he was destined to go out? Fuck. It looked bad, really fucking bad. He stared at Jeff's expressionless face, eyes closed, mouth agape. He looked dead already. He was gone, surely. He'd died. He had. He'd bloody well gone and died. Just like that.

Julie started singing. Bloody singing!

'Ah ha ha ha, stayin' alive, stayin' alive, ah ha ha ha, stayin' alive, stayin' alive,' she sang, pressing hard on his chest on every beat.

'They taught us this at a first-aid class I did at Watson's.'

'But the Bee Gees? Shitting hell, Jeff won't like that. He'll want to be kept alive by rock 'n' roll, not disco,' said Nick, a spasm of black Teesside humour kicking in.

She kept on and on, working herself into a pink-faced sweat.

'Gotta keep doing this until the ambulance gets here,' she said, breathlessly, 'it's his only chance, He's in cardiac arrest, I reckon.'

'Don't we have to do the kiss of life or something?'

'No, just keep the rhythm up on his chest, shit, I'm knackered.'

'I'll take over.'

He began to strike up the same rhythm but instead of Stayin' Alive, he sang UFO's 'Only You Can Rock Me,' hoping that the power of rock 'n' roll might somehow bring him back. It was utterly surreal to be doing this to someone he knew so well while they were unconscious but there was no time to worry; worrying didn't seem to even be appropriate. Just focus on doing this and on nothing else.

Julie wiped the sweat from her brow and then ran to the front door when she heard sirens. The oscillating noise got closer.

'...only you can rock me, rock me, turn around now, do it again, only you can rock, rock me...'

'You'd better not fucking die, Jeff. Right? If you pop your massive clogs, who the hell am I going to talk to about records released on the Immediate label and not just the later pink-coloured labels but the earlier lavender and white ones? No-one else knows about this shit, so you owe it to me to come back to life like a big fat fucking Lazarus, right?'

The ambulance screeched to a halt.

'In here,' shouted Julie. Footsteps. Two paramedics dressed in green overalls appeared.

'He's had a cardiac arrest,' she said.

'We'll take over,' one said, a woman in her early 30s. 'What's his name?'

'Jeff.'

'Okay Jeff, I'm Marion, and we're just going to put the defibrillator on you and get your heart working properly again, okay?'

They hooked him up to the machine and gave him a jolt of electricity, once then twice.

'Did you give him CPR as soon as he passed out?' asked the second paramedic, a man in his late 20s with bright blue eyes who seemed to be measuring his pulse.

'Yeah, within about a minute or so,' said Julie

Marion measured his heartbeat on the machine. 'Well, I think you might have saved his life. His heart is ticking away quite nicely now. Let's get him to hospital Robbie.'

'Is there anything we can do for him?' asked Nick.

'Just pack him a bag, some clothes, a few bits and pieces. He might be in for a while.'

'Will he make a full recovery?' asked Julie.

'Well, it depends on how long his heart stopped for. He may well do...or he may be somewhat...you know...impaired and need help. You did everything you could do.'

They took Jeff out on a stretcher, still unconscious, and the ambulance drove off at high speed.

Nick and Julie looked at each other in shock and hugged. It was all too much to take. The whole affair had taken less than 25 minutes from him collapsing to being taken away. How life could change in such a short space of time.

'Well, he was lucky he had this happen when he was with us and not on his own,' said Julie, washing her hands and face in the sink. 'He'd not have had a chance.'

'And lucky you knew what to do. I didn't have a clue. I've never seen anyone have a heart attack before.'

'A cardiac arrest is different from a heart attack. I can't remember how though. It's more serious, I think. Lack of blood to the brain...you know...he might be...'

'...a vegetable? Christ, poor Jeff.'

Julie dried her hands on a towel and looked at the floor. 'He is massive though. He must've known the odds were that he'd not be well at some point, like.'

'Yeah...he was gambling. Funny though, he mentioned changing his diet.'

'Maybe he'd been feeling dodgy for a while and really was going to do something about it.'

'Aye, mind, he's put some drink away just while he's been here. That can't have helped.'

She sighed and shook her head. 'It's easy to be judgemental; I just hope he pulls through okay.'

'I'll get some stuff together for him. He's probably got some clean clothes in his bag upstairs. He better have because nothing we've got will fit him.'

'We've got that tarpaulin out the back. He could use that as a nightie.'

They both laughed a little wearily, both shocked.

'Poor old sod. I hope he's, y'know...all there when he comes round.'

'Doing CPR is supposed to keep the blood pumping, keeping oxygen in the brain, thus stopping major knackage. You can tell I'm a doctor, eh.'

He kissed her on the forehead.

'Might as well look in on my mother while I'm at the hospital, just for a little light relief, like.'

'Don't eat the omelettes here our Nick, they poison them,' said Julie in a decent impression of his mother's Hull accent.

'That's her big hit. Ten years in and out of that place on and off and she's still on about omelettes. Thank God paranoid schizophrenia doesn't run in the family.'

'Aye, well you love an omelette don't you? It'd be a shame to go all loopy and not be able to enjoy them anymore.'

'I just hope Jeff survives to eat another meal.'

CHAPTER 13

He drove to the hospital with some clothes, Jeff's iPod, his bible - the *Record Collector Rare Record Price Guide,* and the latest copy of *Classic Rock.* That was all he really needed in life. That and a body that actually worked.

Hospitals were creepy. Because his mother had been ill for much of the 70s, he'd spent a lot of time visiting them. The smell never changed. The same stillness, the same suspension of reality, the same ghostly people clinging to life for another day. The same civilians arriving to visit and pretending everything was going to be alright when it wasn't. The only thing that had changed was the nurses 'uniforms, now a blue or green pyjama.

There were coloured lines on the floor to direct you to where you were supposed to go, as if words were not merely enough in this reality; everything had to be colour-coded for the illiterate or those too sick to read. Obviously illness is a step outside of the norm and hardly something cheering to the soul but the atmosphere always seemed to be one of foreboding and doom, as though the threat of death had won out over the prospect of hope and life and that secretly everyone knew it but just pretended otherwise. He had always been haunted by the notion that people were dying all the time inside this building, expiring silently and inevitably.

So it was with trepidation that he entered the building past a phalanx of smokers huddling outside in their nightclothes, seemingly sucking onto their fags with more determination than they had to hold onto life itself.

He held off calling Jeff's mother in case the unthinkable happened and Jeff didn't pull through. It was going to be an awful phone call to make either way, better to only have to do it once.

It was all very shocking yet he felt in control somehow. He was dealing with it. He'd gone into practical mode; the feelings and emotions could happen later. The best friend he'd had since he was 16 was hovering somewhere between life and death, but it was no time for reflection or perspective. It would do no good. It wouldn't help anyone and he knew that Jeff himself wouldn't want him or anyone else to waste precious time worrying about him.

He was a big, brave bloke who'd known the path he was walking. Now it was time to pay the toll for a life of excess. If he came back from this, things would have to be very different. The old Jeff life, full of massive blow-outs and alcohol-fuelled benders, would be over. But then life changes, usually just when you feel it's at its most stable, as recent events had shown all too well.

'My friend Jeff Evans was brought in about three hours ago. He had a cardiac arrest. I've brought him some stuff,' he said to the nurse on the reception desk. 'Can I see him or maybe just take these things in for him?'

She looked at a screen without even speaking to him. This was another thing he hated about hospitals - they reduced you to a faceless drone, a number in the system, a figure on a spread sheet or just a corpse under a sheet. Your character, your life experience, your everything, was left at the door for both patient and visitor. It was like being at school again. You had to report to this one, ask that one, get directions from another, check if this or that was okay with yet another one. You couldn't behave like a sentient adult. It was as though you were a retard or a child who needed their hand held through the system and you were supposed to be grateful as though you hadn't already paid with your taxes. Then again, she was just dealing with her day-to-day job, was overworked and underpaid and probably also tired of all the sick people and the limitless parade of corpses. So you couldn't blame her for being blank-eyed. Not really.

She gave him a ward number and said he could take the bag but that Jeff couldn't have any visitors yet. He walked up three flights of stairs and around an endless maze of corridors until he found Jeff's ward. There was a nurse or sister or whatever she was called on duty in a little side area. She was very fat. At least she was in the right place if she keeled over. He introduced himself. She smiled and took the bag.

'He's stable now. Best wait until tomorrow before you visit him though. He'll need some time to recover. We need to make sure he doesn't have another cardiac arrest. But he's comfortable now and out of any immediate danger.'

She was just trying to be nice, he appreciated that, but it was like being addressed by a teacher in junior school. He felt about ten years old. Jeff would have taken the piss if he'd heard her placating, sing-song voice. 'I'm afraid the fat old hairy bastard is well and truly fucked,' is what Jeff would have said and he wished the nurse was allowed to say that. He smiled to himself and thanked her.

The psychiatric ward where his mother was resident was even more depressing, if only because it was populated by people who ranged from bereft to delusional. Occasionally you saw someone in there who looked sane and wondered whether they'd been trapped in with the crazy people and couldn't get out. Did people look at him and think he was crazy too? Maybe he was. He'd spent a lot of the last year fearing he was some flavour of mad.

'Hello mam,' he said as he walked into a ward of six beds. His mother was in the near corner. She was sitting up in bed reading a copy of *Woman's Own* that looked like it belonged to the 1980s.

'Who's that?' she asked, looking up at him with her usual glassy eyes.

'It's Nick, mam. I was visiting a friend of mine so I thought I'd drop in.'

That sounded as though he wouldn't have come otherwise, which was cruel but true. Thankfully, she was too spaced out to recognise such a verbal faux pas.

'Eeee, hello our Nick. Have they offered you anything to eat?'

'No mam, they don't give visitors food.'

'Good, don't eat it if they do. They poison it. They think I don't know but I do.'

This was a gear her mind seemed unable to avoid engaging every time he visited. They'd diagnosed her as paranoid schizophrenic years ago but these days she seemed relatively untroubled by voices and weird notions. The drugs seemed to have achieved that much, admittedly at the expense of much of her personality. At times it was as though she was adrift in a sea of madness, able to see the shores of sanity but unable to ever get back there. She couldn't look after herself because she had no concept of time and would have gone days without eating, thinking only a couple of hours had passed. He used to just accept her condition, but lately it had started to make him feel profoundly sad. There seemed no quality to her existence at all and it was a hollow end to a life which, at some point, must have held joy and optimism.

'No mam. I won't eat any food, especially not the omelettes.'

'Did you say you've got a friend in here?'

She put down her magazine and looked at him but through him, as though he was a ghost.

'In the hospital? Yes. He's had a cardiac arrest, a heart attack, like.'

'Has he? That's terrible at his age.'

'You don't know how old he is mam.'

'Don't I? That happened to your dad you know.'

'I know mam, I came here and told you about it last year when he died.'

'Did you? Eeee I can't remember anything these days. It's the gravy, I'm sure of it.'

He laughed. 'Gravy, mam? Are you sure?'

'No not really,' she said, managing a laugh, though he wasn't sure she knew what she was laughing about. 'Well that's no good is it? Having a heart attack, like. Not unless he wanted one, but I bet he didn't.'

'No, that's right mam. He didn't want one.'

'I knew it. Not him. Do I know him?'

He laughed a little again. 'You used to, yes. I was at school with him. Jeff Evans. He was a big lad, very tall and broad with long hair. He used to come round our house to play records.'

215

'Oh yes, I remember him. Didn't he have a beard by the time he was 16?'

'Yeah he did', he said, surprised by her actually remembering something accurately for once.

'Nice lad, him. By God he could eat. Do you remember? He ate a whole jar of peanut butter once. I made him a huge pile of sandwiches and he wolfed the lot.'

That made him laugh. Jeff had always had a massive appetite.

'No self-discipline, that was his problem.' she said, gazing into the middle distance, 'you've got to know when to stop, especially with peanut butter.'

Nick kept laughing. She was often unintentionally amusing.

'What are you laughing at?'

'You mam, you say funny things.'

'Do I? I don't mean to.' She let out a huge sigh, a sigh so big it seemed there could be no air left in her body. It felt like she was trying to expel something, the confusion, perhaps. Poor woman. He looked at her, tears in his eyes. It wasn't fair, was it? Not fair on him. Not fair on her. He'd have liked to have a mam that was happy and sentient and sane. Someone on his side. Someone to offer a word of support. He could've bloody used a shoulder to cry on right now. He rubbed away the water from the corner of his eyes.

'You're right though, mam. He hasn't any self-control really. He was a big eater and a big drinker.'

'Of course I'm right. I always was. Nobody listened to me though. They never did. Your dad never did.'

'I do, mam,' he said.

'Aye, you're a good lad our Nick. You always were nice to everyone, even when you were little. Always had a smile on your face. It's not worth being nice though. You just get hurt don't you?'

'You're probably right, mam, yeah.'

'I know...I know,' her voice trailed off, 'no-one took any notice. I could have done anything. I was invisible for years.'

'You weren't actually invisible though mam. We could see you.'

'Hmm? Mind, I used to love a glass of stout. Can you still get stout?' Her mind had slipped a gear.

'Yeah I think so but I've given up drinking booze.'

'Why?' she asked as though he was mad.

'I just thought it was no good for me. I think it helped make me depressed.'

'Depressed? Maybe you should have a drink or something. They say it cheers you up, don't they? It's the cup that cheers.'

'That's tea, mam.'

'Tea? Tea's not alcoholic is it? Everyone would be drunk if it was,' she laughed to herself and shook her head. Her brief moment of lucidity had passed, as it always did, and she returned to talking in circles of ever decaying logic.

After half an hour, Nick took his leave. She seemed to occasionally receive echoes of who she was and the life she'd lived but they only seemed to disturb her, the disconnect between her circumstances then and now only serving to confuse and upset. What a terrible thing to happen to anyone.

As he walked back to the car park he called Julie.

'Hiya. How was Jeff?'

'Stable but still unconscious.'

'And your mam?'

He snorted. 'Also stable but she's conscious, or just about. Are you at home?'

'I'm just driving over to the estate to see if Pinky's there. I thought, well...we've just got to get on with things haven't we? I mean, the Jeff thing doesn't change that. We need to find out who killed Lisa and Myra.'

'Yes. Yes, you're right. Okay, I'll come over too. Give you some support.'

'Okay, I'll see you there in a few minutes.'

He was literally a two-minute drive from her mother's house, the hospital being adjacent to the Hardwick estate. As he pulled up, he could see Julie's Peugeot wasn't there yet so he sat in the car and looked around. The big four-wheel drive wasn't outside; in fact there were no other cars on the street except for an old Mini in the distance. All was quiet. There were still no kids on the streets despite it being a sunny, warm summer afternoon. Where were they all? When he was a kid every grassy area and patch of wasteland played host to children doing something or other with a ball, a stray dog or a stick. Now it looked as though kids had been banned from the streets. It felt weird. Like a ghost town.

As he sat, a black car pulled up ten or 20 yards away and a girl in a bright pink hoodie and black leggings got out of the passenger side. It was unmistakably Pinky. He slid down in his seat a little as though to hide himself from her gaze but she wasn't looking anyway. She fished out a key from her pocket, unlocked the front door of her mother's house and went in. The car was the sleek black Mazda sports car he'd seen her drive from the fire. It pulled away but he couldn't see who was driving, probably Finlay. A minute later, Julie pulled up in front of him.

'Pinky has just gone in,' he said, getting out of the BMW.

'Right, let's see what she's got to say.'

She rang the bell and they waited. No-one replied. She rang it again.

'She's not answering.'

'Maybe she doesn't want it known she's here.'

Julie opened the letterbox and shouted through, 'Pinky it's me, Julie Wells. Can I just have a quick word with you?'

It snapped shut. She raised an eyebrow at him. They waited. A minute passed and there were footsteps coming down the stairs.

The door cracked open and she peered around.

'Eeee hello Julie. I was in the bath...come in,' she said with her nice open smile. It really was her star feature. As he'd thought at the party where they'd first met, once she'd given you the big smile, you really wanted to see it again. It bestowed something almost tangibly pleasurable.

She ushered them in and shut the door behind her, dressed in a pink towelling dressing gown.'

'Give us five minutes. Put the kettle on, Jules.'

Her tone was friendly, nice.

She ran back upstairs and they wandered through into the back kitchen. It was small and smelled of burnt fat and smoke. Julie filled the kettle. They could hear her walking around upstairs.

'Every time we come to these houses, I'm amazed at how small they are,' said Nick. 'It was the same when I cleared out my dad's house. That seemed tiny as well. Barely enough room for a large fart. We lived such small, cramped lives.'

'God knows how six of us lived in one of these,' said Julie. 'We never thought anything of it. It was all we knew so it seemed normal. And I had my own bedroom, being the only girl, like. Luxury, eh. Mind, it was hellish when I was 16, Terry was two and the other lads 17 and 18. The house was a furious cauldron of hormones. Eeee God, the fights we had.'

Pinky came down the stairs in a pink t-shirt and old blue jeans.

'So to what do I owe this visit then?' she asked. 'Not that it's not nice to see youse both.'

She smiled again, looking from one to the other.

'We're trying to find out something,' said Nick but Julie interrupted him.

'Pinks, you've known me for your whole life and you know I'm not one for bullshit or beating around the bush.'

'Yeah, course, that sounds dead serious, Jules.'

'It is. We're worried that someone wants to kill us.'

'Kill you?! What? Who wants to kill you?' she asked, her small face scrunched into a frown.

'Whoever killed Myra LeFevre and Lisa Lambert. Did you hear about them?'

She shook her head slowly. 'Oh, there were two bodies found somewhere on the beach wasn't there? Is that them?'

'Yeah. Lisa was a good friend of mine,' said Nick.

'That's awful, how did she die?'

'She was shot in the head. They both were.'

Her eyes widened and her bottom lip dropped in enough shock to suggest it was either genuine or a bloody good act.

'Good grief...but...how does that involve you? Why are you in danger?'

Julie poured the hot water onto the tea, fetched three mugs and a carton of milk, and put them on a tray.

'Let's go and sit in the front room,' she said, almost as if this was her house and she was Pinky's mother.

It was a small room with walls covered in woodchip wallpaper and painted magnolia. A three-piece suite made from grey leather occupied almost all the floor space.

'Y'see Pinks, Myra had been putting it around that she'd been painting fake pictures - she was an artist, both of them were – and that Jimmy had bought some of them.'

'Jimmy? Fakes? No, that's not right, he always has the expensive ones checked out by experts. Which ones were they, like?'

'The Phyllis Plant pictures.'

She turned her lip up in a sneer. 'Oh that manky stuff. It's awful, that. Beyond me how it costs so much.'

Nick gave a little laugh. 'It does seem mad. That was Myra's point. The art's not important; it's the signature that matters.'

'Well she was right. It's all a rip-off. I don't understand it. Jimmy seems to get off on it though, like. He's always been into art even before he made it as a footballer.'

She sipped at her tea.

'So are you saying that they were both killed because of this faking business?' asked Pinky.

'Essentially yes, killed to shut them up, but I already knew about it,' said Nick, 'Lisa told me.'

'So because of that you think you're next in line? Why don't you go to the police? Or is that a stupid question, like?'

'Well there's been no threat against us or anything so they can hardly offer us protection against something no-one knows is even going to happen, but I've told Dave Sargent about it,' said Nick. 'Did you have any idea that Jimmy's PP's might have been forged?'

'I stay out of all that. I just...,' she clapped her hands together and looked around her as if looking for anyone who might hear, then shrugged, 'I just don't really care about it.' She looked around her again, drank some more tea, scratched her head and said: 'What it is, right, is that it's come between us, like. He's obsessed with it and I can't understand why, it's just a load of squiggles and lines. It makes no sense to us and it's all he wants to talk about. He does all the art business with Frankie and that posh woman, Emmy Green. She's a patronising cow, that one.'

'So why did she come around here looking for you then? Mam saw her,' said Julie.

'Eh? She's never been here, Jules. I see her at galleries and that. She's been around Jimmy's house too. She's too...oh you know...like a teacher. And she talks to me like I'm a thick little kid but she thinks she's being nice to me.'

'But like I said, my mam saw her knocking on the door. She said she wanted to talk to you about an artist's modelling project.'

Pinky looked puzzled.

'Eh? I'm sorry Jules, I'm pretty sure she'd never come here. She wouldn't be seen dead on the estate. I've not told her where I lived and I'm sure mam wouldn't either. Are you sure your mam isn't just making that up or has got her mixed up with someone else?'

'No, she was sure.'

'Well, I never heard the like, I don't even do modelling, I don't want to and I've never said I did. She's never said anything to me about it. Anyway, she's got our number. She could have asked me on the phone at Jimmy's.'

'Well that's what we thought,' said Nick. 'We thought it was odd.'

She looked at her phone, distracted by a text. She tapped out a quick reply and looked back to them.

'Does Maggie know her then?' asked Nick.

'Mam? No. Of course not. Well, she met her at a posh artists' do we went to in Darlo. She wanted to see how the other half live, so I took her. She got pissed. Typical.'

She sneered and looked away as though the memory offended her.

'I think your mam must be seeing things. Emmy has never been around here, not as far as I know anyway, and mam would've said.'

Julie pursed her lips and stared at her. 'I'd like to believe you, Pinky, but I don't know...there's something funny going on here, as I think you already know.'

'I don't know what you mean.'

'Don't you?' Julie said, an eyebrow raised.

Pinky looked uncomfortable under Julie's glare for the first time. 'Yeah alright, look, I'll be honest with you...I'm not sure I want to go back to Jimmy, in fact, I know I don't. '

'Is that because of what happened at the party?' asked Julie.

'Sort of. I do still like him...but I'm err...I'm staying here for now while I work out how I feel. We're so different. I just don't like any of his friends, they're just rude, calling me names and that behind my back and Jimmy doesn't even defend me. It's not right, that. Most of them are creepy wankers and I'm not even remotely interested in what he's really interested in. I mean, he's a lovely, generous bloke and that...but...I dunno. I think I might like him as a friend but not as...you know....most of the time I feel like a fish out of water there. It's not me really, is it Jules? What do you think? That's shocked you, hasn't it?' She sat back with her arms folded.

'No, it's not shocked me at all,' said Julie, finishing her tea, 'you do seem like two very different people, and anyway, you're still having a relationship with Finlay aren't you?' It was her ace card.

Pinky looked up from her phone, her cheeks visibly flushed in an instant.

'I am not! What are you saying, like?' she said, a higher pitch to her Teesside accent.

'Pinks, I'm not being judgemental, right,' Julie put her hands up in surrender, 'but we know all about it. We know about the kidnap scam you set up with Frankie Gray and Finlay. '

Nick watched Julie as she spoke. She was an excellent bluffer. She spoke with a certainty that neither of them actually had.

'It's alright, we've not told anyone and we're not going to tell anyone if you answer a few questions for us...just so we can try to find out who killed Myra and Lisa and so we don't end up getting killed ourselves,' said Julie. 'What you do with your life and relationships is up to you...'

'Fuck you...who do you think you are? I don't want your sympathy or whatever the fuck. Get out of here now! I'm not sitting here listening to you spouting lies about me. I can't believe it. The cheek of you, you stuck-up bitch.'

'Don't be a silly girl. We're not going yet. Sit down,' said Julie, gesturing to her in such a final way and with such authority that it didn't even seem in question. Pinky duly slumped back down.

'I was bloody kidnapped by some blokes, it wasn't a set-up. I don't know why you even think that,' she said, running her small hand through her blonde curly hair.

Nick wasn't convinced. She seemed weary.

'If that's what you want us to believe, then fine,' said Julie opening her arms outwards in acceptance, 'but I know better than most that a girl has to do what she's got to do to get off this estate. You get a chance, you bloody take it. Break whatever rules you need to break. Like I said, it's nothing to do with us but bearing all that in mind, like I said, we need to know a few things.'

Nick watched the girl. He could almost see her brain whirring, working out what to say and do. Her outrage at the suggestion she had set up the kidnap was clearly fake and had already passed. Her aggressive defensiveness was the wrong move, the wrong emotion at the wrong time. It was the response of someone who had been caught out in a lie and hoped bluster would be good camouflage. He knew Julie would have spotted this too. She remained calm, sitting back in her chair drinking tea.

'First, Frankie Gray. You set up the kidnap with him, didn't you? What else do you know about him?' she asked.

'Jules man, I haven't done anything with Frankie. He's a fucking creep. I hate him. I've done nowt, right? He's Jimmy's manager. That's all I know.'

She was still defensive but now maybe a little less so.

'Is he a gangster?' asked Nick.

'Gangster? No. Not in the way you mean. He's just a rich bloke and rich blokes always know blokes who do their dirty work, don't they? He knows them sort of blokes. But he's not the Mafia or whatever. Jimmy wouldn't even deal with him if he was. Jimmy's soft as clarts, you should bloody know that. He'd not be involved with anyone who was a gangster. Frankie just employs hard blokes and lawyers and accountants and that.'

'How long's he been doing that for?'

'Since he played in France, I think. Years.'

'Does he have access to Jimmy's money?'

'He can write cheques and he's got a card or something on one of Jimmy's business accounts but I don't know really, I don't understand it all. It's not something we're brought up to understand round here. Jimmy's got more money than this whole estate put together and then times 100.'

'I know, it's a different world isn't it?' said Julie.

'You haven't a clue,' she said with a wry, knowing smile.

She sat back on the sofa.

'Do you know what it's like to have anything you want, whenever you want it? I do. It's amazing. Just like that, you can get it.' She snapped her fingers.

'It must be great,' said Nick, not believing that for a second. She certainly didn't seem happy. It seemed more like she was pleased with the achievement of having that option, rather than with the actual money.

'When Jimmy bought those Phyllis Plant paintings, did they get checked out in the house for insurance?' asked Nick.

'Yeah, Frankie organised it all. Some old bloke came round. He smelt funny, like off milk. Horrible. He looked at them, said they were all genuine and then went away.'

'Then what happened to them?'

'Frankie sent them to get professionally cleaned and framed and that and when they came back they were hung in the gallery the day before I saw you two at the party. Frankie organised all of it. He does all that sort of thing for Jimmy but he messed up one of them. Jimmy didn't like the frame. I told him to get Frankie to have it done again but he hates having to confront Frankie over anything so he just sorted it himself.'

'So Frankie could have swapped the real ones for the fakes when they were away getting cleaned?' asked Julie.

Pinky laughed suddenly. 'Do you really think they were all fakes? Eeee God I bloody hope they were, that'd be total class.'

'We think he bought real ones but they were replaced with fakes, probably by Frankie,' said Nick.

She laughed again. 'Brilliant. I wish I'd thought of doing that.'

She said it flatly, arms by her side. There was nothing in her body language to indicate she was doing anything other than telling the truth now.

'Look Pinky, I know this might sound weird but is Jimmy bent?' said Nick.

'Is he bent? Is he gay, you mean? No, he's definitely not gay,' she said incredulously.

'No, I mean corrupt. Has he ever talked to you about taking money for match-fixing?'

She crossed her arms, her eyes flicked from Nick to Julie and back to Nick. A different look this time. Edgy.

'Why are you asking that, like?'

'Just answer the question,' said Julie.

'I don't know anything about it,' she said, turning her mouth down.

'But you know it goes on?' asked Julie.

'Whatever goes on, I don't know anything about it. That's all I'm going to say.'

225

'Oh stop trying to be clever, it doesn't suit you,' said Julie, getting up and standing over the girl, hands on hips. 'Tell us what you know about match-fixing or we'll walk out of here and tell the police about the fake kidnapping. We've got recordings of Finlay on the phone, we've got film of him collecting the money and of the bloke he used as a decoy. We've got pictures of you wearing that short black wig at his flat in Seaton Carew. So don't bullshit us any longer, right?'

She leaned over the girl, jabbing her finger into her face. Pinky slapped her hand away and tried to push past Julie but she was eight inches taller and much broader and easily pushed her back down.

'I know you don't realise this, but we're doing you a huge favour, Pinky. Now be sensible.'

The girl flopped back down with a sigh and seemed to give way, slapping the arms of the chair with the palms of her hands as she did so.

'Alright, alright. Fucking hell. Alright. How did you get photos of me?'

'Just luck,' said Nick. 'I followed Finlay to Seaton one day, though I didn't guess it was you in that wig. Not at first.'

'Bloody wig. I don't even have it anymore...dunno where it's gone. Fucking thing itched anyway. Yes alright, he's been match-fixing. Long before I knew him mind, he's not done it in the last year but I heard all about it. He'd let in a goal or whatever at certain times when bets had been placed. It was all Frankie's thing from way back. He made Jimmy do it.'

'He *made* him do it? Jimmy didn't want to do it?' said Nick.

'No.'

'He said that?'

'Not really. He said it was best I don't know anything about it but I could tell when they talked about it. I think they want him to do it again now he's set to play more games for Boro but he's resisting.'

'They? Who's they?'

'That freak Yashie mostly. He's horrible.'

'Yeah, we didn't like him,' said Julie.

'Others have been around but it's mainly him. Frankie set it all up as far as I can tell. He knew all the people. They kept me out of it but they're all so arrogant, they got sloppy and started bragging about it when I could hear. Fucking idiots.'

'So what about the fire?' said Julie.

'I honestly don't know anything about it. Jimmy was away when it started so he can't have done it, can he? Do you think I did it? Well I didn't. I swear. Frankie might have done it but I've heard nothing at all, right? I don't know who shot those two women either. If Frankie was involved in anything like that, he'd never let me or Jimmy know. But if you want a nasty bit of work I'd go and speak to Macca. He's a lecherous creep and always puts his hands on you, touches you up, I hate him and he's got loads of dodgy mates in the East End. He's always going on about them, like he's one of the Krays or something.'

'But Jimmy thinks he's alright?' said Nick.

'He's more Frankie's mate. He worked for him in Spain and he only comes over with Frankie. This is what I mean - all these people - I really don't like any of them and the whole world they live in is...,' she squirmed in her seat, 'it's weird and seedy, like...they're not straightforward...you can't trust anything any of them say. I told you that Nick, at the party, remember? They're all phoney wankers, not real people, like. Not like people round here.'

'Yeah you did. You also said that extended to Jimmy,' said Nick.

'Well, yeah...I was probably just mad at him.'

'You don't think he's phoney then?' said Julie. 'We like him, he's always seems nice.'

'He is. But...I don't know...I mean you don't know what someone is like when they're not with you, do you?' She looked way, squirming in her seat again.

'You've got doubts about him? Has he had affairs?' said Julie.

'I don't know. I don't think so. But he had a lot of girlfriends in

Spain and France. I know that.'

'Well, he's a footballer....'

'Yeah I know...but...it's not just that.'

Julie leaned forward. 'What are you trying to say Pinks? You can tell me.'

'It's nothing. I mean, it's just a feeling I've been getting, like.'

'What sort of feeling?' asked Nick.

'A feeling that I might not know him as well as I thought I did. Some weird stuff.'

She cracked her fingers one at a time, stared at the floor and shrugged.

'And what prompted that?' Julie said,

'I'd rather not say. It's dead embarrassing, man.'

She glanced up at him and then Julie, her forehead creased in a deep frown.

Julie looked over to him. 'Go and put the kettle on for a couple of minutes, Nick.'

She flicked her eyebrows at him to indicate he should leave the room.

He went into the kitchen. It had to be something to do with sex. How did women talk to each other about sex? It had to be very different from how men talked about it. He rested against the sink and looked around the kitchen. There was a cork board on the wall with a calendar. Next to it notes were pinned as reminders to do shopping or pay bills. A yellow post-it note with a phone number but no name was at eye level. Nick took out his phone and called the number. It rang once, twice and a voicemail kicked in.

'You've reached Emmy Green. I'm sorry I'm not available at present, please leave a message.'

Nick rang off and stared at the phone. What the fuck? What was she doing with Emmy's phone number? She must have been here, just as Jackie had said. Maggie must know Emmy.

Julie poked her head around the door. 'You can come back in now,' she said.

'What was that about?'

She made a face. 'I'll tell you later.'

He pointed at the yellow post-it note. 'See this? It's Emmy's phone number.'

She opened her eyes wide. 'Really?'

They went back into the front room.

'Please don't say anything to anyone about Finlay. Mam would go spare if she knew. We want to get away when the moment's right. I've had enough of being a bloody WAG. I liked the lifestyle for a while but I'd go insane if I had to spend my life living in that world. But I'll never have a chance like this again. Jimmy is worth over 150 million, so he won't miss the cash. Finlay says it's a victimless crime and he's right, isn't it he? Please don't shop us. I swear down it's nothing to do with Frankie Gray. I swear. Me and Fin came up with it all. Mam didn't even know until I told her. I'm sorry he had to threaten you, Nick. For what it's worth, like, he thinks you're a nutter. You put the shits right up him on the phone.'

She gave him The Big Smile. The old trick. It worked.

'We're not bothered, man,' he said.

She looked pleadingly at both of them.

A big scam to get out of a dead-end life was almost noble. And she was right, Jimmy could easily afford it, though he might well have given her the money if she'd only asked.

'Don't worry, we won't say anything,' said Nick in return for another smile.

'Not unless you've been lying to us,' added Julie. 'Are you sure you didn't do the kidnap scam with Frankie? Don't lie to me.'

'I've not been lying Jules, honest,' said Pinky, shaking her head, her almond eyes wide open, 'it was me and Fin. We came up with it.'

'Where's Maggie?' asked Julie.

'She must be at the club or in town. I've not seen her.'

'She's got Emmy Green's number in the kitchen,' said Julie. 'You might want to ask her why.'

They stood up to leave.

'She's not has she? I don't get that at all. I'll have it out with her about that,' said Pinky, wiping her palms on her thighs as she stood up.

'Okay, well...good luck with...with everything,' said Nick as they advanced to the door.

'Yeah you too, I hope you find who killed your friend.'

He turned to look at her as they left, hoping for one last smile, but she was closing the door quickly and firmly.

They walked around to Jackie Wells' house.

'She's quite a kid that one and I believe her about not being involved with Frankie,' said Nick as they went in the gate.

'Yeah I do too – though you only believe her because she was giving you the full love headlights. You melted like snow in a fire.'

'True. I even knew that as it was happening. So what was she too embarrassed to say in front of me? I assumed it's something to do with sex?'

Julie tried the front door; it was locked.

'The thing is, right, you don't understand how weird some blokes are about sex,' she said.

'I'm not naïve, Jules. I know blokes can be total bastards.'

She cleared her throat and looked up at him, almost a little embarrassed to say the words.

'She said Jimmy wouldn't have sex with her unless she'd removed all her pubic hair and he was really insistent about it.'

'Isn't that the fashion anyway?

'Yeah but think about it man... pubic hair is a symbol of adulthood in a way, isn't it?' It says you're no longer a child because you've gone through puberty, so to my mind, if someone doesn't like it to the point of refusing to have sex with you unless you're bald down there, they don't really want to have sex with an adult, and she says he insisted from day one.'

There was no reply from the house. They walked back to their cars and leaned on his BMW.

'Are you really saying Jimmy is some sort of...I dunno...some sort of paedophile? Surely if he was, he'd not be with Pinky at all because she's 21 and very much a woman, not a girl, pubic hair on or off.'

She pursed her lips. 'I know what you're saying but she feels it's not right. In fact, I think she's really creeped out by it. But it didn't stop there. She also said that he was rough with her.'

'Rough? You mean he hits her?'

She shook her head. 'No, I mean rough during sex and not in...you know...in a normal way...I mean wanting to inflict pain. Like he was turned on by it. She's had to stop him.'

Nick shifted in his seat uncomfortably. This sort of thing made him feel awkward and a bit prudish. Julie was far more worldly-wise on such matters.

'What does that, you know...what does it mean?'

'Don't be naïve, Nick. You know what it means - making demands, being aggressive and overly physical. Forcing your...your lust on someone or dominating them. It's one short step from rape. It might even be rape. It certainly shows disrespect. And Pinky really doesn't like it, I can tell and she's right to, mind. I told her not to go back to him and that she must follow her instincts. Too many women don't and end up in trouble one way or another. I don't want that to happen to her. She's not told her mother...she's too embarrassed to say anything. I think she just needed someone to be on her side.'

'Bloody hell, I'd never have thought he was like that.'

'Neither would I. But like I said, some men are weird about sex. Trust me. It changes them.'

'I'm not sure I even want to know. I was always just grateful a woman would grant me the favour. I hated the idea of being to be one of those guys who hassles women for sex so I always waited to be waved in. It just seemed safer. Probably missed out on it sometimes because of that but...I dunno Jules, I mean, you don't want to be a bastard just because you're horny. That's always been my take.'

'A lot of men are not like you, I can tell you that for nowt.'

'I was never like that with you when we first met was I?'

'Quite the opposite, you never even realised when I was waving you in. I had to actually put my hands down your pants before you twigged.' She snorted a laugh. 'I'd have had your pants off on our first date if I'd had even the slightest encouragement, actually. Don't you remember?'

'Not really. I mean, I'd never have guessed that. I remember we got on really well and were laughing a lot. It just never occurred to me that a woman would be instantly physically attracted to me like that, especially not someone I'd actually want to have sex with.'

'Maybe that's what turned me on – the fact you were oblivious.'

'I've never understood where people get these perversions from, whatever it is...pissing on people, dressing up as a nurse, S and M, bondage, all of that. Is regular sex not enough for people? Are they really so jaded by orgasms? I mean, sex is very pleasurable as it is. Why all this messing around? Surely there's only a couple of positions worth doing it in...after that it's just rearranging the furniture for the sake of it.'

She unlocked the Peugeot and looked around.

'Yeah, but sometimes you don't know or realise until it's too late that you've got into bed with someone who's weird. I bet if you asked them most women have been in a sexual situation where at some point they've suddenly realised that the bloke might be a bit strange and they've just had to go through with it and then get out as soon as possible. It happens all the time to one degree or another.'

'God. I don't like the real world, Jules. Has that happened to you?'

'Of course it has. Sex becomes a power trip for some men or an excuse to unleash their worst side. Whatever words they say beforehand, if they don't really respect women, it always comes out during sex. The trick is to spot what they're like in advance.

Usually you can; but not always. Jimmy Repp being offended by something as natural as pubic hair, like I say, that's fucked up and it won't stop there. That's not an isolated, freaky thing, it's part of a theme. It tells me he likes girls young. He doesn't want an adult woman for sex. That's what it says to me. Even though Pinky is 21, he wants her to look under-age. That's his preference. All those models he went out with in Europe were 16 and 17, remember?'

'And she wasn't just making this up to get sympathy, was she?'

'Oh no. She was for real. I'm sure she's quite sexually experienced. She'll have been at it since she was 15 or 16 like most lasses on the estate were in my day. So she knows his attitude is out of the ordinary. I think he's nice to her most of the time but she's freaked out by what he wants from her in the bedroom and I think that's made her want out. Remember the rapey alarm I talked about? Hers has gone off. The kidnap was just a way to make the split happen with an added bonus and I don't blame her one bit. Shit. You know what?'

'What?'

'I think my good guy radar might have stopped working with Jimmy Repp. Let's get over there now.'

CHAPTER 14

The Teesside International hotel was busy with some sort of conference of sales executives dressed uncomfortably in ill-fitting business suits.

'This reminds me of the life I left behind when I went back to college. God, I really don't miss it,' said Julie looking around as they walked through the lobby to Jimmy's suite.

'But you were good at it. You don't get to be a legal PA at one of the north-east's biggest law firms without being any good,' said Nick as they strode through the foyer.

'Oh aye, I could do the job, but it sucks your soul out of your eyes having to kowtow to the corporate bullshit. I don't think I can ever go back to it now I've had a year out. I like my freedom. I like not having to take orders off someone.'

'You've been hanging around me too much.'

They went upstairs, where Nick knocked on Jimmy's door and then put his ear to the wood.

'Sounds like someone's in.'

A voice came from inside: 'Just a minute.'

'Probably thinks we're the cleaner.'

When the door opened, Jimmy stood there in jeans and a hoodie. Was he really some sort of pervert? He looked so normal, so regular.

'Hey guys!' he said with a smile. 'How nice to see you, come in, come in...ah, you've got the picture. That was quick.'

They walked into the suite. Nick wasted no time.

'It's bad news Jimmy, It's not a Phyllis Plant. It's a fake.'

His mouth dropped open and he looked blankly at them.

'You're kidding me. Shiiiittt.'

He ran his large hand through his floppy dark hair.

'Yeah, it's a bummer but there you go,' said Nick, dismissively.

'I don't understand that. Harrison saw all the pictures I bought, every one of them. Frankie was sure about that. He should have spotted it then.'

'Yeah, he said he'd seen the originals but that he hadn't seen this one before,' said Nick, putting the picture on a table and looking around for any sign of Jimmy's business manager.

'I'm stunned...I'd better get in touch with Emmy and Frankie then. They should know about this.'

'Is Frankie around, Jimmy?' asked Nick.

'No, he's been in London on business, but he's on his way back.'

'Ah right. Well, I wouldn't go running to him just yet because there's something you've got to know. We think the real pictures were swapped for fakes so the fakes got burned in the fire. That's what's happened Jimmy. This one only survived because, unknown to Frankie, you pulled it out of the gallery because you didn't like the frame. The real ones are somewhere else now, awaiting re-sale in a few years, no doubt. Frankie did this. He organised it all. He was in charge of the cleaning and re-framing, wasn't he? He must have done the switch then. You didn't realise because, although you love art, you don't know a fake PP from a real one. He knew that. He pulled the wool over all of our eyes at your party.'

Jimmy laughed awkwardly and flopped down on a sofa. 'You're not serious, surely?'

'Deadly serious. Why do you think you've got a fake picture here?' asked Nick, pointing at the picture.

Jimmy shrugged and gave them an innocent look. 'I guess this one was a mistake by Harrison or Emmy or by someone.'

'That's crap. No-one ends up with a fake painting by mistake,' said Nick, a little impatiently. For the first time Jimmy's 'aw shucks' act was annoying. He should be outraged but instead he was just shrugging. He did this with everything; it was a character fault. Maybe he did have something to hide.

'It's not just a small thing this, Jimmy. Myra LeFevre almost certainly painted this and she was murdered and so was Lisa Lambert. That's no coincidence. I need your help to find out who killed them.'

Jimmy shrugged and smiled.

'I don't know Nick....this sounds too weird to me. I've known Frankie a long time and he wouldn't do something like this, he's not a killer, and I'm sorry about your friend but you know, until there's some proof, it just sounds like a crazy story. I don't think I can help you.'

Nick looked at Julie. She wore an expression of disdain.

'I'm sorry you feel like that because, you see Jimmy, I don't want to have to do this but if we're going to catch the killer – which, if it's not Frankie, it's someone he's paying – we need your help and if you don't want to help us then I'm going to have to make you help us. I shouldn't fucking have to ask you to do the right thing but if you're going to be awkward...'

'I'm not being awkward. This is just a lot of rubbish,' he said, almost but not quite losing his temper.

Nick put his hands on his hips and stared down at him.

'We know about your match-fixing scam,' he said as plainly and unemotionally as he could.

'What?!' He stood up, towering over Nick.

'But I'm not here to beat you up about it and I've no interest in taking it to the police.' He stared the big Dutchman in the eyes as he spoke.

Okay, he had actually already told Sarge but he was prepared to lie as much as was necessary. He went on, 'I'm sure you've got reasons and on the scale of human wickedness it's pretty low. I know you don't need the money so if you're being bullied into it, if Frankie Gray has got something over you or is making you do it, we need to know that as well. He's not going to get away with these murders. You might as well be on the side of the good guys, Jimmy.'

'It's where you usually want to be,' said Julie, setting her jaw against him just like her mother.

His heart was racing now. The Dutchman held his hands wide and interrupted her...

'I really, really just don't know what you're talking about. I feel

236

like I should be insulted but maybe it's the language or something. Maybe I just misunderstand you. So we'll shake hands and say goodbye, yes? No more of this talk now. It's all just bullshit from another planet...you're crazy.'

He got up to usher them out of the room but they stood their ground.

'...look, forget all that, the fixing is all bullshit to me, I couldn't care less, we really just want to find out who killed Lisa and Myra. We need your help, we need information about Frankie's movements, about what he's been doing,' said Nick, pleading with him.

He picked up the painting and thrust it at him.

'Don't you understand? This is her work and she was killed because of it so forgive me for not giving a fuck if you're offended by our accusations. Women are dead because of this shit. So shut up and listen to me...'

He strode into the centre of the room.

'...you obviously didn't know this was a fake.'

'No, of course not,' Jimmy said, defensively.

'So like we said, the pictures were exchanged for fakes before the party because they were genuine when you bought them. That must have been done by Frankie, or organised by him. Right? It must have been. He was the only one with access. That's right isn't it?' He leaned into him, jabbing his finger into Jimmy's face.

'Again with this crazy talk. I'm calling security...I'm not having you say these things...I think you must have gone mad,' he said, picking up the phone and calling down to reception.

Nick saw no point in getting thrown out of the hotel.

'Okay, so you don't want to talk about it or even consider that your manager is behind the deaths of two innocent people, okay, so we'll go, but you fucking hear me good, Jimmy. We'll get to the bottom of these murders...and if I have to take you down for this match-fixing or for anything else, I fucking will. Right? Don't fucking doubt it for one fucking minute, pal.'

He yanked the door open and marched out with Julie right behind him.

'What did you make of that?' asked Nick as they got back into the car, wiping sweat from his brow.

'Pffff...I don't know. I can't read him. He seems genuine on one hand but then all I could think about was what Pinky had told me and it made me feel queasy just looking at him. Christ, I just don't know. I can understand why he wouldn't even listen, but I do understand why he wouldn't just confess to being a match-fixer, especially if he is being bullied or blackmailed into it somehow. We need some leverage over him. When we get back why not call Sarge and tell him everything we now know from talking to Pinky. Give it to him to sort out. I don't fancy Repp will hold out for long when he's given the good cop, bad cop treatment by Sarge and his cronies.'

'Yeah but that'll put Pinky in the shit, won't it? It'll bring her scam out into the open. She'll do time for that, man. Is that what you want? I mean, I know it's illegal and all that but do I want to send a kid like her to jail for years and years? The answer to that is 'no' isn't it? It's no because we don't really see it as much of a crime. No-one got hurt, all that happened was a rich bloke was made a little less rich. And like she said, it's her way out and we both know that you need a way out of a shit start in life.'

Julie rubbed her face with the palms of her hands and growled: 'Yeah yeah, I know...oh God...I don't know what to bloody do.'

When they got back at the farmhouse he made tea and took it out into the garden on a tray. Julie was standing by a wild, unruly sprawl of honeysuckle which grew up, over and around an old fence. It was in full flower and its scent was overwhelmingly heady, rich and silky, almost like someone had lit a whole packet of joss sticks.

She turned towards him and, with a smile, put her arms around his waist. They kissed as a soft, warm wind blew their hair together, intertwining strands of dark brown and blonde like a marble rye loaf.

'It's such a lovely afternoon, you know you could travel a long way and not find anywhere as beautiful as this,' said Nick, looking around at the peaceful rural scene.

As he spoke he noticed a glint, a flash of light from the footpath that ran the length of the back field out into open countryside.

'Yeah, good old Teesside, both bloody ugly and yet bloody beautiful,' she said wistfully, putting her arms around his neck, smiling into his eyes.

He was about to reply when there was a small popping noise on the summer breeze, a noise like the crack of a piece of wood, not loud but distinct.

Julie let out a piercing strangled cry, a noise like none he'd ever heard. It was distress, shock and pain all rolled into one short and brutal expulsion. Her face contorted, her eyes closed and he felt her weight fall onto him.

'Jules? Are you alright?' Her answer was a guttural moan as she slumped to the ground. He looked down at her, his brain numb with horror as a small patch of dark red blood oozed through her white t-shirt. What the fuck was this? What?

'Julie! Oh my God. Jules! Jules! What the hell...?!' He sank to his knees and tried to look at her face. She was unconscious. Instinctively he touched the blood soaking through her shirt as if to confirm that this was real. It was. She had been shot. Shot once. In the back.

He grabbed the phone from the table, dialled 999 and screamed into the phone: 'Get an ambulance here now! My girlfriend has been shot. Yes shot!' He gave the address and then threw the phone down, scrambling on his hands and knees around her, not knowing whether he should try and move her. He heard another crack and a bullet whizzed somewhere in his vicinity. What the fuck? He scrambled for cover behind an old concrete coal bunker. She was still in reach, slumped on the grass, and he kept talking.

'It's okay Jules, just take it easy, the ambulance is coming, we'll

239

get you fixed up. Don't worry.'

He stroked the ends of her soft, yellow hair, too scared to look close enough to know if she was still actually breathing. Please still be breathing. Please, please, please. The sun burned down onto her back, her head in the shadow cast by the bunker. She hadn't moved since hitting the ground except for an occasional twitch. Oh Christ...she was dead...she was going to die here. That bastard Frankie Gray had shot her like Lisa and Myra. The bastard.

Where the fuck was the ambulance? Don't die. Please God, not Julie. Not her. Was his love not big enough, not strong enough to keep her alive? He loved her with every ounce of his existence. That had to count for something, didn't it? His head felt like he'd drunk half a bottle of whiskey, weirdly dizzy and numb and disorientated, totally unable to fathom or grasp the speed at which his life had changed in that moment, in hearing that gunshot. One fraction of a second he was holding her in his arms, the next she had gone from him. Surely there had to be more of a warning, a run-up, a steady introduction. Death couldn't come that quickly, could it? One moment she was alive, the next she was on the ground and dying, the life draining out of her by the second.

As his brain spun like an engine in neutral there was another cracking noise and then another. More gunshots. He didn't see it but felt it as one bullet and then a second whizzed just past the bunker and embedded themselves in the wooden fence. Fucker. Anger rose up in him, bursting through his mental fuzziness and incomprehension, something more primal taking over his soul, a profound inner fury at this injustice. This would not stand.

He ran at a half-squat into the kitchen, reached into the drawer and pulled out the gun along with the bag of ammunition. The fucker wasn't getting away with this. No way. He loaded the gun just as Ricky had shown them, put all the ammo in his pocket and ran back outside, positioning himself behind the old coal bunker, looking up towards the footpath. It was defined by a long row of ash and birch trees. Gaps between them showed the land beyond.

The anger burned brightly in him now.

'Come on then you fucker!' he yelled, standing up with his arms out wide, the gun in his right hand, 'Show yourself! You fucking pussy! Fuck you!' He yelled it with all the power his lungs held, spitting out the words like poison.

As soon as the sounds left his lips he dropped to his knees behind the concrete bunker just as a bullet passed overhead and into the woodshed.

But he saw them. In firing, they had given their position away. He saw exactly where the shot had come from. Yes. Yes, you fucker. Now let's fucking have you. They were maybe 20 yards away but he needed cover to get close enough to shoot them. He kissed his fingers, investing every atom of love he had for her in that kiss, and held them towards Julie's still body. The cops and the ambulance wouldn't be far now; he had one chance to avenge this.

Furious but focused and with a clear head, he ran around to the front of the house. The pathway was obscured by the mature oaks that lay to the west and north of the house. He ran low and fast into them. He was wearing an olive shirt and khaki combat trousers so he knew he would not stand out.

Now no more than ten yards from the track, he caught his breath, his heart banging in his chest like it was demanding to get out.

Movement. There was movement on the track. There. A flash of...what was it? It was a flash of pink and jet black short hair. It was fucking Pinky?! What? It made no sense. That kid was the killer? She'd come for Julie, had she? Come for him? The cold-hearted bitch. Right, let's see who's the biggest bastard here.

If she was still looking towards the back garden, she wouldn't see him run across the patch of grass that separated the trees from the old footpath. But if she was looking directly at him, for a few seconds he'd be a sitting duck. How did you do this? His only reference point was the movies. They always ran in a zigzag to avoid being shot. It was a roll of the dice. This was it. He was not going down without fighting.

He took off at a speed he hadn't known his legs could achieve and covered the ten yards in seconds. No shots were dispatched. She can't have seen him. She'd assumed he was still with Julie and was looking at the back of the house.

He spat out thick foam, squatted down beside a tall birch tree and peered out and along the dry, well-trodden path. Sirens wailed out in the distance as he looked for Pinky. Fucking hell. He had to get her now. He had to kill her. Kill her before the police came. Get it done. Do it now. Wipe it all away with one shot. Make it all stop. For Myra. For Lisa. For Julie. *Go hard or go home. Fuck them up, Nick. Fuck them up.* He emerged from his cover and stood in the middle of the grassy path. It had worked once, it could work again.

'Let's fucking 'ave you then!' he screamed, arms out wide, bouncing on his toes like a football hooligan gesturing to opposition fans.

As he shouted, he dived for cover behind a fallen tree and rolled into some shrubs. Crack. Crack. Two shots. Fucking missed. And there she was. She'd come out of hiding to fire. Now she was side on to him, squatting low, arms extended, holding a pistol. She must have thought he'd dived the other way. Yes. He had her, right here, right in view. Raise the gun and shoot her. Clean Julie's blood away with one shot. This was the moment. Her pink wrist band glowed in the shadow of the trees. She wore the short dark wig, black jeans and t-shirt - a small but perfectly formed target.

Trying to remember how Ricky had said to use the damn gun, he gripped it in his left hand and took aim at the back of her head. He'd never killed anything before, not until now. Now would be the first time. Why the fuck not?

'Instant fucking karma's gonna get you,' he said under his breath and squeezed the trigger. His first split-second thought was how easy it was to kill someone as she fell to the ground, the next split-second realisation was that the shot had missed because he'd let the recoil affect his aim. It went right over her head, missing her by a couple of inches, allowing her to dive into the overgrowth for cover.

Now gripping his left-hand wrist with his right hand, he let off two more shots as she leapt, almost cat-like, behind a large fallen oak. She let out a piercing scream.

He'd hit her with the second bullet. Hit her somewhere. But where and how much damage had he done? Now she was out of view again. He scuttled from tree to tree, peering out, trying to find her, approaching the big dead oak, one tree at a time. No more shots were fired. Was she dead behind there? She'd better be fucking dead. Sirens were now close, almost at the track. Last chance.

He squatted behind a tree adjacent to the fallen oak and listened for her breathing or for any signs of life. Nothing. He leapt out from his cover, prepared to fire the gun as soon as he saw her. But she'd gone. No sign of her. Fuck it. Sirens loud now.

Emerging from the tree-lined path he stood looking up the field of short straw wheat that waved in the summer sun. There on the brow of the low hill was a figure of a woman running in between rows of golden wheat. She'd got away using the crop as cover and was now nearly 40 metres away. His bullet must have only caused a flesh wound because she was moving without restriction and she'd covered a lot of ground quickly. He took aim, not knowing whether the gun would be able to hit her over that sort of distance and shot three times. She clearly heard it go off and dived out of view. Nick turned to see four police cars coming down the farm track with an ambulance in tow. She'd fucking well got away.

Nick ran back to the house, putting the gun into a rucksack beside the front door along with the bullets. The police were in full body armour and emerged from the vehicles with guns drawn, pointing them at his head as he approached with his hands raised.

'I'm Nick Guymer, I called you,' he said. 'Julie's in the back garden. I think she's badly hurt. Someone shot her from the path over there. They got away up through the field.'

The police frisked him as they waved in the paramedics. It was the same two who had attended Jeff. He didn't want to see them working on her. He couldn't stand it. She was surely dead now. In his brain all he could hear was her voice, her last word. Her last word had been 'beautiful'. Like her. That was all he could think. He held the word as a last memento of her life. He couldn't let himself even think about her being dead; his brain just wouldn't compute it. All he wanted to do was hunt Pinky down and shoot her. Kill her. His rage was incendiary and atomic deep and wouldn't be swallowed down. Now, what Julie had said, '*go hard or go home*', made sense. That was their philosophy on the estate. '*Fuck them up, Nick, fuck them up*.' Lisa's voice now. Echoes of dead women in his brain. But he wasn't going to tell the police his plan. This was personal. He would hunt her down. He would finish this. Where would she go? Back home? Seaton? Wherever it was, he'd find her. He cursed himself for not being a better shot and killing her when he had the chance.

Two officers went to the path, guns drawn. More cops soon arrived until there were about 20 of them shutting down the crime scene and beginning to collect evidence.

He sat on the old park bench against the front of the house as it all unfolded. Soon, Julie was taken into the back of the ambulance on a stretcher. As they closed the door, he got to his feet and called to the paramedic he knew was called Robbie.

'Is she dead?' he asked plainly, bluntly. She was. He knew she was. The look in the paramedic's eyes told him he was right. It was a look of pity, not of hope.

'We'll do everything we can for her,' he said, clearly avoiding the question. They took off at high speed.

Then the questioning began. The re-living of the experience was sickening. He wasn't even at home to himself anymore. He had locked himself into a dark room away from all this shit and just left the auto-pilot switched on to deal with the practicalities. His inner voice conducted a different conversation to what his actual voice communicated. Kill Pinky. Fucking kill her. The fury didn't dissipate one microgram.

A familiar figure soon arrived. Dave Sargent.

'Sorry to see you so soon in these circumstances,' he said, patting Nick on the back and sitting down next to him. 'When I saw the call come in, I came right over. '

'Are you in charge of this?'

'I will be, yeah. Look Nick, I realise this is difficult and that everything in your life has fallen apart and you're obviously distraught, but right now is the best chance we have of catching this killer.'

He said killer. He already knew Julie was dead. They just weren't telling him.

'Do you have any idea who might want to do this?'

If he told him, they'd probably find her and arrest her and he wouldn't have his revenge. Putting her in jail wasn't good enough. He wanted her to die and he wanted to shoot her. It was the only thing that would re-balance the universe. *Fuck them up, Nick. Go hard or go home.* Over and over in his brain. He'd promised. But he had to say something. It still had to be something to do with Frankie Gray. Set them off on that chase. It was all bullshit now anyway. He didn't care...only wiping away Julie's death mattered.

'I don't know who it was. Someone paid by Frankie Gray. I think,' he said, putting his head in his hands to give the impression that he was too distressed to talk.

'You don't have to wait here, is there anywhere else you can go? Anyone else you'd like to stay with, maybe?' Sarge asked.

'No. I've got to get to the hospital... for Julie, like, and Jeff.'

'Yeah, of course. I can call you if we need any information. Are you okay to drive?'

'Yeah, I'd rather be doing something even if It's only driving, anything to occupy my mind. I don't know what to say or do. I feel like the sun has gone out. I feel dead inside.'

He arrived at the hospital car park in an expressionless daze as though the rest of existence was passing him by at an entirely different speed. How could everything keep happening as normal? He was disconnected. In the forefront of his mind all he could see was Julie's dark red blood on her white t-shirt. He couldn't even see her anymore, just the blood, the lifeblood, the death blood. Oh God. No Julie. No Julie! Just when it had all been so perfect. Too perfect. No-one is allowed that much pleasure or happiness. That much love. Their love. It's not allowed on this bastard cruel earth.

He wiped his eyes dry on his sleeve and explained the situation to the receptionist. She told him to wait but he couldn't wait, sitting still was something people who had an ounce of contentment with life would do. He had none. He just had a deep, visceral, hollow pain. This was not life, this was a living death.

So he went for a walk around the hospital, walking aimlessly, following coloured lines until they ran out, knowing that somewhere in the building were his mother, soul-mate and best mate. Eventually he found his way to Jeff's ward, almost by accident. The dark-haired nurse recognised him.

'How is he?'

'Not much change just yet. He's been awake on and off but he's not been making much sense. It's quite normal after this sort of thing. We're just letting him rest. You can look in on him if you want but he's asleep.'

Nick looked around the corner to see Jeff lying in bed. His hair had been tied back in a ponytail. He looked washed out but was breathing easily as he slept.

'I'll check up on him later,' he said, taking his leave and going back down to the reception area. A doctor was waiting for him.

'Mr Guymer?' he said.

'Yeah?'

'I understand you are Julie Wells' next of kin.'

'I'm her partner. We live together.'

He wanted to steel himself for what was to come next. He wanted to be brave, stoic, accept it as part of the unpredictable travails of life, but he couldn't. All he had was numbness and fury.

'Okay, well Julie is in the operating theatre now. We're removing the bullet, assessing the damage and trying to fix what we can.

She's lost a lot of blood, so we need to sort that out and to stabilise her.'

'So she's actually alive?'

'Well...yes,' he said, slowly, awkwardly, and then looked away from him and at the floor, 'but she's very unwell, Mr Guymer.' He tipped his head, almost as though flinching from the pain of saying those words.

'Unwell?! What, has she got the flu or something? Unwell? She's been shot in the back. That's more than fucking unwell, isn't it?!'

The doctor nodded apologetically and a nurse looked around at the raised voice.

'Sorry, yes, I mean, she's in a bad way. But rest assured, we'll do everything we can for her. She's in good hands but you should prepare yourself if things don't go...,' he trailed off, seeing the wild look in Nick's eye.

'She was in my arms when she was shot,' said Nick, placing his hands around her again. 'It didn't do any good. I couldn't protect her; all I wanted to do was love her. That's all. It's not too much to ask, is it?'

Why was he even talking? Killing Pinky would be a better use of his time.

'No. Not at all. Do the police have any idea who...'

'Not yet.'

'Okay, well let's hope they catch them...you're free to stay here if you want Mr Guymer, but we probably won't have any news until she's out of theatre. Even if all goes well, she'll be in intensive care. Might be best to go home and come back tomorrow. We'll call you if anything happens.'

Happens meant dies. He knew that. Don't fucking call, pal.

He nodded, went back to the car, took the rucksack out of the car boot, took out the pistol, loaded it, put it in his waistband and drove to Pinky's mother's house so he could blow her pretty little head right off her fucking shoulders.

How could she treat Julie like this? She'd been like a big sister to her. It made no sense. He had to tell Julie's mother what had happened to her daughter. If he told her who had shot her, the brothers would swing into action. They'd get Pinky and they'd kill her, swiftly and mercilessly. He didn't want that. This mission was for him and him alone. *Fuck them up, Nick. Go hard or go home.*

He pulled up outside Pinky's house. There were no cars outside, the curtains were drawn. It looked like no-one was home. A knock on the door didn't produce anyone. He walked around the back and peered in through the kitchen window. Three doors down, he saw Jackie Wells sitting in her garden in the evening sun. He went round to her house and walked down the side to the back garden. She looked up at him.

'Alright there, son. Lovely weather isn't it? What are you doing here?'

'Yeah. Lovely.'

She looked him up and down.

'What's wrong? Where's our Jules?'

He stood opposite her. She narrowed her eyes and drew deeply on a cigarette.

'What's up? What's happened?' she said, reading the look in his eyes.

'I'm sorry Jackie but Jules has been shot.'

She continued to look at him with hard, lined eyes and immediately asked: 'Is she dead?' Confront it face on. That was her way.

'No. They're operating on her now. It doesn't look good though. She lost a lot of blood. They told me to prepare for the worst.'

'Where the hell did this happen?'

'Our house. Someone shot her in the back from a footpath.'

'What? And they got away?'

'Yeah. Sorry. I tried to...'

'Who was it?'

'I...I..I don't know.'

'Don't you, like?' she asked with some degree of disbelief.

Her responses were so calm, cold, unemotional. He envied her this rationality right now. Maybe she'd always thought this day might happen and some part of her had been ready for the horrible death of one of her kids.

Jackie shook her head and looked past him.

'I don't understand. Why would anyone want to shoot our Julie? Any number might want a go at our Ricky and Kev but not our Jules, unless it's someone trying to get back at them.'

'They wanted to shoot both of us.'

He let out a deep wavering breath of air.

'Our Ricky and Kev will find out who's done it, mark my words. They'll find out.'

'Aye, well, if they do, tell them to tell me before they do anything. I want first fucking chance of some revenge.'

She lit another fag, stood up and reached out to touch his waistband.

'Is that why you're carrying that gun, is it? Listen son, don't ruin your life by acting like a fucking cowboy. Whoever did this will get caught one way or another. You don't have to play Clint Eastwood. Look, our Jules is strong as a bloody ox, she always was. If she's alive now then mark my words, son, she'll survive. I know her. I'm her mother, aren't I? She'll bloody fight to see you again, if for no other bloody reason. She loves the bones of you. Hey! Hey! Don't bloody look away from me, son, I'm telling you something you need to know.'

She slapped him hard across the right cheek with a rough, hard hand. It stung and then burned.

'Listen to me. Right? She'll pull through and I don't want her having to visit you in jail for the rest of your life for some bloody stupid thing you do now when you've gone radge.'

'Alright, I hear you. I hope you're right about her living because I really don't want to live without her, Jackie. The thought of that is worse than death. Much worse.'

'I know son, I know. You've got to be strong though. Keep

yourself together. Don't go bloody daft.'

She punched him hard on the shoulder as though to emphasise the point.

'I don't know how to do that, Jackie. I feel so fucking crushed. Seeing her there bleeding. She's so beautiful, such a lovely spirit...I love her so much. I feel like I've let her down. You lot are hard bastards. I'm not. I can't get the thought of her blood out of my mind. It's fucking torture.'

He began to cry, wiping the tears from his eyes with a shaking hand, his breath shuddering.

She grabbed his chin with her yellow-fingered, nicotine-stinking right hand, forcing him to look into her eyes.

'Look Nick...we're only hard because we've had to be. This sort of shit is what life dishes out to people like us. We're born into sod all and if we get anywhere at all in life it's never without pain and a lot of hard sodding struggle.'

She sucked hard on the cigarette and blew out a cloud of blue smoke.

'Maybe it's partly our fault, like, maybe it's the fucking system or whatever but we're born drowning here and we have to learn to swim quickly even if it's always against the tide. You feel like you're always about to go under, so you end up fighting for the sake of fighting because it's all you bloody know. Do you understand me?'

He nodded, her voice talking him down from the red anger in his blood. She put an arm around his shoulder now. It felt like being comforted by an adult, by a mother, a kind of mother he'd never really had. He instinctively leaned into her for some sort of protection.

'So this is another fight, the fight to keep Julie alive and the fight to catch the bastard that did it to her. There are no easy rides for us, son. This isn't the home bloody counties, this is Teesside. We're northern and we're hard and that's just the way it is, the way it's always been. Take bloody strength from that. She'd want you to be strong and she'd be really bloody furious with you if you did something stupid, wouldn't she? Well? Wouldn't she, son?'

She shook him.

'Yeah, she would,' he said.

'Yeah is right. So don't go shooting that thing. Leave it to the coppers or to certifiable lunatics like my sons. Don't go being like them. You're a good lad, a really bloody decent boy, and our Julie deserves you. God know she went through enough blokes to find you but when she did I always knew you were the one for her. So don't let me down now. Alright?'

'Alright Jackie, yeah.'

He debated telling her who shot her daughter. She was being so tough and supportive. She deserved to know what he knew. As she was getting her things together to go to the hospital he spoke up.

'Jackie...'

'Yes, son.'

'You know I said that I didn't know who shot her...'

'Aye...you said, like'

'Well...I was lying...I do know.'

'You do? Why didn't you tell me then? Who is it?'

'I wanted to have my revenge first. I know Kev and Ricky will hunt them down.'

'Bloody right they will, though I'll be giving them the same bloody talk I've just given you. They're no use to me in jail on a murder charge...so who was it then? Did you see him?'

' It's not a him Jackie, it's a her.'

'Eh?'

'It was Pinky.'

She stared at him with her wizened mouth agape. She looked more shocked at this news than at the news that her daughter had been shot.

'Are you sure?' she asked with incredulity.

'I chased her. She shot at me but missed. I shot at her and I think I nicked her but she got away. It was her. She was wearing the short black wig I'd seen her in before. She was dressed in all black but with a pink wristband. I'm sure it was her.'

'The fucking little bitch,' she said, spitting it out with acid venom. 'The fucking get! What the fuck does she think she's doing? Shooting our Jules...she was like a big sister to that kid. I might have bloody known and to think all we've done for her and Maggie.'

She pulled another cigarette out of a packet of Silk Cut.

'She must have got mixed up in something. Maggie is a hard-faced bitch but Pinky I had down as a clever kid. I thought she was going to do a Jules and move out and up. Stupid pissing cow.'

'I went round there but there's no-one in. I was going to kill her Jackie.'

'Well you're not bloody doing that for a start. You'll have me to answer to if you do. Right? I'm going to the hospital. I'll call Ricky and tell him what's gone on.'

'She still wants to kill me, so she might not have gone far. She's got to kill everyone who knows about the fake paintings scam she's set up with Jimmy's manager Frankie Gray. She's a clever liar. She spun me and Jules a tale, painted herself as the innocent.'

'She'll have got that from her mother. Devious little shit.'

'I should tell Dave Sargent about Pinky. I held it back. I wanted to kill her.'

'Sargent? Well you're not going on a fucking killing spree now. So it's a good idea to tell Sarge. Come on son, you can drop me off at North Tees.'

The sun was setting as he drove away from the hospital after letting Jackie out. He called the policeman and got his voicemail.

'Dave, it's Nick Guymer, call me when you've got a minute. I've got some news for you about Julie's kill...err...shooter.'

Jackie was right. If there was a chance Julie might live, he wanted to live with her, whatever state she was in. But he still had to avenge what had happened to her and to Lisa and Myra; that hadn't changed. He had to do it, to purge it from his brain, from his soul. It was his duty. He had to catch Pinky and see her punished.

He dialled Jimmy Repp's mobile but withheld his number.

'Jimmy, it's Nick.'

'Nick...I don't think we should talk after what you said earlier.'

'Forget that - something awful has happened. Julie has been shot. Someone tried to kill us both.'

'Good God....oh my God...is...is she alright?'

'No. She's nearly dead. She's fighting for her life. They're trying to keep her alive now at the hospital. She lost a lot of blood.'

He listened for Jimmy's response. It was one of disbelief.

'Oh God...my God - who the fuck would do that and why on earth…?'

Jimmy shock at the news was palpable. He may have been guilty of some things, but Nick was sure that he knew nothing about Julie's shooting.

'I know we had bad words a few hours ago. I've got to lay everything I know on the line for you. I have to tell you about it all. I know who did it. Julie being shot has changed everything. I'm coming round.'

'Okay, yeah, come over here, man. You can come here.'

He parked up at the Teesside International, put the gun in his waistband and walked up to Jimmy's suite.

'My God, you must be so freaked out, ' said Jimmy as he opened the door, sympathetic as ever.

'Yeah I am.'

He walked in and turned around.

'Do you know who did this terrible thing?' Jimmy asked.

'Yeah I do Jimmy, but you won't like it.'

'Me? Why? Can I get you a drink or something?

'Have you got any tequila?'

'Yeah, I'll have one too. Jesus, this is a bad world sometimes. I can't believe this is happening.'

He fetched two tumblers of Cuervo Gold and added ice.

'Here. It might calm you down. When did all this happen?'

'Just after we left here.'

'Wow. So who did it and why?'

Nick took a drink of the powerful tequila. He hadn't had a drink for over nine months. It tasted like poison. Acrid, bitter and strong. How the fuck did he used to drink this stuff?

'I'm just going to tell you this straight out Jimmy. I'm not bullshitting you because I saw her with my own eyes. She tried to shoot me as well.'

'She? It was a woman?'

'It was Pinky.'

The big Dutchman looked at him in silent disbelief, his head cocked at an angle as though trying to figure out if he'd understood properly. When he spoke again, he spoke slowly.

'Pinky? Are you sure?'

'Yes. It was her. She was wearing that short black wig to disguise herself, the one I told you about before.'

Jimmy took a large mouthful of tequila and stared at the carpet trying to take it all in, shaking his head, his face pale as ash.

'This makes no sense to me at all. I don't even know what to say.'

'I'm not fucking around with you Jimmy. This is serious shit. No-one is going to kill Julie and get away with it. No-one. Right? So this is what I know and I don't want any bullshit from you, nothing...now is the time for total honesty. It all stays in this room. Right? Whatever. Illegal, legal...everything. This is now all about catching Pinky. Fuck the rest of it.'

'Okay, okay, right,' said the big Dutchman, 'cards on the table...everything...'

'This all starts with the fake paintings scam we told you about. The real ones Harrison saw were replaced with the fakes Myra did. Pinky worked with Frankie on this and they have all the originals somewhere to sell at a later date. But it's not just that. You know when she was kidnapped? Well that was all bullshit as well. It never happened. She invented all of that with Finlay. She was never kidnapped, got me? It was a hoax to con you out of a million quid. She confessed that to me and Julie. I now suspect Frankie was in on that as well.'

Any colour still left in his face drained away.

'Wha?!' he exclaimed, his face a picture of helpless astonishment.

'She's never stopped seeing the kid Finlay - they plan to run off and start a new life with your money. As soon as Myra started shooting off her mouth about doing the fakes, Pinky must have shot her to shut her up because if that scam was revealed, everything would have unravelled. I thought Frankie had hired a hit-man but it was her. Then she shot Lisa and then Jules and she damn nearly got me too. She's trying to close us all down and shut us up but it's too late now...too many people, including the police, know about it. So she's really fucking dangerous. She might come here and shoot you...she's killed three people already...why stop there?'

He shook his head in disbelief and shock. 'The fucking crazy thing is I even paid for her and her mother to have shooting lessons a few months ago. They were always at the club.'

'Really? Fucking hell Jimmy.'

'Jesus I'm sorry man, I never had a clue, honest. I thought it was a hobby, a sport. I used to target-shoot when I was younger. I never bought them guns though, I swear. She must have got that herself. Shit. Shit...this is so bad. I can't believe it. I hadn't a clue. Believe me.'

As he spoke there was a knock at the door and someone let themselves in - it was Frankie Gray. Dressed in an immaculate cream linen suit, white shirt and red tie, he was surprised to see Nick; so surprised he jumped a little.

'Oh, sorry, I didn't realise you had a visitor.'

'Come in, Frankie...something terrible has happened,' said Jimmy, warily. Nick stiffened his spine. Should he shoot him?

Frankie stepped into the room and held out his right hand towards Nick, who instead stood and grabbed the camera dangling from his left hand on a strap.

'Hey what the fuck?' shouted Frankie, trying to hang onto to the Pentax. Nick grabbed his left arm and twisted it up behind his back.

'Drop the fucking camera,' he shouted into Frankie's ear.

He did as he was told.

'What the hell is this about? Jimmy? What's going on?'

'Some really bad shit has happened,' he said again, unable to look at his business manager.

Nick looked at the camera and began skimming back through the photographs.

'You fucking piece of shit,' he said, 'you fucking cunt, I'll fucking kill you for this. You gave her these didn't you? You her and her...you're as thick as fucking thieves.'

He ran at him and swung a right-handed punch into Gray's guts with as much force as could muster, sending him onto the floor, doubled up holding his stomach, trying to catch his breath.

'What? What?' shouted Jimmy, who clearly had no idea what to do but shout.

'Why have you got photos of me and Julie and Jeff on here? Eh? We saw you taking them, you cunt.'

He threw the camera onto the sofa, from where Jimmy retrieved it and took it to his laptop on the study table.

Frankie got to his feet and staggered to the door to get away. Nick pounced on him, pulling him to the ground by the shoulders and then pinning him to the floor. He felt physically immense, able to overpower and defeat anyone. The pyre of fury inside him had turned into raw energy. Holding his enemy's head by his hair, he forced it down onto the carpeted floor as hard as he could.

'Right you fucker. Start talking.'

'Fuck you!' he said, wriggling under Nick, trying to get away. But Nick was too strong by far, straddling him and pushing him back. He grabbed his hair again and slammed his head onto the floor with a thud. He could have shot him dead but he wanted to hurt him.

'I can fucking beat this out of you or you can tell just tell me. Frankly I'd prefer to beat it out of you and I fucking will beat it out of you unless you start talking within the next three seconds. One.

Two. Three. Too late, you lose.'

He slapped Grey in the face with the full palm of his hand. His jaw fell rough against his skin.

'Urgh...alright, alright....'

'No, no, you had your chance to talk, now you get the fucking kicking you deserve,' shouted Nick and sank a right fist into his eye and his left into his neck. Frankie howled in pain.

'Get off him...get off him Nick.' It was Jimmy's voice invading the red cloud of rage in his head. The big goalie dragged him off Gray and away across the room.

'Let him speak, you'll fucking kill him if you go on like this.'

They were words of sense, sense Nick needed to hear. He had lost his mind.

'Frankie, explain these pictures to me,' said the Dutchman, giving his manager a damp flannel to wipe away blood trickling from his nose.

On the laptop he'd downloaded the pictures from the camera. There were nearly 30 - 15 of Julie, Jeff and Nick, sometimes individually, sometimes in a group in Masham and on Yarm High Street, and other images of their cars. There was a photo of Nick and Julie's farmhouse and one of the footpath next to the house that Pinky had used.

'I don't think he needs to explain anything, these are all incriminating enough. He took these of us so that Pinky would know who to shoot and where to do it, just in case she didn't remember what I looked like and because she doesn't even know Jeff. Except Jeff has had a heart attack, the poor bastard, so he wasn't there. Didn't you, you twat? You've been working with her all along to con Jimmy out of millions. You fucked him over for the pictures and on the kidnapping as well, didn't you? No wonder you were so quick to assume control of the situation, you fucker. This was all your idea, wasn't it?'

'You are out of your tiny mind,' said Gray, rubbing the swelling on his face from Nick's fist. 'This is the first I've heard of any of this. I work for Jimmy, not Pinky. She's just a kid. And what's this shit you're telling me about the kidnapping?'

'You heard. It was all a hoax you cooked up with her,' said Nick, wiping a thick spit crust from his lip.

Gray laughed bitterly and repeated himself. 'My friend, you are out of your tiny mind. A hoax? Do you believe this, Jimmy?'

'Nick is sure, yeah.'

'She told me herself man!' shouted Nick.

'Well she's fucking lying. I've done nothing with her. If she's cooked up a hoax she's done it without my help. The fucking bitch. I told you not to trust her didn't I?' he said to Jimmy, spitting blood onto the expensive carpet. 'I didn't know that - for real - I never knew.'

'What about these photos?' asked Jimmy, pointing at the computer. 'These are secret photos, not holiday snaps.'

'Just in case you haven't heard yet, which I seriously doubt, Julie, my Julie, was shot this afternoon. She's on the slab now, her beautiful body getting cut open to try save her life,' shouted Nick the fury rising in him again as he said the words. He couldn't calm down.

Gray turned away, shook his head and then held up his hand. 'Christ, that's nothing to do with me. None of the shootings are anything to do with me. I swear blind.'

'You're a fucking lying toe-rag,' spat Nick, pointing at the photos.

'I took those because I thought you were up to something. I thought you were plotting something against Jimmy...'

'Bollocks!' Nick's anger flooded into his arteries again and he swung at Gray, this time missing as the manager swung back out of the way.

'Alright...I admit, I wanted photos of you in case I had to get some muscle to err...let's say, dissuade you from whatever it was you were plotting...I thought you might be planning a kidnap. You'd been sniffing around. You all looked dodgy to me. I thought the big fucking bloke was your muscle.'

'Don't judge everyone by your own standards, Gray.'

'Nick's a good guy Frankie. You're crazy. You know that. You....you're a fucked up guy, man.'

Gray spat out some more blood.

'Me? Looked in the mirror recently, have you? Remember what happened in Amsterdam, do you? Remember how I got you out of all that shit, do you? Well shut the fuck up or you know what you'll get.' He sneered at Jimmy and jabbed a finger at him. 'Remember why I fucking own you. If I choose, you're gone, just like that. So don't fuck around with me, Jimmy boy.'

He turned to Nick.

'If Pinky is the shooter it's nothing to do with me. She's working alone or with that piss-head bitch of a mother.'

'Yeah? And how did this fake painting end up in Jimmy's collection then?' asked Nick, for the first time half-believing what Gray was saying as he picked up the bubble-wrapped picture from a table.

'Fucked if I know. I had old man Harrison check out all that shit. What more could I do? You've got the wrong man and I mean that in more ways than one. Nobody does this to me and gets away with it. Nobody.'

He yanked open the door and stormed out.

Jimmy closed it behind him and swept his hair off his forehead.

'Man, that was fucking terrible.' He stood with his hands on his waist, caught his breath and then let out a guffaw of laughter.

'What?' said Nick.

'He was scared of you, man. I've never seen him like that before. He was in...what do you say...in pant-shitting mode, yes? Ha ha. You scared him big time.'

Jimmy held a hand out for him to high-five but Nick didn't feel like celebrating anything.

'So like I said, cards on the table, is he blackmailing you over match-fixing and did he organise that with the Yashie fella from Singapore?'

'Ah the bloody match-fixing thing again?!'

'Well?'

'I've no doubt Frankie has had his fingers into match-fixing and Yashie is the King Fixer but it's nothing to do with me, I swear. I'd tell you if it was...especially now, after all this.'

'You're kidding me. Really? I mean, I don't care, man...it's not important except if Frankie is using it against you.'

'Yeah really,' he smiled and held his arms out wide.

'But I watched all those dodgy goals when you threw it in and gave away penalties. They were all legitimate mistakes?'

'I'm afraid so. I'm just a bit shit sometimes.'

'But there was someone in an orange hat behind the goal at most of your games. I was sure they were giving you a sign.'

Jimmy laughed again. 'You're crazy. I can't believe you thought that meant anything. That was probably my goalkeeping coach Jans. He's not over here but he worked with me in France and Spain. He'd stand behind the goal and watch what I did in real time. He thought it was the best way to see what I was doing rather than just rely on tapes.'

'But he was behind both goals.'

'Yeah, he could go from one end to the other, though sometimes his brother Patrik helped in the big stadiums.

'But why wear an orange hat? I thought it was to make him more visible to you.'

Jimmy shrugged. 'They're Dutch. It's our colour isn't it? We are The Orange. There's nothing to it Nick. You've added two and two and made something that isn't four.'

'So what was he talking about when he mentioned Amsterdam?'

'That? It's not good, I'm afraid. I picked up a lovely girl there. Really pretty. But she was a sort of hooker, I guess. Only I didn't realise that – I don't know why – I'm naïve like that. And the worst part of it was that she was just 15. She seemed much older to me. Anyway, you know, it was all great at first and she was really hot but she said she was having trouble with her landlord so I let her stay in this flat I have over there. I didn't know she was also a druggie and sold herself for money for drugs and then I got a call when I was over here to say she had overdosed in my flat and died, poor kid. Frankie paid off the police officer so that no questions were asked about it and it was all kept quiet. It did look bad because she was under-age and I had sex with her. Frankie thought it might damage my career. You know how the tabloids love a scandal about footballers. He's holding it over me, or so he thinks anyway. He thinks he can threaten to expose me. But if he did, I can explain it all...he doesn't scare me. It was really upsetting though, the poor girl.'

'Is that it?'

'Yeah. Totally.'

'Fuck me.' Nick sank onto the sofa exhausted and covered his eyes with his hands.

'Where's Pinky likely to be now?' he asked.

'I don't know but wherever she is she'll be using her debit card which is on my account.'

'Doesn't she have a credit card?'

'No. No point. You only need credit when you've got no money. I have a lot of money. So I can look it up on line on the bank website. Hold on, let's see now.'

He logged into his bank account and began noting down transactions.

'It's 24 hours behind but she's only bought stuff in this area up to eight o'clock last night. She's been in Seaton Carew, she withdrew £300 there, and then at shops in Yarm, Stockton and Middlesbrough.'

He printed off a list of transactions from the previous three days. There was a pattern. She was in a coffee shop on Corporation Road in Middlesbrough at 11 o'clock each morning; she had a meal in the same restaurant on Yarm Lane every day at around six.

'I bet she's in Seaton Carew at Finlay's flat,' said Nick, kicking off his boots and putting his feet up on his sofa.

'We could go round but my feeling is she's too bright to be there. She'll be staying at a hotel somewhere and paying cash. She's taken out well over two grand in cash in the last couple of weeks. If she pays cash we won't know where she is,' said Jimmy.

'Is she that clever?' asked Nick.

'Yeah, super-clever. Not educated clever, you understand. Street clever, you might say. She's got a bright mind and thinks fast. She's a great kid, really.'

'She tried to kill me and Julie, may I remind you, and she's already murdered twice. So you might want to revise that opinion.'

'Sorry...yeah I didn't see that coming from her. How could you? You think you know someone, eh.'

'She took you and me and Julie for a ride, Jim. She even told us you were weird about sex.'

'Weird? In what way?'

'That you didn't like pubic hair...and were really aggressive in bed, like. Rapey.'

He shook his head.

'She was shitting you, Nick. That's not me at all. She was trying to twist your mind. Her mother brought her up to be a good liar. She was great in bed, my God, yeah. The English girls get trained well at that I can tell you this.'

Nick managed a laugh of sorts. 'Yeah, well she's a Teessider, isn't she? We breed top-class shaggers on Teesside. Always have done. A man hasn't fully lived until he's had it off with a Teesside lass. Look Jimmy, I'm knackered. It's been a horrible, stupid day. I can't go home. It'll kill me to see where Julie was....y'know...can I just sleep here and then tomorrow I'll speak to Sarge and we'll try and find her before she either disappears for good or kills me. Will she come here do you reckon?'

'No. But I'll tell the desk not to let her up if they do see her. You can sleep in the second bedroom if you want.'

'Here is fine,' he said as he was falling asleep. It was a relief to lose consciousness.

CHAPTER 15

For perhaps two seconds, as he came back to consciousness, he had no recollection of previous day's events. Then the tsunami of heinous evil flooded back.

Fuck them up, Nick. Go hard or go home. Their voices. His conscience. Still in his brain.

It was 7.15am as he washed his face with cold water and rubbed his beard stubble.

Jimmy appeared in the kitchen.

'I'm off to the hospital. Do you want to help me catch Pinky?'

'Yes, of course. Anything. She's got to be stopped before she gets away. She can't kill everyone who knows about the fake pictures though, can she?'

'No. Not now. But that might not stop her trying. I'll ring you later in the morning and we'll try to get hold of her in Middlesbrough at that coffee shop on Corporation Road around 11. She might not have sussed that we can track her movements by her spending. I'm hoping Dave Sargent calls me this morning. Seems odd he's not rung back yet. Ideally I'd like his mob to pick her up because if I get my hands on her I might just wring her fucking neck.'

'Okay. I'll see you later then and I hope Julie is doing good.'

That bloody hospital smell. The smell of slow, depressing death. It clung to him as he walked into the reception area, introduced himself and asked for the doctor. What had happened during the night? His mind churned and churned restlessly, only able to focus on whether she was alive or dead. Please be alive. Please. One chance God, please, just one chance. She's a good person. Rather me than her. Please. His palms were sweating and he couldn't stand still, pacing up and down, side to side as he waited for the doctor to arrive, an empty, sick feeling in his guts.

Then suddenly he was there, stepping out of an elevator, dressed in what looked like baggy green pyjamas but which had to be operating theatre garb.

'Morning Mr Guymer,' he said with a curt nod. He was unshaven and looked very tired. He ushered him through a plywood door into a small room. The small room wasn't a good sign. Having to be told something in private wasn't a good sign at all. Oh God. She didn't make it, did she? She died on the fucking slab. Dead. She was dead. They'd worked on her all night but couldn't stop her dying. That was the news. His mouth was desert dry.

'Well?' he said, unable to cohere any more words.

'She's...she's still alive, I'm *very* pleased to say.'

'She's not dead?'

'No. She's still very much alive...though it's something of a...of a...surprise, perhaps, because she lost so much blood and we struggled for some time to stop the internal bleeding caused by the bullet.'

'But you've managed it now?'

'Yes, finally, in the early hours.' He nodded solemnly.

'But she's still in danger?' It was obvious he wasn't exactly celebrating.

'Yes, I'm afraid so. By losing that much blood she risks organ failure and that could prove fatal. The next 48 hours will be the most dangerous for her. In her favour, she is a healthy, strong woman and seems to have been pretty fit and she has already proved to be something of a fighter to survive this far. She's in intensive care right now if you'd like to see her. She's unconscious, of course.'

'Would it help her?'

'Well, I don't know if she could hear you. Personally, I think not. I was thinking it may be of some comfort to you.'

'I...I can't bear to see her like that. I already feel like I'm losing my mind. I feel like I'll never not see her lying there, bleeding. It's burned on my eyes. It seems cowardly I know...but if she doesn't need me there, I'd rather get on and keep busy.'

'No, no, that's very sensible. Her mother was here half the night.

She wanted to wait until Julie was out of theatre. Quite a lady...quite a command of what you might call, industrial language,' he said with a small smile.

'Yeah, she's...she's something is Jackie. Tough old bird.'

'Yes, when Julie was out of theatre, I did hear overhear her admonishing her daughter for bleeding so much...which I thought was a tad harsh.' He managed another thin smile.

'That sounds like Jackie. It's her way.'

'We all deal with these things differently, I suppose.'

'Well thanks for saving her life...at least so far. Thank you so much. We say those words so often that they don't mean anything really but for once, let those two words, thank you, have as much meaning as is possible.'

'That's why I'm here. Do go to your GP for some help with the stress.'

'Right. Well, my best mate had a heart attack earlier in the week and I need to go up and see how he's getting on.'

'Good God. It never rains but it pours.'

'It doesn't stop there - my mother is in the psychiatric unit. In fact, everyone I know seems to be in this hospital.'

He was relieved she wasn't dead, but the panic at her being so near to death wouldn't just disappear. To lose her now after a glimpse of hope would be even crueller. He took the lift to Jeff's ward. As soon as he walked down the corridor he heard a familiar sound: Jeff's booming voice. 'Ah tea...more delicious than the sweat of angels.'

'Jeff! You're awake!' he said, looking around the corner and into the room where Jeff lay in bed.

'Aye aye fella,' he said with a tired, washed-out grin. His face looked drawn and his hair was tied back in a long ponytail. His beard had been cut back from its normal thick bush to something closer to stubble. He was sitting up in bed with his laptop.

'They've done some facial topiary on you and you've got a massive bruise on your head. Looks like you've nutted a truck.

How are you feeling?'

'Like I've had a massive long sleep after nutting a truck. I just came round in the wee small hours and have been feeling better ever since.'

'Well you did have a massive long sleep...well...a sort of sleep.'

'Aye, they told me I'm lucky to be here.'

'Yeah, you had me worried man, especially when I was beating on your chest.'

Jeff laughed. 'Yeah, it was your CPR talents that kept me going, they reckon. David Crosby had a band called CPR for an album didn't he?'

'Yeah he did. Early 90s. Well it wasn't my first-aid talents that got you through, it was Julie. She knew what to do right away. I just took over when she was knackered.'

'That lass is an angel and I shall tell her when I see her.'

'Yeah well...err...well...things have taken a turn for the worse in that regard while you've been out of it'

'Oh aye? What do you mean?'

'Long story...she got shot. She was in theatre all night, they kept her alive but she's not good, man. Lost a lot of blood.'

'Fuck me. Shot?! Who shot her?'

'Pinky.'

'Get outta here. Fucking hell. She killed Lisa as well?'

'Yeah, seems so.'

'The fucking little shit.'

'Yeah.'

'Fuck.'

'Yeah.'

They went quiet. He didn't want to say anything to make Jeff's blood pressure rise.

'So you've got to take it easy from now on man y'know, you've got to get well. You might have to cut down on your intake of Stella and pizza.'

'What? You mean ten pints a day isn't healthy? I can't believe you're telling me this now.'

He shook his head and then smiled.

'I've got all the lifestyle advice to come. Much needed I suppose. Maybe I should've listened to you about all that. Truth is, like I said, I was thinking about cutting back on carbs and the ale, but just never quite got round to it. I'd been feeling a bit shit for weeks and now I know why. I feel like I've been in a fight with a tractor and lost. Every bit of me hurts and I'm as weak as a kitten. But on the up side, I'm alive and sodding glad to be alive and thanks to you, I've got a laptop and a copy of *Record Collector*, so it's not all bad.'

'Well that's your basic life support system right there, isn't it? Have they said how long you'll be in for?'

'Nah, not yet. At first I didn't know where I was really, had a vague idea I was in jail after a massive piss-up. So they'll assess me later. They'll probably dope me up and kick me out soon enough.'

'I've not told your mam yet – I thought...well I'd wait, like.'

'To see if I died, like? Rightly so. No point in having to make two awkward phone calls. Okay. I'll e-mail her later.'

'Look, I'd better go. I've got to find Pinky and get Sarge to arrest her. The shit that's gone down since you keeled over, man. You'll not believe it all when I tell you.'

'So Jules is in here?'

'Intensive care.'

'Poor lass. Fuck. That's a real shocker. Christ, you've had a bit of a shit 48 hours one way or another.'

'I've had better.'

'Will she...will she pull through?'

Nick wobbled his hand from side to side. 'Touch and go, man.' Saying the words made tears rise up in his throat. He swallowed them down hard.

'Mind, don't go kicking off like a nutter and end up getting shot; all three of us can't be in here at once. I need someone to buy me grapes and give me a bed bath.' He gave him a half-powered smile.

'Glad you're feeling better, big man. Really glad. I thought you were going to visit the big record store in the sky.'

'Aye it was a bit 'walk towards the light my child' for a while...then I thought hang on, that's not the light of heaven, it's just one of those Whitesnake 12-inch singles on white vinyl we get in the shop all the time. So I came back, like.'

Nick had just got back to the car park when his phone rang.

'Hello?'

'It's Dave Sargent. Sorry it took me so long to get back to you. I was busy. There's been another murder, I'm afraid.'

'Christ, who?'

'Never mind that now. What have you got for me?'

Nick gave him a brief account and the police officer listened in silence, making only occasional surprised grunts. He didn't even admonish Nick for not coming clean earlier that it was Pinky who had shot Julie.

'Jimmy looked up her bank account activity and she's been in the Boro Bean café on Corporation Road around 11 each morning. So there must be a decent chance she'll be there today.'

'Okay, okay, we better get a team together and get down there. We have to be careful though, we don't want anybody else getting shot.'

Nick gave him the location of the flat in Seaton Carew where he'd seen her and Finlay and told Sarge about him working at the Boro ticket office.

'Right, we'll pick him up, get to the bottom of all this and put an end to this killing spree. I took so long getting back to you because a body was found in Northallerton. It was another woman killed with a single shot to the head.

'Do you know who the woman was?'

'Oh yes. It was Emmy Green.'

'Oh God. She's killed again? When did she do that? Emmy was just at our house two days ago. Terrible. God I feel so sorry for her. You never got to speak to her, I take it.'

'No.'

'I told you, didn't I, that Julie's mother saw Emmy at Maggie Gull's house one day. No-one was at home but it was definitely her knocking at the door. Jackie identified her from a photo.'

'Yes, I remember you saying that.'

'Emmy came round our house and we thought she might have been the killer....but obviously we were wrong.'

'I shouldn't tell you this but Emmy Green was found in her house along with a number of Phyllis Plant pictures, all of which, initial assessments suggest, were fakes. This is off the record but so far, all the evidence is pointing to Emmy commissioning the fakes from Myra. But if we add in your latest news, it looks as though this was a scheme suggested and run by Pinky. She must have been behind it all and that's presumably why Emmy was looking for her.'

Nick sat for a moment to take it all in. Bloody hell, Emmy Green had lied to them. She'd looked right in their eyes and denied knowing anything about the fake pictures. She said she would never be associated with anything criminal. She lied even with a gun pointing at her. As long as you believe the lie, it becomes the truth. That was exactly what he did when he lied. She'd insisted so convincingly that she had nothing to do with any fakes that all of them had believed her totally. It just showed that you really couldn't trust anyone.

'You're obviously now her number-one target. I've got a copper at the hospital to protect Julie, just in case, like. I can get you some protection too. You should stay away from all this now, Nick, let the professionals do their job.'

'Bollocks. I'm not staying away from anything, Dave. This became fucking personal when they put a bullet into Jules. I'm going to see Pinky go down.'

The policeman sighed. 'I was afraid you might say that. Okay, let me organise this. What time do you have?'

Nick looked at his watch. It was 9.23.

'Check. Right. I've got to organise everything. I'll meet you at 10.30 on Scott Street – it's right by the water, across from the

269

Riverside, just off Dock Street. It's a dead-end but there's some old gravel waste ground there. Okay?'

'I'll be there. Hang on a minute though Dave, what about Frankie Gray? He must be involved in the fakes swap.'

'We've nothing on him yet. I'm still trying though. His record is clean. Or he's done a good job of clearing up after himself. We'll keep trying. There might still be something incriminating at Emmy's.'

Nick put down the phone and sat in the car quietly, letting his brain settle down along with his ever-bubbling sense of anger. The gun was still in the boot of the car in the ruck sack. Dave wouldn't be happy if he went in armed but he was damn well going to do it anyway. He didn't want to rely on Cleveland Police to keep him alive.

He absolutely reeked of sweat; the stink of yesterday's fear and fury still clung to his t-shirt. He drove into Stockton, parked off the High Street and bought a new black t-shirt. Stripping off the old one in the shopping centre toilets, he began to wash himself. Getting clean in public was usually the preserve of the homeless. Looking at himself in the cracked mirror, he certainly looked bereft. With his hair matted on the back of his head, beard dark with grey flecks and dark rings underneath his eyes, he could easily pass for someone sleeping on the streets. He certainly felt feral.

His reflection looked back at him, sad and disturbed. Would life ever get back to normal or was this the end? Somehow, in his soul, it felt like the end. In his guts he believed it was all destined to end badly, probably in his own death. Life was off the rails. Broken. Yet shoppers were all going about their business as usual. Here it was, another day, same as the last day, same as tomorrow. Life unchanging. But not for him. How could it twist and bend out of shape like this? How could it be transformed from sane to insane so utterly, so completely and without warning?

He took one last look at himself, dried his face on a paper towel and exhaled deeply, suspecting this was the final time he would see himself. It had all been leading to this. All those years as a kid in Stockton, treading these same pavements, unaware that years later it would be where the beginning of the end of his life would kick off. So be it. It's everyone's fate to die somewhere, sometime. We have little or no control over the length of our own mortality. None of us are important. We're all million-year-old carbon and not much more.

He got to the waste ground in Middlesbrough at 10.20. At one time it had housed heavy or dockside industry. Now it stood naked, awaiting reinvention. Across the dock inlet was the Riverside Stadium, looking like a spaceship that had landed on a planet which had recently suffered some sort of devastating war. It was the home of so much energy and emotion, so much of his and Julie's energy and emotion. The thought of that made tears rise in his throat again. They'd loved going to the football together. With a deep snort of air he pushed the emotion back into his belly. He took the gun out of the rucksack and jammed it into the pocket of his jeans, putting ammunition in the other pocket. Thankfully it wasn't big; nobody should notice.

A breeze blew off the water but the sun was bright and warm. His phone rang. Jeff.

'Hey man, what can I do for you? I'm just waiting on Sarge and his boys before going in mob-handed to get Pinky.'

'Are you playing Starsky or Hutch?'

'I think I'll have to be Hutch because I am one cardigan short of the full Starsky.'

'He only wore that in the first four of 93 episodes, you know. Funny how it stuck in everyone's mind. Anyway, look, as I've got time on my hands here, no energy to walk around and sod all to do, I thought I'd do a bit of research into the people who are at the heart of all this shit you've been going through. Frankie Gray, Jimmy Repp, Pinky, Emmy... all of them.'

'Emmy is dead.'

'What? Dead?'

271

'Sarge just told me. Shot in the head in Northallerton.'

Jeff whistled. 'Poor old Emmy, eh. Fuck me, that Pinky is a ruthless hard-core bastard.'

'You got that right.'

'Well I started with her, the easiest name first, Pinky Gull, real name Kelly. I did a trawl of some newsgroups, births, marriages, deaths and all of that.'

'You're a loss to MI6 you.'

'Aye well, it helps she's got an unusual name. Much harder to find someone called Jane Smith. Anyway, I don't know if you know this but Pinky Gull had a sister.'

'She had what?!' Nick looked out at the Riverside Stadium in disbelief.

'A sister. Well, a half-sister actually.'

'You're shitting me. No-one has ever mentioned a sister. Not her, not anyone.'

'Weird stuff indeed, but it gets weirder...I say 'had' because she died.'

'My God. Julie's mam knows everyone's business - she would have mentioned it if she'd known of a sister, especially one who died, so it must be a big secret.'

'Well, I reckon the kid never lived in Hardwick. See, as I'm a big clever hairy bastard, albeit one with clogged arteries, I thought I'd do an electoral roll search. I found Pinky and Maggie and a bloke called Seb Gull living in Hardwick until 2002. Then the bloke seems to have left so only mother and daughter from then on. Then I did a broader search for the name Gull. Long story short, I looked through this list of kids born with Gull as a surname since 1990 and found a Jasinder Margaret Gull. Same middle name as Pinky, that. Her father was Khalid Khan, Indian dude, her mother is listed as Margaret Lynne Gull. The birth was registered in Stockton in July 1990. That has to be Maggie's kid. There are no other Gulls on Teesside. As Jasinder wasn't on the electoral role in Hardwick, I guessed she was living with her dad and had taken his surname when she was a kid. Then I looked up Jasinder Khan and found her listed as living with Khalid Khan up to 2005. Their address was in one of those big houses on Darlington Back Lane. So maybe she was estranged from Maggie and Pinky's side of the family and they simply didn't talk about her. Julie's mam probably didn't even know she existed.'

Nick jotted down some notes on a napkin as Jeff talked.

'But Maggie would have been pregnant with her in 1990 when Pinky was four or five. So Jackie and others on the estate must have seen that.'

'She can't have done if she never mentioned it, can she? Maybe she was living at the father's at the time but kept the council house on – as insurance, like. You know what families are like with council houses...they cling on to them to pass down the generations. I bet if you asked Jackie, there was a period of time when Maggie went away.'

'Yeah, I'll do that now. I'll call her. Wow. Top research there Jeffrey.'

'I've not finished yet. Like I said, Jasinder died.'

'How did she die?'

'I did a search of some newsgroups.'

'Newsgroups? You're so old school.'

'She took a huge amount of sleeping pills, washed it down with vodka and blackcurrant and it was Lights Out in London...or in Amsterdam in this case because that's where she was found.'

'Poor kid. Hang on...in Amsterdam?'

'Yeah. She was only just 15. Had run away from home. She was found OD'd in someone's flat.'

Nick blew out air.

'Jeff. A teenage English girl was found dead from an OD in Jimmy Repp's flat. I couldn't find her name in news reports but they said she was a runaway. Frankie Gray paid off some cops to keep it all quiet. Jimmy told me that himself.'

Jeff made a barking noise. 'Nah man. That's too weird. It can't be the same girl. And even if by some weird chance it was, Jimmy couldn't have known Pinky was her half-sister. Maybe no-one knew except Maggie.'

'Yeah, well whatever...it's worth knowing. Keep digging, Jeff. Who the fuck knows what else you might find out?'

'Aye, I will do. Gull is an unusual name, like - interesting record label, though.'

'Of course, jazz-rock specialist wasn't it?'

'Not really no...though all those Isotope albums were on Gull and some of If's stuff as well.'

'Bloody love If...'

'Yeah, great jazz-rock band. Some early Judas Priest was on Gull as well you know...back when they were good. Mind, Typically Tropical's big summer hit of '75 *Going to Barbados* was on Gull too. So it was an eclectic mix.'

'Ha, I hated that record. So was it an independent?'

'Yeah but distributed by Decca. Hang on...what the fuck are we doing? We're getting distracted by rock trivia.'

Nick could see a white car approaching. It had to be Dave Sargent.

'Sarge is coming. I'd best go.'

'Okay, good luck...and be bloody careful, right?'

As the car approached he called Jackie Wells' phone.

'Hello?' she answered with her default tone somewhere between annoyance and indignation.

'It's Nick, Jackie. Look I've not got long; I need to ask you something, right?'

'Aye...what is it?'

'Did you know Maggie had another daughter apart from Pinky?'

'She what?!'

'I'll take that as a no, then. She had a kid in 1990. A daughter called Jasinder.'

'Are you sure? I never heard about that.'

'Yeah. Her dad was an Asian bloke, Khalid Khan.'

She rasped a cough. He could hear her drawing on a fag.

'I remember him, I think.'

'She must have been away from Hardwick for most of the pregnancy.'

'Aye, well she did go away when Pinky was pre-school age. She had to look after some old auntie or something.'

'That was when she had the kid then. She never lived in Hardwick - always lived with the dad on Darlington Back Lane. He probably had money. Look, I've got to go...thanks Jackie.'

Dave Sargent got out of the car.

'Now then Nick...good God, you look rough, more like a bloody desperado more than a football journalist.'

'Some would say there's very little difference.'

They leaned against his BMW, the July sun hot now. The policeman was dressed in an open-necked blue short-sleeve shirt, black pants and shiny black shoes, with a silver watch on the left wrist of his tanned arms. Somehow, he was obviously a copper.

'Now look Nick, this is serious. I've got an armed team getting into place around the Boro Bean café as we speak. We're going in mob-handed to catch her, that way even if she's armed, we can surprise her before she makes a move. We'll have six officers in there by 11. I need you to make a positive ID on her. We don't have a picture of her on record and we don't want any mistakes, right? If you're not sure it's her, say so. No hoping you're right, no guessing. Right?' He jabbed his finger at Nick, dark eyebrows knitted into a frown. 'If you're not sure, then that's fine, we'll pull back.'

'Okay Sarge.'

'We've got an observation point on the eighth floor of Centre One - it looks right down on the café so we should be able to see her walk in. There's only one entrance.'

'Funny...that's the building where me and Jules watched the kidnap money drop.'

'So is that all clear? You'll tell me when you see her and then we'll watch the fun unfold.'

On the short drive into town in Dave Sargent's car, Nick told him Jeff had just survived a heart attack.

'Well let's be honest, I've always liked Jeff, he's a funny sod, but he brought it on himself, didn't he? You abuse your body for long enough and it's going to object at some point and then just pack up all together,' he said unsympathetically. 'I hope he's learned a lesson and is going to turn his life around.'

'I'll believe that when I see it.'

'Yeah, well, there's no helping some people is there?' said the policeman.

They parked in a restricted zone behind the town hall and then made their way to the office block. It was 10.50am when they got into position. From the north side it looked down onto a pedestrian area which began at the Boro Bean.

Police officers handed them both binoculars as they arrived.

'Everyone is in place, sir,' said one of them, a neat man with cropped blond hair.

'Good. Thanks Johnson. Do we know for sure she's not arrived early?'

'Yes sir, there are only three people in, all of them males.'

'Good. Right Nick, keep your eyes peeled, we're near to the end game now.'

'It can't come too soon for me. That bastard is going to get what's coming to her,' said Nick, feeling the bulk of the gun in his pocket.

CHAPTER 16

Nick focused on the door of the café and waited. Nothing. No-one. Eleven o'clock struck. Business was slow. Maybe the warm weather was making people turn to cold drinks or to have their coffee outside on the move. The modern obsession for drinking coffee while walking through the streets is clearly designed to make you look busy but reduce the quality of yours and everyone else's life simultaneously.

He took the binoculars from his eyes and looked up and down Corporation Road. Middlesbrough wasn't a fast-paced town and people rarely looked in much of a hurry to go anywhere, sensibly realising that a life lived slowly was likely to be a happier one.

Suddenly, there she was.

Pinky. The killer. He felt a surge of electricity fire up his spine.

Dressed in a blue v-necked t-shirt, tight blue jeans and Cuban-heeled boots, her blonde hair flowed behind her as she walked at a confident pace. Cool as you like.

'Dave. There.'

He pointed as she crossed the road past the town hall.

'Is that her? I thought she always wore pink.'

'She does.' He looked through the binoculars. 'She's wearing a pink necklace, maybe made from coral.'

'She's a real looker, isn't she?'

'She's got one of the nicest smiles you'll see on a cold-hearted killer, that's for sure.'

The policeman spoke into his radio to tell the team on the ground that their target was approaching.

She reached the café and then stopped to make a phone call; standing outside with her back to the shop, she looked up and down the street and directly up at them. The call took less than a minute and then she pushed open the glass door and went inside. If she was armed, the gun had to be in the black leather Chanel shoulder bag hung over her right arm.

'The target has just entered wearing blue t-shirt and blue jeans with a black bag,' Sarge said into his radio. 'Wait until she's standing clear of any member of the public before you take her. I don't want anyone else hurt.'

'I don't think we'll have any trouble with her,' said Dave, giving her a few seconds to get to the counter and away from the door before giving his order. 'Okay, if it's safe to do so, let's pull her in.' He received affirmation from the team leader.

It was odd. Nothing changed for at least a minute before his radio came to life and said: 'We've got her.'

Dave Sargent grinned and held his thumb up to Nick.

'Where will you take her?'

'Stockton station. I was hoping she might be with her mother. We need to question her too. She doesn't seem to have been at home for a few days but I'm sure Miss Gull can help us find her.'

As he spoke, the café door opened and two officers, one male, one female, marched out Pinky, securing her by each arm. In tow were four more officers. She wasn't resisting and wore the wry, sarcastic, defiant smile that he'd seen before. People on the street stopped to watch her get marched away.

Dave Sargent turned to Nick with a nod.

'Okay, thanks for your help, Nick. I'd better get down there. The law will take over now; you can be sure about that. We'll put her behind bars for what she's done. It's all coming together.'

Nick was just about to reply when the doors crashed open and clattered against the rubber door jams, quickly followed by two loud cracks. In less than a single heartbeat he knew what that noise was, it was already burned into his synapses. Gunshots. He flung himself to the floor behind a pillar, scrabbling for the gun in his pocket. The two shots had killed the two officers instantly. They fell where they had stood.

Sarge's baritone voice rang out in disbelief as he turned around from the window to see them slain.

'What the hell do you think you are doing?!' he bellowed with righteous indignation.

It was a woman by the door holding a pistol in her out-stretched arms.

It was Pinky. Surely.

But no. It can't have been. She was in custody.

No, this wasn't Pinky.

This was her mother, Maggie.

Wearing Pinky's short black wig, dressed in black t-shirt and jeans and her daughter's pink bracelet, he could see her face up close now. Physically she was so similar to Pinky it was impossible to tell the difference between them at a distance, but here she was no more than 25 feet away and staring straight at him. If he'd seen her this clearly yesterday, he'd have known. She had a bandage on her right arm, presumably from where he'd caught her with a bullet.

The two officers were lying on the floor, not moving, blood running from head wounds. Dead.

'Get the fuck out of the way Dave!' he yelled as he pulled out his gun, but the policeman just stood there, shocked and stunned at what he had seen

'Dave, man! Get down!!' he yelled again.

But now it was all too obvious what would unfold. He saw it happen a split-second before it actually did.

She fired twice - one shot to the throat and then one to the head which knocked a hole of viscera from him and onto the glass windows in a wet splash. He was dead before he even hit the floor.

Nick stuck the gun around the pillar and pulled the trigger twice. He'd forgotten again that the kick from the gun was so strong and the shots ricocheted off the far wall, missing her by more than three feet. The crazy fucking bitch. So this was it, was it? This was it. A fight to the death? Well come on then. Let's fucking 'ave it. No messing around now.

She fired back; her gun had a silencer fitted and made a muffled, dull, thud thud sound. The bullets shattered the plaster on a pillar, fragments flying everywhere.

Now the shit had well and truly hit the fan, Nick felt calm and focused, not shocked, not now. Dave was dead but that almost seemed normal in this new world. Maybe there was only so much profound shock the human body could register within 24 hours. If so, he'd hit his limit. He'd been through this shit before so his brain locked into logical mode. Shoot her and all the problems end. It really couldn't be that hard. One good shot was all it'd take. Even if she shot him, as long as he killed her, justice would be done. And now he had an excuse – self-defence. She'd shot at him first. She was already a murderer. He couldn't get sent down for defending himself to the death. That felt good. You get what you give. You reap what you sew.

'Go hard or go home. Fuck them up, Nick. Fuck them up.'

Yes.

Now to the death.

The pillar was good protection. She couldn't get him without stepping away from the door and coming into full view. She knew he was armed so she was clearly reluctant. She fired once more, again into the pillar, an impotent shot, and then he heard the swing doors clatter open as she left the room.

He ran to the door and peered through the glass panel. Outside were the elevators and the stairwell. She clearly hadn't used the lift because it was still on that floor. Had she gone up or down? Down meant she would risk running into the arms of the police, but going up meant there was no way out. No-one would have heard the gunshots because there was no-one near enough. But within minutes, Sarge's unresponsiveness would be an issue and someone would come to investigate why the boss had gone quiet. Until then, nobody would know that shots had been fired. The nearest occupied office was four floors down, the ones above all empty until floors 13 and 14, again too far away to hear the shots.

He stood and listened. Footsteps. They were going up the stairwell. What the hell was she playing at? Why didn't she want to get away? Was she trying to set a trap? He went after her, two at a time, but she was quick. By the time he got to the 18th floor, she was almost in view, one flight of stairs ahead of him, her heels visible.

She was clearly heading for the top floor. Was this part of her plan? Had she heard what was going to happen to Pinky or had they interrupted her well-laid plans? The latter seemed more likely as the decision to arrest her daughter was only two hours' old.

He reached the top-floor landing and looked around. She was nowhere to be seen. He caught his breath and listened, wiping sweat from his brow with the back of his hand. The abandoned open-plan floor space was behind two swing doors, one of which was propped open. He walked in. These big vapid, character-free spaces offered no place to hide whether you were an employee or a killer; they were designed so that everyone could be monitored in the name of workforce unity and efficiency. The concrete pillars were literally the only hiding places. She wasn't there. That could only mean one thing. She was on the roof.

He turned to go back out and heard something behind him, but it was too late. She was on top of him before he could even turn around, emerging from some kind of store cupboard. She stuck the barrel of the gun into the back of his neck.

'Move and you're dead, son,' she said. He froze.

'Maggie, man, what's all this about?'

'Shut up. Go and stand by the window where I can see you.'

He walked to the north-facing window, all of Teesside spread out below and into the distance.

The black wig was the same one Pinky had worn in Seaton, the one Pinky had said she'd lost. It made them look so similar. After all, she'd only been 16 when she'd had her eldest daughter and now she was in her mid-30s and Pinky in her early 20s. They could have been sisters. 'Why are you doing this?' he asked again, calmly. She obviously didn't want to shoot him or she could have done it by now. She obviously had other plans.

'I don't have to explain myself to you,' she said, pulling over an old swivel office chair and sitting down to get her breath after the chase.

Sweat ran down his back.

'The cops will find Dave soon and they'll find us up here eventually. You know that. Is it really worth any amount of money, Maggie? All of this? You've shot six people now and for what?'

'You're more stupid than I thought you were,' she said, lighting a Benson & Hedges, 'I'll get out of this easy, like. No-one knows I'm here apart from you and I'll have you dead before I leave here. I can walk out of here just like that. You thought it was Pinky who shot at you and you've told everyone else it was her so when you're dead, the truth dies with you.'

'You're setting up Pinky for your crimes, Maggie. You think that's fair?'

'There's nothing fair in this world. And she's a clever kid, she'll prove it wasn't her...there's no evidence it was her because it wasn't... they'll know that when they find you dead but by the time they work it all out, I'll be long gone with or without those bastard fucking pictures. I don't care. All I want is revenge now.'

'Did you know they were going to arrest her here today?'

She shook her head and blew out smoke.

'No, but it didn't surprise me. And I knew Pinky goes to that café.'

'So you were just here anyway?'

She took some bullets from her pocket and re-loaded her gun.

'I was here to set something up. Now, even better, you can do it for me.'

'Bollocks. Why should I help you?'

'Because I'll kill you if you don't. See, you think you're such a clever twat but you're not. Julie is still alive, somehow...fuck knows how, so if you don't help me I'll kill her somehow, sometime, somewhere. Then I'll kill your fat fuck of a friend. Is that enough of an incentive for you?'

'Alright, alright. What do you want me to do?'

'We're going up on the roof and you're going to call Jimmy Repp and tell him to meet you outside the town hall steps on Albert Road.'

'Jimmy? Are you going to shoot him? But what'll the Boro do for a keeper if Schwarzer gets injured?'

He couldn't help it. The gallows humour that was every Boro fan's inheritance was never far from the surface even in times of the greatest stress.

'Don't try and be funny.'

'On the roof? Jesus Maggie, when did you train to be a sniper? You weren't on the grassy knoll in Dallas were you?'

'Stop your fucking prattling. You know nothing.'

'Why don't you tell me then? Tell me why you're doing this. You can't shut the fake paintings scam down now, man. Too many people know about it. Dave Sargent knew all about it and there'll be paperwork. It won't disappear if you kill me.'

She grinned at him, a smile like Pinky's only really bloody nasty and cold. Then she spat at him. Thick white foam hit him in the face.

'I fuckin' know that, don't I? I should've killed them sooner and killed you yesterday. I waited too long. But sod it. It makes no difference now. I'll still have my revenge. That's the only thing that matters now. Now, get up and walk in front of me.'

She pushed the gun at him.

'Revenge? How the hell do you know the way up onto the roof of this building?'

'Because I planned this, didn't I? I'm not fucking stupid.'

She pushed him up a set of concrete steps that led to a barred metal door. He kicked it open and a warm breeze blew in.

She jabbed the gun in his back as he walked up and out onto the roof of the Centre North East building. The view was phenomenal in all directions. To the south-east were acres of red-brick housing and on the horizon were Roseberry Topping and the Cleveland Hills

283

where he and Jules loved to walk. To the north-west, the industry of Billingham, all factory units, cooling towers, wasteland and the twisted metal digestive tracts of the chemical industry. Just north was the legendary icon of the region, the Transporter Bridge. The Boro's Riverside stadium looked little more than a stone's throw away. He thought he could even see his car parked up. To the east, the Tees curved out towards the sea. To the west and south was the open countryside, Yarm and their home. In the far distance, the Pennines stretched up into Teesdale. It was a 360-degree panorama of Teesside in all her catch-your-breath, beautifully ugly, twisted glory.

Making sure the gun was never far from his head, she lifted an old piece of tarpaulin near an air-conditioning unit which was blowing out hot air, bringing out a powerful-looking rifle from underneath. It was resting on a stand to make shooting more accurate, presumably. Its angle suggested it was to be fired at the town hall steps. Damn right she'd planned this.

'Christ Maggie. Don't do this to Jimmy, I don't know what he's done to deserve this...'

'No...no, you fucking don't know why I want him dead...so don't be so quick to judge.'

'What's he done, like?'

'Done?'

She quickly checked the rifle's position.

'He as good as killed my daughter. Is that good enough for you?'

'He what?!'

'Pinky had a sister....a half-sister she never knew about.'

'You mean Jasinder? She killed herself, didn't she? She overdosed.'

That shocked her. She looked up at him with wild eyes and flushed cheeks.

'How the hell do you know about her? How?!'

She jammed the gun into his neck painfully.

'Jeff worked it out. He just told me,' he said, trying to pull his neck away from the pressure of the gun.

'She was just 15. Just 15, man!' she screamed it at him then leaned on the wall, the pistol still pointing at him. 'That's what all of this is about.' She waved her non-gun-toting hand in a big circle. 'All of this. He was responsible. He's a despicable shit. He was fucking her when she was just 14. Huh...didn't know that, did you? Didn't know he was such an evil man? Well he's a fucking pig.'

'What? Are you sure?' But even as he said it, pieces began to fall into place in his mind.

'Of course I'm bloody sure. Him and Gray prey on young kids like our Jas. They're part of a gang that give vulnerable kids somewhere to live, drink, drugs and you can guess the rest. All of them 13 or 14. Jas suffered it for over a year. They took her to Holland to traffic her amongst all the other perverts. One of the girls she was with found me and told me a couple of months ago. They're dirty, evil bastards.'

'Oh Christ.' He didn't want to hear this. It was all his worst fears come true.

'She was a vulnerable young girl who had fallen out with her family one day and they saw their chance, took her off the street, swooped in and they exploited her for sex, the fucking depraved bastards. After a year, she was so messed up that death must have seemed like a relief when she took those pills and drink.'

'Jesus Maggie, that's terrible. It seems unbelievable. Gray, I can imagine, but Jimmy, I mean, he's always seemed so nice. Are you....I mean...are you sure it's true?'

That seemed to enrage her.

'Of course I am! Stop saying that you fucking prick!' She reached into her pocket and threw some prints of photos at him.

'Look at those! This girl she was friends with, a girl called Karen, she gave us these. They're disgusting. I wanted the police to get involved but they'd already paid everyone off. We got nowhere. We had no chance. I wasn't having that.'

He picked up two of the five A4 sheets. It was enough. They

showed three naked men and one young, naked girl with their bodily fluids and her blood. One of the men was Jimmy Repp, another was Trevor 'Macca' McMahon and another was Yashie. Some featured other men he didn't recognise. Photo after photo of hard-core porn all involving the same girl, who must have been Jasinder. They were appalling. He couldn't even look at them with more than a brief glance. He'd never seen anything like this. How could this sort of evil exist? How can men be like that? You heard about this kind of thing, you heard the words or read the stories, but here it was in full and appalling colour. It was incomprehensible that anyone could inflict sexual violation and assault on anyone at all, let alone a vulnerable 14-year-old kid. This was undeniable proof. Repp was bad. Fucking bad. Good manners or not, he was an evil swine and so was everyone he was connected with. Everyone at that party. Jesus Christ. It made his guts roll over.

'You could still take these to the police or to a newspaper. You'd get justice for her Maggie. You would. They'd get sent down for this – I know who some of these men are. I'll help you. I'll do whatever it takes. This is proof – it's clear evidence.'

She shook her head.

'No. It's too late now. They let us down once by taking Repp's money and believing his excuses. Anyway, I don't want him in jail; I want him dead. We take care of our own on the estate. We're not afraid of a fight. I want him dead. Simple as that. I have to take revenge. The system doesn't want to help people like me. We're fucking scum. The shits off the estate. The toe-rags. The underclass. What happens to us doesn't matter. But before I killed him, I wanted some of his money, not for me, for Pinky and to help other lasses like our Jas.'

'But why let Pinky live with him if you knew all this?'

'I didn't know what he was like until two months ago, did I? I was stupid, like you, I thought he was a charmer. I encouraged her to be with him. Its my fault. That's why I don't care what happens to me.

I fucking deserve it. I've still not told Pinks what he's really like. I didn't want her to know because she'd have left him before I could get proper revenge.'

'He didn't know she was Jas's half-sister though, did he? He couldn't have?'

'Did he fuck. It's just a horrible coincidence. He tricked me like he tricked my daughter. He's going to pay for that with his life and I don't think that's especially unreasonable, like. Those photos are just one moment in time – imagine how many other days were like that for her? For a year! And for all the other lasses too. He's got it coming. It's not wrong. And you know it's not wrong.'

A soft summer breeze blew the fringe of the black wig as she talked, her cheeks pink with stress and exertion. He understood how she felt. It was how he felt after Julie had been shot. Shot by her.

'I'd worked out how to get some of his money and then set up his death without anyone knowing. Or at least I had until Myra LeFevre started shooting her mouth off to anyone and everyone who would listen. That was the only weak link in the chain. I had to shut her up.'

'But she lived down in York. How did you even know she was bragging about it?'

'Emmy told me, didn't she? She'd been with her at some gallery opening and she'd told her to be quiet but she wouldn't. She did it again the next day at another do...and some other folk got back to Emmy after hearing her saying she'd been painting fakes. She said she was joking but it was too dangerous. I thought Frankie's ten grand would make sure she kept quiet but it didn't. Silly cow.'

Nick looked down to the street. All still looked normal. No sirens. They mustn't have found Dave and the other coppers yet. Surely it wouldn't be much longer. He had to keep her occupied.

'So you're Grace Edwards?'

She nodded. 'Sorted them out, easy. Myra told me she'd told Lisa so I had to do her as well.'

'Jesus Christ, Lisa just wanted to find her friend...she would have been on your side. She would have said, yeah, fucking shoot the cunt. Why did you have to kill her?!'

She was unflinching, no humanity left in her now.

'She knew about Myra. Maybe I pulled the trigger too quickly but she found my number and came up to see me thinking I was the gallery woman. So I drove her out to South Gare, left her there and shot her from an old building. She didn't suffer, like. One shot was all it took.'

'Maggie, she was my mate...she was a really good person, she didn't deserve that.'

'So was our Jas,' she answered bitterly.

'But Julie man...Julie! What were you thinking? She's done you no harm. She would have been on your side too. She'd have gone into bat for you, man. Surely you knew that. You know what she's like.'

But looking at her, he knew she didn't regret any of it because it was clear she'd lost her fucking mind. She was so deep into this that she couldn't see outside. All normal values and standards had fallen by the wayside. She was some flavour of insane. He could see that in her eyes. They'd shut down and were not seeing anything anymore. All she could do was live inside the plan she'd created and literally execute it.

'There was bound to be collateral damage. Alright, it's not gone as smoothly as it would have done if Myra hadn't started shooting her mouth off, but when you're dead I'll be away and gone and no-one will ever find me. I'm shutting all this down as soon as I put a bullet or three into Repp's head. It's all his fault. I'm just putting his wrongs right. I'll get the rest of them eventually.'

'...yeah but I held the woman I love in my arms, bleeding to death. So forgive me if I don't sympathise too much,' said Nick, but she obviously didn't care. 'So Pinky knows all about this murderous fucking rampage you've been on? She knows about Jas?'

She peered over the wall.

'Does she hell as like. She never even knew about her sister. I never told anyone, her father insisted...it was all messed up. He had money, and could give her a life I knew we'd never be able to match on the estate. So I give her away. I didn't even know she'd run away or was in trouble or anything. Not until I got those filthy pictures.'

'You must have been worried for Pinky though - when you found this out.'

'I know my Pinky, and I knew she could handle herself when it came to Repp. I knew she'd see through him and that's when she came up with the fake kidnap scam. It was brilliant.'

'So you had something to do with that?'

'Nothing. I never knew until she'd got the money and then Finlay told me.'

'So she doesn't know anything about the fake paintings or you playing at Dirty Harry either?'

She shook her head.

'Nothing. That's why it was such a great scam. I did a deal on the fake paintings with Emmy and she arranged it all with Myra.'

'Which was why Emmy called at your house...of course...to see you, not Pinky. You had her number on the board in the kitchen.'

'She was a pushover. Desperate for money. Pathetic really, posh woman like her. She couldn't get involved quick enough when I suggested it.'

'And so you had to shoot her in Northallerton?'

'I think I did her a favour. When the pictures were done, I took them to Frankie Gray to swap for the real ones. Sucker. He went for it as well. I've got them all in our loft. He thinks he'll get a cut when I sell the pictures but he can whistle for that. I had planned to take his fucking head off as well but never got the chance. I'll save him for later. Hopefully he'll turn up here with Repp and I can kill the both of them. That would be sweet.'

'So Gray really didn't know anything about the kidnap?'

'No. He thought it was for real. Our Pinky outsmarted him totally.' She grinned at the thought. It was the first emotion she'd shown that wasn't fury.

'Frankie Gray, eh. I never liked him. Did he start the fire?'

'Course he did, like I told him to. Like a good little boy.'

'Does he know it's you doing the shooting?'

'Does he hell as like. He thinks he's the boss of me, the boss of everyone. He wouldn't think I've got it in me. I know his sort. Patronising bastard. He's a lying, scummy pervert. It'll be a pleasure to kill him.'

Where were the police? Come on for God's sake. Keep delaying her. Keep her occupied.

'So what does that guy Yashie do? The Singaporean bloke. The match-fixing?'

'Yashie? Yashie is the evil swine who organises the girls over in Holland. He traffics kids around Europe for sex. I wanted to shoot his fucking head off but he's left the country. He'll get what's coming to him eventually though...and yeah, he is some sort of betting scam fucker as well. Up to his neck in filth, the evil little shit.'

His memory flashed to that day on Roseberry Topping walking with Julie when they'd seen Yashie and a young girl in the field. Jules had said she was no age. God knows what had happened to her since.

Jimmy had lied to him about everything. Everything. Even when he'd gone around to see him after Julie had been shot. Even then, in his hour of distress, it was all a lie. The only thing he'd told the truth about was his ignorance of Pinky's plans and what Frankie had been cooking up with Maggie. Everything Pinky had said about him was right. He was sick. A pervert. The utter bastard. Who the fuck is for real in this world? Gray had maintained the lie about the fakes even when he was beating the shit out of him.

It was time to get his brain into gear in order to get out of this. As they talked she held her pistol in her right hand pointed directly at him and had put his pistol into her back pocket. She had the high-powered rifle set up with a silencer and ready to fire. She was all set. He didn't want the conversation to end because as soon as he'd made the call to Jimmy, that ended his usefulness. He had to buy some more time somehow, he had to buy time to get a chance to escape but she held all the cards.

He took a deep breath as she thrust a phone at him.

'Right go on...call him. Disguise the number then tell him to be at those steps in less than ten minutes.'

He dialled. 'Jimmy? It's Nick.'

'Hi Nick. Where are you?'

'Err...weirdly, I'm on top of the Centre North East building. Can you be at the town hall steps on Albert Road in ten minutes?'

'The big tower block in the Boro? Has something happened, Nick, you sound stressed?'

'Yeah. Well, I'll tell you when you get here. On those steps, right?'

'Okay. Take care.' Polite and friendly to the last. It was like he was two different people living in the same body. He rang off.

'He's on his way.'

That call was all she needed him for. This was it. This was the end. She was going to kill him.

'Right. Stand next to the rifle,' she said, flicking the gun at him.

He tried to swallow but he couldn't. His throat was too tight with fear.

'On your knees.'

'Come on, Maggie. Not this. I'm not a bastard. I don't fucking deserve this, do I?'

She ignored him and held the handgun to his head.

'Put your right hand on the rifle trigger and put your left on the gun handle. Don't bother to try and fire it, it's not loaded.'

Nick did as he was told.

'You're framing me for the shooting?' he asked.

'Now stand up,' she gestured at him with the gun. 'I told you, I'm not stupid.'

He stood up again, her gun still in his face.

'Good. Now, you're going to shoot yourself.'

She grabbed his right hand and took his gun from her back pocket and slapped it into his palm while keeping him covered with her own pistol.

'If you don't kill yourself, I'll kill Julie and Jeff. You know I can do it, you know I will do it. If you kill yourself, I'll let them live. You've got my word. You have to kill yourself to save them. If I have to kill you, I will kill them. So kill yourself now. There's one bullet in there. Put it to your head and pull the trigger. Get it fucking done!'

She stood square on to him, her pistol pointed at his head. He gripped the black Kel-Tec PF-9mm in his shaking right hand.

Just a second, just one blink, just one moment of doubt, one pause, that was all he needed. But now he was standing next to death, his finger on the trigger of the gun, pointing to his own temple.

'Do it!' she screeched. She would shoot him if he could not pull the trigger. He knew that for sure.

'It's no good Maggie. Not my right hand. I'm left-handed....it's...it's no good...I'd shoot myself with my left hand – I shoot with my left....they'll know something's wrong if they find me with a gun in my right hand...I'm not bullshitting...hang on...what the fuck am I trying to help you for?!'

There it was. Yes.

He saw it in her eyes, a flash of doubt. Was he telling the truth, had he used the gun in his left hand earlier or was he lying? She didn't know for sure.

That scintilla of doubt lodged itself in her mind and in that second, she was ever so slightly distracted.

She took the gun out of his right hand to put it in his left hand and in doing so, dropped her own gun just slightly so it pointed over his shoulder and not in his face.

One punch.

One big bastard punch to save your life.

Better make it a good one.

No back lift, all power from the shoulder.

Bang.

He hit her right in the fucking face as hard as he had ever hit anything. Every last calorie in his body went into the punch, every fume of pent-up anger, every ounce of emotion.

It sounded like she'd been hit with a cricket bat as his fist connected to her flesh and bone, echoing into the Teesside summer air and blowing off towards Hartlepool.

She staggered backwards and stumbled and for a moment he thought she was going to fall over the wall. But she didn't even go down. How fucking hard were these Hardwick women? Her nose was smashed up and bloodied and briefly she looked dazed. She staggered a little but still had both pistols, one in each hand now.

'You fucking twat!' she shouted, trying to shake the mist out of her brain.

She raised both guns to shoot him dead but he was already gone, diving behind the air-conditioning unit, a large metallic toast rack of a machine, belching hot air from the building below. It gave him just enough cover. She fired once and twice and then a third time, still dazed. The bullets bounced off the metal as he scooted low and fast to get better cover further behind what looked like a brick cupboard, probably some sort of storage area for tools.

His skin prickled, all the hairs of his arms and neck standing erect with the adrenaline thrill. He'd fucking done it, he'd got away from an almost impossible situation. One fucking nil, now don't lose a cheap goal. Remember, you're at your most vulnerable when you've just scored.

The only escape from the roof was via the stairwell about 60 feet away. He would be too exposed for too long if he ran. She'd have time for at least three clean shots and she was obviously good enough to hit him at least once. But he offered no threat to her - all he could do was avoid being shot and try to escape down the stairs or waste enough time for them to be discovered. How much longer before the police found their dead colleagues? Jesus, they were so slow.

He licked his dry lips as he caught his breath and spotted three places across the big rooftop where he could dodge a bullet but which were close enough together to run between without offering too good a target. Keep on the move. That was the thing to do. Keep going around in circles. He sprinted over to a large tank, perhaps for holding rainwater, then on to another brick structure which housed lightning rods and aerials. Each time he moved he caught a glimpse of her, still standing where he had hit her. She had the gun raised and followed his movements, firing a shot each time she caught sight of him but unable to hit.

She was distracted by Jimmy Repp's imminent arrival and glanced over the wall down to the ground. Seemingly happy that her enemy had not yet arrived, she sprinted at pace towards Nick as he squatted down. She could really move, covering the distance between them in seconds. She put one gun in her back pocket and ran with her right arm extended, firing as she moved, trying to flush him out of his hiding place.

He took off back the way he had come, running fast and low as the shots rang out, weaving in and out of obstacles and structures. Her aim was inaccurate because she was running. She'd be out of shots soon, surely. He dodged and weaved but still she came after him. Two shots pinged off the metal water tank as he dived, rolled and ran again, all in one movement.

Glancing over his shoulder he saw her pulling ammunition out of a pocket. Now was his chance. He sprinted at high speed across the open space towards where the rifle was resting on its stand, grabbing it as he flew past.

Squatting low behind the cooling unit he looked at the weapon. It looked like a toy but he'd noticed it had what could be an ammunition clip stuck into the underside, a curving rectangle of metal that jammed up into a hole. It had to be an ammo clip, didn't it? She must have been bluffing when she said it wasn't loaded. Only one way to find out. Freedom wasn't far away now.

He had the long sprint to the stairwell ahead of him. It would take him five seconds to cover the ground but there was nowhere to hide. She didn't even have to move from where she was reloading in order to take careful aim and fire.

Now or never. He pulled the rifle's trigger twice and dispatched two bullets – so powerful it knocked him back a pace. He missed her hopelessly but it scared her into jumping for protection.

One sprint, that's all it was. He took off as fast as any legs could carry anyone, heading for the stairwell, turning as he did so and pulling the trigger, once, twice and a third time without even looking at her, firing and running, firing and running. He could hear the bullets hitting hard objects and hoped it would mean she had to keep her head down while he headed for the stairs.

Time seemed to pass so slowly. Those few paces to freedom were like wading through mercury. For a few elongated seconds it didn't seem to get any closer at all but then came within reach. Three strides to freedom, three strides to escape, three strides was all it would take. He fired one last bullet behind him. One stride. Another stride. Yes, he was away and free. He'd won. Two fucking nil.

It was then that he felt the hot explosion of pain in his foot.

Instantly it was as though his right leg was on fire. Oh Jesus Christ, the fucking pain. It was excruciating, as though the end of his leg had actually exploded. The bullet has struck him on the underside of the foot and ripped apart his sole and toes. He let out a bitter howl of pain and hit the floor, now unable to support his own weight on the wounded foot. As he went down, the rifle fell from his grip, skidded down the steps and out of view. He clawed desperately after it. Arghhhh, fuck it! So near but so far.

Down below, the first police sirens began to blare out, echoing around the buildings. They must have found Dave and raised the alarm. Too bloody late. Typical. Maggie came running towards him as he tried in vain to drag himself the few feet to the stairs. The pain was so intense that his body wanted to black out. He could feel himself shutting down. He looked up at her standing over him.

She was panting, wiped her mouth and said, 'You put up a

fucking good fight, I'll give you that, but I fucking win, son, I win.'
She extended her arms, gripping the pistol with both hands to shoot
him in the head.

There and then, in that moment, staring down the barrel of her
gun, he was prepared and he knew he'd been prepared since the
moment Julie had lay in their garden, her life bleeding away. Fuck
it, go on, do it...do it...you fucking stupid bitch...what the
hell...everyone dies in the end. And in that instant, he let out a sigh,
lay back, closed his eyes, heard footsteps, heard the explosion of
the gun, accepted it and fearlessly took the bullet to his head like
the fucking stoic, tough northern bastard he had always been.

Two seconds passed. Then three. Then four. The summer breeze
blew on his face. Sirens still rang out below.

He wasn't dead.

He open his eyes and rolled on to his side, propping himself up on
an elbow.

Maggie Gull was lying on her back, her feet almost touching his.
The top of her head had been removed by a high-powered bullet
and looked like a pink and red blancmange; her eyes open wide in
surprise. She was seriously dead. The rifle lay to one side of him.
He hadn't shot her. He knew that. So who the hell had?

No-one was around. The gun had gone clattering down the steps.
Someone had come up those steps, picked up the gun, shot Maggie
and immediately left. But he couldn't move to go after them. He
spat out a thick gob of sticky, foamy spittle, pulled out his phone
and dialled 999. They clearly thought it was a hoax at first but
within three minutes, two officers shouted up at him from the
stairwell. They were in body armour and had drawn their own
guns.

'I'm the only one alive up here,' he said, 'and I've had my foot shot
so I can't walk.'

They radioed for back-up. Down below he could hear an
ambulance arrive. His foot had gone cold and numb, which felt

weird but marginally less horrible than feeling like it was on fire. The pain throbbed up his whole body and blood oozed through his good leather boots. He felt very disjointed suddenly, his brain losing grip of reality. Blood coming out of your shoe is never a good thing. He laughed out loud. That sounded like something Jeff would say. Him playing at Dirty Harry on top of Middlesbrough's tallest building with all of Teesside spread out below, what a fucking joke. Teesside, home of the sodding psychotic gun-toting woman. He laughed again thinking of how hard he'd hit Maggie in the face and she'd still not dropped.

And then consciousness ebbed away from him...he could feel it disappearing like water spinning and spinning down a plug hole. Soon it had all gone and he blacked out.

Disembodied voices and noises drifted in and out of his mind for an indeterminate amount of time. In some moments he thought he knew what was happening but couldn't hold onto consciousness for long enough to come to the surface of reality. He wasn't even really sure why all of this was happening, only that it was.

Then nothing. He was totally gone.

Slowly he swam back up from the depths of unconsciousness and the pain in his foot exploded all over again. It was the sort of pain that hurts right to the core of your bones. It was obvious he was in a bed. A hospital bed. He began to piece together the jigsaw of his last hours, the gunfight on the roof. How the hell had he survived? He owed his life to whoever pulled the trigger and killed Maggie.

The room had a window looking out onto a corridor with a small venetian blind to give him some privacy, but he could see nurses and other people passing by. It felt like he was in a side-room to existence as life passed him by.

This had to be North Tees, so somewhere near were Jeff and Julie. Shit, how was she? Had she made an improvement or taken a turn for the worse? He had to know as soon as possible. Had she survived? His stomach began churning in knots again at the thought of her dying. How did you attract anyone's attention in here? Was there an alarm or a bell to ring for service? Seemingly not. Briefly he considered getting up but his foot was resting under a tent.

He resorted to waving his arms in the air trying in vain to attract someone's attention. Eventually a nurse opened his door and looked in on him.

'Ah you're awake Mr Guymer. How are you feeling?'

'I'm alright. My foot hurts like hell though.'

She came in and nodded. She was dressed in the uniform blue pyjamas, had short, cropped hair and spoke with a broad Teesside accent that suggested she'd grown up in nearby Hardwick or Roseworth.

'I can give you some painkillers for that. You only got out of surgery a couple of hours ago. It's going to be sore for a while, like.'

'What did they do to my foot?'

'They took the bullet out and...you know...fixed it up and that.'

'Will it work properly again or am I going to limp around for the rest of my life?'

'I'm sure it'll be fine,' she said in a manner which suggested she didn't have a clue one way or another. 'The doctor will be in soon to see you, he'll tell you everything, like.'

'Can you do me a favour?'

'Yeah if I can.'

'My girlfriend is Julie Wells, she was in intensive care...hang on...how long have I been here?'

'You were brought in just over 24 hours ago.'

'Christ, okay so Julie was in intensive care two days ago...can you find out if she's...if she's okay...she was shot as well...by the same woman who shot me.'

'Oh yeah, everyone's talking about it. You were on Look North and everything.'

'Is she okay? She was really ill last time I was here.'

' 'I don't know but I'll find out for you.'

'Thanks. What's your name?'

'Georgie.'

'Thanks Georgie. Can you do that as soon as possible? I'm really worried about her.'

She smiled at him nicely. It was a small glimpse of human warmth that he badly needed.

He blew out air, feeling tired and very hungry. He could have murdered a steak with blue cheese but there was nothing he could do, he was powerless in there. He might as well just lie back and let things take their course, don't fight it. But even so, it was really bloody frustrating not being in control of anything; he couldn't even put a kettle on and make a brew.

Half an hour passed really slowly before a welcome sight appeared at the window.

'Here he is, Hopalong Cassidy,' said Jeff as he opened the door and peered in.

He was wearing a blue dressing gown.

'Who was Hopalong Cassidy anyway?' Nick asked.

'No bloody idea. Some one-footed geezer from the old west, I suppose. So how are you feeling then? Nursie said you'd woken up.'

'Hungry and thirsty...how are you?'

'I am now the proud owner of a stent the size of a house brick, or it feels like that anyway.'

'To keep your arteries open?'

'Yup. I feel pretty good really, all things considered. Everything is working. My brain wasn't fucked up or anything they reckon. Lucky me, huh? I could have turned into a Cabbage Patch Kid. Still feel totally knackered, mind.'

'Do you know what happened to Julie?'

He nodded and sat on the bedside chair. 'Aye, I went down to intensive care this morning. I didn't get to talk to her but they said she was conscious again.'

'Fucking hell. She's alive then? Are you sure? She's not...you know...a vegetable or something?'

'Like I say, I didn't get to speak to her but the nurse down there said she's 'making progress' - you know how they talk, it's all deliberately vague so you can't sue them. But she's 100% alive.'

'Thank fuck for that.'

'You nearly gave me another heart attack though...when I saw the news reports. Man in shoot-out on the roof of Corporation House – I'm not calling it Centre North East, I refuse. It's like League One and Two, I'm not having that, it'll always be Third and Fourth Division to me.'

'Aye, me too...bloody awful name Centre North East, makes it sounds like a leisure centre. Corporation House had civic pride, didn't it?'

'I had a feeling it was something to do with you even before they said your name. Sounds like the sort of shit Guymer would be caught up in, I said to myself. There's still a news crew outside.'

'It was insane, man. I shouldn't be here. I should be dead. Maggie Gull had me down, she was standing over me, about to shoot, when someone shot her in the head with the rifle I'd dropped.'

'Rifle? You had a rifle?'

'I had her rifle, the one she was going to shoot Jimmy Repp with.'

'She was what?'

'It's a hell of a story man.'

He explained what had happened to their old school friend Dave Sargent.

'I saw her blow him away just like that,' said Nick, the vision still clear in his mind, 'he didn't stand a chance. If only he'd dived out of the way, he had the time, but he just froze on the spot like he couldn't understand what was going on.'

'Poor old Sarge, eh, I heard he'd bought the big one on the news. I've been trying to work it all out and what you've said fills in some of the blanks, but when that Emmy Green woman came to your gaff, what was she up really up to, do you reckon? I can't work it out.'

'I think she really did want to know how much we knew about the murders. She must have suspected it was something to do with Maggie or Frankie and she really was probably worried for her own life. Rightly so as it turned out.'

'Christ, what a fucking killer that woman was...she'll go down in history. So the Pinky lass knew nothing about any of the murders.'

'No. Nothing.'

'I wonder what she feels about her mam today. Must be a bit of shock to have a mass murderer in the family.'

'Aye, Maggie decided to shoot everyone who had found out about the fake pictures. That was going to be her big treasure trove. Between her and Frankie they'd have pocketed 30 or 40 million quid.'

'Aye but even so...I mean...that doesn't turn many people into a mass killer, does it?'

He closed his eyes. 'No. It wasn't really about the money it was about revenge. She went mad. Simple as that. Insane. When I was on the roof with her, she was...y'know...she was gone. Flipped out. Proper woo-woo. She just wanted to kill Jimmy and then disappear.'

'Why him?'

'Turns out Mr Nice Guy is nothing of the sort. Turns out he's part of gang whose speciality is raping young girls. I saw the pictures, man, though God knows I wish I hadn't. The daughter you found out about, she killed herself after a year of fucking heinous abuse at the hands of Repp and his cronies in Amsterdam. She'd run away from home.'

Jeff pulled an incredulous face, part shocked, part disgusted.

'Bloody hell. I never met him but everyone liked him, didn't they? And then he meets her sister. That's just weird synchronicity, man.'

'Yeah, maybe he saw a similarity or something, though he can't have known Pinky was related to girl in his flat. Pinky didn't even know. Maggie Gull only found out a few weeks ago and it sent her over the edge. The grief and pain was too much for her to deal with and she was just on a rampage, trying to somehow make it all right again. I know what that's like. I was exactly the same after Julie was shot. I lost it man. I mean, I really fucking lost it.'

'Yeah?'

He opened his eyes again and licked his dry lips.

'I didn't care who I killed or who got in the way. I just wanted revenge. It burnt inside me, like physically burnt. Only killing her would put the fire out, that's what it felt like. Nothing else mattered. I was raging, man. I went round to Julie's mam. Eventually she talked me down. It was just as well Pinky was in custody because I'd have shot her dead just like that, without thought or hesitation. I wanted blood. I nearly popped her mam in the woods but I'm a lousy shot. Retribution was all I could think about. So maybe that's what Maggie was going through, only she didn't have anyone to talk her down.'

Jeff puffed out his cheeks and blew out air.

'That's some heavy shit. Doesn't sound like you at all. You've always been a moody sod but I never had you down as a murderer. Not even when I sold your Van Halen ticket for 50 quid that time.'

'I'm still mad at you for that. It was their first tour, man. City Hall, Newcastle, middle of the front block.'

'Aye but I needed rent money.'

'Not as much as I needed to see The Halen.'

'Aye but even so, you'd not have shot me for it, would you?'

'Only because I didn't want to go to jail.'

'Rightly so, no man could stand that amount of sex in a confined space.'

Nick let out a laugh. Fuck knows he needed a laugh.

'Did you know the police were here last night? I heard the nurses talking about it. They'll be back to interview you now you're awake, I reckon.'

'Aye, the nurse said. As soon as I tell the whole story it's going to pile a whole heap of shit onto Repp and his mob. They'll have already found Maggie's photos on the roof, I should think. That's about all the proof they'll need to arrest them. I suppose Pinky's still in police custody.'

'I've not heard otherwise. But maybe they'll let her go when they realise it was her mam. Do they know about the kidnapping?'

'Nope. I don't think so. Jimmy and Frankie know about it – I told them – but I assume they won't have pulled them in yet.'

'I hope she gets away with it then.'

'Yeah I do. I'm not going to lie to the cops about it but if they don't ask me, I'm not volunteering any information.'

Georgie the nurse returned with a smile.

'Good news, Nick, Julie has regained consciousness. She's still in intensive care but I can take you down there later this evening. The police will be here in an hour to speak to you. Can I get you something to eat? Then I can give you some painkillers for your foot?'

'Roast him a hog, the boy is famished,' said Jeff. 'Roast me one while you're there.'

'Two roast hogs coming up,' she said again with a nice smile.

'Lovely lass, her,' said Jeff, watching her go, 'I was hoping she might give me a bed bath but I'm not bed-bound enough for that, apparently. It seems unfair. There should be perks to being in hospital. Soaping a chap's thighs and buttocks is a cheap and simple pleasure. After all, we're keeping all these people in work, aren't we? Being ill is a selfless act in order to keep the economy moving.'

'Nothing wrong with you anymore is there?' said Nick, laying back and closing his eyes.

'Must be this new stent - the blood is flowing properly for the first time in years. Now if I can only walk around without feeling like I'm pulling a ball and chain around...'

'I'm very happy for you but I'm going to have to have a kip before the coppers show up.'

'Alright mister. I'll see you later. We're turning this place into our own personal social club, aren't we?'

He was brought some terrible cheesy pasta mush and over-cooked broccoli - all carbs when he really needed protein and fat.

The police interview carried out by two detectives was long and exhaustive as he went over every detail of the last two days. As he suspected, they'd already found the abuse photos. He realised he had been carrying an illegal gun and debated whether he should try to hide that but the truth was too difficult to conceal. To take it out was impossible and he didn't have the mental strength to sustain the lie except to say that he had bought it from a bloke in a pub in South Bank rather than Julie's brother. They didn't ask any questions about Pinky's kidnap, thankfully.

They talked to him for nearly three hours and then a doctor came to tell him about his foot. They'd taken out the shell but it had removed his middle toe altogether, or rather it had been shattered so badly that they'd had to amputate. That was a bit upsetting but the doctor said that if you were going to take a bullet from a lunatic murderer, then taking it through the foot wasn't a bad choice. He gave him some super-strong Codeine and assured him the pain would subside over the next week, but it would be about a month before he could walk without aid.

That evening the lead on the local news was a breaking story about the arrest of Jimmy Repp and his business manager Frankie Gray. They were unable to give details but said it was connected to 'last night's dramatic shoot-out on the roof of Centre North East in Middlesbrough'. Further arrests were expected, they said. He grinned to himself. All his own work.

Afterwards, Georgie brought him a pair of crutches and helped him hobble across the hospital to intensive care, where Julie had been installed.

He saw her at first from a distance. Jesus, look at her. She was thin and gaunt in the face and a sickly shade of white. Her lips were a pale version of their normal crimson and her straw-coloured hair was pulled back into a ponytail. It was heart-breaking. His big, warm, loving, lusty woman reduced to this. She really did look half-dead. As he approached she had her eyes closed, but turned to look at him as he rattled in on the crutches.

'Bloody hell, it's Metal fucking Mickey,' she said with a wide if weak smile.

'Aye, there goes my tap-dancing career, eh. How are you feeling?' he asked, sitting down on the side of her bed and taking hold of her cold hand.

'Weak....,' she paused, licked her lips and added, 'but I'm getting stronger.' She squeezed his hand. 'I saw the news report on the telly and the nurses said that was you...on the roof...,' she shook her head, 'what are you like, man? I can't let you go anywhere on your own.'

'You won't believe half of it when I tell you.'

'I sort of worked a lot of it out from the news reports. So Maggie was the murderer? The sodding cow. Mam always said she was a devious get.'

'Yeah, maybe we should've listened more to your mam. Has she been in?'

'Yeah, once. I was pretty out of it.'

'She spent most of the first night in here swearing at you from what the doctor said.'

'Sounds about right,' she said with a faint smile.

'She was fantastic when I had to tell her about you getting shot. It felt like talking to a proper grown-up. I was...shit man, I'd gone crazy, Jules. I was running around town with that gun, looking to shoot Pinky. I was sure she'd shot you. I swore I saw her in the woods. But it was Maggie. Your mam talked me down from this insane place in my head.'

She patted him on the hand as he spoke.

'Aye well, she's always been good in a crisis. I'll give her that. I'm glad Pinky wasn't the killer - I always liked her. Have the police got her?'

'As far as I know. They've just pulled in Jimmy and Frankie too. Jimmy turned out to be a wrong 'un.'

'Really?' She let out a moan. 'Oh fuck, how tedious. See, that's

305

how I ended up going out with so many unsuitable men. Not got the sense I was born with.'

'Your mam said you'd got a good radar.'

'I like to say I have. But clearly I have no fucking clue when it comes to men. Didn't I say he was the sort of bloke I'd have dated? Christ. Remind me to shut the fuck up if I ever mention this radar thing again.'

'Well he took us all in, like.'

'It's porn or something, isn't it? Something sleazy.'

'Yeah. I won't curse you with the details now but yeah, it's in that sleazy ballpark. Remember what you thought after our chat with Pinky...well it's all of that and much, much worse too.'

'Fucker,' she said, bitterly.

'They're all going to get sent down though. I've already given the cops a statement and there's photographic evidence, no getting out of it.'

She took a glass of water from the bedside cabinet.

'Will Kev and Ricky be getting a visit from the police about the gun?'

'No. I kept them out of it.'

She nodded and closed her eyes again. 'Good. Well done that man.'

'Least I could do, I'd have been dead without that gun. The thing is Jules...somebody saved my life by shooting Maggie in the head. She'd fucked my foot up and had me down and was going to shoot me in the head but someone shot her from behind me. I heard their footsteps but I couldn't follow them because of the foot.'

'Who could that have been?'

'I have no idea. I'd love to shake their hand, whoever it was.'

As they talked, Jeff walked in and held his arms out wide.

'Hey hey, welcome back to the land of the pyjama men.'

'Hello you,' said Julie, 'you look like you've got a purple potato growing out of your head.'

'I've got a nice pair of plums as well if you want to see them.'

'The last time I saw you I was pushing down on your chest to the Bee Gees' 'Stayin' Alive,' she said.

'Don't worry, I took over to the rhythm of UFO's 'Only You Can Rock Me' - I thought you'd dig that more,' Nick said.

'Thoughtful but actually I'm not averse to the Bee Gees, especially their psychedelic pop period. They did an album called *Cucumber Castle*, you know. Rates as one of the worst album titles ever. I mean, how can you have a cucumber castle?'

'You could definitely carve a castle out of cucumbers but you'd need a fuck of a lot of cucumbers,' said Julie.

'It'd be a bit wet and slippery,' Nick said.

'And it'd only last for three or four days,' added Julie.

'Ah, but this was 1970, so it's really a metaphor isn't it?' said Jeff, raising his index finger in the air. 'The cucumber castle is the anti-castle. It's made out of cucumbers which, if they were any good in warfare, would have been used for thousands of years for general shafting and abuse. But the fact is, anything made of cucumbers is going to be easy to invade and cucumbers make terrible weapons. So it was really a statement of peace. All castles should be made of cucumbers and the world would be a better place...or...you know...some shit like that.'

They all laughed wearily.

'It's nice to have you back with us, Jeffrey,' said Julie.

'Aye it is big man, it really bloody is,' said Nick, gripping his friend's hand.

'We all made it through, that's the main thing,' said Jeff, pulling his finest crazy face.

'Aye well, we're all Teessiders aren't we?' said Nick. 'It takes a lot to take us down.'

'Too fucking right, man,' said Jeff, holding up his hand.

'Yeah, too fucking right,' said Julie and they gripped their hands together, a Teesside triumvirate.

CHAPTER 17

Events moved quickly. Jimmy Repp was deported to the Netherlands to stand trial for a litany of sexual offences against minors. There would be charges of fraud to answer at a later date as a full-scale investigation into match-fixing was launched right across European football.

Frankie Gray was also arrested and charged, initially with arson for starting the fire at Jimmy's house. Other charges involving the trafficking of children as well as fraud were expected to be made once investigations were complete. He was held on remand in Durham jail while the legal machinations took place.

After initially being arrested at the Boro Bean café on a murder charge, Pinky was released a day after the death of her mother. Within 24 hours, she and Finlay disappeared along with the kidnap money which had been hidden in the Seaton Carew flat. No-one knew where they'd gone and no-one really tried that hard to find out, even when the police learned of the scam from notes in Emmy Green's diary. The original Phyllis Plant pictures were found stored in the roof space of Maggie's house.

Jeff returned home to Harrogate and his record store to try and put a life of heavy drinking behind him, armed with instructions to lose 100 pounds.

Nick's foot healed quickly and he spent August painting and decorating the farmhouse and making some attempt to organise the garden. A couple of days before Julie was due to come home in early September, he had a visit from Colin Harcombe, a detective from Cleveland Police who had taken Dave Sargent's job. A similar age to Nick, he'd been a regular visitor since he'd left hospital.

Nick showed him into the garden and brought out a jug of iced water and two glasses.

'I've got good news for you. You won't be charged for unlawful possession of a stolen firearm or for discharging it, not given the circumstances. But I've got to officially caution you and it will remain on your record for three years. Everyone felt that was a good political solution,' said Colin.

'Well that's a relief.'

'I'll call you into the station when we're ready to do that. And how is Julie this week?'

'Recovering well now, thanks. She's still underweight but that aside she's almost back to normal. She just needs feeding up to get her strength back now. I've been cooking decent meals for her and taking them in; no-one can get healthy on hospital food. But the doctors seem pleased with her powers of recovery.'

'Well she's a tough lady that one.'

'Yeah she is. They told me that they thought she was a goner when they brought her in. But somehow she just hung on. Thank God. So how's the investigation going?'

The policeman took a drink of water and nodded.

'Very good. It's all falling into place. Interpol have taken over the Jimmy Repp and Yashie cases. Both are in jail in Amsterdam awaiting trial. Trevor McMahon has just been picked up in Spain - he went on the run but they found him in Ibiza. We'll continue to liaise with Interpol but with so many charges it's going to be a long time before it all gets to court. There's so much evidence to collate.'

'What if he just pleads guilty?'

'I imagine that is what he'll be instructed to do – try and plea-bargain his sentence down – and if he takes a few others with him he might get a few years knocked off, but there's no way out for him.'

Nick shook his head. 'I still find it so hard to believe when every time I saw him he was the nicest bloke. Couldn't do enough for you. It's disturbing. I want evil bastards to be easily identified as evil bastards and not go around being confusingly nice.

'By all accounts he was like that with everyone. In one sense, he was a really nice guy. Helpful, generous, well-mannered, all of that. But he had this one area of his life...this terrible, dark sickness, if you like...humans, eh. We're a complex animal, capable of the best

309

and worst of things.'

'You can say that again. And he was such a great liar too – he lied even at times of most stress, at times when you think it wouldn't be possible to lie.' He let out a groan. 'So do you need something more from me? Will I have to give evidence in any of these trials?'

'That depends on their pleas but you may well have to, though not anytime soon. I just came here today to show you something.

He unzipped a flat black leather briefcase and took out a DVD and laptop.

'Do you remember I told you that in the course of gathering evidence, we requested all the CCTV from in and around the Centre North East building and then out into Middlesbrough town centre too?'

He loaded the DVD into the computer.

'I've put together a compilation of clips for you.'

'The Boro's greatest hits, eh?'

'Something like that...first up, you remember that Myra and Lisa both rang who they thought was Grace Edwards but was actually Maggie. We pulled this CCTV footage from Middlesbrough Station.' He tapped the screen with a Biro. 'See, this is Myra meeting Maggie as she gets off the train...and...here...,' he loaded another image, 'here's Maggie meeting Lisa in almost the same spot at the station. Obviously, from here she took them to South Gare and...well, we know the rest.'

The frozen blurred images were awful – like looking at images of ghosts. Knowing what was about to happen to those innocent women, to his friend, was unbearable.

'I can't look at those, Col. Really. Take them away...take them off the screen...I don't want to see them. I'm...I'm not really over Lisa's death yet. I don't know if I ever will be. I'm happier thinking about Maggie trying to kill me than I am about...about that.'

He turned away and took a drink of water.

'Sorry, I didn't think...yes...it must be...well...okay. I'll move on. Remember you called Jimmy Repp from the rooftop?'

'Yeah, at gunpoint. You tend to remember those kinds of things.'

'That call was made at 11.23am. Now you said you told him you were on the top of Centre North East. He took that call just outside the Cleveland Centre.'

Nick angled the screen against the glare of the sun.

'Yeah, he said he was in town when I called him.'

'Uh huh. And now we can follow him along Grange Road. He turns left on Albert Road and heads towards Centre North East.'

He showed him a slideshow of CCTV images, all a few seconds apart.

'Now, he was supposed to be going to wait for you on the town hall steps on Albert Road, that's what you'd told him to do, but he doesn't. As you can see from this shot taken on the town hall camera, he actually goes into the Centre North East building. At the time, no-one even knew what was going on up on the roof - the noise of the shots was lost in the traffic noise and no-one had found Dave's body yet. So he's gone there presumably because you said that's where you were.'

'Yeah, I told him where I was thinking it might help me in some way. I was desperate.'

He continued with the slideshow.

'These shots are from cameras located on each floor next to the lifts. Look, he presses the button and gets in at the ground floor. The next time he appears is 30 seconds later as he gets out on the top floor. He's not had time to get out on any other floor. He gets out and looks around for you. But it's deserted. Then he must have heard gunshots. Look...there...he jumps and looks around, and then runs towards the service door to the roof. Meanwhile, you're having your shoot-out with Maggie. Now watch....he goes out of view and then 15 seconds later he comes back, gets in the lift and goes back down to the lobby and out onto the street. Then he walks off down Corporation Road and away to his car without even bothering to wait outside the town hall. So now we're adding murder to his lists of crimes, albeit a murder which saved your life.'

Nick ran his hands through his hair, scrunched up his eyes and scratched his head.

'This is un-fucking-believable. So he's heard the gunshots, gone to see what it was, found the rifle I'd dropped down the stairs, seen Maggie about to shoot me, picked up the rifle, shot her and then legged it.'

'Yes, Exactly.'

Harcombe smiled and nodded.

'How come his prints weren't on the gun?'

He pointed at the screen. 'If you look, his fingertips are taped up – presumably because he's a goalkeeper. We got some half-prints from the palm of his hand but not enough to identify him. And when we looked into his background, he was actually a good amateur target-shooter. He represented Holland at junior level, so he could handle a gun, no problem.'

Nick sat back and looked out across the garden as two goldfinches landed on the fence.

'I don't know how I feel about this. On the one hand he's a fucking evil child abuser and on the other, on the spur of the moment, he's saved my life. He didn't have to. He must have done that instinctively, like you would if a friend was in danger.'

'From everything I know, everything he's said in interviews so far, he considered you a good friend. He defended you on the roof, but then knew he couldn't be seen anywhere near a crime scene because he had so much to hide. That's why they didn't want the kidnapping of Pinky to involve the police either. Like I said, humans, we're complex animals.'

'The ultimate irony is, by saving my life, he condemned himself to a life in jail because of what I'd found out about him, but he couldn't have known that when he pulled the trigger. He just came upon a crime scene, saw someone with a gun about to shoot me...what on earth must he have thought was going on?'

'He couldn't have known that Maggie was Jasinder's mother. He couldn't have known for sure that you knew about his sex crimes.

As you say, he must have just seen her with the gun and in an instant realised she was the murderer and not Pinky and he's just shot her to save your life. When we picked him up, he was all sweetness and light. He denied even being there. He used that friendly persona as a cover for his dark side.'

'Will you get a chance to ask him why he saved my life?'

'I probably won't, no. But my Dutch counterpart will. I really do think it was simply because he thought of you as his mate. He didn't have much time to think; on some level it must have been purely instinctive.'

Nick stared out over the open countryside feeling confused and shocked. How could you think badly of someone who had saved your life? But how could you think good of someone who was capable of that kind of heinous abuse?'

'He gave me a fake Rolex, you know. Bought it in the Boro.'

'Oh yeah. We found a bag of those at the hotel. He must have bought a job lot of fake Rolexes, or more likely Frankie did. He didn't get them from the store in town though.'

'Fucking hell. He was just a big fucking liar. Twat.'

Colin Harcombe packed up the briefcase and laptop.

'That's the movie show over for today.'

'Thanks for coming over, Col.'

'No worries. I'll see you again soon I should think. When's Julie due home?'

'In the next couple of days.'

'Great news. I wish the both of you health and happiness.'

He got up and shook Nick's hand.

'And try not to get mixed up in any more trouble, eh,' he said with a smile.

The great summer weather broke on August bank holiday, pouring with rain for three days without stopping, but as September turned to October there was an Indian summer. Six days of temperatures over 70 degrees, one last glorious kiss of summer heat. Nick and Julie took a walk up Roseberry Topping for the first time since she'd been home.

'Well there it all is...,' he said, looking out across Teesside sprawling into the distance like an untidy carpet. 'You can even see Corporation House in the distance...look.' He pointed towards the Lego-like brick on the skyline.

'Still can't believe what happened to you up there,' she said with a shake of her head.

'You and me both. It was insane.'

They sat quietly for a few minutes.

'Are you still glad you moved back to Teesside?' she asked, sipping from a bottle of water. 'Given all that's happened, like?'

'Oh God yeah. All the shit that happened could have happened anywhere. And it meant moving in with you, which is the best thing I've ever done.'

'Sorry I bled on the garden,' she said with a snort.

'No worries. It's all good fertiliser, isn't it?'

He put his arm around her as she leaned her head on his shoulder.

'Maybe I should never have moved away,' he said.

'But if you don't move away, you can't get a perspective on what you've left behind.'

'Yeah, that's true. But sitting here now, I don't know, looking out at Teesside all spread out below, this is what I'm made up of...the industry, the countryside, the pollution, the wild nature...all of it, do you know what I mean?'

She squinted into the sun.

'Yeah, I do. You know after I was shot I can't remember anything specific really, but some bit of my brain was still working and though I wasn't conscious, I still had to cling to something, like, something to focus on. It's hard to find words for...you know that voice in your head that you always have...?'

'Yeah...I call him my little man. He's always there - when you're drunk he's the one who says 'you're fucking pissed out your brains, get home to bed' or 'don't put your hands down her pants.'

314

She laughed. 'Yeah, well I have a little woman who does the same job for me. She says 'put the Jack Daniels down, put on some sensible underwear and don't go putting that cock in your mouth until he's washed it'. She's a good mate, the little woman, like.'

'If the little man goes away, that's when I worry. He used to go away when I was depressed and that's when it feels like you can behave without judgement or consequence and you can just do anything. The little man went away when you were shot. I literally could have done anything. I didn't care about mine or anyone else's welfare. Just didn't care anymore. It's scary how you can lose your mind like that. I think I went insane in some sort of way.'

She stroked the back of his head.

'Yeah, well that inner voice of mine was still working and told me to hold onto something, focus on a thought or idea or something while my body recovered. '

'And what did you focus on?'

She gurgled a laugh.

'Two things. As mad as it might sound, I focused on you and me having it off...we'd been having such great sex, hadn't we? Like, lovemaking was the proper word for it...funny and lusty and unselfish and bloody orgasmic...it was...I dunno...it was the essence of what makes life worth living, or something like that. So I hung onto it but also onto Teesside...not one thing, not the Transporter Bridge or anything but just the feeling of the place, everything it's ever meant to me, everything I know and feel about it, good or bad. Not just the physical stuff, the... I dunno...the spiritual stuff maybe. Does that make any sense?'

'Totally, yeah. It's...the core of what we are, so it's natural you'd cling onto that. You're a Teessider, you can never not be a Teessider. For good or bad, this place made you, made both of us. Teesside has been there since the start, it's the stone on which you're built, so that's why you held onto it. It's your roots.'

'If I hadn't, I think I might just have let go and died. I don't know, maybe that's a bit fanciful; after all, it's a physical thing, death, isn't it? If something in me had packed up working then that's what'd have done for me...but there was a time when I knew if I let go then that was it...but this place...all of this...gave me the strength to survive, this and your bed skills anyway, lover boy.'

'So it was Teesside Shaggers 1, Death 0?'

'Yeah, it was a late goal and involved a lot of nerve-racking hanging-on and last-ditch defending, but maybe it was all the more glorious for that.'

He nodded and in unison they said: 'Typical Boro.'

THE END

About John Nicholson

John is a well-known football writer whose work is read by tens of thousands of people every week. He's a columnist for Football365.com and has worked for the Daily Record, The Mirror, Sky and many other publications over the last 14 years.

Other John Nicholson Books
published by Biteback Publishing

We Ate All The Pies -
How Football Swallowed Britain Whole (2010)

The Meat Fix -
How 26 Years Of Healthy Eating Nearly Killed Me (2012)

Books in the Nick Guymer Series
Published by HEAD PUBLISHING

1. Teesside Steal (2013)
2. Queen Of The Tees (2013)
3. Teesside Missed (2013)

Kindle/Ebook/Paperback

http://www.johnnicholsonwriter.com